The
Heart of the Rose

The Heart of the Rose

June Barraclough

Manufactured in the United States of America

CONTENTS

To my great great great grandmother
for providing the inspiration.

'It brightens as it burns.'

ONE

ANNE TESSEYMAN
1818

Virtue is like a rich stone, best plain set
Bacon: *Of Beauty*

Mr Larkin the carrier had let his horse feed on the grass verge of the lane down by Ranbeck when two passengers had got down. Now there was only the young woman inside, clutching her bundle of clothes and her basket. When the horse had had his fill the carrier urged him on again with a mighty 'gee up' and the young woman was jolted from side to side as they lurched along. The seat was hard and there was a smell of dust and grain but she did not notice it at first for she was too excited about making the journey at all. It was the longest journey she had ever made, even though her destination was only a wandering eleven miles from the village of Stockton-on-the-Forest where she had been born and lived for eighteen years. The Rector had told her the coach would skirt three parishes before arriving at Fountaynes Castle.

It seemed only yesterday that Goody Aysgill had come in to talk to Mam. They had spent a long time hunched over the hearth sipping tea, a great luxury. Anne had caught a few words: 'a situation' and 'strike while the iron's hot', and had guessed what they were talking about. Darkness had come at the end of the long summer evening and the room rushlight had been lit in honour of their visitor. When Goody finally heaved herself off, Mam said: 'Well, that's settled – thee's to go to the Castle, lass. Mother Aysgill has been right kind to let us know and it's not the sort of work that's two a penny.'

No one had asked Anne her opinion. They had taken it for granted that she would want the work of sewing maid at Fountaynes Castle – her keep and a good wage of five guineas a year and a place for life if she proved a good worker. Since Dad's going to work away the year before, she and Hannah and Mam had been hard put to earn even a few pence. Mam had 'taken in' the Rector's sewing and done her turn at last season's reaping and gleaning and had dug potatoes, joined in the hay-making and manure spreading, but it had not been enough. Brother Dick had married and now had his wife's and bairn's mouths to fill as well as his own. It was work 'out' or Parish relief. Anne had helped out at the Rectory when they needed her and Mrs Hart, the Rector's wife, would have kept her on if she could, but even the Rector had no money to spare. Sister Hannah had gone over to Tollerton to work for a farmer there and now it was

Anne's turn.

'I'll send you all I can, Mam. You're not to worry,' Anne had said as she clasped her mother's thin frame to her and they clung to each other a moment as they said their goodbyes. The Rector's friend Mr Ridsdale would ride by for messages twice a year and take her mother her wages. Anne accepted it all as she had accepted being hungry and cold on the days when there was no work at the Rectory.

It was a hot August afternoon, but as the carrier rattled along the lanes she was still too churned up to notice the blue sky or the gold of the first harvest. She'd noticed her friend Jane standing by the verge at the far end of the village with the gander, and she had waved but Jane had not seen her. When they had rounded on to the coach road she had settled back with one hand on her familiar basket and, in spite of the heat, drawn her shawl round her in a self-protective gesture. If only they would take Hannah too at the Castle. Her seams were as neat as Anne's: the Rector's wife had taught them both. Hannah though had preferred to work for the farmer out Tollerton way and Mrs Hart had said that she, Anne, must look for daintier work. The Castle post seemed providential – she would in any case have to leave the village unless she wed and there were no likely lads in Stockton. Since the enclosures the young men had drifted away and folks were reduced to their cottage patches where the 'owd uns' grew what they could. *She* had grown flowers. She liked flowers and would rather grow them than kale or rhubarb, but flowers didn't fill your belly.

What would the Castle be like? Goody Aysgill's lass who had found her the position had tried to describe it, but it all seemed fantastical. 'It's bigger nor our village but it's got lakes and fountains and a big farm and stables and grand gardens – and the *house* – wait till you see it, Anne! It's the biggest palace in all Yorkshire – as big as where the King lives down in London.'

Anne shifted her bundle and looked out of the window. How much further? They had passed the farthest villages whose names she knew and now they were entering upon a long sandy lane edged with trees – it seemed like a forest stretching on each side. Through the trees on one side though she saw little hills and then they turned with a squeak and a groan and came to rest by a signpost.

Larkin got down and poked his head through the window. 'Have to get out now, lass. Steward's servant with t' fly'll pick ye up – I can't go right up to t' Castle.' He broke off as a fly appeared as if by magic from a side lane that curved round the wood. It was being driven by a youngish-looking man. Anne got out of the carrier's rickety contraption, stumbling a little in the sudden hot sunlight. She pulled out her bundle and scooped up her basket on one arm whilst Mr Larkin lumbered up to his perch and was soon off again on the road which the signpost said was to Malton.

'Afternoon, Miss,' said the young man. 'If you're for the Castle, get in, will you?' Anne clambered into the fly and sat back still clutching bundle and basket. It was cooler at least. Thank goodness someone seemed to expect her. The pony pulling the fly was soon turned and they entered a long straight ride through beechwoods, with fewer bumps than formerly. This must be the Castle grounds.

The man turned round and grinned: 'Nearly there. Only a mile if we go this way. Off to work at t' Castle then?' His tone was not unfriendly.

'Yes, sir. I am a seamstress.' That sounded rather grand, she thought.

'Aye well, we've nigh on a hundred servants.' He said 'we' as though he employed them. Anne was emboldened to ask him more.

'You'll never have seen the like as our Castle. You're a lucky lass and no mistake. What's your name?'

'Anne Tesseyman.'

'Well, Anne lass, work hard and you'll be welcome. I'm servant to his lordship's steward.' He spoke as though this was work of high degree. 'Amos Thorne to you!'

'We're nearly there,' he added. 'When you get down, take yourself and your bundle past the stable entrance and knock on the door at the side through the archway. That's where the housekeeper's rooms are. They'll show you where Kitchen Court is. Aye, you're in luck,' he went on, 'to work for an Earl – why there's not a lass in England wouldn't give her eyeteeth for your job!'

'Yes, sir – Mr Thorne. I know I'm right lucky.' She felt she would hardly be up to this honour. It seemed that a sewing girl who worked in a castle was of some high degree herself. There were hardly any servants in Stockton, except for the Rectory, and a mile or two away at the Hall. How would she manage? Perhaps there had been a mistake and she would not be good enough?

'Ask for Mrs Gibson, or Miss Sharpe – and tell her who's sent you,' said the young man and then he turned the fly on to a gravel road and set a spanking pace for its final spurt. More avenues of trees on each side, and then in the distance but slowly getting nearer a long high wall with arches and battlements set in at regular intervals. Behind this there came into view a great golden dome. Anne did not know what it was but terror mounted in her, mingled with excitement. Even the pony seemed to have changed into a noble steed as they rounded another corner, went through an enormous outer gate, passed an obelisk, then went through a cobbled courtyard surrounded by long low buildings surmounted by a clock in the middle – and came to a sudden stop as with a 'Whoa! then!' Amos Thorne sounded out the importance of his arrival. No one seemed to have heard him for there was silence.

Anne got down and looked around. Apart from the driver, who pointed with his whip to a door at the far end and then was off in another direction, there was no one around. Where were they all? Was this the village? She knew there was a village near the Castle, but this must surely be the Castle itself. Now, though, even that gold thing had disappeared.

She smoothed her hair, picked up her basket, hoiked her bundle more tightly under the other arm and moved in a daze towards the door indicated by Amos Thorne. She felt slightly sick but knocked on a high wooden door set straight above three sanded steps. Then she noticed a bell-pull and gave a timid pull at it. It shot out of her hand but she heard a faint clang.

It was some time before anyone came and she was wondering whether she had come to the wrong door (and where *was* the Castle? – it must lie beyond the inner wall) when she heard brisk footsteps and a curly-haired young woman with a white mob cap and blue print dress covered by a long white apron opened the door and said 'Well?'

'Please Miss, I'm Anne Tesseyman from Stockton sent by Goody – I mean Mrs Aysgill – for the sewing.'

Her voice seemed to lie in the air for some time as the girl looked her up and down: 'Well – you'd better come in. Have you a letter? Mrs Gibson doesn't receive till five.'

Anne crept in and followed the curly-headed girl down a long, stone-flagged passage and into a large room with long deal tables and high windows. 'Servants' Lower Hall,' said the maid, and then, kindly: 'They're all out at front, waving off the Family. Will you have a cup of tea? I could make you one – or will you go and look?'

Tea was what Anne longed for, but she thought she had better be polite and so she replied: 'Can I go with you?'

For answer the maid took her basket and bundle, placed them on one of the tables and said 'Follow me – but you'd better be quick.'

She sped off through the room, Anne following, then down another stone passage and through another door and Anne found herself in a cobbled yard. There was cheering on the other side of a high wall and the maid put her finger to her lips and then squeezed herself and Anne through an archway.

Lines of footmen, maids in caps and blue print gowns, valets, stewards, bailiffs, men, women and their children were ranged round a great lawn between the stables and the side of an enormous building topped by the golden dome. She saw that the real entrance to the Castle was on the far side, for a red and gold carriage was standing over there and on the other side from the ranks of servants were a tall man in blue set apart from the crowd, a woman almost as tall and several children with their nursemaids and governesses.

'That's the Family,' said the curly one and pushed a way through for them both near the front of the massed servants who were now cheering enthusiastically.

'Strong beer for us tonight,' said a thickset man to his neighbour, who wore an under-butler's apron.

'What *is* it?' whispered Anne to her companion. 'Why are they cheering?'

'It's our Hardow and his Lady and the bairns off to Norpeth for the grouse,' said her new friend. She took her arm and pointed over the lawn. 'That's the *young* master,' she said. Anne just had time to glimpse a youth in dark clothes coming out of a door in the great building, followed by another soberly-dressed man. 'That's his tutor – but he's going to Oxford in October,' she went on. Then the tall man and the tall lady and the young man and all the children began to climb into the red coach and into another carriage behind it, and when their servants had been fitted into yet another coach there was a 'Huzzah!' and a 'Three cheers' from the crowd and the departing party were all pulled through a large wrought-iron gateway, very slowly, by sets of gleaming horses. 'There you are! You've seen them!' said the curly girl. 'There'll be a feast tonight. We'll go over to the quarters now. Come on.'

Anne found herself whisked away as the assembled servants dispersed. She felt dazed. She hoped the cup of tea would be offered again. She didn't like beer. She need not have worried. The women servants were all collecting in the room she had first entered and she was relieved to find her basket and bundle still there. How far away Stockton and Mam and even Mr Larkin the carrier seemed.

'There you go. Knock at the door at the end – it's next to the housekeeper's stillroom. You'll find someone there – Miss Sharpe or even Mrs Gibson.'

'What's your name – if I can't find you again?' asked Anne shyly.

'I'm Maria, but they call me Curly. Don't fret – you'll get used to it.'

Anne wondered whether they would want her in this grand bustling place. Would they put her somewhere else to sew? Where would she sleep? She knocked at the door, which was immediately opened by a dark thin woman.

'Yes?'

'Please mum – madam – I'm Anne Tesseyman that was sent by Mrs Aysgill from Stockton for the sewing,' she managed all in a rush.

Again she was asked for a letter. 'I've lines from our Rector. I was to take the place of Mary Aysgill that's got wed.'

Another woman who had been listening as she sat at a table piled high with linen said: 'I know, Miss Sharpe – you may let her in.'

Anne advanced. At last someone knew who she was. 'Please ma'am, there's the lines from our Rector in my basket here.'

'Give the letter to me,' said the other lady, who seemed quite young. She took it, motioned Anne to wait, opened it, scanned it quickly and looked up. 'We'll start you off in the sewing-rooms tomorrow, I think. You will have to show us you are a good worker, Tesseyman.'

'Yes, ma'am.'

'You can leave your bundle here and one of the girls will take it up to the attics for you before you go up. You can eat tea with the others and then they'll take you up to your bed. Where is Stockton-on-the-Forest?' she added, looking at the letter again.

Fancy not knowing where Stockton was!

'Please mum – ma'am – it's in Yorkshire,' said Anne.

'Well, so are we here. I meant, is it far?'

'Yes, I've come a long way,' replied Anne. 'It's nigh on twelve miles away.'

She looked at Mr Hart's letter in the lady's hand and felt she had handed over her past life in it and was now embarked upon a new and strange existence.

Mrs Gibson stood up. 'We'll sign you on tomorrow and explain your work and wages. I see this says you are honest and dependable and that you have done general maid's duties and also some sewing. We are a good house here, a generous house, and if you behave yourself you will do very well I hope,' she said, pocketing the letter. 'Go now and try to find some of the other sewing maids. They'll tell you we've a lot of linen to prepare for her ladyship's next lying-in.'

'Yes, ma'am.' Anne curtsied and turned to go. The thin woman was laughing as she closed the door: 'A long way! Twelve miles or so!' she said.

Anne found her tea, and Curly, and managed to ask that her bed should be shown her later as her things were to be taken up for her. She still clutched her basket. It was all so strange. How would she ever settle? There were so many people around her. It was like a fair. And would her sewing be good enough? She supped her tea quietly and felt a little better. The men's table was full of servants swigging beer which seemed to come from taps at the far end of the hall and the talk was loud and the cheering and laughing raucous. It did not help her headache but she sat on amongst a bunch of young women and Curly came and sat next to her.

'Don't worry about your bed – I'll show you where to go – and don't worry about *them*,' she added, dismissing the men with a toss of her head. Then one or two of the younger men came up.

'Who's this then?' one enquired.

'This is Anne – and I'll thank you not to bother her,' replied Curly before Anne could summon up the courage to pronounce her own name.

'Howdy do,' said the other man and advanced a brawny paw. Anne took it and shook it. 'Aye, she'll do, won't she, Jim?'

'You leave her alone. Come on Anne. I'll show you where to go,' said Curly, and the men turned away but not without winks and nudges. 'You'll have to do some waiting on later,' she said, 'but you needn't today.' Anne was not sure what this meant.

She followed Curly out of the hall, through the cobbled courtyard and into a building where they climbed hundreds of steps, up and up and up to the top where lay the servants' attics. Her bed was to be one of twenty in one of these attics, the sleeping quarters for the women servants who did not live on the estate.

'Don't mind the lads,' said Curly. 'They mean no harm, but they like to look over anyone new.' Anne thought they had stared at her as if she was a piece of new property. She hoped they would not be able to get up to the women servants' dormitories, especially on 'beer nights'. Curly guessed her thoughts. 'They won't come up here – haven't you been away from home before?' 'No, only in the village. We haven't got many lads left now, there being no work.' 'Aye, they say things are right bad,' replied Curly sympathetically. 'Our servants are lucky, so they behave themselves – 'cept they get a bit rowdy sometimes.'

To her great relief Anne found her bundle deposited efficiently on the bed which was to be hers and she decided to undress and go to bed as no one seemed to require her services that evening. Even the singing from down below did not prevent her from falling asleep. She tried to mutter a prayer but nervous exhaustion overcame her so she did not hear the other girls when they crept up to bed.

'Did you see the new lass?' said one. 'A right bonny one,' replied another. 'Now don't you go putting ideas into her head. She looks a right good lass to me,' said an older woman. They laughed as Anne slept on.

She woke once though in the early morning and knew that today was the beginning of her new life and that this great grand strange place was to be her home.

'Was that young man they were cheering yesterday the Earl's

son then?' Anne asked Curly. They were sitting up in the servants' sewing-room in the big East Wing. Curly was not, it seemed, a seamstress but sometimes helped out. They needed extra help at present because her ladyship was to be lying-in again in November with her eleventh child and needed sheets, linen, and baby clothes.

Anne had been led up a special staircase into this top room at the back, facing a green sward, with a lake in the near distance. Between the lawn and the lake was a long wide field, now gold and dusty-looking. Miss Sharpe, the maid to the housekeeper, and one or two other girls, had accompanied them.

Miss Sharpe had been called away for a moment and Anne had seized the opportunity to ask questions. Now that they were all sewing she felt a little less shy though still somewhat bewildered – but too busy to be homesick. Even this sewing-room at the top of the East Wing was bigger than any ordinary room she had ever been in – much bigger than the Rectory drawing-room – and Curly said she hadn't seen anything yet. She knew she was 'on trial' for a month with board and lodging thrown in, and after another three months, if she were satisfactory, she would receive a sovereign and two crowns, more money than she had ever seen before. But she was curious about the inhabitants of the Castle. She felt she ought to know for whom she was working, since after all – it had come upon her that morning – Miss Sharpe, and even the grand housekeeper Mrs Gibson, were servants too!

'That *boy*,' answered Curly snapping a thread with her teeth, 'was young Mr George.'

'Is it true he'll be the Earl one day then?' asked a girl with a drip on the end of her nose.

'Not till his dad and his grand-dad are dead,' replied Curly. 'It's his grand-dad who's Earl of Fountaynes and his dad is Viscount Hardow. Mr George is the eldest son and so when the old Earl dies, and after Hardow dies, Mr George will be Earl.'

'So – H-hardow is the young Mr George's father, then?' said Anne shyly looking up from the long white expanse of linen sheet she was hemming.

'Yes, and the Earl of Fountaynes his grandpa, like I said.'

'And you'd better mind *him*, lass,' said another girl. 'He's the governor here. They all like it better when he's away but he don't go away much.'

'So there are lots of other bairns then?' asked Anne, remembering that Mrs Gibson had said something about the next lying-in. She was shy but curiosity had overcome her shyness.

Curly was launched on her favourite theme. She knew all the names and ages of all the Viscount's children and all their cousins and second cousins – and all the gossip, since her mother and her father were both on the estate.

'Mr George is seventeen. Then the two young ladies, Miss Caroline and Miss Georgiana – only a year between them – sixteen and fifteen. Then Mr Fred – he's fourteen but a great big lad – off at school most of the time. Then our Miss Harriet – she's thirteen and a right character *she* is – and there's Master William and Master Edward, younger than her but older than little Miss Blanche. She's nearly seven, and Master Charles is four and little Miss Elizabeth is nearly three.'

'What a lot of them,' breathed Anne.

'Well, there'll be another soon,' said Eliza, the sallow-faced girl, holding up her seam to the light and squinting.

'You're not used to big families then?' asked Susan, a round-faced girl with large red hands. 'How many are there of you at home?'

'Only my brother and my sister, but they work away too. There were two little ones that died and the other ones who are all married,' replied Anne. She bent over her work. Hannah and Dick seemed so far away.

She didn't really want to talk about them, or about the little ones that had died, especially little James. Of course Mam too had had eleven childer all told!

'It's a big family. They take a bit of getting used to – not that we see them much unless they put us in the nursery. They do that sometimes, if they think you'll do.'

Perhaps earls' children did not die, Anne was thinking. Curly was also pursuing thoughts of her own. 'Poor little William,' she said suddenly without explanation, then: 'Heigh up – she's coming back!' said Eliza and Miss Sharpe was suddenly once more among them, looking rather flustered but with her customary tones that did not belie her name.

'Gossip, lasses! Silence if you please. You're already behindhand. I have just been explaining to one of her ladyship's maids that stayed behind how much we have to do.' They all bent down to their work again and Miss Sharpe walked to the window. 'If you don't finish mending the large sheets today you will have to do them by candlelight and his lordship doesn't like that,' she said. After a pause she said: 'Tesseyman!'

Anne looked up. The effect of Selina Sharpe's voice was to make her heart into a heavy pebble that dropped to her boots.

'Yes m'm.' 'Girls here are expected to keep their hands clean. Let me see yours.' What a sad and angry face she has, thought Anne. I don't like her, that I don't. She has a look of Mother Scott in the village – the one they said was a witch but the Rector said it was all nonsense. But she got up, held out her hands and Miss Sharpe looked them over, turned them round in the light of the window and sniffed. 'They'll do,' she was forced to admit. Anne went back to her stool and shivered a little but bent further over her almost invisible stitches. She had brought her thimble with her that had been Mam's and Grandmam's. It gave her comfort to think it had been on their fingers too.

Miss Sharpe was silent for a moment, contemplating the bent heads; then she moved among them again and soon found something to criticize. Mary's cotton thread was getting dirty. Eliza's stitches were too big. She dared not say anything against Curly and the others knew it. Then she sat down in a chair which she placed near the window. The new girl was a pretty thing, she thought.

Mrs Gibson had said that Tesseyman looked quite refined in spite of her rustic background and that she wouldn't be surprised if Mrs Copus asked for more help in the nursery when the family returned from Norpeth in September. Margaret, one of the nursery maids, did not look at all well, she had said. They hoped the air of Norpeth would revive her, but if it did not, and if the sewing were done in good time, they might ask Mrs Gibson for a maid to train up in the nursery. Mrs Copus was chief nurse to the children and continually grumbling that they were understaffed, as Mrs Gibson well knew they were. The new girl might go over there if she proved reliable. It was a pity that Viscount Hardow didn't have more say in the management of the household. After all it was his wife's money that paid his own servants.

Miss Sharpe did not like children and resented all the work they made. However could they keep the sort of house the nobility expected if they were continually harried by the old Earl over costs? Everyone knew where *his* money had gone. She smiled. As for the children – they were the weak link for all the ladyships – they fretted and worried over them and then didn't see them for weeks when they were off to London or to other great houses. Her ladyship here would have preferred to stay put, they all knew that. There was not much the upper servants did not know about their employers. Breed 'em and let someone else bring 'em up – all the ladies who came to the Castle were the same. But Lady Georgiana was a better mother than most, she must admit. Well, she had to be!

Miss Selina Sharpe was lost in thought as the girls occasionally sneaked a quick glance at her and once or twice caught each other's eye and made a face. They all sewed on for another three hours, their backs and necks aching and their eyes smarting. But soon they would get their tea and bread and cheese, and a rasher of bacon from the Castle farm pigs.

As soon as Miss Sharpe gave the sign they were off down the East Wing stairs, hungry and stiff. Once out in the open they crossed the great courtyard on their way back to the Servants' Hall. Anne looked at a huge door as she and Curly passed by the West Wing of the Castle. 'Where does that go?' asked Anne. Curly was plodding along, her arms crossed under her cloak, for the weather had suddenly changed and become spitefully cold for August. 'Chapel,' she answered briefly. 'You'll see, one day.' So the family had a special church all of their own!

'They choose two servants every Sunday, so you go about twice a year. The women like it – other times you go to church in the village.'

Anne pondered this. She loved church. All that she had so far seen in her life before she came to this great place, all that was beautiful apart from flowers and babies, was to be found in their little village church. She liked the sound of the words and the peacefulness of it. She looked forward to going to this family church – if they kept her on of course! She hardly dared hope that they would. But, oh yes, she did want to stay. Thank goodness that Miss Sharpe hadn't found anything wrong with her hands. At least they didn't sweat, though she had pricked her finger after Miss Sharpe had sent her back to her stool and there was a tiny dot of blood which she had tried to hide under the hem of some seaming she was doing. How hungry she was now. She looked forward to getting her tea after she'd 'waited on' the other servants, and almost skipped after her new friend Curly.

Perhaps life was not going to be too bad after all!

A month soon passed, working hard, sleeping like a log and listening to the gossip of the other servants. Curly and she seemed to agree on most things. She had never had such a good friend before and could not imagine what she would have done without her during those first weeks. Then the day came when she was told by Mrs Gibson that her work was satisfactory and that she would be paid her first wage after another three months had passed. She was to continue sewing under Miss Sharpe – 'for the present', added Mrs Gibson.

The day came when the family was to return. Curly was full of it all that evening when they went down for supper. Anne had seen nothing as she had been up in a smaller sewing-room stitching baby-bands, but Curly had been over to her mother's cottage and gathered all the news. Anne had got used now to serving the other servants before she ate herself although she was still bothered by some of the sallies from the younger menservants and tried to ignore them, not being yet used to using her tongue in self-defence. When she finally sat down, Curly said mysteriously: 'A little bird tells me you'll be wanted somewhere tomorrow', but she would say no more. Anne went to bed that night a little worried but when next morning Miss Sharpe called her out from her sewing saying 'Mrs Copus wants to see you', she felt even worse. Her heart sank down once more into her boots. Had she done something wrong? Just when things seemed to be going along nicely. The other girls looked up with interest. 'Go on, Tesseyman, down to the sitting-room on the left at the bottom of the wing facing Stable Court.' Anne put down her sewing and allowed her cap to be adjusted by Miss Sharpe. 'Get along with you then', she said and went back to her post near the window.

'Tesseyman?' said the fat middle-aged lady, as unlike as possible to the neat and trim Mrs Gibson. 'Yes, ma'am.'

'You may be seated,' said Mrs Copus. She had a stately but comfortable manner. Anne curtsied and sat. What had she done wrong? Yet Nurse Copus did not sound annoyed.

'When you and the other girls have finished the sheets and the new layette it will be some time before the next consignment of linen arrives,' she began. Anne waited politely.

'You know the family have returned?' went on Mrs Copus regarding her keenly. 'Yes, ma'am.'

'Have you any experience of babies and small children?' She kept her large brown eyes fixed on Anne. Experience? What did that mean. Anne hesitated. 'I mean – have you bathed, washed, tended young children and babes? Did your mother have small children whose care was sometimes given to you?'

Anne's face lit up. 'If you please, ma'am, my younger brother – that died' – she bit her lip – 'I looked after him. And I helped sometimes with the Rector's bairns.'

'Ah. It was . . . this is a delicate matter . . . no negligence of yours that led to the demise of your brother?' Anne looked blank.

'Why did your little brother die? Was it a fever or convulsions? You did not drop him?' 'Oh, no ma'am. He was ever so weakly – the Rector said it was not nobody's fault. Jesus wanted him to be an angel, he said, but Mam was so grieved. It was her last you see. We looked after him right well.'

'Yes – I can see you would. And I had a very good impression from the letter Mrs Gibson showed me from your Rector's wife. Well, Anne, your services may one day be required in my nurseries when sewing work is low. That is all. Continue as you are for the present. Miss Sharpe will still report on your work, of course.'

She inclined her head gracefully and Anne got to her feet, curtsied and somehow found the door. 'She'll do,' thought Mrs Copus when she had gone.

No more was heard of this for some time. Anne confided in Curly who said 'I told you, didn't I?' Life went on as usual and Anne began to count the weeks till she would receive her first money at the end of December. She was told she could bank it with the housekeeper until the Rector's friend should visit. There was nothing she would need to buy. The nearest village was a mile away and one day she thought she might buy a ribbon or two there for Sundays. Her clothes she had brought with her, and the Castle had provided gown, cap and apron – not new of course but new to Anne. Her boots would still do – she hoped her feet would not grow any more for she had put on weight in the last month or two with all the good Castle food. She still felt sometimes a little anxious, a little fearful, and then sometimes happy and excited, and these emotions quite bewildered her. She told herself that she had never been away from home before and it was a lot to manage. When she was able to stop working, which was not often, she felt terribly tired. It was not just the work, it was all the new faces. They made her wonder who and where she was. But gradually moods of happiness seemed to predominate and the Castle began to feel more like 'home'. She found to her surprise that people were not all equally likeable – some of them she did not like at all, Miss Sharpe for instance. At home and in the village she had known everyone and been known by everyone all her life and got used to their differences. And there had always been Mam and sometimes Hannah to chat with and to discuss people's peculiarities and disagreeable sides. One of the maids, Susan, annoyed her because she giggled a lot at nothing; and Eliza always looked as though she needed her nose blown. But Curly never annoyed her and she did not seem to get across Curly, who was shrewd and kind. Anne wondered what Mam would have made of it all, and whether she would have shared her opinions. Now she was alone with no Mam, and had better make up her mind to 'fettle herself' – one of Mam's favourite expressions. She wondered what all her new acquaintances thought of her. It was a novel idea, that. She hoped they liked her and thought they did for the most part, for she tried hard to be pleasant and not too quiet. She'd always kept things a bit to herself, even at home. It was strange, seeing yourself suddenly as a separate person, just as all the others were separate people. It was a queer sort of shock. Sometimes she would look at her hands, with Mam's thimble on the third finger of her right hand, and think: 'These are *my* hands.' After a few weeks these feelings faded a little and her animal spirits reasserted themselves and in spite of her fatigue she would have liked to run round the park or sing. Of course she did neither, but now she knew she was going to be all right the tiredness seemed to become less too. She even felt like answering back to Miss Sharpe who was very hard on them all. That surprised her. She found she had a strong sense of justice. Miss Sharpe tormented Eliza most. Eliza was indeed annoying but her being victimized occasionally over a less than perfect piece of work put Anne on her side.

As autumn drew on the maids were sometimes allowed a free hour or two in the afternoon when the sun began to set earlier and earlier. Anne had still not been called for again by Mrs Copus and had begun to feel she would be staying in the sewing-rooms, except that Curly said they were always short in the nursery, there being so many children still not old enough for school or schoolroom. It began to be chilly up in the sewing-rooms and they would sit round the fire in the Lower Hall, or if it were fine, walk to the big lake. She had still seen only a small part of the Castle and grounds – and others spoke of other wonders she would one day see, gardens and statues and woods and other buildings. Neither had she ever yet seen the 'state' rooms or the Family rooms, though Curly promised to smuggle her one day over to where the family and its guests lived and slept and entertained, far from the Kitchen Court and the stables and the servants' attics.

All the servants seemed to Anne to work hard and not flag, but the chief steward and the housekeeper and all the upper servants kept a generous house and knew that the younger servants could not be worked to death. If every hour of daylight were worked they would weary and their work suffer. They knew too that the Earl of Fountaynes' bark was worse than his bite and that he knew they did their work well even under his necessary economies.

Economies there had been, what with the old man gambling his youth away and spending great sums in his middle age finishing the New Wing. But the 'young' Viscount and his Lady were less rash in their spending and were slowly beginning to exercise more influence on the household as the older servants died, particularly when Fountaynes – Fred, as he was affectionately called, though not of course to his face – was bedridden with gout, which was more often as time went on. Curly said that servants were often deployed on work they had not originally been taken on for. The organization, though immense, was rather lax, and 'economies' were often not in the right places. The farm with its dairies and cheese-rooms gave work to both men and women; as did the gardens and laundries. The whole of the great castle building with all its rooms, boudoirs, salons, gallery, kitchens, nurseries, and library had to be kept clean and shining by the women servants. The family had its own close servants too, both men and women of all degrees – and there were the stables with their own hierarchy of coachmen, grooms and ostlers. Anne was still bewildered by them all and in order to save trouble curtsied at first to everyone. The man Amos Thorne she had met on her journey had been right: it was like a village with its own laws and customs. Over a hundred servants and servants of servants, servants of children and servants of horses! The coachmen had their stableboys; the steward his bailiffs and understewards; the head gardener his under-gardeners and his boys; the housekeeper had Miss Sharpe and many other housemaids. And there were parlour maids and sewing maids and serving girls and milkmaids and kitchen maids under the cook with his under-cooks and other minions. When the family returned she saw other faces – governesses and ladies' maids and nursery maids, and glimpsed the butler, more footmen, valets and boot-boys. She felt she was not quite at the bottom of a vast heap.

Curly was proud of it all. 'My mother says it's a beehive,' she said to Anne. It did hum with activity all day and half the night and yet you could walk across the field to the big lake and under the trees of the nearest woods where all was quiet. So long as you kept sober and punctual and did what you were asked, you could stay all your life!

'If you get to be a nursery maid you're lucky,' said Susan. 'It's luck, you know. They take a fancy to you – don't worry, I'm not jealous, I don't like children.'

'Oh, I'd rather look after bairns than sew,' replied Anne. She often thought of that first day when she had glimpsed the children and their big brother in the distance getting into the red carriage. How long ago it seemed. She did hope Mrs Copus would not forget and would let her learn to work in the nurseries.

It was almost time for Lady Georgiana to go to London in time for her lying-in, which was expected in mid November. She had just a few more days before leaving for Grosvenor Place and was sitting peacefully in her dressing-room writing to her sister Harriet. Lady Georgiana Hardow was only thirty-five but was already the mother of ten children, and her thoughts were constantly on them as well as on her next 'petit paquet' which was disturbing her night's rest. Harriet was the great comfort of her life at this time and to her she could pour out all her problems and vexations of the spirit. There were plenty of them, though her nervous fears – that something dreadful *might* happen – were even worse than her true difficulties, particularly the angry feelings she was sometimes ashamed of having for her father-in-law, the old Earl. For nearly twenty years, since her marriage at seventeen to Hardow, she had tried to repress them, but could not help enjoying her life more whenever the high-handed old man was away, which was unfortunately not very often. She had known of course before she married that she would have to live with her in-laws: that was to be expected. But she had not known what a constant trial she would find one half of them, nor how her husband's moods would be exacerbated by his irascible father. For her mother-in-law, the apparently hare-brained Countess, she had nothing but pity, especially when that lady tittered and laughed at her husband's jokes all through the long meals they ate together as a family. She had always tried to be patient with them both. Her husband had at one time called her an angel of kindness and she strove hard to go on deserving that appellation.

She laid aside her letter to Harriet. What was there to write about except alarms? For example, that her daughter Harriet, her sister's namesake, a tall well-developed girl, had had another argument with the governess who had been found in tears, that poor little William was no better, that dear little Lizzie's nursery maid had had to be sent away with symptoms of decline after they had returned from Norpeth, that the bull had got out of one of their fields and chased a guest, that she was weary and longed for her confinement to be over.

She took up Byron's *Beppo*, which she had found so amusing last week. Her sister had had something to say about Byron in her last letter – so clever and so wicked he was, one could not help feeling. But she did not feel like reading Byron tonight. Harriet seemed to have more time for reading than she had, even with her more crowded social life and her continuous moving round the country house circuit. But of course Harriet had not gone on to have any more children after her fifth. Dear God, if only she herself survived the next baby. How did Harriet manage it?

Lady Georgiana put down Byron, finished her letter to seal the next day, and picked up *The Heart of Midlothian* which was really more to her taste. Soon she would have to dress for dinner and perhaps she might just peep in the nursery before she went in to dine. Thank goodness Copus and her helpers were so wonderful with the children and understood that she herself liked to

26

keep in touch perhaps more than was warranted. She loved her children and knew that Copus needed more help now that William was back, but Hardow would groan when she broached the subject. She had made too many economies in her staff already. Grand, as they all called her father-in-law, though ever talking of economies, never actually seemed to cut down on anything. No, it was no good speaking to Hardow about it. His way of dealing with his father was, as it had always been, a policy of smiles and silence. What Hardow really thought about anything was a mystery to her even after all those years of marriage. But she knew he must fume inwardly at the old man, for he avoided him whenever possible and sought sanctuary in the library. He still visited her bedroom now and then of course, which resulted in the constant state of being 'gravida'. She hoped and prayed for all their sakes that this baby would be their last. Her stomach was quite deranged and no doctor seemed to know what to do with her nervous fears. It was not the place nor the people which set her fears abroad, nor could she complain of the silent Hardow. Nor was it that life was dull. She liked the even tenor of country life – her sister would have found it duller than she did. Perhaps it was that any good luck seemed to allow her nervous anxieties to crowd in when she had nothing better to worry about than the bull or overturned carriages. Harriet said 'Fear is a coward', but Harriet, who was not entirely free of anxieties herself – chiefly connected with her husband's gambling – *would* say that, because Harriet was not a coward, which *she* was. She smiled reminiscently over Harriet's last letter. She was so amusing, even about the Prince.

Down at Brighton, of course, even she, Georgiana, could make the Prince laugh. Another self seemed to emerge from its country blankets there, to dazzle and delight. Of course the Prince had been *so* fond of her dearest mama and liked her because of that. Fifteen years ago he had stood godparent to her own little Georgy, who did perhaps look rather like mama. She was going to be prettier than the other girls, she thought – prettier than she herself. Not that *she* could ever have been a beauty but she was well enough still in face, still tall and her hair had kept its gold. Her sister Harriet worried more about plumpness than she did. That was just luck of course – she had never had much appetite and it was no good worrying about plumpness when another little Hardow was soon to make its way into the world.

She must make an effort to be cheerful tonight. They had one or two old acquaintances staying but no one really to her taste. If only young George were home! He was such a love when he dined with them, kept the conversation going and did not seem to fear his grandfather with whose outbursts he dealt subtly by teasing him. But George had just gone off to Oxford to keep his first term. She knew that George did not really approve of Grand for he had told her so, more than once. He disapproved of Grand's past life, of his gambling and his *affaires*, though of course he did not speak of the latter to his mama. Young George was going to be – already was – a scholar, and could always retire into the world of books in the library like his father. That at least he shared with him. They would both pore over folios her brother sent and even the old Earl would join them, for he too was a connoisseur, though apt to prefer his own productions to those by anyone else.

She did hope her guests were warm enough in their various rooms in the vast place. She had a good fire and would have liked to sit over it with Walter Scott, but she must dress and descend in her finery. Perhaps they would excuse her tonight? She could plead a headache, but then they might send for the doctor and there was nothing he could do. Women understood these matters better, but they did not fix the order of things. At least there was less drinking now among the men. It seemed that men drank when they were bored, but that women had headaches – which if *they* drank would only get worse. Perhaps at Christmas, when the baby had been safely delivered, they would have a small houseparty for the christening, and get up charades. There might not be much hunting or shooting going on: not all the men of the family liked it, many of them being of a rather scholarly disposition.

She sighed for young George again but she must not become one of those mamas who pinned all her hopes on her sons and was loth to let them go into a wider world. George was already in a different world from that of women, she thought. Everyone said he was brilliant at Greek and Latin, though his French and Italian had only been picked up *en passant*. In a year or two he would make the tour. She shuddered, thinking of overturned coaches and Continental chicanery.

She must ring for her maid and stop dreaming. Had the flowers she ordered up from the glasshouses been seen to by Mrs

Currey? She must tell Marie to put the warming-pan in earlier and to change it before she retired. Thank God the rain had stopped: the girls would be better tempered, she hoped. She must remember to praise Caro's sketch of the shepherd's hut, for last night she had overpraised Georgy's piano-playing and Caro had looked sulky. It was not her fault that she was so much plainer and so much less clever than her sisters. And Harriet must be dissuaded from dancing, up in the schoolroom, and started on some fancy needlework. Maybe tomorrow afternoon they could all go for a drive. No, she had better not. After dinner perhaps they might discuss a visit by the girls and their governess to the village school. Harriet said it was quite *de rigueur*, and their brother in his great house in Derbyshire was taking an interest in the church's plans for a better building for the school of the children of favoured tenants, so she ought to make sure her own girls were primed. The old manners were beginning to change: the church had found new wings and was actively encouraging people to take religion seriously. She always had of course. Something had to be believed in, surely, and in her own childhood and schooldays in that rich rackety house and in their London 'palace', the two constants had been God and Grandmother. Grandmother had died four years ago, before Waterloo, but she still felt her influence. Grandmother would have approved of the New Thinking, just as she had disapproved – and who more so – of her own daughters' conduct. Oh, that was all past history; no good thinking about it. Harriet had suffered more than she had. At least she herself had married Hardow out of the schoolroom in her first season and the problems of father and his mistress had come later. She did not regret her marriage, though she wished God had not made her so fertile. But she did adore her children. They were such good children. Not all beautiful, and not all clever, but good-natured. Even Grand in a good mood had been known to acknowledge the existence of some of them with a smile.

She looked over at the wall behind her bed with all her engraved miniatures. George on his pony – how uncomfortable he looked! He had never liked riding. And Caro and Georgy with their arms around each other the day they had had their hair curled specially for the artist. And dear tall handsome Fred looking out as bold as brass, carrying his father's gun. And her Harriet, already at three years old the mistress of all she surveyed.

And poor Willy holding his bricks with his brother Edward's arm around him, Ned already taller though William was older. Then the little ones, engraved only last year when Lizzie was one, with Blanche and Charlie. Little Blanket was so pretty, after Georgy the prettiest of all her children she thought, and Lizzie so sweet-natured. Would she have a boy next? Everything was arranged for her in London and she would go up at the end of the week. She prayed it would not rain. Coaches were bad enough, even if you were not expecting. She would try to make a leisurely stop at Chatsworth and Stafford on the way.

At the thought of leaving the Castle she began to bestir herself, and when her 'own woman', Marie, came in she found her ready for the final touches to her toilette.

'You should have seen Miss Lizzie in the new little cart today, my lady. Master Charles was pushing her this afternoon and they were both so rosy. Miss Blanche has a slight cold – Nurse Copus told me to tell you – so she's keeping her indoors tomorrow.'

'Oh dear, Marie, I hope Charlie will not push the cart off the terrace, and Blanket – I must go in and see her. Is she feverish?'

'No, no, my lady, nothing to fret over. Some of the servants have had colds I believe. But Mrs Copus is arranging for a new girl to help out soon. She will have a word with you in the morning if you will allow her.'

'Yes, we must see that Copus is happy before I go away,' replied Lady Georgiana, studying her reflection in the mirror.

'Perhaps the feather *there*? – yes – and the little aigrette. Ah, your ladyship looks beautiful.'

'Thank you, Marie. Did you meet the other ladies' maids? I hope all is to their liking.'

Marie almost answered 'Better than they deserve', but she knew her mistress's kind heart and that she sincerely wished even difficult guests to be happy, so she only assented, adding 'Lady Boringdon has the new curls but, if you will excuse me, I do not think they suit her.'

Georgiana only smiled vaguely. She was thinking again of Blanche's cold. Once dressed she went out of her comfortable room down a long staircase and up again to the next floor on the wing where the younger children's nurseries were. There was a rush of little feet and 'Mama! . . . Mama!' The old nurse and the nursery maids stood aside and the latter curtseyed.

'It ain't *fair*, Mama. Blanche had a hot caudle and me and Willy wanted one too,' said one – Charles – a pugnacious boy of four.

'Hush, dear, Blanket has a cold. How is she, Mrs Copus? Shall I go in?'

'I should just stand at the door, milady, you don't want to go catching cold in your condition,' replied the nurse with the direct manner of the previous century. Georgiana was used to her and always took her advice, so she contented herself with peeping through at her little six-year-old daughter before bidding the others goodnight. It was not night but the children were ready for bed, having had their own supper at four o'clock. They did not yet eat the nine o'clock dinner since bed was at seven in winter.

Georgiana kissed William, who stood awkwardly behind his younger brother. 'I want Edward,' he said suddenly as she turned to go.

'Edward is at school, William. He'll come back for Christmas.' She stooped to kiss Charlie and Lizzie. The little girl was thin and pale, unlike her pretty sister Blanche.

At last they let her go and she met Marie, who took a message up to the girls in the schoolroom. They were not yet allowed down for dinner in spite of their entreaties. Caro, Georgiana and Harriet had been amusing themselves with Mademoiselle Sterky the Swiss governess, but had found the entertainment palled. 'Tell Caro and Georgy they may come down before bed to the drawing-room. Harriet must wait.'

'Miss Harriet won't like that,' observed Marie.

'Then she will have to be patient,' replied Lady Georgiana, somewhat tartly for her. Harriet would soon enough take over the dinner-table conversation, for she dominated wherever she went.

All her tasks done she called the footman who preceded her down to the dining-room. Her thoughts were not with Harriet, nor even with Blanche, but with poor William who should have been at school but wasn't. Not for the first time she wondered if he could have caught sunstroke that year at Ramsgate. He had seemed quite normal when he was born. A little slow, but so had Caro been. She must certainly speak to Hardow about him again. Fear clutched at her heart as she thought of the next unborn child and whether he too might be 'strange'. She must have Willy up in her sitting-room before she left for London.

'Please tell your papa it is cold,' Aunt Julia was saying to Hardow when Georgiana entered the ante-dining-room where guests were assembling. Aunt Julia, the old Earl's sister, was still living at the Castle, a beribboned and lacy memento of the last century with an ugly little face but much vivacity. How hard it was to *like* her, though one had to admire her pluck. As for asking Grand to order more logs – he never noticed the cold, nor did his wife, who often sat out in the middle of the kitchen garden in a gale. The guests assembled: most were related in some way to Earl Fountaynes and his wife. The conversation was not brilliant. No political man, no doctor, no man of the cloth, no dandy or dangler tonight. It had been better when Hardow's younger brother Fred had been with them, but he had perished at Waterloo. Georgiana sighed and decided to listen carefully to everyone so that she might report even a dull conversation to her sister when she finished her letter. Her husband was looking at her when they had finished the entrée and they were all listening to an interminable joke retailed by Grand, a joke they had heard hundreds of times before. The guests' smiles were frozen on their faces. Why did they come to be bored? It was true that the livelier ones only came now when Grand was away or indisposed.

She looked round the table. The old Earl, Grand, still in the middle of his story about a grouse (did he do it on purpose?); his wife the Countess of Fountaynes – Lady Caroline – pecking at her food, giggling and shrieking as though she were not quite all there; the middle-aged Lord Boringdon glumly sipping claret and looking at his usually jolly wife who was for once silent; Lord Dudley discussing his new gardens when Grand was silent for a moment; Hardow quiet as usual but with an occasional clearing of the throat; Henry and William, his other two brothers who lived on and off at the Castle; Lady Julia, chattering, rouged to the eyeballs, attacking her gelée as though it were a partridge; two other nondescript ladies, and herself. She looked down at her stomach and sighed. If only Harriet would come to visit them with her distinguished husband and delightful children. Really it would be quite an improvement when Caro and Georgy came down to dinner, though they would both be paralyzed with shyness at first. It was certainly not very 'sprack' at the moment – no 'sparks' present.

The dishes were changed, the gold and silver sparkled on the snowy cloth, talk veered to the Prince. Fountaynes was interested in elderly royal lovers, it seemed. There were titters and sighs. Fingerbowls were dipped into, the footmen stood like statues, the draughts whistled up the enormous chimney. Fountaynes found fault with some opinion or other, his lower lip protruding as it always did when he was angry. There was a short silence. Then the arrangements for the next season were discussed; the men dispersed to billiards and the ladies to conversation and to patting the drawing-room dogs. Lady Caroline screeched on, her conversation punctuated with dozes, and then a sudden return to life with her: 'Comical enough, so comical.' Hardow had gone to the library to escape his father who was pacing up and down the Long Gallery admiring his own handiwork. It had taken him ten years to have the interior decorated and painted to his satisfaction, for the West Wing had not been finished when he had inherited the Castle as a boy of ten nearly sixty years before, and his gambling debts had swallowed up the money the estate had needed. However, it had finally been done, though not without his grumblings and carpings and quarrels leading twice a month to a change in the workforce.

Georgiana sat round the fire with her lady guests and one or two of the men drifted in and out again. Caro and Georgy came down and played chess with their young uncles. It was quite peaceful. So long as Blanche recovered from her cold and William stopped asking for Edward and Charles did not overturn Lizzie and the baby arrived healthy, and Harriet calmed down – and her beloved George came home at Christmas when she and his father had returned from London with the new baby – then she could perhaps relax and be happy and give her mind to Byron and Walter Scott. If only she could talk over her reading with Hardow, but he was always so remote and it would be even less likely that she could talk over with him her worries about the children.

The winter stars came out over the vast estate; the moon was reflected in the old lake and the little new one; the horses snuffled and stirred in the stables, the garden urns kept watch over the terraces; the maze, denuded of its summer mystery, and the beautiful temple at the end of the grounds by the river that cascaded into the new lake near the new bridge, watched over the spirit of place; and beyond them, rising on its own mound half a mile away, the Mausoleum with its tombs of dead Hardows brooded in the vast silence. Fires died down in the Castle, bedroom candles were lit. The nobility slept. The Swiss governess and the French maid slept. The old Earl and his Countess probably slept. The young Viscountess Georgiana lay trying to sleep. Hardow lay in his own room reading but then blew out his candle. Caro and Georgy, Harriet and William, Charles and Elizabeth slept. Mrs Copus sat by Blanche's bed, in case croup set in, but eventually slept. Old Lady Julia and her nephews William and Henry slept. The indoor servants and the outdoor servants, the upper and lower, the dairymaids and bailiffs and housemaids and cooks, even the great chef himself finally slept – though not for long.

When the sun rose the servants all rose with it, the farmhands even before. The animals had to be seen to, the house cleaned, the parquet floor of the Long Gallery polished, billiard tables brushed, books dusted, tables set, food prepared, fires cleaned out and laid with new coal, nursery breakfast made, children dressed and their flaxen hair combed, their bleary little faces washed. The hens' eggs had to be collected, the pigs' troughs cleaned, the lake fished and the mail sorted, when the Mail Coaches came from York and Malton. The schoolroom had to be prepared for the morning's lessons when the girls had breakfasted next door. Fountaynes had to go out and 'make improvements': he planned them in his sleep as his good-natured spouse lay dreaming of a ride in a gig in 1775. In short the Castle would wake from universal slumber (except for Nurse Copus whose vigil had ended only after the sun had risen) and the busy life would begin again.

Anne Tesseyman was to meet some of the family a few days later, but not before two things happened which frightened her. She had become used to the part of the Castle where she worked and to her bed in the women's attics over the East Wing, and also become used to the everlasting sewing. She had even learned not to mind the various male servants who stared at her. Not having seen Mrs Copus again she was beginning to think she would not be needed in the nursery.

She was looking out of the window one Thursday morning. She was alone in the attic at the time as she had gone to find a clean cap which she had forgotten. The dormitory was at the corner so that the window looked straight down and over to another window one storey down in the main wing across the courtyard. As she stood there, getting her breath for a moment and fixing her cap, she looked across at the other window and suddenly a face popped up behind the glass: a strange young face on a head too large to be a child's. It stared at her and she stared back for what seemed a long interval. It was immobile, with small ears and a tuft of hair. She did not know why but it made her blood run cold. 'Oh mercy,' she muttered, but could not stop staring, and as she did so the face suddenly vanished.

She was not near enough to see whether it was a man, woman or child – it seemed neither, rather more like a turnip with a tuft on the top. She ran down the wooden stairs, reasoning with herself. What was there to be frightened of? Perhaps the glass had distorted. She put it out of her head till the next day when she was finishing off a final ribbon for a cap which had to be ready that very afternoon for her ladyship to take to London. Curly and Eliza had been sent for by Miss Sharpe so that once more she was alone. Darkness was beginning to fall. She had moved to the window – from this one you could see only the lawn and the lake – to hold up the selvedge of a large sheet to the light to see if it needed strengthening, when she heard what sounded like the whine or moan of a beaten dog, somewhere above her. But there was nothing in the rooms above. They had been cleared of old curtains and samples not long before and she had been up there with boxes. She stood stock still, her heart thudding. Then, telling herself not to be silly, she took up her needle. Why did Curly and Eliza not come back? Just then as she threaded her needle the sound came again. 'Aa r-gh'. This time it was more like a woman in labour, but then it changed to a gulping sob and a choked voice saying, 'No, no'. She sat down again and tried to collect herself. She waited to hear it again but nothing happened. Everything was quite still once more except for some young stable-lads who had come round from the West Wing with a curricle and were shouting and laughing.

By degrees her heart began to slow down and when Curly came back, this time with some hats to feather, she was sitting quite composedly. Could she mention it to her? She had said nothing of the strange face, thinking they might think her mad or too imaginative, and she certainly did not want to lose her job for being thought odd. Perhaps she could just ask if anyone had

35

been upstairs.

'I heard a strange noise just now, up above: is there anyone there? At first I thought it was a dog moaning, then it sounded like a lass. What could it have been?'

Curly looked at her. 'You know there's only a load of old boxes up there. Nobody ever goes there – except when we took the things up last week.'

'It was someone, though,' said Anne. 'I wish it hadn't been.'

Curly looked at her strangely. 'Happen it was just a lass having a good cry and looking for somewhere quiet like,' she said at last.

'Aye, happen,' replied Anne and said no more, for it could have been that. But when they walked through the dark grounds round to the Servants' Hall on the other side, away from the kitchens, she could not repress a shudder. The corridors that branched out from the central Hall were ill-lit and stone-flagged and seemed to go on for miles. You could easily lose yourself there. All her initial bewilderment at the vastness of the place seemed to return.

'Tell you what,' said Curly. 'We'll take a walk tomorrow. They owe us our hours. I'll show you summat really grand. Like to come?'

'What is it?'

'You'll see when you get there!' With this Anne had to be content.

The pressure of work had now eased off a little. The layette had been packed and the winter sheets and towels for guests and family were almost finished and they could afford to take time off. Lady Hardow had gone away to her London house. The weather which had up till then been mainly cold and wet changed overnight into a hard frost which made everything look brighter. Even more stars pierced the dark heavens above Vanbrugh's ramparts, and Anne had begun to find certain things beautiful: dusk in the cobbled stable courtyard, and the morning pale pearl sky which could be seen through the high semicircular windows of the attics which were themselves like half moons.

The only person who did not seem cheered by the brighter weather was that under-housekeeper Miss Selina Sharpe – 'Sharpe's her name and sharp's her nature', they would say. She seemed to look daily more pinched and cross and to take delight in pointing out slightly crooked stitches. But this did not worry Anne, for she sensed that the lady was unhappy. Some called her the Earl's spy because she was such an economizer. But she was hard on herself too, for often she would sit tidying and doing endless tasks after dusk by candlelight when the girls were glad to leave the sewing-rooms for the Hall fire or their beds.

The next day, the day of the promised surprise, the girls were free at two o'clock and could walk or go wherever they liked till dusk. Eliza and Susan opted for the village shop. 'They think they'll see Joe Clayton and Bill Holderness,' said Curly knowingly. Although she 'slept in', she also lived with her mother and father in one of the cottages attached to the far end of the Castle. Her mother was a pleasant buxom woman with a crisp white cap and ribbons. She had been a dairymaid but now helped out in the house as she had a great talent for flower-arranging and was often in demand. Curly's uncle was over at the Home Farm and her father was a gardener in the walled garden in summer. In winter he cleared the land and felled trees.

'Where are you taking her then, lass?' asked Mrs Currey after Anne was introduced.

'Just a walk, mother. She ain't seen nothing yet.'

'Aye, it's a splendid place, is our Castle,' replied her mother comfortably.

Anne had noticed that all the servants seemed to think they owned the Castle along with its owners.

They wound round the long East Wing, crossed to the front and walked beside a wood where Curly then turned right along a path that led to the terrace path which continued into the distance. Over on the right Anne glimpsed a sheet of water.

'*Another* lake!'

'That's the new lake. Come on, we're going up this grassy bit. Now shut your eyes.' Anne stopped and shut them.

'Follow me – take my hand. It's a little steep. In spring there are thousands of Lent Lilies here – Mother makes baskets of them. Now . . . ! Open your eyes.'

Anne opened them and saw, about fifty yards away, a sort of house with a dome and cupola and pillared front and sides; a few steps with a stone balustrade led up to it.

'What is it? Who lives here then?'

'No one, silly. It's the *Temple*.'

'Is that a church then?'

'No, it's a temple – it's where the family come in summer for pique-niques and to rest and play. They sit in the room under the dome and look out over the gardens. You can even sleep here. Isn't it pretty?'

'Can we go and look?'

'I should think so. No one would be bothered to come in winter. Not inside mind – but you can look through the window.'

It was really the size of ten cottages of the sort Anne had lived in, but compared with the Castle of course it was small. She realized she was now comparing everything with the Castle!

They climbed the steps and walked over the sward, climbed more steps with two stone statues, larger than life, guarding the entrance, went under the arches and up to a large window whose panes stretched right to the ground. 'It's a door really,' whispered Curly.

'Oh, isn't it pretty!' breathed Anne. The place felt a happy place. There was a feeling of lightness and gaiety about it even on a winter day.

'It's the same round four sides,' said the guide Curly.

'What do they call it? Just the Temple?' asked Anne.

'The Temple of the Four Winds,' enunciated Curly. 'That's north, south, east and west you know.'

'Oh, I'd like to stay here – can we look round the other side?'

They walked solemnly around the building. Anne felt unaccountably happy.

'But you ain't seen nothing yet,' said Curly. 'We're going on further. There's another surprise.'

'Oh, can't we stay here?' But her friend drove her along, laughing.

They ran down the further slope behind and then across a long, long field to a little bridge across a stream.

'That's where the Castle grounds really end – but if we walk on further up here, up to the top, there's something else.'

They plodded on. Anne's boots were beginning to hurt her. As the ground began to rise Anne saw in the distance, looming ahead beyond some trees, what she vaguely assumed to be a church. They came upon it suddenly – a great domed building with circular pillars standing on an enormous plinth like a rock.

The whole area was bounded on all sides by a curious high wavy wall.

'What *is* it? It's like a picture our Rector showed us of St Paul's!'

'Ah – guess what it is.'

'A church?'

'No.'

'I don't think I like it, Curly. Let's go back to the other one, the little one, the Temple. This one's too – too big.'

'It's where they bury our Lords and Ladies,' whispered Curly. 'Deep down underneath. Like to look? We *could* go in.'

Anne shrank away, though usually she quite liked graveyards. It was so big, so heavy. She felt the weight of the stone down her back though they were only standing inside the wall looking over to the big platform on which rose the circular mausoleum on its high raised plinth, looking like an abandoned ruin.

'I don't want to go in. It gives me a feeling like a pain,' said Anne slowly, not looking at Curly.

Curly was a kind girl and did not press her invitation. 'You're a right rum lass, Anne. It's only dead people buried there.'

'I know. I just don't like the shape,' said Anne. How to explain that this strange building gave her the same feeling of terror as the face she'd seen looking in at her from the barred window and the queer strangled moaning she thought she had heard over the sewing room.

Anne did not want to spoil Curly's surprise, so she added politely: 'It's very grand, Curly – I'm sure I've never seen such a thing before. What do you call it?'

'Oh, we call it the Mouse Museum. I don't know why.'

They stood for a moment and then turned back, scrambled through the outer wall and ran, ran, ran, with the high spirits and energy of youth down and down past the wood and the bridge and the far field, once more past the Temple and the near wood and back after what seemed hours on to the path with the little lake glittering in the winter sun. Another walk across fields and they were back at Kitchen Court with the fields stretching down to the big lake.

Now Anne's boots were an agony to her so she asked permission to take them off at Curly's cottage for a moment. They were given a cup of tea and told to get on with it or Mrs Currey wouldn't answer for the consequences with Mrs Gibson if the girls were late serving tea to the upper servants.

In bed that night Anne had a strange dream. When she woke it seemed for a few moments all to fit together – a face, a cry, a vast tomb – frightening but somehow familiar. She was long in getting to sleep again. Before she did she thought of the little Temple. Perhaps it was a place you could say your prayers in? The next morning after breakfast she was summoned to Mrs Gibson's and told to present herself at Mrs Copus's apartments at eleven o'clock to receive new orders.

TWO

THE CHILDREN OF HARDOW
1818

'Nourish thy children, O thou good nurse;
'stablish their feet'

Apocrypha: 2 Esdras

Anne sought out Curly as soon as she had come out of Mrs Gibson's room. She was trembling again, a thing she had not done for some time. She *did* prefer children to sheet seams but the summons was sudden. She had had a good breakfast before she had heard she must go to Mrs Gibson but it now lay heavily on her stomach. Perhaps she had eaten too much – at home they were lucky if they ever got bacon, and tea was remashed from wetted leaves, if they had it at all it had to last. Here there were oatcakes for breakfast, and beer for the midday meal, even for the girls. She had acquired a healthy appetite, though at first she had felt her stomach was not large enough for the Yorkshire puddings and the meat. Even so she had gone on eating, fearful that the food might suddenly disappear. She suddenly felt ashamed – had she been greedy? What would the upper servants and even the children think of her manners, if it were true she was to go to the nurseries. She wondered why she had been chosen out of all the other sewing girls. She knew the Rector had given her a good report – 'honest, cheerful and industrious' – but was ignorant of her own attractive manner and of the fact that Mrs Gibson and Mrs Copus had sensed an intelligence under her country ways.

How would she get used to a new day, she wondered, thinking she had managed the sewing so well because Curly had been so friendly. Who would now be her friend – particularly if she had to leave the now familiar servants' dormitory and sleep in the nursery attic? Mrs Gibson had only said: 'You are to go to Mrs Copus, Tesseyman, about new work.'

'Don't fret – they'll probably only want you for the day at first,' Curly consoled her, having rushed up to the sleeping-quarters knowing Anne was looking for her and would be getting herself ready for her interview with Ma Copus. 'And you'll get out more – the children go out a lot more than their lordships and ladyships – on the estate and for walks. Lady Georgiana believes in "fresh air" – my mother told me.'

'But what if I have to sleep over there?' said Anne, sticking hairpins in her thick golden-brown hair. The nursery floor was on the north side, a long way from the main family bedrooms, which faced the gardens near the dome. Curly said nothing.

'Oh, how shall I ever get used to it? What if I do something wrong?' Anne uttered for the twentieth time. 'They usually take you on to help the others first,' replied her friend. 'Then if Ma Copus thinks you are satisfactory you take them out – with Delia Turner I expect. A lot of girls have gone away in the last year and my mother said Mrs Copus will have too much on when the new bairn comes back with Lady Georgiana – they need someone to help with little Miss Lizzie. Miss Blanche is nearly old enough to go up to the schoolroom, and Master Charlie – he's a handful – will soon have a tutor. 'Course there's William . . .' she broke off.

Anne swept up her basket and her needle and bobbins and thimble. 'You got used to the sewing all right, and you can come round and see me at teatime with my mother if you like, if the family want the childer then – or if Ma Copus gives you a break.' 'Thank you, Curly, you're very kind.' 'And anyway,' continued Curly, 'it's easier with little children – just imagine having to learn to be a lady's maid!'

'Oh, they'd never want me for that.'

'No, I expect not. I'll tell you a secret – if you promise not to tell the others.'

'What is it, Curly?'

'Well, my mother's going to put me in to learn to be a lady's maid one day soon! They all know our family and my mother's always wanted that for me.'

'Oh, Curly – then you'd be in the house too!'

'Yes, but not with you, over in the apartments. Don't breathe a word though.'

'I promise,' replied Anne, and the two girls went down together. Anne thought, well, even Curly wanted a change, and wanted to better herself, so why not her?

At eleven o'clock punctually by the stable clock which the old Earl always set five minutes fast in order to have punctual servants, Anne presented herself in Mrs Copus's comfortable chamber. That lady was sitting in a low chair, her hands folded. Anne noticed this time that her hair was greying and that she looked tired.

She beckoned Anne to come up to her.

'Let's have another look at you, Tesseyman.'

She saw a girl of medium height, transformed by good food, her bonny face no longer pinched, the dark blue eyes now even larger, her thick brown hair tidied away under her cap. She rose with some difficulty, took Anne's hands and turned them over. 'Do you know why I've sent for you, Tesseyman?'

Anne thought it was more diplomatic to say she was not sure.

'You're to go to the nurseries, Tesseyman.'

'Oh, ma'am!'

'You must be sure to keep your hands clean – soap will be provided over there. One can't be too careful with children. We may also give you a smallpox inoculation – all the children have had one.' Anne was silent, not knowing what that was.

'I see you've pricked your finger with a needle.'

'Yes, ma'am.'

'See you get a patch for it. Now as for your duties. You'll help Delia Turner, who is chief nursery maid, with Miss Lizzie and Master Charles. Miss Blanche will be with you sometimes – and Master William. There's other help of course, but we're a bit short. Miss Blanche and Master Charles won't be in the nurseries more than another year of course and I shall be occupied with our new babe when my lady returns from London.'

Anne said another 'Yes, ma'am.'

'Do what Turner tells you to do. You will not have to prepare the food but you may have to collect it and take back dirty platters to the kitchens. You will make the children's beds, clean their rooms, sort out dirty linen, darn, mend, and if Delia Turner needs you you may accompany her with the children on walks. She may need you to dress and wash some of the children too – there's plenty to do, as you see. I usually preside myself over the main meal of the day which the children take at four of the afternoon and if you watch me or Turner you will see how we teach young children to behave. If you are dependable you may be given further duties.'

'Yes, ma'am.'

'You may have to iron the clothes again after they come back from the laundry. I like my children's hair and person to be always clean and tidy and their clothes in a good state of repair, and nicely pressed. Later of course, as Turner thinks fit – always referring to me of course – you may be allowed to play with the children.'

Anne felt that under her plump and quite kindly exterior Mrs Copus saw herself as a queen. The queen walked to the window and looked out at the West Wing across the great courtyard and said, as though absent-mindedly, 'There is one more thing. They keep a very liberal house here, Tesseyman. Do you understand?'

'Yes – I mean no – ma'am.'

'You are not always overlooked when I am not there. You are trusted to do your work well – I shall of course be there a good deal at first to see your duties are well done – but you may be left with Turner and another girl from time to time to keep an eye on the children in addition to your domestic duties – and you will be trusted to see they come to no harm. And no "flirting", as I believe they call it now, with the footmen, no nipping off the children's toast unless you are offered it. Yes, they keep a very liberal house.' She was silent for a moment and Anne stood awkwardly.

'See you don't abuse it,' said the lady, looking up as if from a great distance.

'No, ma'am.'

'Well, that is all.' She turned and said more gently: 'I have been here many years. We've had our trials and tribulations – for a poor young woman like you there are always temptations. This is not just a house for gentry, it's a palace for noblemen. But remember, Miss Lizzie and Miss Blanche are only children, and children need the same things to my mind whether they are paupers or noble and rich.' She paused, perhaps feeling she had gone too far.

'Remember they are children, like anyone else's. Don't envy them, Tesseyman. I believe you have an affection for little ones?'

'Oh, yes, ma'am, I *do*.' Anne spoke with bright conviction.

'Yes, well, go up to the nursery – the stairs are opposite my door – turn right and knock. That is all. You may go.'

Anne curtsied. Her cheeks were hot – she felt she had been told something of significance but was not sure what. She bobbed another curtsy and walked out with a springier step, as she followed Mrs Copus's directions and went up the stairs. Mrs Copus for her part sighed a little and went back to her armchair. The girl seemed willing enough, she thought. She was still shy and unpolished but she had come on. She had often taken girls as young as fourteen in the old days when there were fewer children and they had done well enough. She was quick – you could see that – and honest. She listened carefully and respectfully. Still the main thing was that she was warm and kind and liked children. If Molly, the other nursery maid under Turner, did not return after her mother's funeral, and Mrs Copus shrewdly suspected she would not, there would be even more for Tesseyman to do. It was a very awkward time and Mrs Gibson had needed some persuasion to let her go, once the bulk of the autumn sewing had been finished. She could mend quite well too and that was necessary for an under nursery maid. Turner had many virtues but her skills as a needlewoman had not been as perfect as she would have wished. Ah well, you couldn't have everything, and Delia was firm with the boys without getting too fond of them. Children grow up and belong to their parents, not to the staff who have brought them up, not even to their tutors and governesses, however many airs *they* liked to put on.

She looked out of the window once more before ordering her tray. No good sitting brooding. Well, fancy that, there was the old Countess already getting into her gig and it was not yet twelve o'clock. How long would she ride up and down the avenues today? Such energy at nearly seventy, though her mind was weak. If only the daughter-in-law had as much. What would the next baby be? Would it be the last? She hoped so, for Lady Georgiana's sake. Eleven children were quite enough, though nicer ones you couldn't find anywhere. 'I like that Tesseyman,' thought Mrs Copus as her tray was brought in to her by a footman. 'A pity though that we are so understaffed. I ought to have at least two more nursery maids.' She sighed. A pity she no longer had her old energy and relied on Turner probably too much. She couldn't see to everything that was going on, but Tesseyman would do – and she was sure she would be kind to little William.

Anne went across the courtyard again and in at the stone door at the bottom of the nursery wing. She climbed up and up a narrow stone staircase which duplicated the stairs of the servants' wing and eventually found herself at a dark oak door on a landing, outside which was a red carpet. She knocked and waited in some trepidation, hoping she had come to the right place. The whole Castle was so confusing and she had only seen a bit of it so far – it was so big and so dark. She supposed the front of the building would be brighter. The door was opened by a very tall woman of about twenty-nine with her hair piled up at the back and frizzed at the front.

'Good morning, ma'am. I'm Tesseyman, the new nursery maid,' said Anne, dropping a curtsy to be on the safe side.

'Come in, come in. Thank goodness they've sent someone. Let's have a look at you. Hm – seen Ma Copus, have you?'

'Yes, ma'am.'

'You don't need to curtsy to me – or call me ma'am, Tesseyman,' said the woman with a short laugh.

She led the way into a little anteroom in which was a table piled high with dirty crockery and another with folded clothes and bedlinen.

'I'm just Turner to you – Delia Turner. What's *your* given name? I hope you can sew – all this to be gone through!' She gestured to a white cambric nightshirt hanging over a chair.

'Please – I'm Anne.'

'Well, Anne – soon you're to take these dirty pots down to the kitchens, and then this afternoon I've a tidy bit of mending for you.' Anne was just about to say that she had come to the Castle as a seamstress, when a little voice cried 'Turner!'

Delia beckoned Anne to follow her, through a door on the left and into a sunny room in which there were little low chairs, a large table and a small one, a rocking-horse and a big fire surrounded by a heavy iron guard. The curtains of this pleasant chamber were, surprisingly, of a deep red and there was a Turkey carpet on the floor. Anne thought what a lot of cleaning that would need if the children dropped things on it. One little girl was sitting at the table with a big piece of paper on which she was pencilling feverishly. A boy sat astride the rocking-horse and another girl was on her knees in front of a large dolls' house.

'This is Miss Blanche,' said Delia Turner, nodding to the writer at the table, 'and this is Master Charles.'

'Gee up!' shouted Charles on his horse.

'And this is Miss Elizabeth.'

The little girl looked up shyly and then got to her feet, holding a small wooden doll.

'Hello, girl – I'm Lizzie,' she said. 'Do you want to see my doll, girl?' she went on.

'How old is your doll then?' asked Anne.

'She is nearly three, like me,' replied the child solemnly. 'And my other doll Belinda is only one year old. She's my baby.'

Anne looked at Delia who just stood there smiling and saying

48

nothing. She took her courage in both hands and went up to the child and looked at the doll.

'Does she have a brother or a sister then?' she asked.

'No, just her. Belinda is not her sister – this doll lives in here.' The child pointed to the house, a beautiful wooden town house with steps up to a red door with a knocker.

'Oh, how fine,' exclaimed Anne. 'Do you look inside?'

'Dolls are silly,' shouted Charles. 'Please, Turner, I want to go out. Why is this girl here?'

'Hush, Master Charles. You know Molly went home. This is a new maid,' replied Delia briskly, sitting down at the table. 'We must tidy up. Mrs Copus will be coming up later.' Then, turning to Anne: 'You get to know the children, Tesseyman – I can see you like dolls!'

'Will you call me Anne?' asked Anne of the child Lizzie, shyly. She did not want to be called Tesseyman by a baby, that she did not!

'I'll call you Nan,' said Lizzie.

'Anne,' said Delia without more ado, 'you play with them till it's time to go out whilst I work – break you in easy like. I've got the beds to do and the night nursery to tidy.'

Every movement Delia made was brisk and angular. She looked extremely efficient and a little overpowering with her height and her scraped-up hair and her snowy apron. Yet Anne found herself liking her. There seemed to be no nonsense about her and the gruffness did not seem unkind.

Soon she was plunged into listening to Lizzie explaining the dolls' house and Blanche wanting water to paint with and Charlie running round in circles in an excess of energy. He had had enough of the rocking-horse.

'Don't let Lizzie on my horse,' he said. 'She'll fall off.'

Anne thought that the child would perhaps object but she looked at her brother steadily and then turned back to her house.

'If *she* can't get on your horse, *you* can't play with her dolls,' remarked Blanche, sucking her paint brush and making trouble.

'Here, Master Charles,' said Anne, going to a cupboard. 'What's this?' She held out a box. 'Is it a toy?'

'No, it's my dissected map that was George's. Look, I'll show you.' Soon he had the jigsaw on the table and was poring over it. It was a map of England. 'That's our place,' he said, pointing to Yorkshire. 'Can you read? The other girl couldn't.'

Just fancy, thought Anne, he was only about five and Miss Lizzie nearly three and they spoke like grown-up people! She found herself attempting to make her accent less broad, more like her old Rector's voice, in order to be understood.

'Yes, I can read,' she said. 'But can you?'

'I've begun with Mama. When I'm seven I shall go to Edward's school.'

Lizzie came up holding a wooden musical box. What wonderful things there were to be sure in this room. Better than the toy shop she had heard of in York.

'Play it for me, Nan,' Lizzie said.

'She's not Nan, she's Anne,' said Blanche, not looking up. 'Ain't you, Anne?'

'Miss Elizabeth can call me Nan,' she replied, taking the little girl on her knee. She seemed to know what to do. If only Mrs Copus didn't suddenly come in and tell her she shouldn't!

Charles occupied himself with the dissected map and Blanche with her writing and drawing so Anne had a good opportunity to look at them more closely. They were all fair, Blanche with silvery gold hair, Lizzie with dark gold and Charles flaxen. The two older children had rather long noses but little Lizzie's nose was snub and her eyes brown unlike her brother and sister whose eyes were light blue.

'Tell me a story,' said Lizzie.

'She doesn't know any,' said Charles.

'That's rude, Charles,' said Blanche. 'All the girls know *some* stories.'

'Once upon a time,' said Anne, 'there was a little girl who lived in a cottage near a wood.'

'We know *that*. That's Red Riding Hood,' interrupted Charles.

'No it isn't,' said Anne boldly, wondering whether she should ever contradict the children.

'Go on,' said Charles.

'The girl was five years old and her name was Hannah.'

The three children all looked up and waited for her to go on.

'She was not rich like you. She had a poor mother and her father was dead and she worked all day picking up sticks and feeding swine.'

'What are swine?'

'Pigs,' replied Anne briefly. 'One day she went for a walk in the woods.'

'And she sawed a wolf,' said Charles.

'It's saw,' said Blanche.

'No, she seed – saw – lots and lots of pretty yellow flowers all over the ground under the trees. And blue flowers. And she began to gather them. She liked the flowers so much she lost her way and came to a funny old house in the middle of the wood.' As Anne rapidly invented she saw that nasty old building Curly had shown her the other week. That would not do. She must not frighten the children! It must be a fine, pleasant house.

'A window opened in the house and a head poked through.'

'It was her grandmother,' muttered Charles wearily.

'No, it was a beautiful young man,' said Anne, warming to her subject. 'His name was Mr Charles!'

'Oh!'

'And he showed Hannah the way back home and put her flowers in a big basket and walked along with her. The sun set and he said "Goodbye" and her Mam – her mother – was *so* pleased to see her she forgot that Hannah should have brought the sticks home and so she did not punish her but gave her a bowl of gruel. And she went to bed and fell asleep straight away.'

'What's gruel?' asked Charles. Elizabeth was now almost asleep on her lap, her thumb in her mouth, and Anne was trying to explain that gruel was porridge when Delia came back into the nursery from the night nursery, her arms full of sheets.

'Lizzie can have her rest and the others their dinner. Kitchen will send up – I've seen to it. Then this afternoon you can come for a walk with me and the children and Sarah – that's the maid that was Master Edward's but he's at school now and she's helping out with Master William.'

Delia's voice was not that of a village girl and Anne wondered where she had acquired her rather superior accent and her efficiency. The table was cleared, the toys put away, Lizzie put down to sleep and trays taken in from the anteroom where a junior footman had left them – mutton and pease pudding and stewed apples. The two young women ate with the children. Anne felt quite hungry. The day was passing quickly enough. She was pleased that when Lizzie woke and when she went in to her the child said 'Nan', and smiled before she was properly awake.

'I can see she's going to be your favourite,' said Delia, her mouth full of pins.

Anne was brushing all the children's hair and putting on boots and cloaks. 'She is a nice little girl – but they are all good children, I think,' she said shyly. She felt much more shy with Delia than with the children, though Blanche had a rather distant air.

'They are not haughty – not like some I've known,' replied Delia, now deftly pulling up stockings. 'We should have more staff – you ought not to be doing their hair – but never mind, Mrs Copus knows we do what we can.'

They were off for their walk after a lost hair ribbon had been found and Lizzie's pleas to be carried had been acceded to.

'Have you seen the new little cart?' asked Blanche.

They found themselves in the hall under Mrs Copus's chamber and went along another long corridor. It broadened out under another grander staircase and a young footman was to be seen wheeling out a little carriage like a miniature curricle, with a hood and two plank seats and a recessed seat behind.

'You *push* it,' said Charles.

Lizzie was put in the recess with Blanche walking along and Charles, aided by Anne, pushed the contraption. They got it out safely into the courtyard, Delia standing rather aloofly to the side. Sarah the maid came down from another corridor off the courtyard. Once round the corner of the West Wing, a part of the house Anne had never yet been in, they all walked slowly round to the front to a great lawn where stood a large cedar tree; stone terraces fell away in the distance to the little lake.

Anne looked at the front of the house; it was more beautiful than the back and a large double flight of stairs in the centre led up to a great grand porch. It was quite chilly so they wheeled Lizzie down a gradually sloping path to the next terrace.

'There's flowers here in summer,' volunteered Delia.

'What's that big vase, then?' asked Anne, and then saw more of them placed in a straight line along the terrace.

'The urns you mean? His old lordship's always planting them – gets them from abroad. I think they're ugly.'

Just then some dogs came running up and Anne shrank away from them. She was not used to dogs as pets.

'Come, Wellington, good boy,' shouted Charles. 'There's grandpapa.'

'He's too busy to talk to you now,' said Delia firmly. 'You may go down and see your papa before supper.'

'Where's my mama?' said Blanche. 'Is she at Chatsworth?'

'Your mama's in London – gone to fetch a new sister or brother,' answered Delia.

'When will she come back?'

'Quite soon, as soon as matters are arranged.'

'What does that mean?' But Delia was spared an answer as Lizzie wanted to get out of the buggy.

'You carry her. I'll push the carriage. Come, Master Charlie, Miss Blanche – we've to go to Nurse Copus now,' decided Delia. 'It's too cold to stay out.'

'Her rheumatics was bad this morning – she wouldn't have let the children out today, I'll be bound,' said Sarah.

'She likes babies better than children,' replied Delia shortly.

'Can I have my ball?' asked Charles.

Delia had been prepared and fished out a wooden ball from her inner apron pocket. He rolled it happily before him as the small party circled round the great house once more and came in again at the East Courtyard.

How grown up, yet how indulged – how childish too – these children were, Anne was thinking. At Charles's age she had been shooing geese and weed-picking and her only toy had been Mam's old peg doll with the ribbon Dad had once bought her at the fair. And nobody in her family had ever answered her questions! Yet it was fun answering children's questions and looking after them, especially when you were going to be paid for it. She wished she were a proper nurse like Ma Copus.

'You'll be tired,' said Delia stiffly but kindly. 'Your first day – they do tire a woman out, no mistake, do children.' Anne thought of what Mrs Copus had said that morning.

'Children are all the same really, aren't they,' she offered, and was quite surprised to find herself giving it as her own opinion.

'Oh, you've found that out have you? Of course they are! I don't expect you had toys and nursemaids – I know I didn't – but if we had, we'd have been just like this lot here.'

'But most children have to *work* when they're very small, don't they?' Anne had distant relatives who had travelled to another part of the county and worked at home with their looms and the children were not spared.

'Master Charles and his sisters *work* hard at playing,' answered Delia enigmatically.

When they got back in Charles wanted to play with his

soldiers but Delia insisted they spruced themselves up for a visit to Mrs Copus.

'She finds it hard to climb all these stairs,' said Delia. 'That's why she doesn't spend all her time with us. Like Sarah said, she's got the rheumatics – but she decides everything really. She's very good with little babies, once the monthly nurse has been and gone. But she doesn't like London anyway and so they let her stay on here and take over when the babies come home. We'll have more work when Lady Hardow comes back.'

'Have you worked here long then Miss – I mean – Delia?' Anne asked.

'Nearly three years, since Miss Lizzie was born. I was trained as a maid to an old lady but she died and so I had to find another place.' Anne was curious as to the rest of Delia's story but there was no time for more chat as they had to go down to Mrs Copus.

'Take some sewing, Anne. There's Blanche's nightrobe. The lace came off and it wants mending, and Charlie is very hard on his hose. They need a good darn.'

It seemed an age, not just a few hours, since Anne had gone in to see Mrs Copus that morning. What a lot had happened – she felt quite exhausted. No wonder her Mam had always said children tired a body out. But when Lizzie wanted to climb into Anne's lap in Mrs Copus's parlour and Mrs Copus did not object and a good cup of tea was drunk, she felt much better. Mrs Copus even seemed to approve of the way she talked to the children. Charles, jumping up and down and begging for bonbons from his old nurse, whose favourite of the three he obviously was, said 'Hey Copus – do you know this girl Anne? She's played with us.' Mrs Copus darted a swift look at her and seemed to smile. Anne bent over Lizzie and fed her soaked toast. It was very homely, almost like *her* own home except that everything was so clean and gleaming and food came in like magic. 'So long as the rest of the work is done, Tesseyman,' said Mrs Copus.

Later, after bathing the children and tucking them up in bed (their papa was too busy to see them in his room that evening) Anne was allowed back to Servants' Hall for a proper meal and found Curly waiting all agog for news.

'Oh, it's lovely work, Curly, but I'm right tired! I told them a story and we went for a walk. Oh, it's better than sewing sheets!'

'What did you tell them? Still I expect you *are* tired – come and sup and you can tell me all about it.'

And Curly too had some more news. They were definitely going to train her up as assistant to the lady's maid, that post much sought after, ending as it did in being lady's maid herself one day.

'Oh, I'm so glad – that's what you said this morning!'

The two girls supped and soon went to bed. Anne did not think of home before she slept, nor did she have any nightmares.

The weather turned cold the next day. Anne saw them bringing up bunches of carrots from the icehouse near the kitchen garden. They looked like frozen amputated fingers, like she imagined dead bits of limbs at Waterloo. As she walked across the courtyard to enter the nursery wing hailstones lashed at her face. She put her head down and ran. When she got to the nursery floor Mrs Copus was in the nursery, the bearer of great glad tidings.

'A boy, girls – a great grand boy and I am told he is to be Master Henry.'

'Oh, Master Harry, then,' said Delia.

'Well then, my dears,' said Mrs Copus to Blanket who was standing one shoe on and one shoe off, and to Charlie who was whizzing round as usual. 'A little brother.'

Anne went in to finish Lizzie's toilette. 'You've got a baby brother,' she said softly.

'Where is he? Where?' asked Lizzie immediately.

'Your mama will bring him back from London soon.'

'I wanted a sister,' said Lizzie as Anne brushed her fine baby hair.

'You *have* a nice sister. Miss Blanche is your sister.'

'I mean a *baby* sister, like a doll, Nanna.' Here was a child not much less than a baby herself wanting a baby sister to cuddle!

The day passed quickly as they were all so excited and the news had spread through the whole Castle.

'When will Mama come back?' Blanche kept asking over and over again.

'Does her ladyship usually stay long in London?' Anne asked Delia.

'Oh – they're supposed to rest for a month but she'll want to be back. I suppose it depends on the roads. If there is snow for several weeks they'll keep back the coaches.'

They were washing some small dresses which Delia said were too fine for the Castle laundry. Afterwards Anne took the flat-iron and Delia played with the children whilst she ironed the tiny pieces of cambric.

Charlie was restless. 'He's been asked for by the Family,' said Delia. 'Miss Georgy will probably send Sarah for him or even come for him herself. We'd better get him clean. Look – I'll finish the ironing and you can get him ready and take him with Miss Georgy to the little drawing-room. They won't keep him long. They like Miss Blanche better up there.'

Anne was just putting the finishing touch to Charlie's face and hands when there was a knock and without warning John, the outside footman, opened the door to a tall, fair, pretty girl of about fifteen.

'Hello,' she said as Anne curtsied. 'I've come for Master Charles. You're new, aren't you?'

Mrs Copus then came up holding Blanche, whom she had taken down to her room, by the hand. 'Miss Georgy, this is a new maid, Tesseyman. She will accompany you with Master Charles,' she said rather formally but did not curtsy.

This was the first time Anne had been near the Family's apartments. She followed the young girl and the footman; Charles was rather quieter than usual and held Anne's hand. They went downstairs and along a corridor and upstairs and down again till Anne realized they were at the front of the house. They stopped before a large door and Anne was just wiping Charlie's nose and seeing he looked perfect when two other girls sidled out of the door. Anne caught a glimpse of the room – a great crystal chandelier hung from the ceiling and the walls seemed to be papered with silk the colour of dark roses. The younger of the two young ladies seized upon Charlie: 'Come and cheer us up, do. Grand has been *difficult*.'

'Sh – Harriet,' said the other girl nervously.

'You can go now,' said Georgy over her shoulder. 'Can you find your way back?'

Anne did not think she could but was so mortified by shyness that she gulped and said she thought she could.

'John will bring Master Charlie back,' said Harriet, turning as the door closed and Charlie was lost to view.

Anne was all in a turmoil and began to walk, she knew not where. She pushed open a door – but surely that was not the way they had come? She peered round the door – no, it was not! – for this room was much much larger than the one that had swallowed up Charlie: a great long room with tall windows and paintings of queer people in gold frames. She was just about to shut the door when she felt a hand on her shoulder and nearly jumped out of her skin. A tall old man was looking at her.

'Where are *you* going?' he barked.

'Please sir, I've lost my way. I'm from the nursery.'

'Let's have a look at you, girl. By God – I don't know my own servants!'

'Turn round – you're going the wrong way – down there, turn left; down the stairs, turn right and along the corridor. You might recognize your surroundings by then.'

Anne curtsied and flew. Down, left, down the stairs, turn right – oh, thank goodness, here was the familiar nursery corridor. What a fool she was! She ran to the nursery door and burst in, panting.

'Whatever is the matter?' cried Delia, in the act of folding clothes and putting them back in the anteroom oak chest. 'Have you seen a ghost?'

'I lost my way – and an old man shouted at me and told me how to get back,' she got out.

'An old man! What did he look like? Tall? With a mouth like this?' – she thrust out her underlip. 'And black eyes, I'll be bound!'

'Yes – he did look like that. I hope he didn't think I was going in that room on purpose – a long room with pictures.'

'Bless me, she's been in the Long Gallery! And talking to Earls, I'll be bound!'

'Talking to *Earls*? – oh! – no! was it, Earl Fountaynes, that old man then?'

'That it was – be thankful he didn't tick you off!'

'I remember he said "I don't know my own servants any more" or something like that.'

'Oh well, can't be helped. You weren't doing anything wrong. Put Miss Lizzie to bed. Miss Blanket's drinking her milk. Master William's coming back tonight. You knew he'd been away?'

'Why does no one ever see him, Delia?' asked Anne, carefully unbuttoning Lizzie's chemise.

'Pas devang les enfans,' said Delia.

'What's that mean?'

'That's French – I'll tell you later.'

With that Anne had to be content. Delia was busy putting Charlie to bed when a carriage stopped in the courtyard. Charlie had returned highly excitable and noisy and it took time to calm him down. Anne was going in to help Delia control him – he was standing on a table at the time – when Mrs Copus came in once more.

'Girls, girls – and Master Charles. Look who's here!'

Charlie stopped just as he was about to jump on Anne and Mrs Copus led in a little boy, a short stumpy boy with a rather big head and a tuft of hair stuck on top.

'Oh!' Anne jumped with shock.

'What is it, Tesseyman? This is Master Willy. Come and say "Hullo" to your new maid, Master William my boy.'

So *that* was the face at the window, the swollen, blurry face! It was just a little boy – a rather strange little boy. It was Master William. Mrs Copus was looking at her so she quickly recovered herself and said: 'How do you do, Master William.' Was it the wrong thing to say?

'Yes, sir,' replied William.

He had rather a loud, jarring voice and continually moved his hands across his face.

So he was afflicted. That was it. Poor child – and she thinking the face had been a ghost or a monster. She resolved to be specially kind to him.

'Master William has his own tutor as well as Sarah,' said Mrs Copus. 'But *he* can't be with us this week. You must manage as best you can.' She patted the boy's head and turned to go. 'Anne, Turner will need your help. He sleeps in the little room with Master Charlie.'

Charles had jumped down and taken William's hand. 'Come on, William – we'll play building bricks.'

'Not now,' said Delia. 'Bedtime. Tomorrow, I promise.'

'Want Edward,' said William, and continued to twiddle his hands up and down.

'Miss Blanket will talk to you as we get you ready for bed. Come on, Master William.' Together the two women undressed him. He was uncomplaining.

'William is ten but I am nearly as tall as he is,' said Blanche.

'Well, he didn't get his height from his mother like you did,'

58

said Delia. 'Even Mr George isn't *tall*.'

'But George is grown up!' replied Blanche in a puzzled tone.

At last they were all settled and Anne was sent down to Servants' Hall for her supper. She had a lot to tell Curly. Now she had seen nearly all the family, except her young ladyship and her husband. And Master Fred and Master Edward – and young Mr George of course. Perhaps he would be back soon from Oxford?

The weeks soon passed. Mrs Copus was busy preparing a room for the new baby when he should return from London with his Mama. Miss Sharpe seemed to have gone away: no one seemed to know where or why. Anne heard them discussing it whenever she went down for her evening meal which she sometimes took in Servants' Hall if she had not eaten with the children. She was no longer required to serve at the upper servants' table and this was a great relief. She did not even see much of Curly who had gone to Marie's room to begin her training. She heard that by Christmas guests would be arriving and Lady Georgiana would return with her new baby, little Master Harry. He would stay with his mama when he returned so Mrs Copus would be over in an adjoining room to her ladyship's along with the wet nurse. 'She'll send the monthly nurse away – you'll see,' said Delia. 'I don't know why she didn't get married herself if she likes infants so much.' 'But she is *Mrs* Copus,' said Anne, puzzled. 'Mrs by courtesy is what they say,' replied Delia. 'She's never been wed – can't you tell – neither has Mrs Gibson!'

Anne was moved on one momentous day from her bed in the servants' attic to one in the night nursery next to Miss Lizzie. Molly had not returned and Sarah had her hands full with William who took hours over every meal – he could not or would not feed himself properly. 'Will Mrs Copus come up here then when she bring Harry back when he's weaned off his wet nurse?' asked Anne. 'That she will not – I think she's enough on her hands without supervising us all up here like she used to,' replied Delia.

The day came when Lady Georgiana arrived back in the red coach from London, accompanied by Hardow who had gone south expressly for the purpose. Many of the servants had stood cheering her arrival and reported it in the Servants' Hall, and the children were dressed up and taken to pay their respects to their mama by Mrs Copus and Sarah. Next morning Anne was asked to take over some baby sheets to Lady Georgiana's rooms and give them to her maid. Mrs Copus was waiting down the stairs from the nursery to accompany her. 'It's right she should know you've been taken on,' was all she said and Anne realized that this meant she was to stay in the nurseries and was overjoyed. What would the Lady be like? She did hope there was nothing she would find fault with, and brushed her hair and washed her hands and face very carefully.

She followed Mrs Copus round the usual endless corridors up stairs and down and in and out and was told to wait at the door to her ladyship's maid's room. Perhaps Curly was somewhere in there? Then Mrs Copus came out and beckoned Anne in and the footman opened the door of an inner room and she saw the lady in her chair and knew she need not have worried. She dropped the deepest curtsy she had ever essayed. The lady had a kind face and a very gentle voice. She was fair, like her daughter Blanche, with a long nose and clear blue eyes, but she looked rather tired with rings under those eyes. She smiled as Anne looked up after her curtsy.

'Tesseyman, your ladyship,' said Mrs Copus. 'Taken on for the sewing in August and moved to the nurseries.' Anne blushed.

'I hope you are happy in my nurseries. Mrs Copus, see she comes to Chapel on Christmas Day.'

Anne muttered 'Thank you, my lady', and curtsied again and waited. What a sweet woman she was. Mrs Copus signalled her to leave and then turned to her mistress. As Anne was ushered through the door by the footman, who winked at her, she heard Mrs Copus saying in a low voice: 'We needed more help with Master William – and Thwaites has not returned.'

This time, thought Anne, she must not get lost. What if Earl Fountaynes or Viscount Hardow was to find her wandering again? As she went down the nearest flight of steps feeling like an intruder she passed the music room, though she did not know it, and heard music coming out of it. That would be one of the older young ladies playing, she supposed. Curly had said that Miss Georgy and Miss Harriet played the harp. If only she could stay to listen. She loved music. Perhaps she would hear some fiddle playing in the Chapel at Christmas? But probably services for noble people had a different sort of music? It was a sad tune, this one. Then she heard a girl's voice singing, but it didn't sound like English words. Reluctantly she crept round the next flight of steps and found herself in one of the stone-flagged corridors she recognized. Thank goodness.

There was no time to think about the music when she finally arrived back in the nurseries. Master William wanted someone to play with him and Sarah was out on an errand for Delia, so Anne patiently built up his bricks and put his lead soldiers on top for him. Charlie called this game 'Waterloo'. Then Charlie wanted toast and fruit and Delia came in and asked her to get a pineapple from the glasshouse. Then Sarah returned and they made the children's beds together and collected the soiled linen. William produced a lot of that. Poor bairn, she thought. A nobleman's son and poorer in spirit than lots of the children of farm labourers she had known.

Little by little, through running errands and walking out with Delia and Sarah and the children, Anne was beginning to find her way around so that soon she felt she had been in the nurseries for years instead of a few weeks. Christmas would not be an occasion for great present-giving but was still a family reunion and great was the excitement in the nursery when big brothers Fred and Edward returned from their schools. The house had other new faces too – a small party of guests invited for the christening of the new baby and one or two politicians and other friends of Hardow's from London. The servants grumbled at all the extra work this entailed. It was said that Lady Georgiana's sister was to have come but could not at the last moment. When Mr George came down from Oxford the house party would be complete. The servants were rushed off their feet lighting fires and warming beds and bearing trays. Dogs belonging to guests barked everywhere, and Lady Georgiana kept to her room but would get up on Christmas Day for the christening in the Chapel. Some very important guests were to come just for a day or two to stand as godparents.

Just a week before Christmas Anne had deposited Lizzie and Charlie with the schoolroom maids, as their sisters wanted to see them, and was on her way back down a staircase which wound behind a pillar of the Great Hall under the dome. She heard the excited voices of Edward and Fred down in the hall and peeped over the balustrade. Viscount Hardow was standing with a young man at the door, which was open – the great door which led down a long flight of steps to the terrace in front of the house.

'George! George!' the boys were shouting. And, oh heavens! there was William too – she thought Sarah was with him in the nursery. Then she saw Mr George bend down and embrace William who stood stock still. Then William butted his eldest brother in the stomach in a gesture of what Anne recognized as the utmost affection and George and his brothers went off in the direction of the family drawing-rooms, George with his arm round William, Hardow standing somewhat to the side.

When Anne got back to the nursery Delia was told of the new arrival and how Master William was down with his brothers. 'We couldn't find him,' said Delia. 'He always knows when Mr George is back.'

Delia also said that her Ladyship was suffering from low spirits which she often was after the birth of a child. 'Mrs Copus calls it her "heart's alarms",' went on Delia. 'I hope she will feel better for the christening,' said Anne.

Anne wished, not for the first time, that she could write to Hannah – there was so much to say – but Hannah could not read very well. She, Anne, had been taught to read and write by the Rector's wife who had found her quick and intelligent. Perhaps if she wrote to the Rector's wife, they would read it out to Mam and Hannah. Yes, she would do that! She would buy or beg some paper and borrow a pen from Miss Blanche: she had seen an inkstand in the nursery. Then she would be able to share all this strange new world. If the Rector's friend should come at Christmas or soon after for her news and her sovereign, she would have a letter ready.

Dear Rector and Dear Mrs Hart [Anne wrote],

I wish you a Happy Christmas and I will ask the messinger to take this to you to send you my respects and will you please take them to my Mam and sister and read them what I write here.

I am very well though we are kept right busy. All the Family is here now, that is the Lordships and our Young Ladyship with her new babby. It is a boy. I help with Master Charlie and Miss Lizzie along with my new friend Delia. And I made a very good friend Maria we call Curly on account of her curly hair. Yesterday I was shown the Chineeze dressing room – that is all the paper on the walls with birds and flowers.

We arc going to Chapel here on Sunday at Christmass and the babby will be christened. One of the young Ladies plays harp music it is lovely.

I do not like all the buildings here but the lake is beautyfull and the Tempel. Mrs Hart you can come to look if you ever had the cost of carridge. The estate is open to the Publick who come on the Footpath to see the buildings.

I miss you dearest Mam and my dear Hannah and I want to know how you are keeping and arc you eating well and is there much work? I shall send you all the brass I have yet got and hoping to hear from you one day. I send the Rector my respects and to all the village and friends and grandmam and Mistress Aysgill and the girls and all the babbies at Church. My love to all the family,

And to the Rector, and Mrs Hart respectfully yours
Anne Tesseyman

It took Anne several days to write this and she was very proud of it but reading it through she wondered if she had been too full of herself. She should have started it with queries about her mother. But the Rector would understand. It was rather difficult writing him a letter meant for her mother.

The baptismal ceremony was to be conducted after the service on Christmas Day and would of course be confined to the presence of the family and friends. Servants were however allowed to stand at the back during the collect for Christmas Day before filing out for the more important event of baptism, and Anne was among them as Lady Georgiana had ordered. Curly's mother was going and had been told to bring along her son and daughter. Her son, another solid footman named Jim, had declined the privilege and Anne was to sit by Mrs Currey and Curly. So far Anne had only managed to attend the church in the nearby village and that only once, and had never yet been in the family Chapel. Its decoration, more in keeping with a hall than a church, startled her as she stood with Curly in the massed ranks of servants. But her attention was soon turned to the front and side rows where the family were filing in. Not yet Lady Georgiana, who had been told to avoid chills until the last moment when she, her sister, friends and maids would bring in the new little future Honourable; and not yet her husband or her father-in-law, and certainly not *all* the fashionable friends who were staying at the Castle, but, in a long line with their governesses and maids and tutors, the older children, followed by Mrs Copus and the younger ones, except for William. Anne had herself looked after little Miss Lizzie that Christmas morning, got her breakfasted and dressed and was pleased to see she looked a little angel, holding Delia's hand. Perhaps next Christmas she herself would be allowed to accompany her!

There were nine of them and as they filed into their seats she stared avidly at their faces. What exciting news to tell Mam and Hannah next time she wrote – all those Hardows in order from the eldest to the youngest. The young man whose departure to Oxford she had witnessed eleven weeks earlier and whom she had seen from the hall staircase, that Mr George, was back with them and led the procession. It was true he was not tall, unlike many of his brothers and sisters, but what a kind, good face he had with quite long wavy hair, and big eyes. He was looking round now at the others and she saw him whisper to Mrs Copus, and that lady whisper to a maid who went up to a steward and Mrs Gibson. She wondered what he had said but found herself looking now at the next boy, taller than his brother though he was three years younger. 'There's Master Frederick,' whispered Curly. Behind him came Edward, a handsome boy of ten, holding little Charlie by the hand. And walking gracefully after them with Mademoiselle Sterky, the Swiss governess, rustling along with bowed head, there came the three almost grown-up girls – Caroline, rather gawky and long-faced, the pretty Georgiana with big eyes and slender arms and, taller than either of them, fair, blue-eyed, hair carefully curled, the dazzling Harriet who at thirteen looked much more confident than her older sisters. Mrs Copus had now joined Blanche and Elizabeth. Who was now coming up to her side? George turned his head, smiled and advanced to – William – whom he must have expressly sent for. So that was what the whispering had been about! George had wanted William to be there.

Anne hoped the poor little boy would not disgrace himself. But George put his arm round him and showed him the prayer-book he was holding and soon after that the service began. The Psalms and responses were familiar to her though the short sermon was almost unintelligible. Whoever was taking the service did not come from round those parts. At home the Rector spoke another language but one you could learn – this preacher was different. Her eyes kept straying to the side pews and she thought she saw that fierce old grandfather but was not sure. What lovely bairns they all were – it did your eyes good to see such a grand family. She hoped to see Lady Georgiana and the baby but was disappointed. The harmonium began to be played after the Blessing and the servants knew their place and turned to go. William was fidgeting, she saw, and Mrs Copus was looking a little grim. Her last sight of them all that morning before Lizzie and Charlie and Blanche came back to the nursery for Christmas dinner was of George smiling, with his arm round his little brother, and a sunbeam, that had unaccountably managed to creep through the plain glass of the end window, playing over his head.

At servants' dinner, a magnificent affair with plum puddings and beer and beef, the talk was all of the christening and little Harry. But afterwards in the Christmas dusk, a message came from Mrs Copus that they should go, she and Delia, to the front house where the younger children would be ready to return to their quarters after their specially granted hour or two with their mother and the new baby. Anne was full of pudding and good cheer and excited by the day and the unaccustomed merry-making, so she was less anxious than usual about losing her way across the great north courtyard to the East Wing door and down inside the house to the front, and up the stairs to the private rooms. It needed only Mam and Hannah to make it all perfect! The footman opened the door to the anteroom and beyond it was light, and sound, and laughter.

'Better wait – they'll bring them out,' said Delia. 'I wish we could see the new baby and her ladyship,' replied Anne. But it was not Lady Georgiana who stood at the suddenly opened door with Liz and Charlie, but a pleasant young man with wavy hair, a large nose and deep-set eyes.

'Here y'are, nurse!' he said cheerily. 'They've eaten well and should be sleepy.' It was Young George. Delia curtsied.

'Is Master William to come too and Miss Blanche, sir?'

'*I'll* bring them along later. They're enjoying themselves,' replied the young man with a smile.

Anne could not take her eyes off him though the children were cavorting round as usual.

'Nanna, Nanna,' cried little Lizzie. Anne bent and picked her up.

'Saw my brother, I saw Harry,' Liz went on. Anne unselfconsciously tidied a strand of her hair which the child had disarranged.

'That's a right nice name, Harry,' she said as she and Delia turned to go with Charlie back to their quarters.

'George, this is Nanna,' went on the little girl. Anne blushed and tried to curtsy but the child made it difficult.

'Merry Christmas, Nanna,' said the young man as he turned to shut the door.

'He wished me a Merry Christmas!' said Anne to Mrs Copus as that lady for once came to oversee the children's bedtime.

'But you shouldn't have let him think it was *his* work to bring back Master William and Miss Blanche, Delia,' Mrs Copus was saying. 'It's not the done thing coming to the children's quarters. Their mother, of course, and even once or twice their papa, but Mr George takes too much interest in everything. You saw how he made us fetch Master Willy this morning!'

'I expect he meant to be kind,' said Anne boldly.

'Master William has to miss out on things, it can't be helped,' replied Mrs Copus. 'And I will say Mr George kept him amused and he behaved beautifully *most* of the time all through the christening.' Mrs Copus had been allowed to stay – it was the eleventh family christening she had seen, having come to the Castle the day before George himself was born. Mrs Gibson, of course, as head of all the female household, attended every ceremony.

They had just settled the over-excited Charlie and Liz when there was a knock at the door. Mrs Copus was in the inner room with Sarah, telling her to tidy up the toys. Christmas was Christmas but no disorder should be allowed.

'You go, Anne,' said Delia.

Anne opened the inner door and found Blanche and William each holding a hand of the democratic George.

'Here are your charges, not too late I trust,' he said. This time she could give a slight bob.

'Thank you, sir.' And then she thought – well, why not? – he said it to me – 'May I wish you the compliments of the season, sir, Mr George.' She was abashed at her daring. Perhaps it was so very wrong that she would be dismissed? But no, he inclined his head, patted Blanche's curls and, before he turned to leave, said: 'Thank you.' She thought afterwards in bed before she went to sleep that he had actually *looked* at her. Thank goodness Ma Copus had not heard her!

The house party went on for two weeks and the servants were tired to death. The children of the house, though, led rather Spartan lives, except when they were allowed into their mama's boudoir or occasionally to be shown off to the guests in the music room or one of the tapestry rooms.

Anne grew used to the five children who were together for the holidays although the ten-year-old Edward disrupted Charlie's routine. William was not always a problem: she wondered how she could ever have been afraid of him. George had given them all a good example by showing him affection. Blanche and Elizabeth were no trouble at all so long as you talked to them. Anne wondered who was teaching whom: she explained things to the little girls and they in turn revealed some of the secrets of the aristocratic household to Anne.

The baby, Harry, was going on well and soon his mother was leading her normal life again. Mrs Copus took him off to his special nursery. It was when the baby's wet nurse and personal nurse joined them in the other children's nurseries sometimes for an hour or two that Anne heard all the house-party gossip.

'Her ladyship is *so* good, and she never grumbles. If it were *my* father-in-law with his carryings on, I'd tell my husband straight,' said Dorothy the baby's nurse, who had been with the family before. 'They were gambling last night and I know Lady Georgiana was ever so worried Hardow would stake too high.'

'He's not as bad as his Dad though,' said Delia. 'Wouldn't *you* gamble if you had money?'

'I certainly shouldn't,' replied Dorothy. 'I'd gamble to get it but I wouldn't gamble it away.'

'They say the Regent and all the Royal Family are dreadful gamblers,' said Delia. Anne listened to the names they bandied about – she had heard of some of them – Prime Ministers and great men, some of whom had stayed at the Castle, and the future King of England even.

'I'm sorry for Lord Hardow – his father treats him like dirt, and his wife's always expecting,' said Delia.

'Well, whose fault is that?' replied Dorothy, giggling.

'Sh-h, not before Anne. She's young and innocent – aren't you, Anne?' said Delia. She seemed in a tricksy mood.

That evening they sat with their feet on the fender, their tasks done for an hour or so. Curly had joined them but *she* never said anything rude. The others said she had so wanted to be a lady's maid she had never said *anything* against the family.

'Go on, Anne,' pursued Delia. 'Who would you have if you could choose? You've met that old Grand, and seen Hardow no doubt, and all the children, and the Duke – remember, he's our lady's brother and godfather to Harry. Which would *you* have?'

Anne was silent. 'Oh – I think Fred'll grow to a lovely young man,' said Dorothy.

'*I* like his lordship, our Hardow – quiet and got hidden depths if you ask me,' said Delia.

Anne thought of young George's face in the Chapel and when they had gone for the children on Christmas Day, but said nothing.

'Young George is too small – he's not for the girls,' said Delia, divining her thoughts, as it seemed to Anne. Still she said nothing and the conversation changed to other great houses the maids had visited.

'Chatsworth's a lot grander nor this,' said Delia.

'I don't believe you,' cried Dorothy.

'Nowhere is as beautiful as our Castle,' said Curly loyally.

'But down in London,' said Dorothy, who had accompanied her ladyship there, 'it's ever so much finer – you wait till our Miss Harriet has her Season! Why, I think she could marry a Royal, that I do.'

'Girls, girls,' Mrs Copus bustled in. 'Do I hear my maids discussing danglers and scorpions?' Anne wondered what on earth she meant. As soon as she had gone in to see Blanche – she dosed her personally with calomel if she suspected the advent of a cough – the conversation reverted to men. They whispered so as not to be overheard.

'I'd have our Fred,' sighed Dorothy. He's so handsome and big. And always joking.'

'Oh, I'd have our lady's brother – he's the richest,' said Martha, who had joined them as nursery maid the week before to 'do the rough'. Mrs Copus had evidently grumbled to some avail.

'Go on, Anne. Who'd you have?' She was silent once more, then: 'Do you mean to wed?' she asked finally.

'Oh, to wed or to bed!' They choked with suppressed laughter.

'Anyone who liked George would have to pay attention to book-learning,' said Curly suddenly. 'He's ever so clever,' she added loyally.

How could anyone not see, thought Anne, that George was the kindest and cleverest and most beautiful young man that ever was? And he'd marry some great lady one day and take over the Castle. How could they talk of these things in such a foolish way?

Most of the guests had left and the Castle was quiet again. The family would stay on for January and February and then all the adults would be off at the end of February for the Season. In one year Miss Caro would go with them but at present the three older girls were still stuck in the schoolroom with their Swiss governess. Young George went off to Oxford again. Anne did not expect to see him again before Easter.

She was now allowed to accompany Lizzie on walks without Delia, and it was one January afternoon when she was out on the terrace with her in a little cart that she came across the two statues. It was a cold dark day and the mists had crept over from the low hills. They had gone for a walk by the side of the new lake and had admired the waterfall which fed it. Anne had glimpsed the Temple standing at the end of the grounds but had not strained her eyes to see the 'Mouse Museum' for fear it might give her a nightmare. Returning by the ornamental garden to the South Terrace she saw a lady in the distance but did not realize who it was. Then two statues came into view. One was of a young man, almost a boy, with a bow and arrow, his back arched gracefully and the arrow just tipped to go. Anne touched the boy's ankle and smiled – it was an airy thing, though made of marble. Fancy having a marble statue in your garden! She had once seen one in Stockton church but had supposed it was of an angel. As they walked across to the terrace, another statue came rearing up and Anne disliked it immediately. It seemed to be of a scantily clad male person with a big head and powerful arms. A beard fringed the more than life-size chin and he was clutching a dead ram, its heavy weight curved in the green marble. The man was naked too, with large calf muscles, and he looked somehow foreign – or at least as not belonging to the place. She shuddered and averted her eyes, bending down to Lizzie whose hands were cold. The lady on the terrace came slowly towards them.

Anne looked up as Lizzie shouted: 'Mama!' She stopped the cart and, reaching for her wits, dropped a curtsy. This glimpse of Lady Georgiana was unusual. The lady was most gracious. She bent down to her little daughter, smiling.

'Take me out, Mama!' said the child imperiously.

'Your ladyship, let me,' murmured Anne, and scooped Lizzie out, setting her little feet in their light blue kid shoes on the terrace.

'Will she catch cold do you think?' mumured Lady Georgiana. 'Perhaps boots?'

'Shall I wheel her in for you, ma'am – your ladyship?'

'Wait a moment. You are the new girl Mrs Copus presented to me. Is it Tesseyman?'

'Yes, your ladyship.' Fancy her remembering!

'I hope you are happy with us.'

Anne curtsied again. 'Oh yes, my lady, that I am!'

'I will take Miss Elizabeth indoors – perhaps you would like to come for her in an hour?'

Anne wheeled the empty cart back. Her ladyship was such a good sort though she often looked so sad.

On returning an hour later, after a blissful rest, spent darning, Anne approached the room where she had left the children on Christmas Day. She dared not go into the front of the house though Lady Georgiana's boudoir and dressing-room and bedroom were at the corner. She found no footman so stood in the anteroom and was just about to knock when she heard an angry voice. Two men seemed to be having an argument.

'And I say no. There is no question of it. I do as I wish.'

'She has been shamefully treated,' another voice broke in.

Anne crept away. It would be terrible if anyone found her eavesdropping.

Where could Miss Lizzie be? She would have to pluck up her courage and try the larger doors at the corner opposite the staircase. Just then another door opened and out popped an old lady. She ignored Anne and went humming off down the corridor, a little lapdog behind her. Anne followed her and coughed.

'If you please, ma'am, would you tell me where to find her young ladyship? I've come to fetch Miss Elizabeth back to the nursery.'

The old lady turned, peered at her, scooped up the dog and hemmed and hawed. 'What is it? What is it? Whom do you wish to see?'

Anne tried once more to explain but further words were not needed as another door opened, a footman came half out, beckoned to her and announced 'Her ladyship is expecting you.' He winked at the back of the old lady and shrugged his shoulders.

Dorothy joined him, Lizzie holding her hand. 'Here you are, Tesseyman! By the way John said there was a message for you. A Mr Ridsdale – "from the rector" he said – come for you, down in the Back Hall. He's going on a tour of the Mouse Museum – it being public day, he said he'd like to see it after seeing you.'

'Oh, thank you.' It would be the Rector's friend come for Mam's money, earlier than she had thought – three months' wages anyway, and her letter would be delivered! She hurried off, being careful to hold Lizzie's hand going down the stairs.

Mr Ridsdale was a bluff hearty man, cousin of Mrs Hart. 'I saw the lady housekeeper and we are to go and collect your earnings. My, what a fine place you are in!'

'Are there any messages from my mother?' Anne burst out. 'I've writ a letter to her if you will please to deliver it to the Reverend Hart – Mrs Hart might read it to Mam. I'll be right glad to send the money.'

One sovereign and six bright shillings were counted out for the quarter's wage and signed for in Mrs Gibson's room and Anne went up for her letter which she had kept under her mattress so it would not get creased.

'I shall say I found you well. My goodness, who would not be well here!' Mr Ridsdale went on. 'Your mother and sister are just about managing, my cousin said to tell you. But they will manage better with this.' He jangled the coins in the bag Anne had sewn for them. 'Don't worry – it will be with them tomorrow, and your "missive". Well, well. Fancy that! Who taught you to write? My cousin, I'll be bound.'

'Please sir, what else about my Mam. Is she in good health? Is Hannah still in Tollerton? Do – do send my love, sir. It was all strange here at first but now it's better. I'm keeping very busy as you can see – I must go now to feed Miss Lizzie.'

'Mrs Tesseyman says you are not to worry about her. Your sister is well and still working for Farmer Eden. The Rector sends his blessing and my cousin her good wishes. Now my dear, show me the path to that *wonderful* building –'

'You mean the Temple?'

'No, no, the great, the inimitable Maus-o-leum,' he enunciated.

Anne shivered in spite of herself. 'It's the same way, just beyond,' she explained and saw him off on his tour. 'Please, sir, you have the money and the letter. Tell them – if the Rector's wife – if your cousin, could just drop me a line – I know she's busy – but just to hear about Mam.' She did not voice her fear that Mrs Hart would have written if the news had been good.

'Do you have a mama?' asked Lizzie suddenly as Anne was putting her hair in curling rags that night.

'What? – of course I do, Miss Lizzie! I wish I could see her. She lives in a little village with my sister.'

'Poor Nanna. You have no one to curl *your* hair,' replied Lizzie. Really, that child – it was almost supernatural the way she guessed your mind! But Anne was not thinking of Mam as she finally laid down to rest that night. Rather she was remembering the sound of angry voices behind the door, and seeing that nasty statue. What if it came to life and shouted at her? She hoped Mr Ridsdale had liked the Maus-o-leum better than *she* had.

Yet, after all, she *was* used to this new life now and it was little Miss Lizzie who had helped her most.

God bless little Elizabeth, thought Lady Georgiana as she lay back on her yellow-curtained bed. Somehow that child had never been a worry to her. And they seemed to have found another reliable nursery maid. What a pretty young woman she was. Still, faces were not always fortunes. Copus was good at choosing them. She trusted her judgement. The servants Copus or Mrs Gibson had *not* chosen were the unsatisfactory ones. Not that they could always be blamed when trouble came. Gibson said Selina Sharpe was to be taken on again: she had had her orders. Poor Gibson was almost in tears! She had not made any reference to where those orders had come from but Lady Georgiana understood. It was most distasteful. If only Hardow would put his foot down. But there was little hope of that. Even George had apparently guessed something earlier, but of course no one had said anything to *him*. She sighed. After all, there was no embarrassing evidence and the woman was to be employed again under Mrs Gibson, who could keep an eye on her. Fortunately the family would all be in London soon and the whole business could blow over. Lady Georgiana sighed and took up her embroidery. It had the effect of calming her. That and the letters to her sister who had advised she ignore the whole affair. As she lay propped up against the pillows, her brightly coloured silks on the bedspread, Georgiana thought for the hundredth time of the difficult situation Hardow was in: one that most men of his age would not have borne with any grace. She smiled: as long as he had his *rare* books and his *new* books he seemed to be content. Boredom was his worst enemy and that was when his gambling worried her. It was not as bad as Grand's but he did gamble now and then. The worry seemed to set off a fusillade of all the other anxieties in her and then she could not sleep and imagined much worse things. She must never forget that God had spared her once more: she had been quite sure she would die at her last lying-in – or that the baby would die. And here she was – and there was little Harry, as contented and flourishing as any mother could wish. And the men would settle down to some shooting now they were all back. She put down her embroidery and rang for Marie to blow the candle out, draw her curtains and settle her for sleep.

THREE

GEORGE
1819–1820

'Tis virtue and not birth that makes us noble.
Fletcher and Massinger: *The Prophetess*

In the Long Gallery of Fountaynes Castle there was a portrait of a little boy of about ten. He had brown wavy hair and regular features and a rather shy smile. His son often used to look at this painting of nearly forty years ago and wonder how his father had changed from this pretty child ('the prettiest boy I ever saw,' said a famous friend to the boy's father) to the retiring rather taciturn man he knew. He had a good idea why. Wouldn't any man forced to live under his father's roof for the whole of his marriage kick against the pricks? And if the father was of a moody, tyrannical, bitter character in old age, even more reason for the son to be continually ill-at-ease and repress his anger until it turned into frigidity. George would often compare the characters of his father and his grandfather. The old Earl with his testy temper and aristocratic ways was a vain and difficult man, but he was also a man who had inherited his title at the age of ten and who had had to fend for himself. He was clever too, not a doubt of that, though his poetry was not as good as he pretended to think! But his taste was refined: a connoisseur of sculpture and paintings; of drawings and buildings; and a lover of Rome and Italy and France since his first grand tour at the age of nineteen. If only he would not treat his own son so badly. Didn't he know that Hardow sometimes hated him? Or *did* he know and not mind? Even so, there was strong family feeling there; he doubtless loved his eldest son and was proud of him. Perhaps, too, he was a little jealous of him. He himself had retired from public life at thirty-five and had spent long periods of time away from his family drawn by the gaming tables of Brooks's and other similar establishments. His gambling debts had nearly ruined him and deprived his own son, that pretty boy in the picture, of some of the money which should rightly have been his. And the old Earl had never said he was sorry to anyone, of that George was sure! He had become less talkative perhaps of late, which was a grace and a blessing, for the epigrams and the anecdotes were intensely trying to George's own mother, never mind his father. But Hardow had withdrawn into his shell – perhaps he feared to appear to outshine his brilliant papa. Hardow might be quiet but he was also clever, not brilliant in conversation as the old Earl might once have been, but if not of a ready tongue or wit, of an extremely good intelligence, likewise steeped in Greece and Rome and in

Classical and Renaissance painting and with exquisite taste. Ladies liked him, George knew, for he seemed, with his 'air noble' and his quietness and slightly bored and bland expression, a ready target for their sympathy. His father did not like 'showy' women, though. In this he was unlike Grand who had, if the stories were true, been continually in the throes of romantic passions for older or inaccessible ladies in his youth. Hardow came into his own in the library, which was well stocked and a refuge from Grand, whose eyes were failing. Vellum and parchment and old folios attracted Hardow like a bee to nectar. Lady Georgiana never complained that he gave her little society for she was so occupied with her children and just thankful that he seldom gambled, for when he did, it was torture to her. Gambling was the only pursuit that ever ruffled his temper – and one that George, too, hated.

George paused again and looked at the picture of his father as a small boy. He felt rather sorry for that small boy and suspected his father did also. But it was difficult to talk to the grown man.

Why were they all so stick-in-the-mud, Papa especially? When Papa was gloomy it never seemed to be for the reasons George himself would have had for despondency – worrying about the state of England or as a reaction against exaltation – but a steady, dreary sort of gloom. He wondered why the older members of his family were so hopeless, always going on about appearance, or money, or losing at cards. He wished he could cheer them all up. Surely he could, if he put his mind to it. And of course *they* found faults in *him*, faults that he could not always recognize. That he was impractical and rather inactive and a bad horseman, and that he talked too much about his enthusiasms he could admit – but not that he was tactless with Grand or not firm enough with the servants, or a little censorious towards Caro and Georgy. Latterly he had tried to talk less about his own ideas and to show an interest in the girls' doings but girls baffled him, particularly his sisters. They seemed so different from young men. Harriet was quite fun, though. She wasn't really grown-up, of course, but her zest for life was extraordinary, and he admired her. What was such a nuisance, he thought, was being so young and yet often feeling he knew best! Perhaps he had not lived long enough to know himself or others, but older people were such hypocrites; even their kindnesses were often calculated. At least he admitted some of his faults, whereas Grand and even Papa never admitted they had any.

He knew when he hadn't pushed himself hard enough in his studies, whereas all the family thought he was brilliant. The trouble was partly that he had always been indulged by the older women of the family – particularly Aunt Harriet and Mama and Grandmama Caroline. They were adept at flattering and much less hard on him and Fred than they were on the girls. Grandmama particularly, who was no fool, though she often acted like one – *she* flattered him about his accomplishments and prizes, liked to compare him with her friends' grandchildren, boys who were hopeless at Greek and Divinity and didn't care anyway. *Their* grandmamas probably compared *him* unfavourably with *them*: 'Poor George H – can't ride, can't shoot, likes the sound of his own voice – and always *reading*!' He smiled to himself. Once he had quoted Byron to Grandmama and that hadn't gone down at all well since Grand had had such trouble with this noble relative some years ago. 'Not a good example, dear boy,' Grandmama had said, and then, irrelevantly, he thought, 'such a gifted fellow though!'

When he was little, Mama had seemed to understand him and it was probably from her that he had derived his early piety. But recently his religious feelings had undergone a change and had shifted ground, to be replaced by a yearning for something stronger. Everything was in flux. He would have liked to talk things like this over with his father but George could never find out what his father really thought about anything, especially matters of politics or religion which seemed so important to George himself.

Grand was of the eighteenth century: a survival of another age, an atheistic irreverent age which George himself abominated with all the idealism of youth. Not that George yet took his religion perfervidly – that would be as bad as being an old-time Jacobin fanatic on the other side, but he believed that the regeneration of England was being held back only by the Regent and his profligate crew. There were young men writing now – even at Eton he had read them – who had wrenched England out of her old ways and yet had not preached bloody revolution. And young poets who expressed his own feelings exactly.

He wondered what *his* portrait would look like up there one day. And would *he* have sons, more Georges and Fredericks and Williams to carry on this Whig line? He sighed. It was true he wanted the political life that had been his father's and grandfather's. It was in his blood. But he also wanted his long hours in the library, the poring over the old masters of rhetoric and the composing of Latin verse. He had a thirst for knowledge and yet, sometimes, it did not seem enough. He would catch himself dreaming of something else, of some torrent of the senses which would leave him a man among men. He did love his brothers and sisters, and family life, and did do his best to be amiable to them, for he liked to be liked; but he often felt he had little in common with them. Perhaps when they were all older they could all be friends. He was particularly fond of little Elizabeth who he felt was a precocious child in the way he had been. And he always tried to be kind to poor William, for it was not William's fault there was something wrong with his brain. It should not be an effort, he felt, and yet it was and his earlier prayers had often been angry on William's account.

He was a lucky man, he scolded himself, lucky in his brains – though that smacked of pride – lucky in his inheritance and with every prospect for his future. Yet the world was a puzzle and he was a puzzle to himself. In less than three years he would be finished at Oxford, achieve his majority and go on the tour, he supposed. Then what? Perhaps he should go and consult the Delphic Oracle in the Museum, which his ancestor had dragged from Greece. Such a pagan thing to be found in the castle of a Christian gentleman!

He wandered slowly down the Long Gallery and out in the direction of the library. Snow was falling now on the gardens and statues so he felt absolved from the duty of taking exercise. He would make up for it with a long ramble on the morrow when he would examine his conscience once more and probably decide to stop thinking about himself.

He glanced out of the library window before settling himself down with his Georgics (George's Georgics, as Harriet called them). There was Lizzie hurrying back with her maid, that pretty woman he had seen at Christmas. What must it be like to be inside *her* head? No doubt life was simpler if you had no choice. Perhaps it was simpler for all women? It must be a relief to be a woman and not have to initiate action. He shook his head: his mind was wandering again. Two hours of Virgil and then at four he would go up to his mother and exclaim over his new brother. And, next week, Oxford again!

Anne remembered how it had begun – with the sunbeam over his head in Chapel. And even feeling something too on her first day at the Castle when he departed – on her first day! She began to look forward continually to the occasional sight of Young George. Even if she did not glimpse him at all for days, the next time was always around the corner and gave her life an excitement which she never knew she had lacked before. When the girls had gossiped about 'which one you would like best', she had realized that there was a whole world of feeling in her which had begun to flow stealthily towards an object and this object seemed incredibly to be Young George. When she had wished him a Merry Christmas it was as though she had daringly crossed a bridge over high waters, and she wondered at her temerity. At the same time she did not expect that he would ever notice or remember her, any more than he would notice or remember Curly or Delia. And yet he *did* notice and remember people, for Delia said once that he took more interest in all the goings on in the house than his father did. It was only later when George had returned to Oxford and there was no likelihood of catching sight of him in the distance that she began to miss the excitement of wondering whether today might be a day she would see him – handing his mama into her curricle, or crossing the terrace with a dog at his heels. Anne did not understand herself. Why should she be miserable at missing somebody of whose special existence she had not even known a few months earlier? But she wisely kept her feelings to herself and felt somehow older. She did not even notice that one or two of the footmen smiled at her now and then and would have been quite glad of a chat. And there was always the general male attention in the Servants' Lower Hall. She no longer felt quite so scared of their teasing and innuendos but strangely annoyed that they should assume she would be flattered by their interest. It was not to do with their being men of her own rank, or that they were rather rough and that some of them had none too good a reputation. It was more that they seemed nothing to do with *her*. Now that she was so busy up in the nurseries there was of course less opportunity for their advances.

With Mr George it was something quite different, a mixture of the pleasures of daydreaming and a strange feeling that she had known him before – which was stupid . . . She had fantasies of rescuing him from the lake over which he was skating on thin ice, of gathering flowers and giving them to him. She never thought of his rescuing *her* or of his giving her anything whatsoever but a smile or, at the very height of her dream, a pressing of the hand, which she knew must be impossible. Future young lords had that sort of feeling only for future young ladies. It was strange to think that the fearsome tall old man stalking the Long Gallery was his grandfather. Lizzie called him 'Grand' and did not seem at all afraid of him when one day they came upon him in the gardens making his 'improvements'. Anne was pretending not to be able to catch Lizzie who was running on the lawn like a little fawn when out popped a noble head with a strange hat, from behind a laurel bush. He straightened up, stood for a moment regarding the child who ran up to him, patted her on the cheek as she prattled away to him and finally gave her a sixpence. Anne had hung behind but came up when the old man creaked away.

'Your shoes are all wet, Miss Lizzie. We must go indoors.'

'Look what Grand gave me,' Lizzie held out the sixpence. 'Do you know that man? He is my grandpapa – because he is *grand*.'

Anne smiled. The child was forever playing with words and Anne caught herself doing the same. When she played with Liz she felt completely herself. Lizzie's father, Hardow, was not often visible. He lurked in the library and was often away in London but once or twice he condescended to call on the nursery wing, to discuss alterations to the rooms, accompanied by Mrs Copus. He would then smile a little at his boy Charlie and listen to Blanche who was always pestering to go up to the schoolroom with her big sisters. To all this Hardow would only reply: 'Ask your mama, my dear.' Although he looked bored and kept his distance, Anne thought he was quite fond of his children. It was, Delia said, very unusual for a gentleman to come up to his children's quarters. Anne even thought he had glanced at her too and therefore made a busy show of counting linen in the background. Once, again when she was out in the grounds with the children, they saw him on his horse in the distance. He rode up, dismounted, handing his horse to the groom who came rushing up, and stood looking at the Castle. His favourite outdoor dog came bounding up and Anne shrank away. 'Tesseyman fears dogs,' shouted Charles rudely, and Anne hoped Hardow had not heard. It was such a foolish thing to be frightened of. Her other fears seemed to have receded since George had begun to enter her daydreams, so that when one day Copus told her to take the children on a long walk in the direction of the Temple she did not worry. It was a beautiful March day; the frost was still sparkling on the grass though it was white under the trees. Although it was very cold the sun shone splendidly and Anne began to imagine what the place would be like in summer. A shooting party had been out – hares and rabbits were the objects of the guns that day and Charles was excited and wanted to walk round the house to the wood.

'No, Master Charles, my instructions was to keep to the path, then we'll come to no harm. They don't shoot round this side of the house.' He sulked but she persuaded him not to stray. 'What if you was to get shot, Master Charles – they would put me in prison for neglecting you.' Blanche looked at her curiously.

'Mama doesn't like the guns much,' she said. Lizzie was holding Anne's hand and would soon have to be carried. Her mental powers were stronger than her physical ones. Sometimes when they went on walks like this, Anne would pretend that they were *her* children and that she was their real mother. She took her responsibilities very seriously and wondered if she would feel the same if she ever had children of her own. The children did love their real mother who also loved to have them with her but was always able to send them away when she was tired or they were noisy. If they were *her* children, thought Anne, there would be no one to send them to! Children must be terribly wearing on an ordinary woman. It was she or Delia who got up in the night if these children had nightmares, not Lady Georgiana. Perhaps Lady Georgiana worried about them so, because she felt she should be more with them. This was a novel view and Anne considered it, but then was called out of her reverie once more by Charles.

'Can we go in the Temple today?'

'No, it's locked till summer,' said Blanche. 'But we can jump off the stairs.'

When they eventually arrived at the slope leading up to the Temple, Lizzie began to cry.

'It's the statues,' said Blanche, as usual aware of everyone's shortcomings. 'She doesn't like them.'

'Then we needn't look at them,' replied Anne. 'Come, Miss Lizzie, we'll sit on the stone stair a while and the others can run round. But mind, no straying, Master Charlie.'

'William and Ned like coming here,' said Blanche, in no hurry to 'run around'.

'Does Master Ned like his school?' asked Anne.

'Oh, not much, I don't think. Isn't it lucky girls don't have to go to school!'

'Well, they have to learn things,' said Anne, taking Lizzie on her lap.

'Oh, I shall soon go up to Mademoiselle Sterky for French and globes and I shall dance with Harriet. What does bot-ernizing mean?'

'I don't know,' replied Anne, truthfully. 'I'll ask.'

'Caro and Georgy say they are going to do it this summer. Don't you think if I am eight years old I could do it as well?'

'We shall have to wait and see,' replied Anne.

She looked up at the Temple and saw, peeping behind it in the distance, the dome of the Mausoleum. Instinctively she shuddered. It had just popped into sight in a thoroughly spiteful way, she thought. Perhaps Lizzie disliked the statues here on their plinths outside the Temple in just the same way. They seemed harmless enough to Anne – nice quiet ladies in long robes. Curly had said all the family would one day be buried under the dome. She seemed to think it quite natural that a great big place should be built for their bones, along with their ancestors'. Just imagine, one day, all of them – the eldest sons anyway and most of the other boys, would be nothing but heaps of bones there. She had imagined the bones strewn inside the building, but Curly said they were under the ground in special tombs. With a start she thought, one day *George* will be in that building, along with Hardow and the old Earl. It was horrible.

'Please can we go now,' murmured Liz. 'I'm very cold.'

'Yes.'

Charlie came hurtling round the side of the Temple, pausing to stick his tongue out at the nearest statue. If *this* building had had dead people in it, would she still have liked it? But no, she had disliked the 'Mouse Museum' before she had known what it was for. If people came here to the Temple for a view north, south, east and west they would be bound to see it. Perhaps it was there to remind people that they would not live for ever? We were all mortal – and sinners. The Rector had continually dwelt upon that fact back home in Stockton.

They all trailed back to the house. The sun had gone in and

Anne was worried lest Blanche should have taken cold.

'Do you know what that is?' asked Charlie, pointing to a door in the wall by the terrace on the left. 'That's a *maze*. In summer you can hide in there.'

'Well, you'll have to show me in summer,' replied Anne, hurrying them along. As they went into the East Courtyard Anne saw Miss Selina Sharpe with a shawl round her shoulders hurrying into the house. So *she* was back. Pity the poor girls in the sewing-attics if she were no better tempered.

Fortunately everyone revived round the bright nursery fire and Blanche was given a hot caudle. Anne was offered an hour or two's freedom by Delia who took over the children, so she rushed down as was her wont to Servants' Hall to chat with Curly. She had got into the habit of taking her leisure down with Curly if the latter had a little time off from her hair-curling sessions. They were teaching her lady's maid work – on Caro's hair! Curly the curler.

'At least she don't complain,' said Curly, sucking in tea through her teeth. 'Though you can't make her pretty, not like Miss Georgy.'

A new dancing master was to arrive the next week to supplement the girls' education. Miss Harriet was wild with joy though he was not supposed to be teaching *her*.

'She does play that harp really fine,' went on Curly.

'I heard her – once before Christmas. I wish I knew that song she played.' Anne sang the tune to Curly who was astonished.

'Why – I declare *you* could learn an instrument, Anne!'

'But find out for me what that air is called, will you? It's so *splendid* – right sad you know but it catches at my heart.'

'You're a funny one, Anne! Ma would say you'd better take care, if songs make you look like that!'

'Like what?'

'Oh, I dunno – ' she searched for a word. '*Passion*,' she came out with. 'Like in those books they've got in the boudoir – terrible tales Dorothy says!'

Anne felt curious but a little mortified. It was true that the tune she had heard always made her think of Young George. She must never, never let any of them know that!

Days slid into weeks and weeks into months and the Viscount and his lady had long ago departed to London. Still no George.

Anne would take Lizzie and Charles down to feed the ducks on the big lake. William was returned to them and often fell to Anne's charge. He would stand motionlessly by the lake except for the hand that twittered in front of his face, like a statue with one small tic. Harry now came into the nursery during the day and the wet-nurse with him. He did not cry much and appeared a cheerful baby.

The servants often went fishing on the lake when the family were away, and Caro and Georgy were often seen in the distance picking flowers and small plants which they pressed into special wooden flower-presses and then mounted on white paper.

'That's botanizing,' explained Curly. *Her* vocabulary was growing and changing now that she was with Dorothy and the stately Marie. Her ladyship had another maid in London apparently, and Marie stayed to oversee the clearing of her mistress's chamber and the mending and washing of her winter wardrobe.

One day Anne could not find William anywhere and guessed that he had wandered off somewhere in the house. She conquered her remaining slight fear of the rambling corridors and unexpected staircases, calling 'William! Will-i-am. There's a good boy. Come back for tea!'

So long as that old Earl did not overhear her! He and his Countess were not in London for the Season. The staff suspected he was frightened of getting involved once more at the gaming clubs in spite of his great age. She heard a slight noise above one of the sewing rooms and saw a dusty staircase leading over it. Summoning her courage and lifting up her skirt, for it was *very* dusty, she went up them slowly. There was a little round window halfway up and through the smeary glass she could see the lake with one of the grooms rowing in a small boat. Everything was normal. The door opened easily at the top of the landing and she blinked a little. The floor was of broad planks and the ceiling looked spidery. William was standing at the window.

'Come on, Master William. You want your tea don't you? Don't be frightened. I'm not cross.'

William turned and said his usual: 'Want Edward.'

'Master Edward will be back for his summer holidays soon. Come with me, do.'

She heard behind her a light footstep on the stair, just as William had been persuaded to hold her hand and follow her through the door. It was dark and a man's figure was standing halfway up the stairs. She was not sure at first who it was. For a moment her heart had leapt, for her first thought had been 'Mr George'. She went down a little way, William tagging on, and realized it was Hardow. But surely he was in London? He did not move and she was obliged to say: 'Excuse me, sir – William was lost – we must go down.' He looked at William, seemed to sigh but then looked at her with a curious stare. He let her pass but as she descended followed her down just behind her. She felt a hand on her shoulder and started with a slight shock. She turned. 'Yes, sir?' William was trudging downstairs now in front of her. Hardow said nothing, just looked at her closely, then let her go. She waited a moment. Then he said: 'Go – go,' and watched her as she descended and took William's hand. Her heart was beating fast, but more from puzzlement than fear. He had looked so sad. She was glad when they reached the nursery, feeling as though she had escaped some danger. Perhaps she should have curtsied.

As soon as she could she sought out Curly. How could she put it to her? 'I thought our Viscount was in London,' she said.

'Why?'

'I think I saw him – looking for William.'

'Oh, he sometimes comes back for a bit. Lady Georgiana's probably with her sister – what's strange about that?'

'Oh, nothing. It was just – that I thought he were – was – away.'

Shortly afterwards Hardow must have gone to Trentham to be with his wife, for Blanche was sent for to say goodbye to him.

'Papa says he will be away with Mama for a *long* time,' she said on her return. So that was that.

The old Earl was, however, much in evidence.

'The attorney is here from York *again*,' said Curly.

'What does that mean?' asked Anne.

'It means he's making his will once more,' explained Curly. There was not much she didn't seem to know about them all! Marie had been telling her about the London season and the delights of Devonshire House and these were faithfully reported as they sat for a moment with their evening meal. Anne wanted to ask when Young George would return but dared not. Instead she asked: 'Will Fred go to Oxford do you think – do they go to learn more there than at school?'

'They say Fred's for the army,' replied Curly.

'And Mr George is very *clever*,' added Dorothy. 'That's why *he*'s at Oxford.'

Selina Sharpe came up just then and there was silence over the teapot. 'What are you all gossiping about, girls?' she asked in a manner rather brighter than was her usual. Anne felt a blush stealing over her cheeks and to distract attention from herself said:

'I expect all the family went to Oxford then – all the men, I mean, the Earl and his son?'

Selina looked at her. 'And what is that to you, Tesseyman?'

Anne was silent and Curly helped her out. 'We were saying what a clever family our family is – all that book-learning.'

Miss Sharpe sniffed, but could not help adding her morsel of information. 'His lordship was at Cambridge I believe, before he went to the Lords.'

Anne wondered whether going to the Lords was like going to the Lord, which didn't seem likely. There was a long silence and the conversation lapsed.

'Well, we mustn't stay gossiping. I've a new sewing girl to see – a pity you left us, Tesseyman.' She went off with a sweep of her skirt. As soon as she had gone the other maids who were sitting round the table began to giggle.

'Before he went to the Lords . . . did you hear her? She ought to write a book about the old man!' Anne was uncertain why they were laughing but joined in. She forgot Hardow's sudden appearance as the days moved into summer.

Haymaking was to begin early that year as the weather had been so fine. Early for that northern clime where hay often lay till August. By June the grass had been mown and lay ready to stook. Anne spent more and more time outdoors and her skin became quite sunburnt. Miss Caro and Miss Georgy put on their large white bonnets with scarlet ribbons tied under their chins and went on dainty walks with Mademoiselle Sterky to the Temple of the Four Winds where they took cold chicken and the *Letters of Madame de Sévigné*. Fred and Edward returned with their tutor, a stern-looking young man who kept them busy. Fred was now at Eton, where Edward would follow him in three years. Anne watched them all and felt she had lived in the Castle for ever. Yet now and again a little stab of worry would stop her in the middle of laying the children's table or calling in at the laundry or taking messages for Mrs Copus to Mrs Gibson, and she would wonder why she had not heard from the Rector about Mam and Hannah. She heard the menservants sometimes talking about the wider world outside the Castle and it seemed things were very bad in the villages and there had been riots in the north of England. The old King was still holding on to life though he was always expected to peg out. The Regent, who was not popular among the servants – though many years before, the year the revolution broke out in France when he was a young man, he had visited the Castle – continued his self-indulgent carryings on in London and Brighton. At the village church, which she tried to attend every Sunday, but did not always manage to, there had been prayers for the King's health and prayers for the poor. Anne began to feel vaguely uneasy – what if Mam and Hannah were ill? They could not be starving since they had her new sovereign, and that would buy them plenty of flour and some bacon for a long time.

As the trees became green and heavy round the fields of hay the maze grew too and was apparent over the wall by the path. Some of the maids, it was said, had got into it with some stable-lads, and their shrieks and shouts had fetched the steward who had sternly chased them out. Anne preferred to peep through the door in the high wall at the other end of the front terrace which surrounded the kitchen garden and once spied the old Countess snoozing on a stone seat with her lapdog at her feet and her parasol askew over her curls.

Would George never return? Perhaps he had gone abroad or was with his papa and mama in London.

'The family will go to Norpeth again in August for the grouse,' Curly explained, and so Anne resigned herself to a long, long summer looking after the children until – perhaps in September – *he* would be there again. She counted the months carefully: for nearly eleven of them now she had been at the Castle.

One golden summer morning when the haymakers were finishing up the nearest field and the lake lay almost blue, she was down by its shores with little Lizzie and a bag of stale crusts for the ducks and the two swans who were nesting on the opposite shore but who could be persuaded to cross to the near shore in expectation of a meal. The grass had not yet been cut by the side of the lake itself except for a narrow path, and butterflies and bees were having a field day.

'Catch me, Nanna,' cried Lizzie and went staggering off. Suddenly she disappeared amidst squeals of laughter.

Anne ran up with her basket. 'Where are you – are you hiding?' she laughed. Up bobbed the little girl a few yards away in the long grass. Then down she went again.

Anne stopped and stared. A young man was standing with Lizzie, whom he was tickling, in his arms. 'Oh I'm sorry.' She stood stock-still.

Lizzie shouted with glee. 'Put me down, put me down, George!' He had a book still in one hand, his shirt open at the front. She curtsied automatically. 'Nanna! Nanna! Look, it's George!'

'It's Bessy's nurse, isn't it?' he said, pleasantly, picking off grass stalks with his free hand. 'Now Bessy, be a good girl and don't hide any more or your "nanna" will worry you are lost.' He smiled at Anne.

'Come Miss Lizzie, let's find the swans,' said Anne. Why did her mouth feel so dry? Was it just the shock of his sudden re-appearance?

'I'll come too – it's too hot to read. That is, if you don't mind,' he said politely. Anne was overcome but seized Lizzie's hand and walked, her eyes downcast, to the lake shore.

Lizzie chattered on to her brother who took some pains to reply to her, Anne noticed. She wondered whether he took so much interest in the other children as he obviously did in William and Lizzie. George certainly seemed to be Lizzie's favourite and they were not unalike, though George's nose was sharper and his eyes lighter and larger. His eyes positively glowed that morning as he chatted with Lizzie in the green shade of a willow by the lake. Anne was unsure whether to stay with Lizzie or wait some distance away. Mrs Copus had told all the maids not to be 'familiar' with the footmen and grooms but had not mentioned the grown-up *children* of the house. Yet George was clearly not a child. He must be about her own age, perhaps a little younger, but seemed to Anne older in one way, because he knew so much more. Eventually after some hesitation she compromised by taking the bread to the swans and hoping the brother and sister would follow. She was glad to see that they did, leaving the willow-tree shade for the dry edge of the lake before it got reedy and muddy.

'Please have the bread, sir,' she said shyly to the young man.

'Nanna must throw some,' said Lizzie.

The swans came sailing up looking as though they were

powered by something other than feet. Anne looked at George covertly as he solemnly threw the bread.

'There were swans in Italy long, long ago,' he said to the little girl. 'And in Greece too.' He looked, as he threw the bread and then bent to his little sister, like the statue of the young man on the terrace except he had put on a cotton cap over his wavy locks and had a smile on his face. Anne found herself wishing she could touch *his* foot as she had touched the foot of the statue. He did not ignore her either. At one point in the enchanted half-hour he said to Lizzie: 'Mama has been too busy to start your reading but now you are four years old *I* shall begin with you, Lizzie. Would you like to read stories – and then you can tell them to your Nanna?'

'Oh yes, please, George. My Nanna does tell stories though!'

'Oh, does she, what about?'

He looked at Anne then as though he were considering her under a different light. The child hesitated and Anne said, looking up at him openly for the first time: 'I make up stories, sir – or little things I heard in the village.' Then she stopped, overcome.

'I'm sure they are very pretty stories,' said George.

'Nanna can read – not like that other girl,' said Lizzie proudly.

'Who taught you to read?'

'The Rector's wife, when I helped her with her bairns – and a bit at Sunday School.'

'Reading is a great comfort,' replied George. What a curious thing to say, she thought. People in marvellous castles must sometimes need comforting, as children did.

'I write myself,' said George, picking up his book.

'We must leave you to your study, sir,' said Anne, collecting her wits. 'Come, Miss Lizzie. Say goodbye to your brother!'

The little girl danced away and Anne stood awkwardly.

'Goodbye Bessy's nurse – see you tell good stories.' He looked at her as he paused before walking on towards the wood, and saw a beautiful young woman like a Greek goddess standing against the lake and the sky – and *she* saw a lonely, clever and kind young man who was human before he was the grandson of an earl and the future owner of all the vast estate in which they stood. The moment passed quickly but it had marked both of them.

Selina Sharpe was already sitting in the nursery when Anne

returned there with the little girl. Delia had taken Charles and Blanche to see their grandmother, the old Countess, and Selina lost no time in coming to the point.

'You know what Mrs Copus told you, Miss?'

Anne, bending to take off Lizzie's sun cap, straightened up, at a loss to know what the older woman was referring to. 'She doubtless told you it was a *liberal* house?'

'Yes, Miss Sharpe. She did.'

'And warned you against undue familiarity?'

Anne remained silent. Could Selina be referring to feeding the ducks?

'And you have deliberately courted a reprimand – your conduct this morning – dallying by the lake, interrupting the young master at his studies.'

Anne's cheeks began to burn. So that was what it was all about! She must have been spying from one of the windows.

'I am innocent of, of . . . courting anything, ma'am,' she replied with a courage she did not know she possessed.

'You are not to take the child in the way of others. I saw you being familiar with nobility – it is not allowed. Doubtless the young master is too gentlemanly to protest.'

Anne felt a rising tide of anger but tried to nip it in the bud. It was no use making an enemy of Miss Sharpe. She would just have to be more careful in future.

'I have been "familiar" with no one, ma'am. He spoke to us first and I was careful not to – bother – him. If he wishes to speak to his sister that is not my affair.' And she added, injudiciously, 'Mr George has always spoken to me *first.*'

'Oh – so he *speaks* to you, does he?' riposted the woman.

'I mean – he wished me, us, a Merry Christmas,' said Anne quietly after a pause. She was determined no one should know the real feelings she had for the young man and equally determined to defend herself. It was true – she had never approached him. The accusation was not only unjust, it was spiteful and wicked. 'And you can tell Mrs Copus that, if she asks,' she went on.

'How dare you speak to me in that tone?' cried the under-housekeeper.

'I am speaking the truth, ma'am.'

'Nanna, what is the matter?' asked Lizzie tugging at her skirt. Miss Sharpe rose to go.

'I shall be careful to approach no one. If accidentally I am in the way of the family, that is not my fault. *I* did not know the earl was in the Long Gallery when I lost my way when I first came here.' She was not sure why she had mentioned this but Sharpe grew pale and with a murmured 'That will do', marched out of the room.

'Well, well,' thought Anne. 'They can't dismiss me for having a conversation with a young man who wants to feed ducks.'

When she reported the conversation to Curly later that day, she first of all began to smile and then said seriously: 'Don't get on the wrong side of her. They say she's the Earl's favourite.'

'But she said *I* was being familiar! What is it exactly, his favourite?'

Curly lowered her voice. 'There were rumours – I wouldn't like to say exactly – but – you know when she went away?'

'Yes – I hoped she'd never come back.'

'They *say* it was because, well, she was going to have a baby.'

'A baby! But she's back – she hasn't got a baby – you mean – the . . .'

'Yes. Sh-h. No she couldn't have had a baby. My mother was talking to my dad and my mother thinks she had an "accident". Don't say anything about it to anyone.'

'But – they must have wanted her back then?'

'*He* must. Lady Georgiana doesn't like her, and Mrs Gibson and Mrs Copus *hate* her, but you see, the Earl is the one with the say-so – and well, I know, Hardow and Lady Georgiana pay their own servants, like us, but, you see, the Earl hasn't *enough* money – but he's still Earl, and Hardow could have lived away when he married. *His* money comes from his wife, you see. But I expect he was sorry for the old man and Lady Georgiana has probably given her husband the money to keep up their style here.'

'What a lot you know, Curly,' whispered Anne, amazed at the revelations of aristocratic problems.

'The old man gambled a lot away and the upper servants got it from his valet that he borrowed money – sold his land up north – I don't understand it all. But he's still the Earl, so be careful of Miss Selina Sharpe.'

Anne resolved to be extremely careful; though she had done nothing wrong from her lowly position, her heart told her secrets that would be better kept within herself. It was all a sort of game to Sharpe, she supposed. But George *had* spoken to her and smiled at her and she cherished that strange moment by the lake when time seemed to have stopped.

It was many months before she saw George again. He was off to Norpeth, off to London, off to Oxford they said and until October the children and the old Earl and Countess were the only constant family inhabitants of the Castle. In August she had had a message from Mam and Hannah written by the Rector's wife. They were not too badly, though Mam was plagued with her chest, and they were very grateful for the money; the messenger would take back another sovereign in September when she had been a year. A year! Anne felt it was more like ten years since she had sat in the coach bringing her to Fountaynes Castle. There were still surprises in the old place. One day the nursery staff were asked to take William and the three youngest children on a visit to the poultry yard which was part of the home farm, and another day they went on an expedition to the pig farm. The children loved it and were given brown eggs by the dairymaids. Charlie dropped his, of course, but William cradled his like a baby. The pigs, although cleaner than any pigs Anne had ever seen before, were less enticing than the pretty fowls. Pigs had no terrors for her, but Lizzie did not like them at all, especially when, being held in Anne's arms to inspect the sow with her litter behind a stable door, an affronted pig lurched up into her face and Lizzie screamed as though the devil were after her. After these expeditions and until the colder weather came they took the children to see the great laundry, the butter-making pantries, the cheese-room and the kitchens, followed by a ceremonial visit to the stables where, his mother in attendance, Charles was given his first pony.

Charles was complacent about all these treats. He loved showing off to the grooms and the farmhands, who all liked him.

'It's a pity', said Delia, 'he isn't the eldest, for of all these boys he's the one who really likes being out doing things. Fred'll be in the army, and poor William – I suppose he'll be looked after by the church.'

'They say young Ned wants to go into the navy,' said Dorothy.

'And the baby,' said Delia quite fondly, 'I wonder what that little mite will do?' Nobody said anything about the girls or George until Anne said: 'Has Miss Caro come out this year then?'

'Oh there'll be a grand ball down in London – let's hope she's made a match.'

'That Harriet'll be married before her, mark my words,' said Dorothy.

'I think Miss Georgy is the *prettiest*,' said Anne.

'How did we get to talking about all this? Oh, Charlie and the title.'

'Well, George will have the title,' said Mrs Copus briskly as she came in and overheard the last remark.

'I suppose he'll go into Parliament then?'

Master Charles would make more *noise*,' said Delia.

'Oh, Mr George is the cleverest, no doubt about it,' said Mrs Copus, who could not resist singing the praises of 'her' first Hardow baby.

'They say he's printed some verses too. About the rose gardens, they said, but it's in some old-fangled language, not English!'

'Perhaps it was French?' said Dorothy.

'Oh no – men don't bother with French – that's for the ladies. Miss Sterky prattles away to those girls in her lingo, you'd never credit it.'

Blanche had obviously been listening because before Delia could say 'Little pitchers' or her favourite 'pas devang . . .', she chipped in with '*My* name is French. It means white!'

'Well, fancy that,' said Mrs Copus comfortably.

Lizzie crept on to Anne's knee. 'Nanna, when will my George come back?' she whispered, putting her arms round Anne's neck.

Oh Lizzie, I wish he would, she wanted to say, but said instead: 'We shall see him at Christmas, I expect, if he doesn't come to the Castle before he goes back to Oxford.'

But it was a long wait. Some of the Quatre Saisons roses gave a final burst of flowering in early September in the walled rose garden. Their scent seemed even headier than in June when there was more competition from others. There had been old moss-roses and cabbage-roses and centifolias and great masses of ramblers, white as snow and pale pink, but now only the painted damasks and the late flowering white Provence roses were left, with a few Rosa Gallicas. Anne was given permission to go to the garden with Dorothy and the baby, now sitting up in his miniature curricle with a cane hood over him. Lizzie went along too of course and tried to spell out the names of the roses which the head gardener had had printed in fancy Gothic script: 'Rose d'amour-virginiana plena', and 'Rosa damascena'. The gardener also allowed the maids to pick any roses past their best, beyond Curly's mother's ministrations. Thus they carried a few velvety blossoms up to the nursery and the schoolroom though the flowers were always put out in the corridors at night for fear they breathed in too much air and poisoned the sleeping children.

But the last roses came and went and Anne still dreamed her dreams of George. Her time was well enough filled but he had been too long away, she told herself. She only wanted to see him, to know he walked the same patch of earth. Selina Sharpe said no more to Anne and usually ignored her. One afternoon, though, when she came up with a message from Mrs Gibson she said to Lizzie: 'Your maid likes roses, doesn't she? Red roses?'

'Nanna likes flowers – so do I.'

Anne was in the next room removing some dirty sheets.

'I suppose you think *she* is pretty like a rose,' went on Miss Sharpe in a strange voice. The child made no reply. 'And when is your big brother coming back?' asked Selina sweetly and went on answering herself. 'Not till Christmas I'll be bound. Oh, there you are, Tesseyman. Would you go to her ladyship's maid for me, please? Her ladyship asked Mrs Gibson for this book. I believe it's for you, Miss,' she continued, turning to Lizzie again, 'but your mama wants to see it first for your reading lessons, so take it now, Tesseyman. I'll stay in the nursery for a minute.'

Anne hated leaving Lizzie alone with Selina Sharpe but duty was duty so she took the book and went off to the South Wing to find Marie. The family must all be back then, Hardow and his wife and the girls who had accompanied them on a short visit away. The comings and goings always bewildered Anne, but allowed her to hope that one day she would discover George back again. This was impossible at the moment, however. Selina Sharpe puzzled her. She was clearly not a happy woman, and Anne found her rather repellent, yet she was not bad-looking. Perhaps she was not as hard as her outward manner bespoke. Could it have been she, she wondered, whom she had heard crying a year ago? She thrust the memory of the sound away from her. It had been harsh and ugly. Perhaps no one was as he or she appeared? Even the old Earl, who still frightened Anne. Perhaps he was just a sad old man. Yet what reason had the folks here to be sad with their bellies full and their thirsts quenched? One of the manservants had read them out the account of the Peterloo massacre not long ago when the cavalry had charged the rioters who were gathered to protest against the price of bread. Many ordinary poor people had been killed and there had been a heated argument in Servants' Hall between those who held that 'the peace must be preserved at all costs' and those who sympathized with the starving and even felt guilty that they themselves were so much better fed.

Thinking these thoughts, Anne knocked on the door of the boudoir. There was no answer and no footman in sight so she knocked again. Still no answer and she was just about to go back when the door next to it in the main south corridor opened and Hardow came out. He saw her and came up to her. 'Good afternoon,' he said softly. 'You are not looking for another lost child I take it?'

'No sir,' said Anne. 'It's this book for her ladyship's maid sent by Mrs Gibson.'

'Give it to me.' He stared at her as she gave him the book and continued to stare for a few moments before looking down at the book in his hands. 'I see. *The Young Person's ABC*. I don't suppose you can read?'

Anne flushed. It was not said unkindly but he seemed perhaps a little the worse for liquor – she was not sure. He was a puzzle, George's father, and no mistake. As she curtsied and said: 'I read a little, sir,' he took one of her hands, appeared to be staring at it, then dropped it.

'You may go.'

She walked away with as much dignity as possible and at the turn of the stair saw he was still gazing at her. She ignored him and pursued her way downstairs. He was, they all said, such a *gentle* man, with his bored silences and subservience to his father but she had glimpsed in his face something far from gentle. George did not look like him at all!

As Selina Sharpe had said, George and the others were back only for Christmas and Anne looked forward daily to the Chapel service the next Sunday when it would be her turn to go with the children, and even more to Christmas Day. Her second Christmas, and she felt so much older and wiser! Then the New Year: 1820. She repeated the number to herself. One thousand eight hundred and twenty years since Our Lord's birth. Charles and Blanche were having catechism lessons from the Rev.

Thorp who came up to the Castle specially for this purpose. William was allowed to join them and sat listening, still for once. Sometimes he looked quite normal and his speech seemed to have improved. Anne would often talk to him as she sat doing the children's sewing. He had stopped saying 'Want Edward', and had learned to write letters on his slate, though he puzzled over 'Marmaduke Multiply's Merry Method of Making Minor Mathematicians', or, in other words the multiplication table, and never got further than 'Twice two are four. Pray hasten on before.' Blanche had got to 'Seven times eight are fifty-six. That fellow merits twenty kicks', which always led to Charles suiting action to words. Lady Georgiana often came for William and tried her best with him and perhaps all their efforts were leading somewhere. She was a very good and loving mother, Anne thought. She never got cross or lost her temper and was as kind to her servants as she was sweet to her little ones. This year she too would be in the Christmas Chapel. All the family would be gathered in before the New Year.

And they were. And Anne rejoiced in the sight of George. He looked rather melancholy. She knew he kept his eyes shut during the prayers for she was standing with Lizzie just across from him and her eyes were not shut though she had her head bowed and managed to look sideways under cover of her prayer book (lent to her by Mrs Copus). Hardow's eyes were not shut either but Anne did not see that. Lady Georgiana next to him was praying softly with her children ranged round her and she too looked melancholy. There was no sign of the Earl though his Countess was there. Of the servants she knew, most were present. She prayed dutifully along with the Rev. Thorp for the old King but more for his namesake George.

And not long after that in the first month of the next year the old King died and it was 'Long Live George IV' and a year remarkable in English public life. But Anne knew little and cared less about all this, though George both knew and cared. Anne cared for the reality of little Miss Lizzie and for the idea of Mr George whose face came near to hers in her night dreams and interposed itself throughout her busy days. She would wake with strange feelings of rapture as though her nights had in truth been spent with the object of her thoughts. And she could give no name to this passion or this rapture but love.

FOUR

THE TEMPLE OF THE FOUR WINDS
1820

Plaisir d'amour, ne dure qu'un moment;
Chagrin d'amour dure toute la vie.

    J.-P. Claris de Florian

Lady Georgiana and her husband went away with Caro at the end of February to London. The older servants said they would be away a long time, might even go to Brighton to see the new King, though they wouldn't take Caro *there*! The old Earl and Countess stayed on, but the Castle was quiet. No house-parties, no George who was off to Oxford. Marie had accompanied her ladyship so Curly and Dorothy were entrusted with Miss Georgy's and Miss Harriet's hair and clothes 'for practice'. Curly might even be sent for in the middle of the London Season when the Hardow party went to Newmarket and she was sure that in summer when the Season was over she would be asked to go with Marie to the castle in the far north. Anne felt gloomy. It was no longer enough to know that George existed; she wanted his *presence*, even if it were only a glimpse of him down by the lake or coming back from the walled garden where he often chatted with the gardeners. She kept herself going by looking forward to his next visit and tried to be kind to William who now had a special room with his tutor. Baby Harry and his nurse were next to the nursery and Charlie's room was to be prepared for the baby. Charlie himself was to go off to school after Easter. How could they bear to be always parting from their children, thought Anne, as she stared at sleeping Harry or listened to Blanche reading a story called 'A Journey to London' to Lizzie. Lizzie was making very good progress with her capital letters but had not yet started on the printed characters. The slate and its sponge were always on the nursery table along with Blanche's paper cut-outs and patterns which she spent hours fiddling with.

But, at last, spring *did* come and Anne's spirits lifted. It was a late Easter but the Oxford term had ended well before and, glory of glories, *he* was to come back after a short visit to his parents in London. Then Lizzie had a letter from him, a real grown-up letter in which he told her he was going to have her study with him when the good weather came and by summer she could walk with him to the Temple. 'Tell your Nanna to lay in plenty of slates and slate pencils,' the letter said, 'for you are not up to quills yet. You will see by my writing that I am scarcely up to them either.' It was true that he had curious cramped writing but had made a special effort to print his letters for Lizzie. The letter ended with 'God bless you Lizzie. This is probably your first real letter – from your loving brother – George.'

Lizzie was entranced and wanted to write back but Dorothy said he would be back before she had finished it. She did draw a picture to give him later – three people, one with trousers, one small one with pantaloons and, holding the hand of the small one, a lady in a skirt and apron. 'That's you, Nanna!' said Lizzie.

The great day came when he *did* return and Lizzie was so excited that Delia said: 'Poor mite. He's like a father to her, isn't he? I'm sure *I* don't want to go traipsing round with slates and pencils. Miss Blanche and I will stay indoors and do our patterns.'

'Perhaps it will rain?' suggested Anne. 'Then we can't go out.'

'Pish! it's only lords and ladies who never go out in the rain. Not people like you, or children – or madmen like our Mr George!'

The next morning no one had yet seen George but Dorothy reported that Miss Harriet had been 'at the harp' the previous evening for the delight of her brother. They were just tidying up the children's breakfast and William's porridge-smeared face when there was a knock at the door.

'That'll be George,' Lizzie jumped up and down. But it was the footman with a message to say that if Miss Lizzie and her maid wished to take a little walk it was a fine morning and Mr George would be over at the Temple.

Anne carried the basket with the slates and pencils and some fruit for Lizzie and they wound their way round the house in the direction of the small lake and the Temple. It was a blue and gold morning, still not warm but warm enough for them.

'I don't know why he can't see Miss Lizzie indoors,' Mrs Copus had grumbled. 'But there you are. Take care of her, Tesseyman.'

Anne had managed to suppress her feelings of joy sufficiently well to appear calm and sensible and had said nothing. All she was worried about was that Selina Sharpe would be hovering round at the windows as they set off. But there was no one and they arrived up the little slope which was now, as Curly had promised, covered with Lent Lilies waving in the breeze.

The door to the Temple at the front was open and she let Lizzie run ahead. Her heart was beating wildly but she was determined not to betray any of her own feelings. She was only a nursery maid, accompanying a child on her walk to a beloved brother. Yes, that was all she was! She too walked through the glass-fronted doors and saw the sun shining on a desk, a sofa, chairs and a little table on which was a vase of flowers and, standing there with the little girl in his arms, George. She curtsied and he put the child down, set her on a chair piled up with tapestry cushions and said: 'Good morning, Nanna. It's good of you to bring my sister. There's a chair for you, too.'

'Do you want me to stay, sir?' asked Anne.

'Of course we want you to stay, don't we, Bessy? If I tire as tutor you can take over. Have you the slates and the alphabet books?'

They all settled themselves. She saw that George had a pile of old folios with him and sheets and sheets of manuscript paper. There was a large well of ink in a silver inkstand and plenty of quills.

'I am composing a poem for a great competition,' he said, seeing her glance at these objects. 'I am afraid it is in Latin but never mind. It will be a relief to return to my native tongue and its ABC. Look, Lizzie, I have drawn an "a" for you and you must copy it. It is "a" for apple – apple begins with "a", as you see.' He drew an apple for her. 'Next time you must bring coloured chalks and that will keep you busy.' Lizzie was delighted and began her copying with great fervour. The small slate sponge had fortunately been brought and there was a stoop of water in the corner.

'I hope you will find it warm enough?' said George. 'We intend soon to have pipes laid under the floor which are to be heated by hot water, so that we shan't get chilblains.'

'I saw there was no grate, sir,' replied Anne quietly.

'You look worried, Nanna. Is it that there should be a chaperone? No – I don't suppose you've ever had one.' He smiled.

'The child is my chape – chaperone,' said Anne, and dared to look him full in the face. Was it, could it be, true, that he was also affected by their meeting? There was a long pause as he held her look.

'Do you remember by the lake, last year?' he said, looking down now at his manuscript. 'I had the idea to write of swans and water, and a young goddess who came bearing food – for the swans I mean – and to compose a pastoral piece round that theme – of plenty and a golden moment.' She only half understood his words but when he looked up at her she felt herself blushing.

'Yes, sir, I do remember!' (It was the happiest day of my life, she wanted to say.) 'I'm afraid I got into trouble later for being – *she* said "too familiar".' She stopped. He looked angry.

'You weren't "familiar", Nanna. Who dared say that?' (And he thought, God knows I can't get her out of my mind even though I thought the poem would purge me.)

'Oh, it was only the under-housekeeper,' she replied, naming no names.

The two sat facing each other, Lizzie still bent down to her slate, happy. There was silence for a moment.

'We must talk of other things,' he said, collecting himself. 'Would you like to learn too, Nanna? You said you could read and write.'

Anne plucked up her courage. 'Please sir, tell me about your studies. What do boys learn at school, and what do you learn in Oxford?' What is it, she meant, that I am missing? What do great folks know that they are so different from us?

He began to speak of history, of times and places, of events long ago, of Greece, of Rome, of learning, of religion. Of how it profited nothing if from one's learning one did not learn how to live. He was an orator, an enthusiast! She listened, tried to understand – but studied *him*! He was too carried away to realize and was plunged in a description of the travels he was to make, of the writing he wished to do, of the laws of England he wished to alter when Lizzie interrupted.

'When are you going away to these places, George?' she asked. The little girl had understood the drift of his words. 'I don't want you to go away, George. You can stay here and write nice things.' These were so much Anne's sentiments that she leaned over and gently stroked Lizzie's hair.

'I apologize. I am being egoistic. You must forgive me. Let me see – Nanna, *you* must write about what *you* see, now, on this slate, and I will be your tutor and correct it for you as I will now Lizzie's work. See Lizzie, the line must come straight down the side of the "a" for apple, thus – "a" – it has to lean on it, look.'

'What shall I write? Do you want me to tell you what I see through the window?'

'Write about that, yes,' he replied and then bent to his own book.

Anne took a slate and pencil and began. Very well – he should know a little of her. As she wrote she was so closed to the world that she did not notice his occasional surreptitious glance at her. It took quite a long time and Anne's fingers ached from holding the squeaky thin slate pencil. 'It is a luvly day and we are sitting in the Tempel. Outside the sun is shining and the flowers wisking in the little wind. Lizzie is learning her ABC and Mr George is writing in his white papers. Mr George is a noble man. He is young but he takes thort for others. I am Anne Tesseyman and I am very happy today. I wish this morning would never end.' There. She had dared. She could wipe it off though. It would soon be time to return for Lizzie's luncheon.

'What have you written, Nanna?' asked Lizzie.

'I will read it,' said George.

'But what have *you* written, George?' pursued Lizzie.

'You would not understand it, it is in Latin,' said George.

> Ego puellam pulcherrimam amo
> Illamque in corde meo teneo.

'What does it mean?'

'I will tell you if Nanna will let me read her slate.'

Anne was suddenly shy and fearful. But it was the truth – and no one could be blamed, surely, for speaking the truth? George took her slate and read it to himself, then looked up at her, in silence.

'You are a poet, Nanna,' he said finally. 'Whisking in the wind, why, it is quite like Wordsworth.' He stopped, still looking at her.

'Go on,' said Lizzie. 'What else?'

'Nanna says she is happy because . . . because it is a fine day, and she wishes it would be like this for ever.'

'With no rain?' pursued the intelligent Lizzie.

Anne smiled. 'No rain,' she said, and looked straight at George. 'What did you write, sir?' she asked boldly.

'Roughly translated: I – er – see the most beautiful girl and I feel – er – emotion – in my heart.'

'Oh! sir.'

They were rapt. Lizzie pulled at George's sleeve. 'And look at my apple.'

He looked down at his sister. Could 'Nanna' have felt what he had been feeling during the past year, whenever, which was curiously often, he had thought of her? It was most mysterious.

'Yes, Miss Lizzie. That is very good and tomorrow we shall do "b" for ball.'

He is so *young*, thought Anne. For all his book-learning and all he knows and his noble manners, he is a child like Lizzie! Yet he *must* know the ways of the world better than I do. Anne had travelled a long way since Stockton, but she was amazed at herself. She felt, in a strange way, *sorry* for George, though she did love him so. She was sure no one but his mama had felt that.

'You learn quickly, Anne,' he said, speaking her given name for the first time.

'Please correct my spelling,' she said levelly.

He took the sponge and altered a few words. 'If you had written it on paper with a quill I would have kept it,' he said slowly.

As Lizzie got down and said she was hungry he agreed she should return to the house.

'But mind, whenever I am free we have our lessons,' he said. 'Perhaps when William's tutor is away I shall teach him too – and your Nanna can come along then as well.'

Did he know that she loved him? Was it enough to say that she wished the morning would never end? And George at the same moment was saying to himself: 'Did she *really* understand the Latin words were meant for her? Are there any words to say what I – we? – feel, or do only actions matter?' He wanted to stay there alone for an hour or two but, 'I am determined,' he said, as he stopped himself from taking her hand, lest she think him forward or dishonourable, 'that these lessons *shall* continue.' But as he bent down again to his writing when they had gone, he felt uplifted yet anxious.

George went on feeling uplifted and anxious, but gave no sign of it to any of his family. Georgy and Harriet, who had heard of his teaching efforts from Lizzie, teased him. 'George is to be an usher in a school', 'George is to undertake the instruction of charity children', were some of their not ill-meant gibes. Yet it never occurred to them that *they* might undertake to help their little sisters and brothers. They were in the schoolroom themselves and though they were both quite clever, both longed to be out of it. Harriet *did* enjoy reading French, and was learning Italian, but this seemed far removed from nursery matters. They tittered at William's tutor who was a gauche, thin man with an eyeglass, and giggled, when they dared, at the stern Mademoiselle Sterky who was herself quite a bluestocking. They took slightly more interest in Blanche who would soon be going up to the schoolroom herself now that Caro had left it. Georgy was now sixteen and surely must have something else in her head but dreams of her first Season and a husband? Harriet had begun to disconcert George. She was knowing beyond her years, witty and somewhat alarming. What would either of them think of him if he confessed to a growing 'faiblesse' for a nursemaid? They would turn their long aristocratic noses down at him and think he meant either something disgraceful or something too funny for words. He did not use the word 'love' to himself, except in Latin when it appeared of somewhat vaguer import, but he could not help recognizing that this strange mixture of feelings he had – of attraction, curiosity, admiration, desire – for the young Anne must surely be connected with that emotion of which the poet spoke. And if it were? It was a complete impossibility. Men did not entertain anything but a sensual penchant for servant girls. It struck deep at the root of the idea of a gentleman on which he had been brought up. It was against all the values of moderation, good sense, and even Christian benevolence, which his better tutors had infused in him. It *must* be just a sensual craving! And that would make him hate himself. Yet it was *not*. No, it was *not*. He liked that young woman, not only because she was 'good'; he knew she was 'good'. She was motherly too, and hard-working and cheerful – and so pretty! What harm if he got to know her a little better? He *wanted* to know her better. What would his friends at Christ Church think, sparks like Kedleston and Greville? They already thought him odd because he was so serious, didn't like getting drunk and 'raved' about his literary and linguistic and philosophical studies. Yet he did not want to hurt Anne, did not want to harm a hair on her head, did not want to lay her open to a masculine siege. With that other part of himself he longed to be near her, to hold her hand, look in her eyes and forget all his previous sorrows in her gentle and yet lively gaze. There would be so many opportunities to see her. No one would stop him, yet he did not want Anne to be 'noticed'. An interfering busybody of a servant had already told her she was being over familiar, had she? No, Lizzie's nurse had always, even this morning in the summerhouse, acted most modestly and circumspectly. When she left, he saw she had forgotten the slate upon which she had written her little piece and so he had taken it back and wrapped it in one of his shirts where his valet would not look.

He saw himself walking in the hayfields with her, climbing the little gills round the estate, following the path through the woods, wandering through the maze with her. *That* would be a good subject for a poem with the Heart's Desire found at its centre! He planned mornings in the Temple – no one would disturb them and they could take William out for fresh air. He wondered what his mother's sister would have thought of the state of his mind if she had known. Manners were doubtless changing – and for the better – but imagine what his grandmother, who had died when he was four and whom he scarcely remembered, would have made of what seemed to be a growing *flamme* as she would have called it, for a maidservant! His grandmother who he gathered, *could* have slept with the Prince of Wales, *had* had a bastard child of her own, and whose sister had produced two bastards as well as her legitimate progeny.

Thus musing, George found himself in the walled garden, though he should have been in the library and certainly must uphold his promise to visit his sisters in the music room in the afternoon. If he were not careful he was so absent-minded that he would find himself in the house again, in the Long Gallery, the prisoner of Grand, who was still admiring the gallery as the result of his own plans finally achieved in the West Wing, and went there every day to flatter himself.

George had all his life before him. He would try to be rational and test his feelings against his conscience.

Anne for her part kept the events of the morning like a little idol's altar in her heart. Even if they never happened again, she knew she had made some impression upon him. He seemed so *lonely* somehow and yet as the heir to all that stood around her, how could he be? Perhaps she herself was lonely and that explained it. The children almost filled her life with busyness and obligations but there seemed to be another sort of life waiting. Of course Mr George could never be a serious *suitor*! Even if young noblemen liked girls such as her and even if the attraction was mutual she knew they never *married* them! Marriage was something different with a lad of your own sort, she supposed, though she had never yet 'kept company' with any young man. Was it not possible just to love someone and not expect anything from them? Oh, there was so much she would like to give George and want nothing back! She kept all these thoughts to herself but could not help wishing sometimes that *she* had been born in a Castle to be a worthy friend for him. She must be a lunatic to imagine he could ever feel for her anything like she felt for him. It was absolutely impossible, against all common sense, and not the sort of thing you could tell Mam! But she still enjoyed her feelings and they buoyed her up throughout the windy days of spring.

She came up to the nursery one day in May and found all the maids assembled in great excitement. She had not seen George for a week or two and had thought him away, or regretting that time in the summer Temple. She had bravely tried to turn her thoughts away from him.

'There's to be a special ball for Miss Caro,' said Delia.

They were all seated round Curly who was holding court. The new maid, Mary Ann, was there, and Dorothy and Susan. Curly did not often come up to the children's quarters now and Anne had thought she must still be in London with her young mistress, it was so long since she had seen her.

'They've decided to give a little country ball seeing as how the rebuilding at the Duke's house is taking longer than expected. Not that it's Miss Caro's *first* Season, so it doesn't matter.'

'She has not been spoken for then?' asked Delia.

'Not a hope,' said Curly.

'And I heard Lady Georgiana was tired and the doctor told her to leave London – and then the next I heard was that they would finish the Season early and come back home here, before they go up to Cumberland or the old place in Northumberland.' She spoke with the knowledge that she was now the main source of information for all the other servants as to the doings of the family. 'You'll all be told today I 'spect and there'll be a right to-do. My lady and her mother are already back – we came last night. The stewards are in a right sweat, thinking they were done for the summer and all.'

'Oo, isn't it exciting, Anne?' said Mary Ann, her eyes round.

'Is it to be a big party then?' asked Delia.

'I heard two hundred – but that's small. Miss Caro was telling me they usually have five hundred but Grand wants to save on expenses so they thought this would be a good way. "It's not the custom, Maria," she says to me, "but we can start a new fashion, and anyway it makes a change."'

'Mrs Copus says it's years since they had a ball here – the last was a funny French word – a Fett Shampeter – like a breakfast, she said.'

Dorothy interrupted the flow. '*I* was told she said that as it's Miss Caro's second Season they won't be expecting an eldest son for her and eldest sons don't bother with the country anyway.'

'Who told you that?'

'It was Miss Harriet – full of it she is. She says there are all these younger sons, you see, who go anywhere to find wives with a good dowry – she calls them danglers.'

'No,' said Curly. 'That's when they flirt with no intention of getting wed.'

'Well, Harriet wouldn't realize that.'

'I wouldn't put it past that one,' said Delia. 'She's got more savvy than her sisters. Plenty of "danglers" around, I'd say.'

'And the younger sons won't inherit the land, you see,' went on Dorothy, 'and so they won't have any estates, unless their elder brothers don't marry, and then they'd have to wait a long time. Now what *did* she call them – *detrimentals* I think she said, and last year they called them scorpions.'

'Well, did you ever!' interjected Delia.

'Well, Miss Harriet told me. She said: "Though I'm the third daughter I wouldn't have a detrimental", and she won't, that's what they'll pass over to Miss Caro!' Dorothy sat back after all this important information.

Anne, who had so far been silent in all this strange talk, asked shyly: 'So would it be better for a young lady to marry anyone rather than no one?'

'Course it would, specially if she were on her second or third Season,' replied Curly wisely.

'So would it be better for a young lady to marry our George than our Fred?' asked Mary Ann.

'You are talking like one of us,' laughed Curly, but noticed that Anne looked away. 'Mr George is the best *party* – that's what they call them.'

'Perhaps they want him to meet someone too at the ball then?' pursued Mary Ann.

'Oh young men can wait – they don't have to "come out" like

girls – and anyway they wouldn't expect him to be looking at a ball in the country, though I wager there's plenty of mamas who'll be all in a tarradiddle to send their girls here just on the off-chance.'

Anne turned and said: 'But it isn't the same for girls, is it – I mean Miss Georgy won't have less money than Miss Caro?'

'Oh no,' replied Curly sagely. 'For girls, you see, it's their looks, but for men it's their money.'

'Bit of a lottery, ain't it?' exclaimed Mary Ann.

They had not noticed that Blanche had crept up and was listening intently.

'Why can't girls inherit titles, Delia?' she asked.

'Well, I don't know. I suppose it's the law,' replied Delia. 'You go and marry your duke dear, you won't have to worry about titles.'

'Well, I shall be a lady too,' said Blanche.

'But is it just *money* they meet men for in London?' asked Anne. 'Not for – love?' It did puzzle her. Didn't grand folk ever marry for love? She knew that what they called love in the village was courting and getting wed in church. The women often talked about some young lad or other and how they 'loved' him. Come to think of it she'd never heard the men call it with that name – not even her brother Richard who was a quiet and gentle young carpenter. And this 'love' often included bundling in the hedges!

'You and your "love" – ' teased Delia.

'*My* mam says there's no such thing,' said Mary Ann. 'She says many a lass feels sorry for a lad, and it does them no good. And Mam always says – then that lass is "Mam to two".'

'What does she mean?'

'Well – she's mam to the lad, fetching and carrying for him – and then – you know – she's a real mam when the first bairn comes along.'

They were silent, digesting this opinion.

'Aye, it's true,' sighed Delia.

'Not for the quality of course – they don't have no fetching and carrying,' said Susan who had come up and was listening.

'My mam says, too,' continued Mary Ann whose mother was a constant and fixed topic of conversation for her, 'she says – many a lass cried out her e'en and was glad for a comforter – when she was lonely, like – and that's how she "fell". That's what my mam said when I was going away. Don't worry lass, she said – look after yourself, there's no one else will.'

'Did you cry?' asked Susan. 'I mean, when you came here?'

'I should think not!' answered the young maid.

'Well, you've no cause, yet, for crying,' said Delia sensibly. Anne looked at Delia and wondered again about her life.

'Did *you* cry, Anne?' asked Susan.

'I felt like it,' answered Anne after a silence. 'But I didn't. Curly helped me, didn't you, Curly? It was very lonely. I'm glad I came when I did – now that you're in the house and not sewing, Curly.'

'Oh, were you a seamstress then?' asked Mary Ann.

'Aye,' replied Anne briefly. 'But not for long – I'm glad they changed me.' But she was thinking over the words about comforters and falling. What did it matter? She felt more like comforting George than him comforting her – and it was funny, why should she feel he needed comfort – after all they'd said about him being the best *party* or some foreign word? She suddenly felt sad. In the end, she supposed, George would make a brilliant marriage and she would, she supposed, also wed someone else.

'Now tell us all about when it's to be, the ball,' said Delia.

'In ten days – they decided last week and messages went up to the steward and Mrs Gibson – eh, they're in a right tizzy.'

'There'll be plenty of work, that's for sure,' said Delia. 'We're always the last to know.'

But by the end of the day all the Castle servants were apprised of the unexpected event and went about grumbling but secretly pleased. Never had there been such a fetching and carrying, such a break from routine. Everyone on the estate was drafted. All Anne could think about at first was that their lessons in the Temple were suspended and she did not know when they would resume. But she longed to see George in all his masculine finery at the ball. She was going to be lucky. She was given special duties and they included 'waiting on' on the great day. She hoped then to catch sight of the eldest son of the house who, it seemed, was to do the honours along with his parents. Grand had gone to bed with gout but had apparently no objection to the junketings. The servants whispered that Lady Georgiana's brother the Duke was footing the bill so that Grand could not complain.

★

The great day dawned at last. Anne saw it dawn for she had woken early with a curious dream and thought she might as well go down and see if her help was needed in the kitchen before waking Willy and Blanche. All the servants had been given special instructions as to their duties for the day. Delia was to keep the children well away from the scene of activity in the State Rooms and drawing-rooms, but Anne, along with Curly's sister Jane, was to help with last-minute mending of linen in the morning and in the afternoon with the final inspection and ironing of Miss Caro's clothes for the evening. In the evening, once the Castle ceremonies were over – and they were to start early, though not as Anne had thought at breakfast time – the Servants' Hall would hold their own jollifications. When Curly had spoken of 'breakfasts' at the London villa, which Caro had attended last year, Anne had understood she meant the mid-morning break for tea and meat. But no, apparently breakfasts could go on till midnight! Fortunately this one was not to begin till the early evening, Grand having put his foot down.

As Anne went out slowly through the Kitchen Court she sniffed the summer air with pleasure, her dream of the night dissolving in the glittering dew-laden grass and the scent of honeysuckle and roses. All was quiet; the old yellow brickwork was gilded with that extraordinary freshness which only a rising sun can produce and she could not help skipping for a moment at the joy of being alive on such a glorious morning and the prospect of all the excitement to come. And somewhere behind those long windows George was sleeping. But strangely enough her dream was to come back to her in little glimpses throughout the day.

It was, as Curly had said, a departure from precedent to have a ball in the country, but as Caro had already officially come out the year before, friends did not shake their heads too much over it, indeed saw it as an extra, an inducement to leave London for a night or two – and a great opportunity for various more provincial nobility and gentry to savour the excitements of grandeur.

Several of the kitchen girls and housemaids were up soon after Anne and she found them there in the Servants' Hall when she finally decided to go in. Mary Ann came up to Anne.

'The Duke's arrived – last night he came,' she whispered to her. The men had all been admiring his carriage and came in soon after. The grooms were still thwacking their legs with pleasure and retailing old stories of horses dead and gone. Mary Ann supped her tea and stared at them.

'I do think that Mr Osborne is a good-looker, don't you Anne?' she asked finally in another of her whispers. She always whispered in Servants' Hall though upstairs in the nursery her voice was loud and clear.

'Which one is that?' enquired Anne for politeness's sake.

'Oh – you know – the blond one just over there, with the nankeen trousers. I do declare he's looking at you!'

This was new to Anne. She had hardly spoken to the grooms. The footmen were more forthcoming in their conversation to the girls and several times Anne had spoken to them, to John of course and to Robert who flirted with them all. But she felt curiously wooden when they would have been pleased to continue their talk elsewhere. The thought of George had for so long constrained her. The men thought it was shyness and several had laid a wager that they would get that Anne Tesseyman to walk out with them, but since she did not come down very often to Servants' Hall now that she was up with the children, their interest had waned. One or two had said she was stuck up, but John had defended her, saying she was a nice lass and was too busy. Anne looked briefly over to the said Osborne but could not agree he was handsome. His face was too red and the way he had of staring at all and sundry was not pleasant. But to please Mary Ann she said that she thought he was looking at *her*. Mary Ann bridled. In spite of her mother's strictures, or perhaps because of them, she was sure that she would find a good husband at the Castle one day. She would like to have continued to talk of these things but Anne stood up with that faraway look she sometimes had and said she was off to the sewing-attics. Just then Mrs Gibson was seen at the door and Anne made haste to follow her. She wondered briefly what Miss Caro was doing on this morning of her ball. Curly would be over doing her hair in the afternoon so it didn't have time to get spoilt, she supposed.

The talk in the sewing-room was of Miss Caro and of the various friends who had arrived the night before with their daughters. Lady Sarahs and Lady Marys and Lady Louisas were all safely housed in the best bedrooms.

'That Lady Charlotte – they say she's very pretty,' said Jane.

'Who are they hoping to get her off with?' asked Susan.

'Oh, I don't know – Curly didn't say. A pity if she gets our

Miss Caro's beau, though.'

'Who is that?' asked Anne.

Delia had been saying something on the same lines to Anne
the night before and that suddenly made her remember a bit of
her dream, which had been about Caro and Caro weeping, and
George had been there saying soothing words but Caro had
flung herself weeping in Anne's open arms, and Anne remembered feeling some strange unaccountable pity for the girl in her
dream as though she were not a grand young lady but just a girl
who was desperate to find a husband – even more desperate than
Mary Ann in reality.

The dream must have come from Delia's saying, meaning to
be comforting – for the maids took the ladies' own problems to
heart – 'If she don't make it this second Season it'll be next year
with Miss Georgy. Doesn't do them any harm to wait. Look at
our poor lady – seventeen she was when Hardow married her
and she's only thirty-six now, and eleven children. Not that you
could find a nicer lady anywhere or sweeter children, but she
ain't got her life to herself any more than us, Anne.' Anne was
pondering this again as they sat sewing. If Miss Caro landed a
beau tonight, was it just to have a dozen children in eighteen
years? Why did they need to have so many? Of course her own
mam had had eleven, counting the two that died, but mam was a
poor ignorant woman compared with these great ladies. You
would think that they had something better to do. Then her
heart thought: 'But I was Mam's eighth and I'm glad I was born!'
And then she thought again of George, being the first child and
special.

'Thinking of the dancing tonight?' enquired Susan. 'You've
got that right dreamy look!'

Anne bent down and persevered with her sewing but she
could not drive away the thought that it was better perhaps for
lasses to dream for a time and not be so hard put to get wed. All
this to-do was to get a husband for Miss Caro and Lord knows
she wanted one bad enough. How much easier it was to be a lad
and even more to be a gentleman.

'She's thinking on the lads,' said another maid. 'Ain't that
true, Anne?'

'Aye – I was thinking how they can pick and choose,' she replied, not entirely truthfully. The table linen had been set up. It
had been laundered, and a few tiny rents had been found which

they were using thread-work to cover, copying the original pattern.

'The old man's too mean to buy new,' said Betty, an older woman who came in only at special times of need.

'Well, we've got to make a good show,' said Susan.

'I don't suppose the guests will notice my darns,' said Anne, with more asperity than usual in her voice.

Whilst Anne and the other maids were busy with the fine linen, away in the South Wing the steward was being given his final orders by Lady Georgiana. She was not an efficient or practical lady of the house and knew it full well. What was worse was that none of her daughters either seemed yet to have inherited any of her Grandmama's organizing abilities. Grandmama was the only female relative who could have managed a ball without either panic or muddle and Lady Georgiana often wished she had been given some of these qualities herself. Still, the main thing was to launch Caro again, and doubtless it would all come right in the end. Thank God for Gibson and Copus and their staff, and the footmen who seemed to know what was expected of them. Hardow always expected things to turn out perfectly as if by magic, she thought. A house-party was bad enough, but a ball – and without the comfort of the London pastrycooks and florists – that was a little too much and she was beginning to wish that she had not acceded to Caro's demands and waited until her brother could have offered the villa, if not Devonshire House. Oh well, doubtless he would do that for Georgy and Harriet. But London would have been harassing too and people would have expected perfection, whereas here at the Castle they might make allowances for provincial shortcomings. She had run through in her head the various items to check with the steward so many times. There would be about two hundred guests – it was only a small fête – but as some of the guests were not young there must be seats on the terraces for them as well as in the anterooms and in one of the State Rooms. The flowers were not yet arrived but she knew she could rely on Mrs Currey. Pray for fine weather! It had looked well enough this morning. The orchestra was to arrive in the afternoon and must be given non-alcoholic refreshment. The lighting must be checked and the special globe lamps put outside. Chef must be asked to have the coffee ready early as the food would be obtainable all evening, after the dinner for the family and close friends. The smaller rooms next to the State Rooms must be prepared for écarté and whist. The carpets must be checked and put away from the small ballroom and the lustres and divans put out in the drawing-rooms. George was saying what a pity it was that his Aunt Harriet could not come but his uncle was to speak in the Lords and she must accompany him. Next week, though, they would all be back in London for a short time, perhaps with Caroline already spoken for and this ball a memory! Now, had she told the steward to check with Mrs Gibson that the upstairs drawing-rooms were ready and the carpets put down? Her mind was in a whirl so she decided to drop in on her eldest daughter to see how she was feeling.

If only one need not bother one's head about whist tables and buffets and hot and cold suppers. And when would the flowers be brought to the temporary conservatory which was to open out of one of the drawing-rooms, and had she ordered the gold chairs to be put there?

What would the dandies think of her eldest daughter in her own home? She did not like many of the fashionable young men and did not think they would be enthusiastic for her daughter either. She had great hopes of one undandified young man but he was a younger son. Now if it were Harriet! But Harriet had been sternly spoken to about attempting to infiltrate after six o'clock and Georgy was to keep an eye on her, for the Swiss governess did not always succeed in curbing her adventures. It was really too provoking to have to supervise all this and to know that Grand, if he did not like the arrangements, was quite capable of ordering different ones, even though he was not paying the expenses. And Hardow would not oppose him, just smile.

'What is it, Mama? You look quite worn out,' said Caro when her mother entered her chamber. 'Don't fret, my dear Mama – everything will be lovely. We have such good servants and you have told them all hundreds of times about the arrangements.'

It was true that Caro was of a somewhat lymphatic nature except in the matter of receiving a 'parti' and Lady Georgiana thanked her daughter and resolved to believe her.

'I came about your dress, my dear. Did your maid think it needed anything?'

'No, Mama. It is perfect, but if it were not I have the other – the one meant for London – and as they are much alike it will not matter which I wear I suppose.'

They went into the anteroom where the dress was hanging. 'I do wish I were not so tall, Mama – but the dress is pretty, is it not?'

'Delightful – and will be even better on you,' said her mother cheeringly.

The dress, of white floss silk with a sash of blue was, indeed, exquisite. A present from the Duke could not of course be otherwise. 'You must wear this one, to please my brother,' said Lady Georgiana firmly.

'I am more worried about my hair, Mama – The comb will slip – my hair is so fine.' But Lady Georgiana was inspecting the dress more closely.

'Have you yet put it on, my dear?' she hazarded.

'Well, no Mama – I thought this afternoon when my maid will see to it.'

'Are you sure the sleeves are not too tight, dear? Remember you have put on a little weight since February when my brother took the pattern to Paris.'

'Oh Mama!'

But her mother was adamant and the dress with its puff sleeves and high waist and low decolletage and embroidered hem was slipped over the horrified Caro.

'Mama, you should not be doing this,' she managed to utter.

'Better see it now, then if anything needs to be altered, there is time.'

'It came only yesterday, Mama,' said Caro, struggling to pull her upper arms through the tight bindings. 'Oh dear, you are right, the sleeves are too tight. What shall I do?'

'Hush, my dear, it is a mercy I asked. Now we shall get the sewing maids to pull it out a little – there are tucks in the hem of the sleeve, see.'

Caro stood there tall in her off-the-shoulder gown, the picture of resignation. 'I am too fat, Mama.'

'No my dear, a little *embonpoint* suits you. I shall see to it at once.'

Thus it was that Lady Georgiana, all thoughts of tables and chairs and food out of her head, sent her maid to find Curly who was despatched to the sewing-attics for two seamstresses.

'Come Betty – and you, Anne,' said Curly. 'There's a right to-do. Dress needs altering – you'll have to do it in Miss Caro's chamber.'

Anne was filled with trepidation, but the older maid seemed used to this sort of thing.

'I thought we were to go this afternoon for ironing,' said Anne as they rushed round Kitchen Court and into the long corridors and up to the family rooms.

Curly was full of her own importance and proud to show her friend the inside of Miss Caro's rooms. 'She'll be with you in a moment. See you curtsy,' she muttered.

'Is that the dress?' asked Betty, casting a professional eye on the seams.

'Yes – it's from Paris but the French must be thinner than our girls. You'll have to fix the sleeve seams – do you think you can?'

Anne had never sewn such fine stuff, not even for the Rector's wife, and gazed at the dress which seemed so fragile, and looked at the rich embroidery on the hem which incorporated a coronet or two. Miss Caro came in shyly from her bedroom.

'You'll have to put it on, Miss Caroline,' said Betty.

Anne curtsied and Curly went into the bedroom with her mistress. They emerged quickly and Betty gently eased the tight hem round the puff of the sleeve.

'You're not to worry, my lady. Tesseyman and I will take out a half inch and you'll be surprised at the difference.'

'Indeed I should have been very uncomfortable,' sighed Caro. 'But do you think the front is all right – not too *outré*?'

'Too what, my lady?'

Lady Georgiana came in quietly and smiled at Anne. 'I know Tesseyman,' she said pleasantly as Anne bobbed another curtsy with pins in her mouth.

'Mama, it is not too *outré*, is it?' asked Caro, whose confidence seemed to have been shattered.

'If your *embonpoint* were *there*, yes, but as it is not, decidedly not. And you want it to stay up without bones,' replied her mother and the two maids looked uncomprehendingly though Curly seemed to understand.

'It don't signify,' said Betty wisely, thinking they referred to the length perhaps. As Caro was tall, her ankles peeped underneath the hem.

'Fine for dancing, my lady,' continued Betty. 'Now if you were to ask Miss Caroline to take it off and put it in its parcel, Miss Curly, you can bring it round and we'll have that done in an hour. Then Miss Caroline could try it on and Tesseyman will see to ironing, though I don't think it'll need more than the hem-line, being as we shall work only on the sleeves and that right carefully.'

'I am much obliged, Betty,' said Lady Georgiana as Caro went to remove her finery. 'Now Maria, have you the flowers for the hair and the waist?'

'Yes, my lady. They are in water.'

Once Curly arrived back with the dress, Mrs Gibson gave them her sitting-room to work in as no one else should see the dress before the evening. Anne was thinking how different Curly was – like a fish in the sea now that she was with the lady-ships. But she was glad to help poor Caro.

'I wonder what we'd look like in a dress like that?' mused Betty after loosening the seams and matching the silk with thread sent down from Lady Georgiana. 'Well not me, I'm too old, but you'd look right lovely in that!'

'With flowers in my hair,' laughed Anne.

'A pity *she's* so plain,' said Betty disloyally. 'But nobility has to lead the fashion, though she's not a lady that cares much for clothes I'd guess. Now if that had been Miss Georgy's she'd have had it out of its parcel and on her back and we'd 'ave known yes-terday and had more time. Still I'm not complaining. Seen the family rooms before, have you?'

'A bit. Curly showed me once when they were away – and we take the children there sometimes. Do you think my hands are clean enough, Betty?'

'There's rose-water for us to wash them and a linen piece,' re-plied Betty, nodding to a basin that had been brought in. They eased and tacked and pulled and sewed and with the tiniest stitches made the right allowances for Miss Caro's rather brawny upper arms.

Curly *was* different now, Anne went on thinking. She won-dered what Delia would think of the dress and all the excite-ment. Delia always seemed so happy when Anne did something well. It was nice of her; she had not been at all jealous that Anne had been told to help out in the evening. Yet Anne *would* have minded missing that – just so as to catch sight of George. At this her heart beat faster and all thoughts of the unfairness of life for girls seemed to take flight. Perhaps Caro would tell him who had altered her sleeves – but no, that was stupid. Men weren't interested in all that sort of thing in spite of the fact that it was all done to catch them.

'A good thing her ladyship didn't take it in her head to tell Curly off for not seeing Miss Caro tried the dress on yesterday,' Betty was saying. 'She should have done really – that's her job.'

Whilst they were thus occupied Lady Georgiana returned to her room and had her jewel-box out. Marie was exclaiming over the pieces and her mistress was enjoying describing their provenance.

'That brooch was given to me by the King when he was Prince of Wales at Georgy's christening and those earrings were my mama's. And this turquoise clasp was my sister Harriet's present to me. I think Miss Caro must wear the pearls though: that centre part, Marie, was given to my Mama by the Queen of France after whom you were named – Marie Antoinette. It's from a larger bauble.'

'Oh my lady, I like those best,' said Marie, pointing to a set of opals and emeralds with a matching necklace, earrings and bracelets.

'Yes, I shall wear those tonight,' mused her ladyship. 'Rather than the sapphire and diamond set. It's too grand for the country. Or do you think opals are unlucky and I should wear the diamond feathers and the turquoise and diamond clasp George gave to me when he went to Eton?'

'I think the opals,' said Marie. 'His lordship's sister will be wearing her diamonds.'

'That is true and very sensible of you, Marie. And Lady Gertrude will doubtless wear her sapphires. Of course I could wear my gold chain,' she went on. 'That was given by the Duchess of Marlborough to my husband's grandfather.'

'I think the opals,' said Marie again after a pause.

'Yes, you are right. Oh dear, *Harriet* would know immediately, but with a cream gown opals *are* best.'

'And with the turban, Madame,' said Marie. 'You must not forget the turban. There is a slight tinge of green in the ribbon which the emeralds will set off.'

'How do you do it, Marie? I am always tempted to put on too much and then take it off again before I go down!' Marie smiled at her ladyship, who was noted for her indecision.

Meanwhile the bandmaster had been told to play quadrilles but no waltzes. George, hearing this, was aghast. 'They can be quite decorous, Mama,' he insisted at luncheon. 'They can adjust the tempo and no one will be tempted to get above themselves.'

'What do you think, Hardow?' asked his wife.

'I suppose it will make a pretty show, my dear, and only the young ones will dance them.'

'But that is just the trouble. They say at my cousin's there were unmarried girls being held quite closely and it gives such an excuse to wander off.'

'My dear, they will wander off if they wish. If Grand has no objection I think we may have a waltz.'

'You do not propose to ask Grand?' the lady cried.

'Well, no – arrange it as you will. You are known for your perfect taste, my dear, and I am sure there will be no scandals. What does your daughter think?'

'Oh, she is too busy worrying about her dress. Have you decided to start the early supper for the upstairs guests at seven?'

'I believe so,' said her husband with a rather bored look. He made an attempt to be genial, summoned a footman and said: 'Tell the steward to pass by my rooms in half an hour to finalize arrangements for upstairs.' The footman bowed. 'There, my dear. You have nothing to worry about.' He picked his teeth with a gold toothpick and yawned.

It was arranged that the principal dancing should be in the Long Gallery with a change of venue to the room next to the Great Hall at midnight for those who wished to continue. The wine cellars were ceremoniously opened by Grand whose favourite pastime it was to judge the claret and champagne.

All seemed to be progressing smoothly when Anne, the sewing done, popped into the nurseries to see Delia for a cup of tea. Her head spun with the tiny stitching and her early rising but after half an hour chatting to the children she felt she had a second wind and they discussed the Servants' Hall arrangements.

'I doubt I shall be able to come,' said Anne. 'They want me to help with the ladies' toilettes when they go upstairs to rest and to see that the flowers don't wither. I must go and see if there's any more ironing.'

The carriages of the guests who were staying over were in the courtyard as she passed Servants' Hall and peeped through the gateway. There were so many types she had not seen before that she stood amazed at the sight of the yellow varnished landaus and barouches. She saw the little ostler they called Osborne giving her a stare as he polished up a halter. He was whistling through his teeth. She was turning away, for she had better see to the rest of the ironing, but heard a 'Keep a waltz for me, will you' from him.

'Too busy,' she shouted back boldly and fled.

When she looked back later to the day and night of the ball it seemed to have lasted a week rather than a night, and to resolve itself into a whirl of colours and scents and rushes hither and thither and glimpses of faces half seen over and over again. From the moment when they looked out at the south lawn and saw the first guests wandering over it long before the strains of music began to penetrate the Kitchen Court, to the moment when a new dawn arrived and the Castle slowly quietened there seemed to be an eternity.

The dandies, carried on their bubbles of champagne, and the whirling girls, the feathered heads of the mamas bent in earnest conversation, the older men drinking in the saloons or sprawled on the divans with their cigars, were all borne through the night on waves of excitement and pleasure, each enjoying the place in his or her own way. The servants too, rushed off their feet, eternally at their service, felt it and were proud to do the honours of 'their' castle. Caroline felt it too as she arrived on her papa's arm and was put through a lively quadrille with her brother George as partner, and for a moment forgot that the beaux had not yet claimed their dance or conversation. Her hair stayed up; her sleeves did not pinch and her dress was not too short. She was a fine figure of a woman in fact, but with none of the grace of her sister Georgy or the sparkle of her sister Harriet. She was statuesque and appealed to the older fellows there, giving the impression of a much older woman, a matron. Even her rather melancholy and large features relaxed in a smile now and then. Her hair was up in a coronet of curls with wispy kiss-curls at her cheeks, and only her mouth, soft and mobile, betrayed her anxiety to please and gave the lie to the impression of maturity. Perhaps in a day or two someone would make an offer, one of the many gallants whom she hardly knew, or even a baronet or a younger son whom Mama approved of – for had she not said to Caro that she and Papa only wanted her happiness, not her glory, and there was the Honourable Mr H..., a younger son but a good family even though they were Tories; and Sir W... W... who had a park and fine mansion in Sussex. How nice it would be not to have to worry about all this business of husband-finding, not to feel so gloomy and hesitant and worried at not pleasing Papa. What would she do if anyone did ask her for more than one dance? She had positively no preferences, found conversation difficult and in the end knew that they would be marrying Papa's daughter, not herself. Harriet would know what to do – if only Harriet had been the eldest and she could have sunk back to number five like her! Still, she thought, she looked well enough and it had been nice dancing with George. Now George had it in him to be quite a social success if he wanted and all the ladies made eyes at him because their mamas had told them to. He seemed indifferent to all this and it was true that he had a rather disconcerting manner and sometimes frightened the girls away because they never knew whether to take him seriously. And there was George's friend from Eton who had come up to ask her to join the next quadrille, probably because George had told him to. He was a kind brother. She would never find a husband as clever and kind as George. The dancing interrupted Caro's disjointed thoughts and for another quarter of an hour she could give herself up to it. If only it need not stop and she need not 'entamer' a conversation (as Harriet would say). Harriet scattered French words like confetti.

Anne was standing at her post next to the white-currant ices with Jane, serving, and piling trays for the footmen to collect and take to the kitchens when they went for the next consignment. She had 'kept an eye' on the flowers on the drawing-room balconies and was doing all she had been ordered to do just as all the other servants were doing, like ants on an anthill where each separate business kept the whole thing going. She had seen her ladyship looking so lovely in her cream gown with green jewels and a big green feather and turban, and was waiting for a glimpse of Miss Caro if she came near in her altered dress. Animated groups of young men pushed by her with a great noise and liveliness. It was a good thing the mamas had everything well under control, but then of course the Hardows were known for their decorum. Not for them the disreputable doings of some of their cousins, about which Delia had told her – even one of the *women* had become notorious for her unbridled conduct. She dared hardly raise her eyes when George was in the room, and was determined not to betray her feelings in front of other servants.

The ball proceeded as balls usually proceed. Some of the lively young men were a little 'heated'. They strolled around in their high white starched collars and embroidered waistcoats over tightly trousered legs that ended in dancing pumps. Except for one or two they did not seem to enjoy the dancing as much as the girls. The girls, with ribbons and bows in their hair and flowers in intricate wreaths in their curls, glided round in their soft shoes.

'Wait for the waltz,' said one young beau to George. 'What was it Byron said? "A lewd grasp and lawless contact warm" – Oh, mustn't forget Byron's not very popular here!'

George smiled vaguely and replied: 'I believe we are to be allowed waltzes, old fellow,' and turned on his heel.

Caro was not thinking of the actual dancing very much, though she enjoyed that. Her mind was still concerned with the dreadful problem: If she were asked to dance more than once by any particular 'parti', would it be forward to accept and would it presage a more than polite interest on the gentleman's part? There were many young men here she did not know; she had been asked by most of them, but none had returned. She felt it was all out of her control, whether they asked her again or no. If they did, then it would be dowries, wedding dresses and trousseaus for the rest of the summer, she supposed. She must wait to be asked and then later if it came to anything she must accept for Papa's sake. After all, it was all for the sake of the family, was it not, that kin should be continued? Her friends Sophia and Marianne and Lady Frances had all been 'asked' this Season and were not here, too occupied with their trousseaus and so on and so on. She had never had any particular women friends, as they were such a large family at the Castle, and Georgy and Harriet were her world. Oh, if only they were here tonight. Georgy was nearly seventeen and so pretty. She would be sure to be 'asked for' next year. Wherever Caro went, accompanied sometimes by Mama or by George, she heard the laughing men in groups. She would catch the words: 'Oh, he is "naughty", is he not?', or 'My dear, have you heard the latest "on-dit"? Too amusing.' But that sort of conversation was not for girls. She wished she were out on her hunter: that was something she did really well, her only accomplishment. They were all back in the supper room now and several elderly relations were being presented to Papa. As she conversed with Aunt Julia, who was rouged to the eyeballs as usual, and then watched that lady demolish a large plate of crème brulée, she wished for one desperate moment that she could say to her only unmarried relative: 'Please take me with you. Teach me how to enjoy myself without a man.' But Julia was expatiating between mouthfuls on the pleasures of being young and gushing over the decorations. 'Such giddy girls we were, just imagine.... O how pretty those urns are full of flowers outside...' And then the Duke came up and rescued her and gave her a dance, but as he was rather deaf it was difficult to carry on a conversation with him.

The Castle did indeed look wonderful. All exclaimed at its beauties, especially the provincial parvenus who had been invited to make up numbers and knew they would never be asked again. Land agents and minor clergy and a few local gentry cast hungry eyes around, the better to be able to tell their wives at home of the glories of the Earl's domain. Outside, the terrace leading to the Temple was now silver in the moonlight and the statues were themselves silvered over. A few sparks were wreathed round them, having imbibed a little too liberally of his lordship's claret.

Some time later Anne was standing out on the balcony, for there was no one else around and for one moment she could be pretending to water the camellias which were to be brought in if others wilted. Then she heard the strains of a waltz beginning from the next room. Surely it was – yes it was – that song, the one Harriet played, but this time much slower. If any man were to propose to a girl or at least show interest tonight, this would be the dance. It was the most lovely sad tune and she crept across the balcony just to see if she could see in through the next windows. They were shut and she was sure no one could see her. It was George she was looking for, not Miss Caro, although she was sure the other servants would be all agog to see if Miss Caro was dancing this with anyone. From outside, the bright lights were seen as through water. Was George dancing – and with whom? He must not see her if he passed. If only just for once all the customs could be turned upside-down and a nobleman could dance with a servant! She smiled sadly at even having the thought and it was thus all unknown to her that George saw her profile at the window like a ghost. He was dancing with his sister. As she had started the dance, poor Miss Caro was still dancing with her brother.

George did not know that Caro, who seemed to be looking the other way, was able to see the look on his face and was following his glance with her eyes. There must be someone in the room on whom his gaze was fixed but she could see no one. The white dresses of the girls were like moths, for they had taken away the big lights, and the candles sent a waxy gleam round the room. What a look he had. She did not recognize her brother, his eyes large and brilliant – such a look! Never had anyone looked at her like that. It was almost as though he were in church at communion, but it was sad too. Yearning, she thought, and was silent. He turned back to her then and made some remark about the music. She wanted to say: 'You love someone then, George', but of course she could not. Instead she said: 'It is haunting music is it not?', and he smiled from far away. No, it was not a marriage look, she thought, it was a look of love and despair. The fiddles were wailing away. Would it never end? But she kept her composure. She had never really expected anyone to make those particular overtures which presaged a proposal a week or two later. But she knew in her heart that no one would ever look at her with that look of her brother's. When the dance was over she excused herself and said she must see to her hair, and fled.

Anne had not known that her reflection could be seen through the pane and she had crept away after staring at George with his sister. Curly had come up then and asked her to join Dorothy in the ladies' boudoir upstairs to see to ladies who needed their flowers rearranged or who felt faint. When she came in, there was only Miss Caro there with an aged aunt. She smiled at her and curtsied and helped Dorothy to tuck the flowers back in Caro's hair and fetched her a glass of water.

'Who is that pretty servant gel?' asked her aunt idly.

'I believe she is in the nursery usually, Aunt,' said Caro, and at that moment was visited by a sudden conviction that this girl had something to do with George. She could not explain it – it was as though someone had whispered it to her and she almost looked round to see who it was. When Anne returned with the water Caro had gone.

It was not the grandest ball the Castle had known, but it was undoubtedly a success for all except the girl for whom it had been given.

'May you be as happy as I have been with your papa,' was what Mama always said, but how could she be happy if no one wanted her? Caro smiled bravely. There would be someone perhaps next year, some worthy, dull young man, some younger or youngest son who would be glad to ally himself with the *éclat* of Hardow Castle.

Harriet and Georgy were not asleep. In spite of dire warnings Harriet had crept to the top of the grand staircase and waved to her uncle the Duke; he had waved back gaily but had thought: No, not that one for my dear nephew, too much for most men; and not Miss Caro, she'll be too old. But he was a charitable man and took Caro once more under his wing that night.

At four o'clock the older ladies and the unmarried girls had retired and the few married couples and younger men were finishing off the food and drink. Caro had smiled weakly at Mama and shaken her head but had gone up to Papa and thanked him for his kindness in allowing the ball. To her uncle she had expressed more formal thanks. So glad was she to get to her own chamber where Curly was waiting to disrobe her that she did not hear the roaring that was coming from the Servants' Hall.

Anne and the younger maids were finishing the carrying over of all the remaining food and drink which it was the custom of the house to allow the servants. The rest of the work could wait till the morrow. Hardow had already sent a message of thanks to them all.

The ostler, Osborne, was watching Anne from the doorway as they came in for the last time with trays and plates. She paused a moment.

'I thought you might like a dance and a sup with me,' he said quite politely.

'I thank ye but I have to go up to the nursery now,' she said coolly. 'One of the children has a sore throat.'

'Well, another time,' he replied and did not attempt to detain her.

It was true that Lizzie had woken with a slight cold and Anne was relieved she need not join the others. As it turned out, most of the girls did not stay in the Hall for some of the men were drunk. Only those who were 'walking out' went off with their flirts. Delia never joined in any of this and was relieved to see Anne.

'I'll sit up with her,' Anne whispered. 'You go back to bed – I'm not tired.' And it was true, she was not. 'I'll tell you all about it in the morning.'

'It is the morning,' said Delia. 'But thank you. I'm too old for broken nights.'

Anne sat on by the child's bed as Lizzie fell asleep again. She looked in on Willy and Blanche and looked out of the window that looked towards the great courtyard. There was a light on in George's chamber. She sat long and alone staring at it and thinking of the glimpses she had had of him. How beautiful he was. His dark suit had set off his fine features and she saw him as he had been dancing with Miss Caro and looking so strange. The shouts of the men in the Servants' Hall were now few and far between. Dawn had come and the air was still, and at last George's light went out. She imagined she was dancing with him as she crept to her bed in the room next to the child's and lay unsleeping, staring at the face which seemed to be lodged behind her eyes.

The night had been an odyssey to her and had revealed inexorably that there was no going back on her feelings. Amongst all the glitter and stir of the assembly only one face was fixed for her, as though on a glazed frieze, and for it she felt she would lay down her life.

Caro awoke crying, but stifled her tears and took late breakfast with her mama. The rest of the guests ate even later and much was the comment on the evening's activities. Lady Louisa had danced twice with a Scottish peer's son and was hopeful of a note later that day. The rest of the giddy girls were either voluble or quiet, according to their natures, but many were the confidential chats with mamas and the reported conversations and the talk of the next ball tomorrow or the day after and of the end of the Season. There was still plenty of time for matches to be made and they took their leave from Fountaynes Castle with many protestations of eternal devotion to Lady Georgiana, who had a headache, and to Caro who, rather pale-faced, thanked them for their attendance. She remarked that George too looked rather pale, but said nothing to him. She still felt a little frightened of the look she had surprised on his face that night. So might Prince Charming have looked at his Cinderella – whereas she was the Ugly Sister, she thought, and went back to her room for a quiet weep. She would never, never forget the expression on his face as he searched the reflection in the window. It was as though he were under a spell.

My dearest Sis [wrote Lady G]. You will want to hear all about our little ball and I hasten to write to you before Hardow returns from his billiards. There is, as yet, nothing arranged for our dear Caro but I expected nothing and would indeed have been rather the reverse of contented if anything had transpired last night with a less than eligible 'parti'. I had advised dear Caro 'discretion always' and am glad to say that she behaved beautifully with that rather shy way she has. I know she was expecting perhaps a little advance from Lord Somers, but he did not come – sent word at the last minute that his grandmama was indisposed. As you have always been pleased to tell me, I manage a tolerable conversation with young sparks so long as they will be gentlemanly and unaffected, but indeed there were none of our sort to converse with and I confess I had more pleasure listening to Sir R's sallies and he must be over fifty. I have the impression that your niece herself prefers an elderly parti – or what to her is elderly – and have great hopes of Lord H who will, they tell me, be back in town next week.

I must say the Castle looked very well but as you know I have a *faiblesse* for the old place and am really happier here than in Town or anywhere else. We had the strawberry baskets done the way you remember at Chiswick (with garlands) and the theme was flowers and fruit. We put scarlet ribbons in the maids' hair – a little *outré* perhaps for Yorkshire, but they looked delightful. George was his usual charming self and most attentive to his sister. Your brother remarked on our fine table but as he will never see anything as fine as his own I always take his remarks with a little scepticism. The crystal sparkled and the chandeliers were all lit – indeed it was very pretty. Our linen all came up as starched as the old Duchess's petticoats (remember?) and our servants' livery was never so fine even in Grand's young days, as he said to Hardow with some tartness I thought. I shall be told, I suppose by Grand, how many bottles of champagne we managed to get through. He is even now on another tour of inspection of the Cellars. The servants were apparently very merry when we had gone to bed but are now somewhat subdued.

I felt that silken cord of sympathy with dear Caro which you know is the feeling for a daughter which nothing can ever break, but I have tried to tell her that nothing matters so much as her happiness and then I shall be happy. *Entre soeurs* I shall tell you that I have prayed for a good outcome next year. Somehow I feel that she and Georgy will set each other off – they are so different and will be better settled before Harriet makes her entrance. Harriet said the other day: 'When *I* leave for *my* season, Mama, these walls will never see Harriet Hardow again!' What an extraordinary child she is and will I am sure have no ordinary fate. But what the future will bring is in the hands of God, as I tried to tell her. She is so agog to enter the social round. Some local families came invited by Grand and his Lady. I believe he meets them on his carriage drives and secretly likes to show us that he can still impress. Whatever the reason, I thought at times that we were a little like one of those provincial assemblies they have after the races here. But they behaved very well and were too impressed to do other than murmur appreciation and thanks whenever they bumped into us.

The danger, by the way, which I thought I might have to confront is now passed. I know you will be relieved and I am even more so. But God's will will be done in this as in all things. Georgy said the other day 'I do not think I would want a large family, Mama.' She remembered when Charlie was born and I was so ill. I tried to tell her that these things were not in our control, but how do you find the words to say such a thing to that dear innocent creature who is the apple of my eye as of yours?

I shall see you in London next week and we shall all be waiting for the latest news on the King and That Lady. You would have loved it here last night, dear Sis, particularly when we had the supper for the older people in the entrance hall through the arches open to the garden with the great door like an arch to heaven. The two large vases which I remember you so much admiring were filled with blooms by Mrs C – a sort of Arcadia and I am told the statue walk was very fine but did not go out to look. As you know at these times I am a little distracted.

Marie was right over the jewels and you should have seen your sister in her green feathers and opals. Lady Julia was dressed up to the eyes and Lady G. C. likewise. I do somehow feel that aquamarines are for *young* ladies. Dear Lizzie has a slight cold. I fear the excitement has given us all a fever. This letter is approaching the length of yours but there is nothing like a sister to whom one can unburden oneself. When you see Caro I know you will not ask too closely of her – well I know you will not. But if you would, enquire about Lord H (in the utmost discretion of course). Your brother is just now come to take me for a drive and I shall be glad of a little fresh air. Hardow has also just come in and says I am to tell you that Grand is threatening to descend upon the Lords but he thinks nothing will come of it. Your devoted sister – G.

A few days later when most of the family had departed back to London, on a sunshiny day when she was sure George had forgotten her and that he had not even noticed her at the ball, Anne was surprised to find the footman at the nursery door very early with a message. Lizzie was still at the Castle and had had a cold but was now better but bored. Anne had tried to entertain her with writing and drawing, but Lizzie had said: 'I wish George were here Nanna – he makes it so amusing.' The message was from George. Slates at the ready and he had some work for Lizzie, and would Tesseyman like to accompany the child to the Temple?

'I'll take my sewing,' said Anne, trying to sound respectable to Delia. Delia did not apparently take much interest in all this alphabet learning and Anne very cleverly played it down. She dreaded the ever-watchful Miss Sharpe on her tracks.

A figure was waiting for them at the entrance to the Temple: George, in an open-necked shirt without cravat, and with a light blue waistcoat. Oh, he was handsome, she thought. Why did the others not see it? Today she did not feel at all shy. George thought, watching her come up the slope: 'She is like a wild rose.' But he determined to ask Anne something sensible, to give all their meetings a point, apart from Lizzie's alphabet. His mama was touched that he should wish to teach the little girl and rather guilty that *she* was away again. George held up the slates as they came in and knelt down to Lizzie's height. 'This will keep you busy all morning. See "b" for ball, all ready for you. Have you brought your slate and pencil?'

'*And* the colours,' said Anne.

'It was a lovely ball, was it not?' he said. 'There was the most beautiful girl in England there.'

Anne wondered, did he mean Lady Charlotte, and a second later was startled to see him looking at her with such intensity that in all her modesty she could not mistake his meaning. It took her breath away and she sat down and occupied herself sorting Lizzie's pencils.

Soon Lizzie was occupied, to her great delight. As they sat there, there came upon them both a shyness. After a silence he said: 'I have written some verses which might amuse you.'

'Are they in – *Latin*?'

'No – in a language you will understand. Plain English. Do you know the poet Gray – No, you will not – don't look so dejected. I'm sure my sisters do not read him either. He wrote a wonderful elegy – that's a sad poem commemorating the dead – about sitting in a graveyard at evening and thinking of all the people buried there. I thought of your village – and I thought: there would be all the women buried there too, who never learned anything . . .'

'Most of the boys didn't like learning even if they could,' said Anne.

'And you *would* have liked it? Yes, that's what I thought. So I wrote this little poem for you.'

She took it. He had written it out in his best copperplate but his writing was difficult to decipher.

'Please read it to me.'

'I will, if you wish.'

He began. It was about evening in a hayfield with all the country girls with flowers in their hair. And then the same people who were old and their flowers had wilted and it was moonlight, but somehow the poem brought them back. Anne understood so far. And then the last verse was a verse about love being like writing poetry because everything lived again in a special way. Anne did not know what to say. It was tender and true, but she was shy of saying that. And she did not know what made poems good.

'Read it to me, Anne,' pursued her new tutor with a melting glance.

She took it and read in her strong northern voice, stumbling over a few words, but not many.

'I love to hear you read.'

'Please, read it to me,' said Anne. 'I like to hear the voices that are different from ours.'

George took it and began and Anne realized he loved doing this. He paid attention to the *words* but he made them sound thrilling.

'I should like to have been an actor – in a theatre you know – but I mustn't like the sound of my own voice too much; it is a fault,' he said, looking up. She smiled at him, just liking to hear him speak, but wanted, too, herself to say something fine, not exactly make an effort, but be seen in a good light. Yet he seemed to regard her in that light, the way he looked at her.

When he asked her to tell him about her life she *did* hesitate. Lizzie was busy, her tongue out, concentrating with the effort of making nicely round 'bs'.

'Then I can draw the ball,' Lizzie said.

'Tell me what it's like to be you, Anne.'

She paused a long time and turned her head away. Then: 'My grandad worked for a farmer though they say he had once been one, at Ranbeck – and Mam, that's grandad's daughter, my mother, she married a farmworker too. Hannah and me and Richard came at the end of Mam's family. All my other brothers and sisters went away. There was no work, you see.' She paused, thinking of the fences that had enclosed the good common land where all the animals of the village had grazed and browsed. 'And the Rector, Mr Hart, he took me in when I was twelve, to help Mrs Hart. They taught me my letters and I went to Church School. But – you see Mr George – there wasn't enough to live on. Dad went away to get work. There was more room in the cottage, but no money coming in. And Goody Aysgill's daughter – she worked here for the sewing – was leaving so

I got the work here.' She took a breath. She had never made such a long speech. George was moved by a complicated set of emotions. If Lizzie hadn't been sitting there he would have taken the girl in his arms. Something in her – not in spite of her lowly birth but because of it, stirred his senses, something over and above the feelings he had already found in himself for her. He, a future landowner, owner probably of all the land Anne's ancestors and father and mother had tilled for generations – and she, if not the lowliest of the low, a child of centuries of near poverty, of the people. Because he could not embrace her he took one of her hands, surreptitiously, under the table and turned it palm upwards. She looked puzzled. Mrs Copus had studied her hands. He saw the hand was not yet red and raw like most of the servants' hands. She was young!

'Anne, when I saw you at the ball – you didn't know I saw you did you? – it was when you were looking at the balcony flowers behind those gold pillars – you were in your blue print dress and I could see your reflection and I . . .' He paused for a moment, then said: 'Anne, it's not . . . like my grandfather . . . or the people in London who make use of others for their . . . their own ends.' He wanted then to say 'I love you', but love must mean a commitment to the life he had imagined he might pass with a woman for the rest of his life, who would bear their children. His mind was also turning on his reading, for several of the new poets had infected him with ardour for a simpler life, for simple integrity and the honour that came from common toil, not from *noblesse oblige*.

He thought of Anne as a separate person with qualities: her voice, now silent, when it spoke with its homely accents was deep and yet clear and strong. Was he thinking of making her into a lady? Such thoughts did enter his head . . . Her clothes – those of a servant girl. He would like to remove the apron and the insignia of servitude . . . These thoughts led him to think of the woman beneath. How could he 'love' her when he hardly knew her? Yet he did.

Anne sat motionless. She had no thoughts of changing, but it was true she *had* modified her speech since she had been put in charge of the children at the Castle. She had never seen herself as rising to anything through the power of her face or her body, and she had accepted the work itself as something very worthy and elevated. Sewing-maid at a castle was an improvement upon anything in the village of course but now for the first time in her life she wondered whether Nature had cast her only for a low estate. How could hands and clothes and accents make any real difference to a *person*? Mr George liked her: she had never met anyone in her life like him. He was different too from the rest of his kind. She felt he was good and felt that others might think him a little odd. Yes, she saw that now. That was why the other girls didn't go for him. But she *loved* him – she had started to wonder about him from the very first time she had seen him, even that day of her arrival when he had left in the carriage for Oxford. Yes, she had. And when the sunbeam had lit up his face that first Christmas in Chapel. It seemed long since.

The faintly sweet, faintly waxy smell of lilies was all around them. It reminded *her* of Easter in church, *him* of other places, of Christ Church meadow and of his grandfather's lands in Cumberland. He sat, still with her hand in his, and a sigh escaped him. She turned to look at him and he looked up from his contemplation of her palm to contemplate her bonny, vivid face.

They sat together, the two of them both young, healthy and strong and both possessed in their different ways with imagination.

George broke the spell. 'I wish Time would stop,' he said. For now they were together and could never be closer as they sat with the whole of their lives before them.

'Let it not sweep me away or make me dizzy; let me not lose my way. Let me *love* her,' George was thinking. 'Perhaps Grand once felt like this, long ago – perhaps he had a heart's desire. And I'm only nineteen and this girl, who is not yet mine, and perhaps never will be, will never be accepted for what she is, but only for what the world sees.'

Anne spoke shyly: 'What is that air – that Miss Harriet or one of them plays on the harp? They played it at the ball for the Waltz.'

'Sing it to me,' whispered George.

And Anne sang in her low pure voice the tune that had haunted her.

'It is *Plaisir d'Amour*,' replied George. 'It is a French song.'

'What does it say?'

'It *says* what *you* sing – you must know of what it speaks. It speaks of the sorrow of love:

Plaisir d'amour
Ne dure qu'un moment;
Chagrin d'amour
Dure toute la vie.

The child Lizzie looked up then and *she* would remember this moment.

'Put it into our language,' commanded Anne.

'Love's joy lasts only an instant; love's sorrow lasts for evermore,' he said and they looked at each other again and this time both were thinking and feeling the same thing.

All that June, with its warm breezes, scents and sunlight, the Temple received its visitors almost every morning. First George would wander there after having breakfasted, followed by Anne and Lizzie. Blanche never visited it but once or twice William's tutor had a headache and William bundled along with them. George had found for him a special book with coloured engravings which William would stare at motionlessly. He was now able to concentrate, or at least not run up and down jerkily as had been his wont. They wondered whether he took any of the pictures in and were surprised and pleased when he would point to objects and give them words in his staccato voice.

Lizzie progressed from 'b' for ball, through the Cow, the Dairy and the Egg to the Fan, and George and Anne would sit, often silently, holding hands under the table. George knew this could not go on for ever. He wanted more than her hand but for the time being was glad to imprison that alone.

One day he decided to show William the maze on their way back to the house. William always turned down the path to the Mausoleum on its mound if given his head and they had to steer him gently back on course.

'He seems fascinated by it,' said George.

Anne shivered: 'I don't like it – I don't know why.'

'You must not be afraid of death, Anne – it's only like the graveyard.'

Then George thought: the Fountaynes were in no churchyard like Gray's Stoke Poges but in a cold classical mausoleum where their bones could not mix with those of the common people. As though they thought they had cheated death! No wonder Anne did not like it!

'But I think how one day all the family's' – she did not dare to say 'your' – 'bones will be there. It makes me think of endings,' Anne went on.

'You must not be afraid of the future – that is in store for us all. Perhaps, as the church says, it is good to be reminded of mortality.'

'I don't mind the idea,' replied Anne. 'It is – the being *real* that frightens me.' She knew, better than George, how short life was. *He* had no dead brothers or sisters to remind him!

'I'm sorry – I understand,' he said gently. 'Come now, William, we will go for a walk in the maze. I'll carry you on my shoulders, Liz. There – shall we get lost, do you think?'

'What is in the middle?' asked Anne.

'Grand used to tell me it was a dragon,' said George gaily. 'But it is not.'

Anne had never been in a maze before and followed George, who seemed to know his way. The trees at each side of the paths had not yet been pruned and grew bushy and tall so that it was impossible to see through them. There were many turns and twists and she knew she would never be able to memorize them on the way back. William plodded on with them, not quite understanding the point of the exercise. After a final 'No, not this one, the next, and then on and to the right,' from George, there was suddenly a gap and through it a clearing. A little fountain was playing and by it there was a low bench.

'Oh, it's lovely!' whispered Anne and Lizzie whooped to get down.

'See Nanna – another little boy!' cried she, pointing to the top of the fountain. It was the statue not of a boy but of a girl in a short shift, holding a bow, with laces round her legs and a coronet on her hair.

'That's a *lady*,' explained George to his sister. 'She's dressed like a boy though. She's Diana the huntress, with stars in her hair.'

'How funny that it should be a girl in the middle of a maze,' said Anne. 'What is she hunting?'

'The moon, I think,' replied George, flinging his head back and looking up at the sky.

'You can't catch the moon,' said Lizzie.

William went up to the statue looking very serious. 'Not dead?' he queried, after a pause.

'Oh! he thinks it's like the statues Grand put near the Mausoleum – of dead gods. I expect someone told him they were dead,' said George. 'He's a clever boy, William – it must be puzzling for him.'

'Did your grandfather put this one here then?' asked Anne.

'I expect it was great-grandfather – when they first laid it out. Do you like it?'

'Her nose is broken,' said Anne, laughing.

'They brought scores of these statues back from Italy and Greece. My uncle still does it – he collects marble.'

Anne was thinking how she would not like to be alone in the maze but how nice it would be to be alone with George in it.

'I think she's got a look of you,' said George. 'But fortunately your nose is not broken!' After a pause he said: 'They say that the first time you walk to the centre of a maze you can make a wish. And you'll have your heart's desire, Anne.' She was silent. 'It is not my first visit so I cannot make a wish,' he went on, 'so you must think of a wish of your own.' She dared not look up at him. He was sitting next to her now. 'If I could wish, perhaps my wish would be the same as yours?' he pursued. 'Send yours with Diana the Huntress to the moon.'

Then she did look up at him but he was not looking at her, rather at the statue. 'It has to be a silent wish,' he added.

'I wish George would love me – but I think he does,' she thought. 'I wish I were a great lady then George might stay with me – but that is impossible. I love George, so there's no point in wishing that. I'll wish then that George gets *his* wish, whatever it was.' She spoke aloud. 'Wish yourself again, Mr George – it will have something to do with what I am wishing.'

'That's too unselfish, Anne – or perhaps not.'

Anne thought: 'Ought I to have wished for Hannah and Mam to be warm and well-fed for the rest of their lives? But I can't help it, they seem so far away! When George is away I shall think of him even more, but when I'm away from Stockton it's hard to think of *them*.'

As though echoing her thoughts, he said: 'I shall have to be away in the summer later on. I wish I did not have to go – but I can't choose.'

It was not yet to be, not for a week or two, so Anne resolved, as they turned back and walked out of the maze, not to think about it, to live in the present as far as she could. But George was restless. He thought of Anne as he lay alone at night in his familiar room when all the great house was quiet. There was so little time to be with her and in the autumn he would be back in Oxford and Mama would take over the teaching of Lizzie. How powerless he was! If only he were older, of age, to choose his own life! Mad plans of taking Anne with him and lodging her in Oxford would shoot through his head. He could never be alone with her here, unless he made a proper assignation and it was beginning to torture him. At the same time he began to feel that his feelings, denied proper expression, would dissolve into dreams. He made an effort and invented two 'excursions' in the house and grounds on which he might justifiably take Lizzie and William with Anne in attendance.

'Where are *you* going then, Tesseyman?' Selina Sharpe's cutting tones stopped Anne as she descended the great staircase, Lizzie and William following close behind. She had never been down these stairs but they were the quickest way to the Long Gallery, George said. He had 'ordered' that she bring the children on a conducted tour of that great room.

'I am bid to take the children to their brother, ma'am,' Anne replied politely.

Selina sniffed and stared after them but there was nothing she could do about it. George had decided that as today was wet, they would meet to look at the pictures, an important part of the children's education. He also planned, as soon as it was fine again, to lead the small company on a guided tour of the Walled Garden. The family, including the older girls, were now all away again and even some of the servants, who were allowed, once a year if the family could spare them, to visit home if they *had* homes. Anne recognized the gallery immediately – it seemed a hundred years since the old Earl had come upon her there! The children began to run up and down, skating on the polished floors. The gallery was certainly long! George gathered them up.

'It is not the only room with pictures,' he explained, waiting for Anne to come up. She walked behind him, trying to appear like an honoured nursemaid, rather than an invited friend, fearful lest the old Earl should suddenly appear and shoo her back to her quarters again.

'My papa and grandpapa both collect pictures and papa's latest ones are in the Music Room and the Tapesry Room, and grandpapa's French pictures are somewhere else. But look,' he said, turning to Lizzie, 'there is your grandpapa in his great robes, and another picture of grandpapa, with Uncle Henry.'

Many of the pictures were over two hundred years old, all of great lords and ladies dressed in strange garbs of ermine and jewels.

'This is by a very great painter,' George continued, pointing to a Holbein. Anne, like Lizzie, was more interested in the more recent paintings which seemed to her friendlier. William was staring at some clocks. There were more statues on plinths, urns on tables and in niches in the walls and, hanging from the ceilings, great crystal chandeliers like tangled pairs of reindeer antlers. At the far end, seemingly miles away, was a large door and an even greater chandelier with branching candles hung before it. Red velvet curtains were draped round it in a wide arch, gold tassels hanging heavily down the sides of their folds.

William was now standing in front of the great figure of a kneeling idol from Egypt. 'That is the oldest object here,' said George. 'That was made at least a thousand years before Jesus Christ. Older than the Oracle from Delphi we have in the Museum.' He came up to Anne. 'I have often wondered if she would speak to me, but perhaps it is better not to know the future – or it is unknowable, in which case the Oracle can either say nothing or can only lie. Do you like our gallery and its pictures then?'

'They are all too much – there are so many – I know nothing about pictures. But they must need a mighty lot of cleaning!' Anne replied honestly.

George smiled. She would never pretend to feel what she did not. 'Music appeals to you more than painting, I think? Come, Lizzie – you will grow up with these pictures and many more. Tomorrow we will go in the kitchen garden!'

At the other end, as they walked back, Anne noticed the door to the Chapel. There was a little recess by it and as William and Lizzie went by, George turned round to Anne who was behind him, seized her hand and kissed it.

'As if I care more for the beauties of Art when there is live beauty for me to see,' he muttered vehemently.

'Oh – George!' She was startled. But he tore himself away and she felt her hand burning as though his kiss had been a sunspot beamed on to her flesh.

Anne was still, in spite of the kiss, a little uncertain as to what George's real feelings were. The shock of realizing that perhaps he felt the same about her as she did about him amazed her – and then told her that she must be wary. He *liked* her – he was a kind man who liked a lot of people, even children! It was true his eyes had spoken for him in their sessions in the Temple and there had been the tone of his voice and the Latin poem and the hand-holding, and he had once adjusted her shawl for her on a cold day when they came out into the garden. *That* had amazed her in a curious way more than the kiss and the glances, for it showed he 'took thought', as she had written on her slate. And taking thought for her seemed somehow different, more tender even than kissing her hand because she was a servant and it was un-thinkable that a future Earl, however far away in the future, would adjust the wrappings of a servant. But the kiss, if she had not loved him, should have made her angry that he dared to pre-sume – unless of course he *knew* that she loved him. How could he know, since she had never said? Was that just the way men were about women, always starting things up? Or was it that he divined her heart and took the first step of showing her he re-ciprocated because, as a man, he would always have to take the first step, unless he was in love with a Princess?

Thoughts like these pursued and consumed Anne. She had never thought anything out before like this and wondered at her-self. To 'make things right' she would have to tell him her feel-ings for him – and women were not supposed to do this, certainly not lowly nursery maids, even if their swains were farm-boys. It was the one way of putting them off you, she had always been told. But he was not a farm-boy.

'You are an unusual girl, Anne,' he had said, and she was beginning to wonder whether there was something wrong with her. She could not confide in any of the other girls, not even Curly, for they did not seem to think these sorts of thoughts or feel these sorts of things. His passionate kiss on her hand made her feel paradoxically alone and lonely. What would it lead to?

The next morning they were to go, she and Lizzie and Charlie too, and, she supposed, William, for a walk in the Walled Garden, the pride and joy of the gardeners and, it seemed, of George. He seemed quite calm and cheerful and after one rapid stolen glance at her, reassured.

As they all walked across the lawn and terraces towards the high wall on whose other side was the carriageway, Anne noticed for the first time the queer-shaped excrescences all along the edge of the roofs of the great house. There was still something new about this place, even now after eighteen months. She wondered why she had not noticed them before.

'What are those funny-shaped things like urns and flower-pots?' she asked. She started her conversation with something impersonal with a sure instinct. Let him come round to other matters. 'Are they goggles like I've seen on pictures of the Minster?'

'Goggles?'

'Nasty goggles, yes, like in York.'

'Oh, gargoyles! No, Anne – and look children too – see, William – those are called finials. They are ornaments to finish off parts of the building.'

'Like icing on a wedding cake?' suggested Anne, remembering Mrs Holt's niece who had had a 'wedding breakfast' after church with a white cake made by the Rector's wife with sugar, something the village had never seen before. 'Like marchpane, a bit?' she continued.

'You call it that – that's marzipan,' replied George. What an observant girl she was! He was tempted to rhapsodize over wedding cakes but thought better of it.

'I shall call them goggles,' said Charlie.

'Now, Charlie, you are to *walk* down the paths in this garden,' said George firmly. 'If you run you will probably fall and get gravel in your knee.'

They went in through a door in the big rose-coloured wall and all before them were walks and alleys and shrub gardens and vegetable and fruit gardens and two glasshouses. Although the garden was large it was entirely secluded by the big high walls and there were twists and turns which made it appear secret.

'It's not quite the season yet for the raspberries and vines but I think the early summer flowers are often the loveliest,' said George. There were a few gardeners working away, hoeing or bending down to tend plants and an old man in one of the glass-houses, but *they* took no notice of them, probably were too immersed in their work, except for one who raised his cap when he saw George in the distance.

'They are wonderful fellows who work here – I think I might like to have been a gardener. Do you know they sometimes tend their fruit-trees in the middle of the night? They make all the espaliers, and the straw screens for when it's cold, and some-times if they think there's going to be a frost in autumn, they light fires under the trees.'

Anne asked whether the asparagus and the melons she had seen in the kitchens at Christmas had come from the Walled Garden.

'Melons in the glasshouses,' explained George. 'Asparagus grown under miniature glasshouses.' Thus conversing they managed to walk decorously along the gravel paths, some of which were planted with box hedges, a little like the maze. 'They bring the water up from the new lake by a stream they di-verted,' went on George.

'What else is in the glasshouses?' asked Anne. Charlie was already off to inspect the stream at the bottom, pausing to open a little iron gate.

'We'd better follow him,' replied George. 'Come Lizzie, I'll carry you. William, you hold Anne's hand.' William complied. He seemed to be in a dream as usual. Through the gate there was a path bowered by mauve climbing flowers. 'There are red-currants and grapes – it's a wonderful smell in there,' George re-plied eventually. 'But we'd better not disturb Mr Laxton. Another time – without the children.'

Anne forbore to ask how she would ever manage to be without the children. It was pleasant walking with George but she realized with a little stab, half-pain, half-pleasure, that she wished he would hold her hand and perhaps kiss it again.

'They say it will be hot next week. I don't know how they know,' said George as they all leaned over a little rustic bridge, looking at the glassy water. After a pause he went on, not look-ing at her: 'You know I shall be away soon? Mama wants me in London before going up north.'

'Oh!'

'But I shall return as soon as I am able . . . Anne, it is torture just to see you like this! Do you know what I am endeavouring to say?'

She was silent. Then she said hurriedly: 'I hardly know when you are to be here with us. Some weeks you are here and then you are away – and then some days I – I – think of seeing you and do not and . . .' she finally got out.

He looked at her, encouraging her to continue.

'And I miss you, Mr George,' she said simply.

'If I knew that I could see *you*, continually, it would be my heart's desire,' said George.

She was holding Lizzie's hand for he had balanced her on the parapet and she, George and the little girl were close together. He made as if to cover her hand and the child's with his but she looked at him steadily as he looked down at her hands. 'Please, Mr George, there is something I want to say – I must say it, sir.'

'Don't call me that,' he murmured.

'But I must . . . I know there is no – no tomorrows in it all you see. I have to live in the present . . . and, ever since I saw you – I wanted to, I . . .'

'Are you frightened of speaking? Do you mean there is no future, Anne?'

'Sir – that is it – but more than that . . .' She struggled to express her thoughts and the feelings she had mulled over for so long. 'It is not given to women to say things to men – and least of all ways because I am your servant – but, *because* I am – and you are a good man, sir, I must say it first – so you know – what you have to deal with, sir. For I think I feel as you do – but I felt it even before you knew my name. So, I am doing wrong to say so – but I' – she stopped a moment, then looking him full in the face whispered, 'I love you.' She caught a breath, trembled, felt – now it is over. He wouldn't want anything now to do with her. She gasped, in reaction to her daring.

But in answer he put Lizzie down, gently took her wrist and made her turn to him. 'You are very brave, Anne! Do you think I do not know it is not – "usual". You have multiplied my love a hundredfold.'

'But Mr George,' whispered the girl, meekly and sorrow-fully, 'it is *because* you are a good man, sir, that if I tell you my heart, I know that you will bear with my weakness. Don't tempt me, please don't, I should like to be always near you – is it wicked? Not that I am a servant but because I want to be closer to you . . .' Tears welled in her eyes. It was a shaming confession and she did not know whether she had said it to make him keep his distance, or to make him acknowledge his own complicity and responsibility in the matter.

'Anne, I know what you are thinking. I feel it too and I have often distrusted that feeling. I want to try to make you happy, but I don't know how. I thought of taking you away, living simply abroad till I am of age. But that will be two years. And I must finish my studies.'

'Oh – I didn't mean anything like that!' Anne was horrified. 'Not to change your life on my account – oh no! not at all, never. I just wanted to tell you that I was equal to you – I mean in my feelings – so you would not be snatching anything from me, or giving me anything I didn't want if you . . .'

'Stop! Oh my God, there is nowhere here I can go, simply to do what my words have to do for me. At least, Anne, let me kiss you, in gratitude. Let us leave to fate what we shall be led to do.'

She turned then and smiled. Was it possible to be so happy? She was almost gay, like a well-born young lady: 'I believe I am a little older nor you – so there!' She took his own fine, pale hand and softly kissed the knuckles.

'That is your contract with me – and I seal it,' said George. He put his hand up to her face and stroked a wisp of hair under her cap. But though their conversation had taken place in whispers, with William standing stolidly beside them and Lizzie staring at the fish she said she could see in the stream, with Charlie running up and down hither and thither, it was not a conversation that could be prolonged and Anne felt even a little relief mixed with amazement at herself that she had got it over. As there was no possibility of continuing it at table, or in a drawing-room, it made their lives to both of them seem to consist of snatched whispers, the pressure of hands, the torment of words said because they had to stand in for more decisive actions – and of other words, lying unsaid, which needed time and peace and a shared life to bring forth.

There was no doubt they were in love with each other. Every manmade barrier of rank and wealth and style and education, of their separate pasts, incomprehensible the one to the other – every one seemed to fall in the glitter and bliss and yet the sorrow of their predicament. From the moment she had confessed her love Anne stopped worrying and gave herself up to her feelings. But she took instinctive, meticulous care that no one but George should guess anything about it; not a whisper of her real feelings did she bring to the ordinary surface of her everyday life in the nursery. Only if she were certain she was alone did she allow herself to think of him. That he had not rejected her unmaidenly sentiments was a wonder to her; henceforth, when allowed, she would move along with her nature.

George was equally careful – and hated himself for it. So little time could they spend together in reality, for what were a few snatched minutes compared with the lifetime of bliss he thought it was in his power to experience with Anne, and to confer on her? His spirit chafed; yet he lay in a daze of gratitude on his carved oak bed, alone, imagining how he would one day when he was free and in charge of his life, sweep her away to the altar! An affair of the heart would not be enough for him. In his private diary with its lock and key he wrote of his love, taking care to inscribe it in Greek characters in case any prying eyes might come upon it. At other times he knew it was impossible, beyond all the bounds of worldly conduct. The world would expect a young nobleman to consummate some feelings and by and by have done with them. And he could not bear it! Were his principles false because they were unconventional? Of course not. Should he then abide by them? How? Did he distrust his senses? No! Did he abhor the desire that rose in him to make this lovely girl his own? No!

He had never before really questioned the sort of life he was born and bred for, even in the midst of his reading of the new poets. He loved his home, his family, even, a little, the power of his grandfather's position; but more than this he had always vowed that he would carry out the duties he owed to others because of it all. He had been a dutiful child, full of gratitude to his Creator for his charmed life. But now he began to sense that none of it would balance in the scale against the power of both idealistic love and awakening desire. And even these last two might have to fight it out. Life was not simple, decidedly not. It was *simple* to devote oneself to the good of England, to try to carry out Our Lord's teachings; not simple to consider the unexpected clash of his temperament with his background, and the fate that had led to this unexpected blessing of a poor, young, beautiful woman's adoration. And what a subtle sensibility she had shown in the midst of her hesitant speech. She had claimed the right to be human. He was full of admiration for her, as well as gratitude and love. 'I cannot help myself,' he wrote. 'Guilt does not enter into my considerations. I feel free of the past but I pray I may be helped to do the right thing.'

All these weighings and ponderings, all these sudden accesses of feeling, all these yearnings and gropings for honour, all his imagined bliss had the effect of making him feel once again old for his years. Did exuberant lust and mixed longings and fears live together in all men's breasts? Was love always like this? As he lay in his richly decorated panelled room with the warm fire in the grate and his beloved books marching in legions across the walls, on the tables, piled by his bed, Anne lay wakeful in her own little bed in the night nursery. Was it a good thing that George was a good man, or was she doing wrong to feel as she did? Perhaps if he had been an ordinary young man she would have worried less? Sometimes Lizzie would cry out in her sleep and Anne would wonder how much the child had heard or noticed. And that very evening, down in Mrs Copus's, William had seen a miniature of George, for that lady's room was full of the mementoes of 'her' children, and had seized it in his jerky way and implanted a kiss upon it. Had he looked at Anne as he did so? She imagined he had. What must he think of them both in his strange little brain. Why, even the ageing Mrs Copus had a brooch with George's baby hair, given to her by Lady Georgiana. The whole family adored George. How could *she* be of any account in all this life which had been going on long before she came to the Castle and would doubtless be going on long after she left it? Still, she was glad she had spoken out as she had, though it had taken courage, even boldness. So long as *he* did not think her a bold hussy! She had meant in a way she did not rightly understand to shift the responsibility from his shoulders to hers, unnatural though folks might think it, and she thought she had succeeded. In her heart she knew she had done right, and in her heart she knew her feelings for Mr George were *good* feelings, though everyone would think her presumptuous and wicked, she knew. That Miss Sharpe had eyed her again at supper to-night as though *she* knew. It was a horrid feeling.

Several days passed and the promised warm weather did arrive.

George did not exploit Anne's feelings but rather grew to the measure of them and the sessions of study in the Temple were secretly full of unexpressed longings. The heat mist cast a haze over the gardens and lakes till quite late in the morning and the scents of flowers – roses now – came in at the door. Célestes and Gloire de France and Maiden's Blush and 'Petite Lisette' and the Portland Roses – he told her all their names and called her Anna Rosa. Their love seemed to have reached halcyon days and to be poised like the heatwave in a blue of happiness. Anne felt radiant and looked radiant. Even Delia had said she looked right well and summer suited her.

George did not abjure his enthusiasms but poured them over Anne. She heard of the French Revolution as a noble act gone wrong, of the new spirit of religion that had come instead to England, of the poets who hymned love, and of his conviction that they were in the last days of the old order and that Reform was round the corner. Anne drank it all in and tried to make sense of it all. She liked the poems best, particularly those about love.

One afternoon the children were tired and had been put down for a rest. In a week or two they were to go up into Cumberland where the rest of the family was to join them later. Anne would not be needed then, could even visit home – but she could not afford that, so would be employed on further sewing and repairs. Curly had been walking round the big lake with her and one or two of the grooms had made complimentary remarks aimed at them both, which they ignored.

'They shouldn't be fishing there either, but when the cat's away . . .' said Curly with a sigh. 'I'm going in to Ma for a bit – want to come?'

'I'm that hot, I think I'll just rest my feet!' replied Anne.

She could never understand why nobility had such a hatred of water. There was that lovely lake, cool to sit by, with the first haymakers on the far shore. Curly went away and Anne wandered down to the water's edge for a paddle, humming and happy, her thinking suspended in the heat. Her humming changed to singing as she slipped off her stockings and thin boots and bunched her skirts up like one of the pagan statues on the terraces round the other side of the house. From the distant field on the far shore some women haymakers waved to her, but apart from them the afternoon was deserted. The water was cold at first and refreshed her tired feet. She leaned down and with one hand scooped some up at her face. What must the sea be like if this was a lake! Shading her eyes, drops of water still falling from her wet hand, she looked at the sky, blue as cornflowers, a Little Boy Blue sky, she thought. Then she gazed at the green wood that sloped down to the grass and at the grass itself, a yellowy green cropped a little to allow wanderers to walk through it round to the fields beyond or to the larger path that wound round to the right. That was the path she and Curly had taken, it seemed long, long ago, when the sky was grey and there was no one to love, not even Lizzie. But even these thoughts did not stay long with her. She was filled with a dreamy zest, part of the landscape, like a red poppy or a wild hyacinth. She wandered back out of the water, cooler now and smoothed her skirts, walking with a smile on her face, released from anything but the present. The sun had bleached her front hair and browned her forehead though she was wearing an old sunbonnet of Curly's. She held her boots in one hand and stuffed her hose in an apron pocket. The grass was soft between her toes. Now she could see round the wood into another field where girls in sunbonnets were raking in the hay and a faint barking of dogs came from the same direction on the warm summer breeze. She found herself advancing slowly to meet their morning path that wound round from the East Wing to the terraces and the Temple. Perhaps, she thought vaguely, she could just walk up the slope and sit down on the steps. George would probably be out riding. It would be pleasant to sit and think about him.

When he saw her walking slowly up towards the Temple, her cheeks flushed and feet bare, George thought for a sudden flash of time that a goddess had taken a mortal form, Pomona or Persephone. There seemed to be a glow around her. His second thought was 'No, a nymph with wet hair – or a shepherdess', and then, lastly, 'Anne!' She was singing as she came up, a little out of breath, and she seemed to be in a dream. Or I am, he wondered as he stared at the vision of her, as no one, he was sure, had ever seen her, before he got up, walked to the door and stood there. She looked up, paused a moment as though uncertain where she was, or who she was.

'Anne,' he cried, and held out his arms and she came up to him and was enfolded in them.

Her cheeks flamed against his. He took her boots and flung

them down, did likewise with her sunbonnet, and drew her to him again. Now she flung her arms around him, murmuring: 'I thought you were out riding.' They clutched each other, found each other's mouths and swayed in a long, long kiss. Then he drew her into an inner room, where she had never been before. Very slowly he unbuttoned her grey dress and then flung off his own shirt. Still in a dream she began to kiss him again until he returned the kisses and was drawn into her own dream.

'My wild rose, my wild rose,' he gasped. 'I love you, I love you, Anne.'

They fell together on a long sofa in that cool inner room and, as though they had all the time in the world, lay together kissing and stroking each other. The feel of their warm flesh, each body against the other's, the gentle smoothness of young skin, was exquisite to them. For a time it sufficed and then without saying a word they slowly drew off the rest of their clothes and plunged into a more passionate embrace. For George it was as though a door had opened for him into another world, a world of ecstasy; and for Anne too a surrender of self, a happiness beyond anything she could have imagined. She felt strong and powerful; not a weak woman but an equal and yet a comforter. When he finally lay against her, exhausted, his heart thudding, she was still there, smiling; her desires had been equal to his.

'I am yours. You are mine,' he whispered and then began to weep soundlessly, long tears, wet against her neck.

'Don't cry, my sweetheart. I am happy,' she murmured, and licked the tears off his cheek.

'I'm crying for you, I think,' he whispered. 'I love you so, Anne.'

He wanted *me* – now he is mine too, for ever and ever, she thought. She looked at his closed eyes, his full mouth and long nose and then kissed them all again. She caressed his wavy hair, wound her strong arms about him again and he clung to her again as if she were his raft in a stormy sea, and yet she was the storm and the sea. The late afternoon breeze wafted through to them and it seemed to them both that when they walked out it was into a golden land.

Afterwards nothing could be the same and nothing was. They met in the maze for a snatched half-hour; they walked in the woods and lay under the beech trees, daring anyone to discover them, and trying to defeat time and turn it into eternity.

'My heart's desire,' he called her, and 'my jewel'. Never did either doubt for one moment that their love had set a seal on their lives which would never be broken. In two or three short weeks in these little spots of time they discovered each other, body and soul, as though they were coming upon new continents.

Once he told her to listen at the door of the music room whilst he played 'her' song on the pianoforte – and she liked it better than the harp. They roamed through deserted rooms in the Castle. Sometimes he would grow sad and ask her questions which she found difficult to answer.

'Do you think William's "difference" is the same as the difference between masters and servants, Anne?' When she did not reply, he said, 'No, you *must* not. There is no difference between *us*, is there?' And he talked about women as human beings, like men, and said he was not her 'master', *she* was his 'mistress'. And Anne said: 'It's the same!' He was not a masterful man, that was the beauty of it. Sometimes she would think he was more like a child – and would talk to him like a mother – except when his passion and desire rose in him and mastered him. That was sweet to her too because *she* had made it so. And she discovered that she too had desires which she would not have liked to admit to any other man. Indeed, other men seemed a different species from her lover.

Once he rowed her to the island on the lake and they felt for an hour or so that no one else in the world existed. George would often recover himself after their love-making and feel remorse, sometimes still a little anxious that his love could be misinterpreted. But Anne did not misinterpret it and that was all that mattered.

'It's only natural, love,' she would say. 'God meant men and women for each other.' In the face of her simplicity and confidence he had not the heart to put her on guard against others who would tell her her feelings and actions were wicked and immoral.

What made *her* saddest was his approaching departure; she was not jealous, did not think that he would do to any other girl what he did with her. 'We must keep it a secret until I am of age,' he kept saying.

He even wanted them both to pray together in the Chapel so that in some childish way – he thought of it as childish – God would bless them; but then suppressed his wish in case it was blasphemous. It was not fair on Anne – he kept telling her so. She took all the risks. He was a man, and was free. Anne listened seriously but all she said was: 'So long as I can stay here! I love the children too', and 'I shan't tell anyone – don't worry, love – it's a secret between us.' He tortured himself that when he was not there, some groom or footman would pursue her. He was so anxious for her, not entirely out of jealousy but from fear that she would be unprotected. That he could not protect her was his greatest anxiety, worse than that they might be discovered and ridiculed.

'I shall tell anyone who wants to keep company with me that I'm keeping company back home at Stockton and plan to wed him,' she said, teasing him but with the serious intent of relieving his anxieties.

When the final morning came and he had to depart first for London and then to Cumberland and his other life – which he said was unreal to him – he gave her a small gold ring with a red stone and promised to send messages through the children and through his valet if there was no other way.

'I can't wear the ring,' said Anne. That was the trouble. 'But I shall be all right. You're not to worry. In September we'll see each other.'

'How *can* I bear it, Anne – and yet I must,' he replied.

'There's work to do for us both. I shall be busy – and you must do all those things you keep telling me about – visits and things – and grand parties – and all those books to read. Please, don't weep' – he had tears in his eyes. They were standing in the alcove near the Chapel preparatory to his leaving from the West Court-yard. All the clothes and books he would need were packed and waiting in the coach and the children were there to wave him goodbye.

'I shall keep a journal for you to read later,' he promised. He looked distracted, pale. She felt she must rally him.

'Cheer up for my sake, love.'

He *had* to go. They were all waiting. Anne slipped down to stand with the children who were with Delia. Anne had had to invent herself an errand to see George. The last she saw of him for over two months was him waving from the blue coach to them all but looking at *her* as it bore him away.

FIVE

HARDOW
1820

The expense of spirit in a waste of shame
Is lust in action; . . .
Shakespeare: Sonnet 129

She stood looking at the coach as it swung through the great gates bearing her love away; it was the same gate the red coach had gone through on that summer afternoon two years ago when she had seen George, in the distance, for the first time in her life: George the popular figure, the Young Master – 'Our George'.

Lizzie was also upset; neither did she wish to go to Cumberland without Anne. But Mrs Gibson was adamant: the staff were sent hither and thither in military fashion but there were not enough habitable rooms for them in their ancient Border keep. Anne might go *next* summer, instead of Delia. This year it was Delia's turn. The change of air was regarded as a kind of holiday for the servants, though Delia said it was nothing of the kind.

Anne was sadder even than Lizzie – more than sad. She felt as if she had had a limb amputated and could not staunch the blood from the stump. It ached dully and then flared up; perhaps for a few moments she could forget her pain but then it would stab her again. She could not very easily write to George but would put a letter in with Lizzie's. Even that expedient would not do for the weeks Lizzie would be away. William, however, was to stay at Fountaynes Castle and perhaps she could write proxy for him too?

After George went away William kept disappearing, sometimes for hours. Anne felt the responsibility. What if he fell in the lake or jumped off a wall and hurt himself? She had other duties, and could not follow him everywhere. The tutor confined himself to tutoring and did not seem to think it necessary that he cared for him too. That was women's work. Perhaps William was looking for George? All the household who were left felt unsettled. The sight of dustsheets over Blanche's bed did not help Anne either. Blanche and Charlie had gone up north already with their uncle, who had fetched them and Dorothy and Curly. Everything looked very dreary but Anne tried to bear up. It was worse for George. He had nothing to remind him of her, whereas every step she took seemed to lead her to a place with memories or reminders of him.

She decided to find as much employment as possible for her hands, thinking it might soothe her feelings of loss. She began to sort and mend all Blanche's clothes, most of which she had grown out of, to make them suitable for Lizzie. Clothes cost a good deal of money and Mrs Copus had impressed it upon her that even noblemen's families made economies when it came to their children. With such a large family savings were imperative.

Before Lizzie left for the north, Anne took her and William on walks around the estate. There were still places she had not seen – the dovecots and the beehives, the soap and candle-making room and the little stone cupboard where they cut rushes for the servants' rushlights. All this would one day be George's, and she knew with a certainty beyond any doubt that it would never be hers. She would fall to wondering whom he would marry in the end. Not knowing anything of London society life except from servants' gossip, she imagined it as an enormous ballroom where bejewelled beauties paraded night and day whilst the new King on his throne sat regarding them. How could any of these beauties *not* love George? Yes, George *did* love her, she was sure of that – but even if he came of age and entered Parliament and had a wonderful and brilliant career, all she could ever hope for from him, and even this was beyond imagining, was that he kept her and their children in a little place in the country – like the King's brother who lived with an actress and had a large family. And who would wish to be spurned by right-thinking society and the Church? And she was not even an actress, just an ordinary servant girl! Yet she loved him truly.

Whilst most of the family were away many of the servants would gather together round the beer and there would be pairings off with the grooms and the gardeners and the footmen. As nurse to the children the rank she would be expected to pair up with would be that of the footmen. Several of them were still trying to get her to notice them, and even arrange to meet her in the village, or to go for a walk after church, but her quietness and self-containedness had eventually put them off. Osborne the groom had apparently gone off to Cumberland with the rest of them, and for this Anne was thankful. There were plenty of other pebbles on the beach for the remaining menservants, so she would sit in the nursery most of the time, alone, when Delia and Lizzie left, except for William or an occasional housemaid. Susan and Mary Ann were working in another part of the house. Selina Sharpe was still at the Castle; she had the job of seeing the housemaids cleaned the housekeeper's quarters. Mrs Gibson was off on a visit to her own family and Mrs Copus had gone north with baby Harry and his nurse. Day followed day and Anne kept going by hoping a letter would come addressed to Lizzie or to William in George's writing. She had written a little note dictated by Lizzie to him before Lizzie left and had added a postscript from herself. But she was shy of committing feelings to paper, partly because some other eyes might see it, though she knew George would be careful. She had not even signed it. 'They are cleaning your Tempel with mops and brushes. The weather is cooler. I think of you every day.' What did ladies write to their loves?

On the sixth of August two things happened. There was a letter for William addressed care of Miss Tesseyman – in case the tutor got hold of it. Anne sat William down, brushed his spiky hair and took his hand. Her own was trembling.

'This is for you, William, from your brother George. Look – his seal! Shall I read it to you?' William looked up at her and smiled.

'George,' he repeated.

She broke open the seal. 'It's from London,' she began. 'He has seen your sisters and your mama who will be writing to you.' George's writing was difficult to decipher. 'He sends you his love – and he will bring you some new lead soldiers when he returns. Do you understand, William?'

'Play soldiers,' said William.

Anne was at the next page on which was written:

Pray read this to William – I write only for you. You are ever in my thoughts. I have been pushed here and there to balls and parties and can hardly call my soul my own. We go to Trentham tomorrow (4th) and thence by easy stages via Chatsworth to our northern estates. I do not think I can break off and visit Fountaynes before September but I will write 'from Lizzie', dearest Anne. Tell me it was not a dream. Write 'from William' to Cumberland and trust me, my darling. The social whirl is not to my taste but it is pleasant to be with Mama. Parliament is prorogued and the men are departing with their ladies and families. A special council is being formed to try Queen Caroline in the Lords. I write in haste as the family is packing to go. Your own G. H.

A line under this said: 'The coach is ready. I dreamt of you last night. I am saying the lines of Byron which I wish *I* had writ for you: "She walks in beauty like the night/Of cloudless climes and starry skies,/And all that's best of dark and bright/Meets in her aspect and her eyes . . ."'

Anne smiled. It was like George to be in a hurry yet copy verses. She wished she knew verses by heart that she could write for him. All those books in the Castle library must have some. Perhaps one day they would ask her to dust them.

That same morning she was told by a housemaid that Viscount Hardow was back on a visit to York Races, but it would not make much difference. He didn't interfere with the work of the household, not like his father. The old Earl had been in London but was back now in his quarters: Anne had not seen him for weeks. She tidied William up in case his father might wish to see him. Perhaps Hardow would be going on up north after York to be with the rest of his family. The housemaid also told her that Miss Caroline had not 'got off' in her second Season, poor lady. To be on the shelf at eighteen! Later that day William *was* sent for. Apparently, the servants gossiped, the races had gone gone well for his lordship, although there were still a few more days of them and he was riding over tomorrow to stay with his uncle in York since the Castle was so empty. Usually they made up a big party, but seemingly Lady Georgiana, who must have had some say in the matter, had decided against it this year, perhaps fearful of her husband's betting propensities. At any rate, Anne was to accompany William to the billiard room. William loved billiards. He had taken years to learn the game but did now seem to understand it.

'They say too that Mr Ross is here – the artist, who sketched the girls. They didn't expect him but he is to sketch William in winter.' Anne would be responsible one day for presenting William in decent attire for this occasion.

At six o'clock she was summoned to take William over to see his father. How strangely quiet all the grand part of the house was. There must be the old Earl and Countess somewhere around and the close family servants but she saw no one and tapped on the small drawing-room door which led to the billiard room at that time.

William bowed to his father, who was sitting before a fire, for the evenings had become unseasonably chilly for August. Perhaps September would be better.

'Come, sir,' said Hardow, beckoning to him. 'We shall have a game.' He looked cursorily at Anne. 'Thank you – come back for him at eight.'

Returning to the nursery she saw the younger boys' school-room door open and William's tutor seated at the table with his books. It was a mystery to her what William was being taught, for she and George had found him sadly deficient in reading and writing and she doubted he would ever make much of it. Poor William. The tutor looked up as she passed but then hastily down again at his book.

Anne felt lonely. If only Curly and Delia were there to talk to! She resolved to do some more sewing and then read a book George had lent her – a book of poems. She had already eaten but still felt hungry. William had left an apple on the nursery table so she ate half of it when the darning was done and then took her book to the window which overlooked the East Kitchen Court. Selina Sharpe was hurrying across it, head down, unaware of anyone watching her. Perhaps *she* was lonely too? She looked thin and her movements were a little jerky. Curly had whispered that she drank too much. All the servants drank beer of course, but Selina seemed to have access to another source of comfort.

When she went for William, he was still in the billiard room playing by himself but Hardow was standing by the fire. At first she thought he looked angry, but it could not be with her.

'Come here, Tesseyman,' he said. 'You are the girl who was looking after William last year?'

'Yes, sir.'

'Does he still run away – stray round the Castle?'

'Yes, sir, he does, but I usually manage to find him.'

'Does he ever go to the Mausoleum?'

'I don't know, sir – I believe – he – ' (she was going to say 'George said' but collected herself) 'I believe he likes the statues and the walls round there.'

He looked up at her. 'William has been telling me that he sees a man with a horse there – that is what I believe he has been trying to say. Do you know anything about that?'

'No, sir.'

'If you ever see a man – and a woman I gather – and a horse in that direction, you are to tell me.'

'Yes, sir.'

He looked at her broodingly. She was a deuced pretty girl. A pity his father was in residence. A man could never be alone in his own place – alone, perhaps, in the library, but libraries were for reading. He made up his mind. 'Take William back and return here at nine. I have some books I want taken to the library when I've finished with them. Where are the other servants?' Anne thought, well, he ought to know, but his manner seemed strange. He kept looking at her, a sort of sidelong glance which she did not like, but perhaps she was imagining it.

'Yes, sir.'

William was summoned from his play and they went back to the nursery.

When she returned after putting the child to bed, the fire had been mended and Hardow was lying on a hard-backed sofa, his feet up and a pile of books by his side on a small table.

He beckoned her in. 'Shut the door carefully.' He swung his legs down from the sofa and seemed to weigh something up, for he walked over to the small inner window for a moment and looked out of it before turning to her. 'Please draw the curtains,' he said, and moved to the fireplace. When she had walked across and was drawing them, she suddenly felt a hand on her shoulder. It had been there before, she remembered – once before, on the stairs the afternoon she had found William in the attics. She shuddered involuntarily, thinking only of George – *his* hand, *his* arm around her. And this was his father, a viscount, Lady Georgiana's husband! She turned and he was looking down at her, his face flushed.

'Don't go away. I want an answer. Are you a maid?'

She was trembling violently but replied: 'You know I am your servant, my lord.'

'You know what I am asking you. You are not stupid – you are a clever girl, I'm sure. Are you a maid? Are you "keeping company" – as I believe your people call it?'

A wild desire to confess her love for George, and his for her, was suddenly upon her – but that would only get George in trouble, and he would not believe her in any case! George had said 'Tell no one – we shall wait until I am of age.' But were they 'keeping company'? She supposed they were, though nobility did not use those words and Hardow seemed to have uttered them in a mocking way. But no, she was not a maid: she knew what he meant. But she was not going to tell him that, unless it was forced out of her. What could he be thinking of? If it had been his father, the old Earl, she could have understood it, even expected it – from what the servants had said, particularly about Selina Sharpe. But – *Hardow*! Should she say she was keeping company with a lad in her own village? How could she tell such a lie when it came to the point. George, oh, George!

At this moment Hardow was hating himself and yet he was damned if he were not going to go through with it. He had remarked this girl when she first came and now that nearly all the servants were away she seemed to have been thrown in his path. Nobody need ever know. This sort of thing happened all the time. He would be remorseful after, but what was he – a man, or a tamed domestic animal? All his bitterness at being for so many years under his father's thumb, all his suppressed anger at that father – which he had never, or hardly ever, expressed – and had certainly never taken out on his wife who was an angel and whom he had hardly dared to touch since Harry's birth, since she was so terrified of dying in another childbed, all this goaded him to act. And even more than this, he desired this girl, in all her youth and beauty, even though she was a little servant. He was becoming middle aged, had sometimes been unfaithful to Georgiana after his marriage but never with a woman of his own rank – why should he not have another little 'aventure', which would hurt no one? But he would not take her if she were a virgin. That he would not do. He was sure she was not, just as sure as he had been, when he had touched her shoulder before and when he had looked at her on the landing, that then she *was*. But if he did conquer her he would not go on with it for long. He would not deceive his wife again with someone under the same roof, not while she was at the Castle. This only left the summer and early autumn, and by that time, he would probably be tired of the girl.

He was not like his father who had deceived his wife throughout his marriage, off and on, even with her own maid. Yet as he looked at this glowing child, only a few years older than his own eldest daughter, he was torn between a mounting desire which her nearness inflamed, and a bitter shame that he should have come to this. It did not stop him though. He asked her again: 'Are you a maid? Have you known a man? If you are "keeping company" I will make it right with your young man.' He meant money – she realized with incredulity. What should she say? He put his arm now round her waist and led her to the sofa. She wanted to resist but was petrified, so frightened that a slow paralysis seemed to have crept also up to her throat. She tried to speak. Was he drunk? She felt as though he were about to *murder* her – was he? Had he lost his mind? Now he had his hand on her breast. She gasped. 'I have a lover, sir.' Now perhaps he would stop.

'I thought so – you are very desirable,' he murmured.

Anne wanted to scream but who would come? She was in his power. And also it was embarrassing. She could not make another sound, nor even cry – what *could* she do? Nothing. Yet she struggled, she did struggle. He was determined though. If she had a lover she was not a maid and so – as they said – 'fair game'. But he must not hurt her – he must calm her, make her see reason, so that she would stop fighting him which only resulted in an increase in his passion.

'Listen. Be still.'

She had flung herself to the other end of the sofa.

'Do you like your work here, miss?'

'Oh yes, I do,' she managed with a piteous look up at him.

'Do you want to keep it? Doubtless your family need your money – *my* money – things are bad, I know they are bad. *I* did not make them so – I wish them to be improved. But for the present,' he spoke hurriedly, 'you wish to keep to your employment here?'

'Oh, please, please – I am right happy here,' she replied, wondering what next and trying to get her wits about her.

'Then do as I say and you will be kept on – I give you my word of honour. Do as I want, just till the autumn – I swear you will be kept!'

'And if I scratch your face?' she wanted to say, but knew what the answer would be.

'You wouldn't like to lose your post?' he muttered, feverishly loosening her clothes and his own.

'No, no,' she managed to gasp, but whether she was answering his question or telling him to desist she was not sure.

What followed was soon over, leaving one of its actors satiated, disgusted with himself and guilty but triumphant; the other shocked, wounded in spirit if not in body. She had not finally been able to resist – for he was too strong – and, in despair, she was mutely sobbing to herself: 'George, George.' For George had made love *with* her, his father *to* her as though she were anybody – a phial for his lust. It was not *just* that; it had been a different act entirely.

'Don't cry,' he said, quite kindly. 'Go now. I shall send for you again.' And he turned away, and walked back to his books. Recollecting his initial ploy for her presence, he said: 'Take these books here to the library tomorrow morning and bring them back next week – this day in a week. I shall be away till then. Knock at the door three times – remember, Tuesday at nine o'clock. You may go. And tell no one, you understand?'

She snatched the books, rushed out of the room, not caring what she looked like and stumbled back to the nursery where she found all as she had left it, the almost eaten apple, George's book of poems and the fire burned low.

She lay seized with a violent trembling unsleeping, the tears stuck at the back of her throat, her eyes open staring at the ceiling. Now, George would never have her again. She would not tell him, no – but he would not want her. And her heart cried out for him, across the sleeping miles to London.

Anne, as a village girl, had always been brought up to be wary of men and had been warned off the act of darkness, as they called it, as soon as she had become a woman. It was reserved for the lad who courted you and whom you intended to wed. That the majority of first babies baptized by the Rev. Hart had been conceived some five or six months before their parents' wedding was a commonplace and no one held it against the babies or their mothers and fathers. There *were* village girls who were 'ruined', which meant not that they had babies without the benefit of clergy but that they moved to the towns and charged for their sexual services. Once you were paid for it, any man could spit on you and use you as he wished. There had been, though, one or two girls who had by virtue of their figures and temperaments passed beyond this and moved to London to charge men of another class for their keep. These men had often picked up a girl at the Races, but by the time the girl had got as far as that, she was no longer a visitor in her own home and had 'gone to the bad' – even if a little later she appeared to have 'done well for herself'. So Anne understood about this but had never thought she could ever become one of them. She was a 'good girl' and her love for George, though it might seem madness, was a noble part of her virtue. She had risked all and received all. George and the idea of George would be enough to sustain her for the rest of her natural life. But Hardow's action was totally unexpected, shaming, terrible – *worse* because it came when she was no longer an innocent little girl but a woman in love. And the only person to whom she could never confess her love for George was his own father. And George himself, how could she ever tell him of what had happened. His own father. *Should* she have spoken to Hardow – said, using his own sort of language: 'Your son and I are lovers – do not touch me or your son will be avenged.' How could she have said that? She could not ask George for advice; there would forever now be a barrier between them, even if Hardow soon dispensed with her services. Never, never again would she be free and pure and lovable; she knew it, so that when George went away in the coach, it was really the end. She tried to convince herself and was far more agonized by the thought of George's reaction to her than she was about Hardow's seduction even. 'Taking advantage', they called it. Rape, in other words. Something which with George had been part of her love and his, and pleasurable in a way beyond themselves, had been with Hardow an indignity, a pain, an embarrassment, a violation. Anyone would have found it so. She could pack her bags and leave on the morrow. Some girls might even have written anonymously to his wife, she knew that. But she could do none of these things. She needed this work for Mam and Hannah, and she loved her work. Why should she leave it? And she loved George – where else could she see him? And she was in awe of and grateful to Lady Georgiana and she would never make her unhappy. And she loved Lizzie. It was all terrible. Her pride made her get up the following morning, bathe her face and carry on as though nothing had happened. But what should she do the next week?

Fortunately when the day came Hardow was still away in York – she knew he was not in the Castle, having made discreet enquiries, saying he had bid her take a book to him. She lived in fear of his next approach. For his part Hardow had made what he saw as a valiant effort to overcome temptation. He had deliberately stayed over in York, had not betted on the races there, had written a pleasant letter to his wife, had avoided the claret and tried to keep himself busy visiting tenants on his farms. All the reasons he had given himself for his forced attentions upon Anne melted away when he reflected upon his conduct – that he was a victim of his rank, of his father, of idleness, of his middle age, of too complacent domesticity, of boredom, of fear of gambling, of his senses. He felt guilty but he knew it was not at an end. She fascinated him, that simple country girl. 'I will make it right,' he had said, and she had given him such a look, as though *she* could tell him something but chose not to. But in spite of his resolution, yes, he *would* have her again, before he went up to Norpeth, at least before the end of September. He should not have threatened her with loss of work; he must have been out of his mind. Yet it had been effective – by God it had! If ever it came to the ears of Lady Georgiana... They did not live in the old rough times now, even with a King such as theirs. He could not act like Grand – he had tried and apparently succeeded, yet his conscience would not let him rest. Well, let his conscience occupy itself over one or two more slips and aberrations to make it worth his while.

The weeks passed and Anne was relieved to find that Hardow was away and that he had not left her with any more lasting memento of his caresses than a few bruises and a bitter taste in her mouth. That was some small consolation. She longed for George to come but feared his coming. She wrote as if 'from William' saying nothing at all of the event, but felt she wrote lies.

William continued to wander off every afternoon and she had the greatest difficulty in restraining him. One day he had disappeared for rather longer than usual and so she went in search of him. It had begun to rain. The tutor took pity on her and offered to search round the gardens and the big lake, and she could go up to the Temple. She hesitated at first but accepted his offer and, throwing on her dark cloak, hurried along the path calling the while: 'William – Master William – come home – where are you?' She scrambled up the slope to the Temple – ah, how different it looked in the rain and with George away. How it brought him back, though. She had not passed this way since his departure. She saw the door was shut and, looking through the window, that William was not there. What should she do? If only he would answer her and then they could go back and she would make him the toast and water he liked. What if he had gone to the Mausoleum? She had pushed that thought to the back of her mind when she set out, being sure she would find him nearer by. Perhaps Mr Coulson had found him? No, perhaps she had better go on. How she hated the place. It came into view as usual from behind the Temple but it was a long trudge. Finally she came up to its enclosing walls, several hundred feet away from the great pillared dome itself on its mound with its double flight of steps. It had a lower door on a level with the ground and another great door at the top of the steps behind a stone balcony. It was about ninety feet high if you included the under-building. She supposed there must be a chapel inside, so it should not be frightening – and George had said she must not fear it.

Now she saw in the distance, not William, but a horse. What had Hardow said about a man, a woman, on a horse? She was trying to remember and still calling: 'Willi-ium', when a man came from behind the curved building and took the horse which had been tethered to a nearby tree and leapt on. He was away before she could try to recognize him but was sure it was no one she knew. Then from inside the building the great door opened and a woman stepped out. Selina Sharpe! Anne stopped shouting for William, praying he had not got into the building and climbed up to the roof, and she hid behind the outer walls that encircled the building. Selina passed a few yards away through a gap in the stones and walked slowly down the rise towards the Temple. What on earth was she doing? And where was William?

Her last unspoken question was soon answered. A small figure came stumping round from the other side. 'William – where have you been? What have you been doing? We were worried about you!'

'Hello,' he said. 'William saw a funny man.'

'Yes. I see.'

'He came on a horse.'

'Yes.' She took the child's hand and walked him down in the direction of the house, bypassing the Temple.

'You know your papa says you must not stray away – *do* play nearer the Castle – or come for me to go with you. Papa would be cross if he knew.'

'Papa knows,' said William. 'Grand was with that lady – William saw that lady.'

'When was this, William?'

'A long, long time ago,' replied William.

Had he been spying on them? Anne hoped not. It was rather distasteful. Some sort of assignation was certainly taking place in the building. It was the last place *she* would choose.

'Papa home,' said William as they approached the house.

'Oh no!' But William knew and William was right. Hardow had come for one night on his way north.

She said nothing, ate in Servants' Hall, talked to Susan in order to put off going back to her room. She knew he would come and order her again. How could she refuse? She was trapped. Perhaps if she stayed in William's room or engaged Mr Coulson in conversation, but he was a stuck-up young man and no help at all. He had been glad to see William back safe and sound but he said no more and returned to his chamber where apparently he had struck up a friendship with Mr Ross the painter, who was still staying over to sketch background and buildings for the painting he was to do of the whole family later that year.

She was sitting again alone in the nursery when the knock came. She opened the door and there stood Hardow once more.

'You will come to my sitting-room near the billiard room he stated.

'If you please, sir – why should I sir?' she said levelly, but quaking in her stomach.

'You want to stay here – I explained. I shall not ask you more than once after this. I shall leave tomorrow.'

'I am not an animal, sir,' she replied. But I have no choice, she thought.

This seemed to encourage him for he was usually of a rather phlegmatic nature. The truth was that he had kept to his good resolution for too many weeks and had decided to make the most of his enforced one-night stay-over at the Castle. The girl aroused him again though he could see she did not intend to.

'Before I do your bidding, sir,' she said evenly, and marvelled at her own poise, 'I must tell you that William wandered away to the Mausoleum today. I managed to find him and bring him back – but not before observing a man on horseback and a woman who were there; I believe William was observing them.'

He flushed. '"Not before observing" – you have a pretty turn of phrase. Thank you for the information. Why cannot you and I be friends? Do you think I desire every Kitty and Polly and Molly in my servants' hall?'

'I don't know, sir,' she replied.

This seemed to excite him even more and he pulled her out of the room and pushed her up the stairs to the attics above the nurseries. Evidently he could not wait. Anne became limp like a rag-doll, determined to suffer it as quickly as possible and forget it. What difference would it make now to her? George would feel the same whether it were once or a score of times! Hardow was angry that her eyes were closed. 'Look at me,' he muttered.

'You cannot make me look at you,' she replied.

'What has happened to you? You were frightened last time. Today you seem not to care – you are so *cold*. Do you want money?' he said afterwards.

'I am a human being – even a person,' she said slowly. 'You cannot touch my soul, for it is not yours.'

He was taken aback and began to think he had underestimated her. Perhaps he had got himself deeper in than he intended. She lay like a fallen statue, pale, her eyes closed. Something in her attitude penetrated his heart. Once, long ago, he had not needed to force a young woman. Long, long ago *he* had loved a woman older than himself – and he did remember passion, by God he did, passion that was not domestic habit, or impersonal lust, but a glimpse of his real self. But perhaps his real self now was only a shell? Perhaps now once more he was just like his father, offering money and protection and taking his old man's pleasures. You will reap what you have sown. His tutor's words came to him from thirty years back. Pray that 'G' would never discover this. Now that he had exhausted himself, he wondered why he had felt impelled to break down this girl. Why were men given such devilish lusts?

'Go now,' he said, not looking at her. 'Go.'

She rose like an automaton, smoothed her skirt, bent her head and was through the door. He had never once kissed her, had he? – never said anything pleasant to her. And the memory of Anne's body mingled with the vague anxiety he had felt half an hour ago when she had told him about the man on horseback and the woman at the Mausoleum. She had not named any names but he guessed who it was, and that Grand was to be humiliated. Grand had been too lax with his own menservants and now that he was old one of them had a hold on him it seemed. That Sharpe woman must be got rid of – Grand would have to be persuaded.

Please God, don't let it happen again, Anne murmured, over and over again. Not that it would redeem her in her own eyes, but – let it not happen. How could she see George now as she had used to see him, happy and oblivious of all else on earth? Those days would never come again. She had not yet been able to cry ever since Hardow had first bent her to his will, but in the middle of the night following his second siege and victory over her, she awoke with tears running down her face and at first did not know why she was weeping. She had felt hollow, light, weightless up in those attics, as though it were not herself he was grunting over but another woman and she was watching him from a corner. She was so far away from the man who was a stranger to her that he had made her feel a stranger to herself. Were these her arms, her legs, her hands? Were they still hers – or had he taken them away?

How strange too that someone engaged in doing such things to her should be so unknowable. She knew as little of him as if he were the man in the moon. He too, like George, read books, was noble and rich. George's *father* – surely there must be something good about him for him to have such a son. Or were parents utterly removed from their children? He had seemed a kind husband too, the little she had seen of him before this summer. But these people could afford to be kind, even the men. She knew men were often not much good to women, except to give them babies. The women bore them and worked themselves to death keeping a family going, earning just like their menfolk. Why had God made men and women so *different*? But George too was a man. 'Why, I always thought of George just as himself, not just as a man!' she thought. The light was coming in at the window; it must be nearly five o'clock. Could she have avoided any of it? How cruel it was, the sun rising and setting day after day, not caring about the human creatures who played out their stories under its rays. Did anyone ever have a person close enough to them, day and night, to support them in this cold world, someone who would listen to them, comfort them and dry their tears, like a good mother did to her children. She thought: when Lizzie grows up, will anyone hurt her like this? Or will the world have changed? Why had she been made so that a man like Hardow wanted her, and with such a heart that wanted a man like George?

Thank God he was going away up north. When would George return? What if he came back suddenly, expecting all to be the same. How could she tell him anything of what had happened? He would surely sense a difference in her. Oh, it was too cruel. Despair welled up again in her but it was better than that cold rag-doll feeling of the night before. She could not confess to anyone, for she would be held guilty for having been George's lover. Did God intend to punish her for having lain with him? Was *that* her first sin? Could she tell George that she regretted it now – to spare him the discovery of her present predicament. I could pretend I had thought I had done wrong and had determined to keep myself pure in future – but he would know it was not true. It is *not* a sin to love with your body when you love a man like I love George. Hardow never kissed me, never. Making love with George was like honey, like warmth, so beautiful. But perhaps I am a wicked girl and it is all my fault. She knelt down in the dawn with her face pressed against the rough blanket of her truckle bed. O God, forgive me and forgive that man, but bless George – for ever and ever, Amen.

After that she felt a little better, though looked still so pale that Curly's mother who was in the dairy when she went down for William's milk asked her: 'Does anything ail you, lass?'

'Oh no, Mrs Currey – I didn't sleep too well that's all. How is Curly?'

'Oh, they're all having a grand time – went out in a boat with Mrs Gibson and Marie and Dorothy. Miss Lizzie's still missing you – I was going to come up and tell you. Mrs Copus wrote with messages. All the family will be up there soon, they say, now the Season's over.'

'All except Master William,' said Anne. 'I do think they ought to let him go with them. He can't come to any harm.'

'Perhaps they will next year – but tell Master William I heard from Mrs Copus that Mr George is going to call here on his way up himself – he needs some books or something for his studies.'

Anne's heart leapt – it was a body blow but she tried to keep calm.

'Next week, I think. There now, there's Master William's special milk. Mind you look after yourself!'

So, next week! She did not know whether to be glad or sad. She was truly relieved though to glimpse Hardow's carriage and himself getting into it round by the West Courtyard later that afternoon. She thought he looked up at the nursery window before he left.

She was in the maze but the paths were corridors along which appeared now and again doors, leading, she knew, to unknown

rooms. She had run out of the servants' attics – thinking Hardow
was beside her bed, and stumbled down the stairs and straight
into the maze. She heard George calling out for her from the
heart of the maze – but how to get to its centre to find him? She
turned right and then left, panic seizing her but driving her on,
in spite of her fear. George, George, she cried, and suddenly the
path in front of her began to slope up and she knew it led to the
heart of the maze. She looked up, and there, planted in the open
space before her, rose the Mausoleum, and standing motionless
in front of it was Hardow. In his hand he held a pistol and the
pistol was aimed at her. She screamed and screamed and tried to
turn and run but found she could not. She shut her eyes and
waited for the shot . . . Then she suddenly found herself in the
Mausoleum. Hardow was not there but the high building had an
interior glass wall divided into vertical sections like upright
tombstones but transparent. As she stared through the first one
the face of George suddenly appeared as though he were lying on
a pillow of stone which had been cranked up against the glass.
His eyes were shut and she knew he was dead. Horror filled her
again and she walked on to the next partition and looked
through it. George's face was not there but this time she saw her
own face as though she were gazing into a glassed-in double; the
face faded and there was nothing there at all. She shouted again
'George!' and found she was now seeing in the third glass case a
little child who was Lizzie and yet not Lizzie. The child smiled
and Anne was suddenly happy, though she could not touch the
vision. Somehow she knew that everything would be all right if
she could get out of the Mausoleum. She turned her back on
Lizzie's face and walked towards a door at the far end which was
now open to the sunlight. But when she came out through the
door she found herself in a meadow with waving grasses.
George would be waiting for her, she thought – and she ran
through the waist-high stalks which were blown by a warm
wind and seemed like the waves of a great lake. Turning and
turning and stumbling she heard his voice: 'Anne! Anne!' yet
whichever way she went the voice came no nearer. And then she
knew that she was in the maze again and that she must find the
statue of the girl and merge with it if she were to defeat Hardow.
For she felt his presence there again, encroaching on the waving
grasses like the shadow from a storm-cloud. Panic seized her
once more – she must find Lizzie! If she could find Lizzie,

George would be there. And in a trice she came to a clearing and there were three figures standing motionless, staring at her: George, Lizzie and, towering over them, Hardow who this time held an arrow in his hand. This time he would pierce her to the heart. She cried out to George: 'Save me!', and he turned his face towards her. It was of stone; and now she saw Lizzie too was a little statue and there was no help anywhere. Hardow lifted the arrow and she closed her eyes and the words of a strange prayer were on her lips. She knew it was Latin though she had no idea what she was saying. She waited to die, could no longer open her eyes – and woke to find herself in her little bed in the night nursery. Shaking and sweating, the waves of panic receding only slowly, she sat up in bed. Alive – and no Hardow there and no pistol, no arrow, no maze, no Mausoleum, no Lizzie and no George. Anne remained motionless until dawn.

In the end it was not Anne who heard first when George was to return, but William who was told by George's valet as he rode up into the stables ahead of the coach from York. Anne could get nothing more from the child but 'George coming soon.' What shall I say? Will he want to see me immediately; must I tell him anything? – the words tossed round her head. Anger, shame and sorrow jostled for place. Would George still feel the same? It seemed years rather than six weeks since he had left. Why should he not approach her just as he had done before? – he knew nothing, of course. Would he have changed? She had had only three letters from him, all enclosed in letters first to Lizzie, then to William – he had been visiting all over the place and she had only managed one or two little missives herself. But she remembered the Byron verse he had enclosed, and wept over it. She knew she was not to blame, had not provoked in any way his father's onslaught, but that made no difference in the eyes of the world. And she would *not* tell him.

For his part, George had been racked by urgent sensual desire since leaving Anne. He had tried always to place her in his thoughts when these urgent feelings overwhelmed him. But he was ashamed of them. It was Anne he loved, he told himself; it was Anne he desired, though there had been plenty of opportunities to indulge himself with others. Anne had awakened not only feelings for herself, but feelings for womankind, impersonal sensations he had always fought against. He was only nineteen and his studies and generous romanticism had so far preserved him from the world. If only he could marry her – and settle down to tame his sensuality, direct it only on her! He was naïve, they said. He believed, like the Prayer Book, that marriage was a guard against lust. And he thought of Anne as a wife. He did not know where the guilt came from; it did not seem to afflict his friends in the same way. And he knew that the moment he saw her, his passion would magically transform itself into love, which yet included passion. Yet – yet – had he done wrong by her, a good, loving girl? He would know when he saw her. It was to be only a flying visit, for his presence was required in Norpeth. Why could they not have sent *her* there too? Leaving her with no friends in the half-deserted Castle! She had never complained. How must it be, never to be free? What was it like to be a servant to others? His youthful rebellion, founded on generous idealism and a dislike of the old order in whose arrangements he could not help being implicated, was founded on an attitude of mind he had had for many years. 'Beware that it does not lead you to abandon God and the principle of Order,' his old tutor had said many times. Surely he knew that he was no violent agitator, no Jacobin?

She stood, pale and agitated, in the nursery waiting for him to knock or for a message. She felt she might cry if she spoke, and she must not. Four o'clock. He must have unpacked. William was with Mr Ross and she was trying to sew but her hands were trembling so, the needle kept knocking against her thimble, and at last she put her work down and sat, motionless. Half an hour passed and there was a tap at the door. She flew to open it. Only John the footman – but bearing a note on a silver salver.

'Thank you, John.'

She must not betray her feelings. Oh God, what if Hardow returned? But he would not, not yet. George would see him up in the north, however. They would say nothing to each other, had nothing in common.

She took a breath and opened the little paper. It was edged with silver gilt – Court paper.

'Dearest – meet me in the Temple as soon as you receive this. Ever your G.'

She put on her cloak, for it was still strange weather for early September. There had been a light gale, and apples were being brought in large baskets from the orchards. Windfalls. There was a pale greenish light in the sky as she traversed the well-known path. She had no idea what she would do or say. Somehow in her head was that idea of God in whom she trusted, and she gave herself up to that, which made her feel calmer. She slowed her walk down deliberately so that when she came up to the Temple she felt stronger. He came out then and was at the door, standing aside to let her in; then he had taken her in his arms and was weeping, his face in her hair.

'Forgive me, forgive me, Anne,' was all he could say.

She looked up at him. It was still George. He did not feel any different. She was not reminded of his father's embraces, not at all, not in the warm, languorous delight of George's kiss, nor in the touch of his young hand on her face.

'Don't cry, my darling. I'm here now.' She stroked his hair.

He stepped back a little. 'It was only . . . My love, let us sit and get used to each other again.'

They sat at the little table hand in hand. A book of Lizzie's had been left there. *The Story of a Good Girl*, it said on its cover, and Anne looked away from it.

'Anne – I have been so lonely – and thinking things over . . . It has been worse than I thought. I couldn't believe you were *true* – and then I felt I had done wrong, wrong to lie with you and wrong to leave you. And I led you into sin – you do not know what temptation is like for men. Perhaps it was a good thing I was away from you for a little time . . .'

'Oh no, George, it was not a good thing.' She leaned over and took his hand. She was so ashamed. That *George* should be asking her to forgive him! And how could she tell him even one tiny part of what had befallen her? Would he discover? Would he know? But he seemed to be thinking about himself, so sure was he that she was good and pure.

'I have been right lonely, too,' she said, after a pause. 'They are all away except William and the maids I don't know so well. I wish – oh I do wish I could have gone with Lizzie.' If she had gone with Lizzie there would have been no Hardow. But, one day, there might have been someone else, might there not? She was so unprotected – how could George protect her?

'You must not despair, Anne,' he said, looking up at her. 'When I am of age I shall marry you, or no one – I promise you.'

'Oh Mr George' – she used the old name. 'You must not say

that. It won't *ever* be possible. I've been thinking things over too ... you see, you will always have to go away...' She stopped, not quite sure what she meant, but continued: 'You are so young, love ... I am just the girl that loves you *now* – I'm sure there will be many, many ladies who will love you – and you will marry one of them and live in this Castle – no, you must let me speak! I know I am very ignorant but I know you need a – a *steady* life, so you will be happy in the way grand folks have to be happy.' She swallowed. She meant 'so you will not be like your father, for you are not like your father now'.

'Anne, Anne! You are only twenty yourself! Give me a kiss if you forgive me and tell me you love me, only me!' He tried a lighter tone. 'I wager those grooms and footmen have been making eyes at you!'

'Oh no!' She drew away, distressed. 'I love *you* George – whatever happens to me, I love *you*.' She flung her arms round his neck and he felt little tears wetting his cheek.

'Don't cry, Anne. We are both too imaginative. I was tortured when I was away – dreams, horrible dreams – but now you are here, and I'll be back in October again. I couldn't bear not to see you when I was so near. They wanted me up with the family straight away but I lied and said I must fetch some books for study. Next year we can both go up there. I'll see you go with Lizzie – and we'll go for walks and I'll show you the dungeons and the keep – and my little Jessamine tree. I think it's like you, warm and sweet. Oh, you are so warm and so sweet...'

He could no longer hold back and they fell back together on the hard Temple floor. He made a cushion for her head with his coat and made love to her and seemed not to notice her initial flinching away, put it down to shyness when he had been away so long. But when he was calm again she was racked with sobs and turned her face away in an ecstasy of shame.

George had been able to get no explanation out of her after that. Not wanting to leave her crying, and being obliged to go to his apartments for dinner he had kissed her, embraced her, said he was a pig, that of course she was upset; he had been too hasty, too passionate. He would try to love her in a different way.

'Forgive me, Anne.'

All she had said, before stumbling away, was: 'Nothing to

forgive – nothing. I love you', and again, turning as she stopped for an instant. 'I love you! . . .'

It was on her way back, still upset but conquering her tears, that Selina Sharpe had crossed her path. Anne had not even seen her, had passed her with set face and disappeared into the Castle to see to William's meal.

It was while she was seeing that he ate – for he would sometimes refuse food, at other times devour it like a hungry animal – that William, running now and then to the window between mouthfuls, exclaimed: 'That lady *not* with a horse!'

Anne looked out of the nursery window and saw Miss Sharpe once more, stalking across the East Courtyard. 'What do you mean, William. That is Miss Sharpe. She has no horse.'

'The man had a horse,' he said, and Anne remembered the couple at the Mausoleum from whom she had hid.

'That lady,' continued William, jerking his head in the direction of the window. 'That lady – was with Grand.'

'What are you saying, William? Was Grand on *his* horse then?'

'Sometimes – and another man was there too,' he said.

Anne did not know what to make of it. But it puzzled her. She began to wonder whether Selina had ever seen her and George in the Temple and shuddered. Would she rather though that Selina had spied on Hardow? Oh no! She could go running to George with *that* story!

Troubled and unhappy, yet still – when she sat quietly for a moment – feeling George close by and remembering the smell of his hair and the touch of his hands, Anne sat long and late into the twilight. The next morning she saw him borne away in the best family coach, the 'gold coach' as the old Countess called it. She stood at the window with William and he looked up and blew them a kiss.

The talk in the Servants' Hall, for most of the older servants still there at the Castle and they loved a gossip, was all of Queen Caroline. They had heard she was going to be put on trial. Prinny, as they still called him, wanted a divorce. He had no right to it! Whatever that unfortunate young consort of his had done, far, far worse things had been done by her husband. All the people were for the Queen. The family – by which they meant the Fountaynes – although they had to keep in with the

King, were sympathetic to Caroline even if they did not like her. They had observed the people, especially the people of London, and dreaded a confrontation between the mob and the King, for he had done little to charm them.

It was all going to be decided in Parliament in autumn. Autumn was already upon them: late September, Anne's favourite month. Over two years now since she had first entered the Castle! A letter from Mrs Hart had had news of Mam. Dad was back and Hannah had work over at Tollerton but Mam was still suffering with her chest. In spring they hoped Anne would be allowed a day or two away to see them all in the village. Anne was more worried about Mam's chest than about Queen Caroline's honour. She had sent her last six months' money back with the messenger and hoped he had delivered it. It was somehow a comfort in a strange way to worry about Mam rather than about the extraordinary entanglement she had found herself in betwixt George and his father.

The family were supposed to return in mid-October and it was said in Servants' Hall that many of the family's friends were in London joining in all the excitement of the trial of Queen Caroline. Anne wondered how all these men could be making speeches about her virtue or lack of it when, from what she knew of one of them, Hardow, his marriage bed was no sacred thing! But she was relieved to hear that he might be off to London and awaited George's return with a mixture of gladness and grief.

The more horrified she was therefore when one day in the first week of October she saw the blue family coach arrive and the grooms and stablemen gather round to meet it, and saw, descending from that coach, not the family, but Hardow.

It was evening and she had gone up to her bed but had not undressed. She prayed he would not send for her. There were no locks on the servants' doors or on the nursery doors. She had put William to bed. When was George coming back? Surely the others could not be long?

There was a knock at the door. Oh God! Anne wondered whether she could pretend to be asleep or just ignore it. But it might not be Hardow. She crept to the inner door and through into the anteroom.

'Anyone there?' shouted the voice of a footman. 'Oh – here you are, Miss. Mr George's valet gave me this for you – I think it's for Mr William.' He handed her a small packet.

'Th-thank you, John,' she managed to mutter and shut the door quickly. She lit a candle, for it was growing dark. The packet was quickly opened, a note for William and a page for her.

'Dearest – I shall be at my aunt's in London for one or two nights and am then to return to the Castle – and to you – before I make my way to Oxford. So I shall see you as soon as we are a week into October.' (What was the date? Anne scarcely knew it unless she asked the housekeeper to look in the family gazette.) 'I am to see Papa in London as he is to follow me there after he visits Fountaynes Castle with my valet to collect his London clothes. I took the chance to write these few words to you to ask you to forgive me for upsetting you when I saw you last. I cannot write what is in my heart but shall hasten to see you and make all right. Expect me in a few days. Ever thine G.'

'Make all right!' she thought. 'Oh – if he could make all right! Poor lamb, blaming himself – oh, poor poor George! Please come to me.' She was crying softly so as not to wake William. He had stirred when she had lit the candle.

She folded the letter and put it in her little box that held ribbons and George's ring and her little pieces of money and one of Lizzie's baby teeth that had come out late.

She sat a long time and was in a reverie when she heard footsteps once more at the door. She started up: 'Who is it? I am just about to retire,' she said in a shaky voice.

'I have a message for you, Tesseyman.' Selina Sharpe's voice? What could *she* want. Anne opened the door. Selina was standing, a candle in her hand which cast shadows over her head and on the staircase walls.

'A message from his lordship Viscount Hardow. You are to take the books from the library which he asked you to bring. He says you will know which books he means.' She stared long and hard at Anne and Anne stared back at her.

'Can he not have these – books – in the morning, ma'am? It is late,' Anne was bold enough to enquire.

'I'm afraid he wishes for them *now*,' replied the other woman.

'Very well,' answered Anne, but she could not hide her trembling. What did Selina Sharpe know about her? The woman turned away quickly and went down the stairs. 'What hope of escape is there?' thought Anne. She supposed she could just not go. And then? 'Did she like her work in the Castle? Did she want to lose her only source of income?' If only George were there – but how could George intervene in his father's affairs? Only by claiming Anne for his own – and Anne knew *that* might perhaps stop the father but would lose her the son.

Wearily she wrapped her cloak round her, slowly she took the book he had given her to 'take to the library' and summoning up her remaining courage she crossed the courtyard in order to avoid meeting any other person on the stairs, and went into the family wing up the side stairs. She recalled her terrible dream – the maze and the Mausoleum. But she was not going to the Mausoleum; she was not in the real maze, she was the fly in the spider's web who could not help making her slow journey alone to the horrible centre of corruption where Hardow waited for her. Well, she would tell him what was in her mind to tell him. She could not betray George but she might find another post eventually since she thought George would not love her any more if he ever discovered. The idea of threatening Hardow by mentioning his wife to him she rejected. It would only hurt Lady Georgiana.

Hardow was waiting for her in his room and immediately opened the door when she knocked. Anne had determined what she would say. He stood there in a long robe like a Turkish sultan's and this disconcerted her.

'I sent for you – to say I shall not want you again – after to-night.' He cleared his throat. She stared at him. He was embarrassed, uneasy. 'What has happened between you and me is something of which I am not proud.'

'I am not proud either, sir – not of what . . . you made me do. But I came to say, my lord – that I must find other work. Perhaps you could find me other work? I have to keep my family, sir. I love your children, sir,' – she blushed as she said this – 'but you have used me ill, sir, and cast me down – and I beg you . . .'

He interrupted her. 'After tonight I shall not see you – but I' – he cleared his throat – 'I was here for another purpose, and I could not refuse myself you, just once. You will not refuse me. I promise not to dismiss you – you must stay here in the Castle.'

This was a great lord and he was seemingly unsure of himself. Oh, of course he had strength to do what he wanted with her – but she felt sure that he was acting in spite of his better nature.

Perhaps, even like George, she thought suddenly, he had desires he is ashamed of. But George has nothing to be ashamed of, nothing.

Now Hardow was on his knees. 'Please sir, get up!' she whispered.

'For God's sake, don't you know how you enticed me, lying up there in the attic, cold as marble, spurning me? I must have you once more – only once. You are a devil, don't you know what you do to a man? I thought you would be like other women I have had, but you reject me, don't you – you hate me. Well, you are right to hate me.' He ran his hands up her back and got to his feet. This time Anne did not feel like stone, passive and fearful; she was not paralyzed with respect either. Something in his tone almost made her feel sorry for him – but no, that was another trap. She tried to push him away. This only seemed to increase his anger at himself, or at her – she did not know which.

'So you have another lover, have you – a strong *young* man I suppose. Oh, but he cannot desire you as much as I do!'

'Stop – oh, please stop,' she shouted. He did not stop. Anger filled Anne now. 'Why should I do what you say just because I am a poor girl? I am not like your Queen Caroline – or your ladies – or perhaps, sir, they *are* like me, ruined by *noble* men.' She began to weep but with hysterical tears: 'I came only to work – I *love* your children – I love a young man – but you have taken away my happiness.'

His face was burning now. But he collected himself and said coldly: 'No more of that. Hate me, but I shall know *nothing* of you in future. You had better be careful.' He began to undress her muttering in a sort of madness. Then he pushed her on the sofa and overpowered her. Something seemed to turn her head into a void and she felt she was wandering inside her own head. Her voice would not belong to her. Her limbs seemed not to be hers. She felt dizzy.

A few moments later she felt sick and choked out: 'Let me go now – I am ill.' He released her. When she stood up the room began to whirl round and she would have fallen but he saw her weakness and was on his feet holding her. She turned her head away.

'You are faint,' he said in a normal way, as though nothing had passed between them. He sat her down and made her put her head between her knees. He threw her cloak round her shoulders. After a little time during which he stood regarding her fixedly she looked up, feeling slightly less sick. The room steadied itself. She knew she had something to tell him, something William had said, but what was it. Obscurely she felt it would punish him. But what was the use of hating him?

'If you please, may I go now?' she said in a broken voice, surprising herself for she felt a little better, stronger.

'Some women would be honoured!' he exclaimed wonderingly.

Now she remembered. 'William told me,' she said clearly, 'your little son William told me – that he saw a woman who works here in the Mouse – the Mausoleum – with your father, with the Earl. Perhaps he too enjoys that sort of sport, sir?'

'Which woman?' said Hardow, a little pale.

'The woman who brought me the message tonight that I should come to you with your book. I thought you might perhaps know her too – and I have seen her with a man on horseback there. If that woman has been wronged, sir, I hope that you will not treat her as you treated me.'

'You don't know what you are saying. It is *nothing* to me, nothing – now go – neither of us will refer to – what has passed between us.'

'And I am to stay here, sir? I am not to go away?'

'Nothing has happened to make you go away. Go now – *pray* for me if you wish! I am not here to settle my father's account.' He picked up the book which had fallen to the floor. Once more he was the noble lord, the good husband. When she had gone, noiselessly, he went to the fire which had burned low and stood for long moments staring into it. It had all been a terrible mistake. He even felt sorry, low in his own estimate and puzzled. There had been something about her tonight – something that had frightened him. He had thought for a brief moment when she went limp in his arms that she was going to die! Stuff and nonsense. He would go to bed, be off to London the morrow and immerse himself there in social and intellectual pleasures. His friends awaited him there. All the busy life of fashion would raise his spirits. He must persuade Georgiana to stay longer in London. He thought of his wife as she had been when she was seventeen on the day of her marriage and how he had grown to respect her. And how he had betrayed her, in the fashion of most men.

At first Anne could feel only relief. Hardow had gone. He would not ask her to visit him again. Of that she was entirely sure. No more terror, her job secure for the present. She felt light in the head as she cleaned the nursery with Ellen. The family would soon return from the north. Indeed they had already overstayed their holiday. But – let George come home first, from London, as he had promised, before setting out again for Oxford. George had said he would make everything right. But what to tell him? She could not, would not reveal his father's conduct to him yet if she did not and he sensed that something had happened, what should she say? What ought she to say? What did she want him to know?

Mrs Gibson was apparently back with some of her house-maids and there was to be a big cleaning and refurbishing; she was in her quarters sitting at her special table, piles of bills and other papers before her. The house must wake up again after its summer sleep. Miss Caro and her mother would be off again on another country house visit soon enough. In the meantime all the bedrooms were being dusted and swept and polished and the curtains that had been to the laundry put back. What could not be washed was beaten and what was not beaten was sponged and shaken. It was like a monster spring clean and Anne had been or-dered to the housekeeper's room.

'You can help Ellen polish up the nurseries – and Mr Edward's room and Mr Fred's. How is Master William?'

'I think he is well – and speaking more,' replied Anne.

'I'm sure you've looked after him very well. You look a little pale my dear. Go for a walk when you've done my bidding. Oh – and tell Master William I hear Mr George is to be up tomorrow – that will please him.'

Anne curtsied and left, joy flooding her veins and immedi-ately upon the joy a sense of dread. Selina Sharpe had been in the room as Mrs Gibson spoke and had looked at Anne blankly. Later Anne went down for some bread and cheese for herself when Ellen said they had done enough for the day. Anne's arms and back ached from stretching and rubbing windows and moving furniture and carrying bed-linen. Perhaps Curly would also be back in a day or two? If only she could open her heart to

Curly. But Curly won't hear anything against the family, thought Anne. Even Curly might think it was *my* fault. She took her earthenware jug to the beer tap. Small beer was laid on in the cellars in great pipes and the servants took what they required. The supply could be stopped if they got too raucous on feast days. As she came back to her place at table between the empty places where Delia and Curly usually sat she was surprised to find Selina Sharpe sitting there. Better ignore her. But she would not be ignored. She waited till Anne had seated herself, then turned to her. Her face was close to Anne's and smelt of candle-grease. Anne knew in every pore that the woman did not like her, had never liked her and was out to do mischief if possible. Let her do her worst though – she could hardly go and tell Lady Georgiana of her suspicions. Would she tell the Earl – and what *had* she seen? Anne decided to strike first and mention the lady's clandestine visits to the Mausoleum – certainly with the Earl, if William were right – and perhaps also, with others. If she had fallen from the Earl's favour she would be looking for another protector. But Selina looked at Anne long and levelly before speaking and Anne turned to her meal. I'll think of George, she thought, if she torments me. I'm sure she has no proof about George and me. And even if she had she wouldn't go running to his father about him, rather she would go to Mrs Gibson and that she had clearly not yet done.

'Did you know you were a little fool?' said that lady finally in an amiable conversational tone. Anne looked at her and held her eyes in an equally level look.

'Why, Miss Sharpe?'

'You know why. You won't get away with it. Trying to enslave a virtuous family man. Do you think Mrs Copus would want that sort of girl looking after her babies?'

'What sort of girl, Miss Sharpe?'

'I don't need to tell you – I see I have hit my mark.'

'Do you mean the sort of woman who meets men in funeral monuments?' replied Anne quickly, looking down now at her plate. Then as there was a silence, she looked up at the other woman. Selina's face was drained of colour and her eyes glittered. 'I have heard from *others*,' Anne went on, 'that there have been men on horseback in the park who had no business to be there.'

Anne was still uncertain of the extent of Miss Sharpe's adventures but there seemed to be something the woman wanted to hide for she said in a low voice:

'I don't know to what you are referring, Tesseyman.'

'And I don't know what you meant either – *I* have never tried to enslave any man, madam.'

The dart went home for Selina's next words were rapid and low. 'Just because you are young and pretty you think you have a right to – be chosen – I know your sort.' But she tailed off and was clearly worsted.

So it was *jealousy*, Anne thought. Jealousy of *her*. Poor woman. Did she want Hardow then, as well as his father? Had *Hardow* had her and dispensed with her? She was as much to be pitied as Anne herself in that case.

'I shall not refer to any of this again,' said Anne and sounded strange even to herself. 'Rest assured – I am sorry for you, Miss Sharpe, as I am sorry for myself.'

Selina was now taken aback; what she had envisaged as a threat had been turned back on her – it was always useful to have some piece of conduct to hold over someone's head. But this girl was cleverer than she looked. She rose with dignity and Anne saw that she was older than she at first thought. She had never looked at her properly, had rather preferred *not* to look at her. Now she saw the pinched lines and wrinkles round the woman's mouth. Selina put her hand up to her mouth and seemed to bite her knuckle.

'You will be brought down in the end – women like us always are,' she said.

In what way am I like you, wondered Anne, but knew sadly what was meant. Selina had once been a beautiful woman – she could see that.

Anne rose: 'I am sorry if I have caused you any pain, ma'am,' she said, and meant it.

Selina took her words to be insincere for she brought out a sound between a sniff and a spit. 'We will say no more,' she finally got out and slid away from the table.

Anne followed her figure as it walked down the Hall to the courtyard door. Had she been hard and rude? No, she would do it again. It was not only in self-defence, but defending George. Selina did not seem to have any suspicions about him and Anne prayed she never would. It had quite taken her appetite away though. Why could not people all be like George and Lizzie –

kind and generous and beautiful? But *I* am not always kind and generous she said to herself. And the one quality Selina had seemed to hate her for was her prettiness, something Anne had never really known she had till others had told her. George had told her of course. Oh, let him come soon!

The next morning they sent Anne out with William on Curly's mother's instructions to pick late roses for indoors. Anne held the long silver hook that reached for the higher blossoms and the cutters and William held a long rush basket. They were to go out at the west door and look for the special roses that grew against the wall and in a profusion in beds alongside. They were all twice-flowering roses, all in their final flowering before winter. Their colours were paler than earlier in the summer but the scent was as powerful. Her orders had been to pick only one of each variety and colour. The old blush roses were of a silvery pine and a scent that seemed to come from Paradise. And the old old roses – which Anne remembered had grown for years in the Rectory garden at home – the old red damasks, the showers of white and the fairy pink ones – they were there too. There were rows also of newer roses, the pride of the gardeners – Rose d'Amour, Rose du Roi, almost black, and the Rose of Paestum which George had told her was almost everlasting. Others of bright pink rambled all over the old walls. Such profusion!

'Are they not beautiful, Master William?' said Anne.

William stood by his basket staring at Anne but did not reply. Then he screamed out: 'George.'

Anne dropped her hook and cutter; her heart seemed to spring upwards into her throat.

He came slowly up the grassy path in the sunlight; his hair, a little longer now, was ruffled in the warm breeze. Slowly he walked up to them and Anne could not take her eyes away. He patted William on the head and knelt at Anne's feet, took her hand and kissed the palm, then put his arms round her skirt and rested his head against her knees.

'Anne, Anne. At last. I thought I should never see you again.'

'Why George – my love – what is it?' She stooped and picked up her cutter and hook. He shook his head, then stood up and took the basket.

'Rose of my heart – Anna Rosa – how beautiful you are. Can't we stay here for ever, in this garden with the flowers? See, I haven't even washed my hands from the journey. They told me Willy was in the rose-garden with you. I thought – I don't know why – that you would be gone. A dream I had . . . it was nothing – I was foolish. Let me just sit here and look at you.'

'You can hold the cutter so Master William doesn't get at it,' said Anne smiling. Everything else in the world seemed of no account when George was there. Why was it? Even sorrow and rage and fear. She cut a deep, deep red rose, one planted only that year – Rivers George IV – and gave it to him. 'See George – it is not mine to give, but will you take it from me? I've never given you a token or a bauble.'

'Never given me anything!' he repeated wonderingly. 'You give me your heart – and a red rose. I shall press it and keep it and I shall call it Rosa Anna – Rosanna as you are Anne among the roses.'

How charming he was, and oh, how young! But she had to ask: 'When will you be going away this time?'

'Alas, tomorrow. I am already late for term and I'm afraid the Christ Church Fellows will think I'm not serious. Oh, I've been reading and thinking. I expect it was too much thinking that gave me dreams. But I have to apply myself to my studies – like you, William,' he went on, turning to his brother who was sitting regarding him fixedly. George went up to Anne again and whispered: 'Can we meet in the Temple?'

'I fear that we might be overseen,' murmured Anne.

'Let us walk there together at four o'clock when you have taken in your roses – I shall bring books for the children up to the schoolroom and you can help me take them over there. It will seem a good reason,' he replied.

They walked together as he had suggested, walked this time down another approach to their Temple of Love, down the grassy ride level with the lake and the waterfall where once a village had stood before the great castle had been built. She was thinking only of whether she could hide what had happened to her for it must not spoil this last afternoon. She felt it as her last afternoon: she did not know why. It did not even make her unhappy; it seemed to be a day cut out, separated from others, mounted like the butterfly in an album Charlie had shown her, its colours preserved. Perhaps it was better to say nothing at all. Perhaps the only thing left to do was to show him how she loved him and in a way that would soften his own guilt. There had been such a shining on his face as she had seen him fall at her skirts among the roses: such hunger, such devotion. As they walked along they passed statues she had never seen before. There was always something to discover in this great grand place.

When they were out of sight of the house, George took her hand and held it. 'See, that statue is "The Boy with the Thorn",' he said. 'Do you think he has plucked it from a rose? There should be a statue of A Girl Carrying Roses, shouldn't there?'

She smiled and squeezed his hand.

They entered the Temple by another door round the side from their little 'schoolroom', directly into the room with the sofas. The late sun was softly shining through its windows.

'It is so safe with you, George,' she whispered.

'We are safe with each other, my darling – do you not think that I too need a refuge from the world? Come, sit by me and we shall talk. Forget that I must go tomorrow,' he whispered and stroked her hair, rolled up the long sleeves of her working blouse and lifted her arm to his lips. 'Look, your hair is like fine down – golden – on your arms. All of you is golden, all your skin. Were you fair as a child, Anna Rosa? – now that the hair under your cap is golden brown.'

'I think so – I do not remember – there were no glasses to look in,' she replied.

'I have often thought of you as a child and it makes me think of all those thousands of children in the villages of our land. Such beautiful children, and rich in heart – yes, rich in heart – and you are the richest.'

'Oh, George, you must not flatter me so. Wouldn't you like me if I were a rich girl and did not make you think of villages?'

'You are right – you bring out romance in me, my *poor* girl – but I am not wrong. When I am an old man I shall think of how *rich* I was when I was young, but you must grow old along with me, Anne. Who can stop us when I am of age to marry?'

'Hush, George, don't think of the future.'

'No, you always turn from it, I know. But don't you believe me? What must I do to make you believe me?'

She said slowly: 'Love me George – don't talk – just love me.'

'Oh Anne – when all I want is to bury myself in you – it is not right. I want to know you and understand you in different ways – I think it will help me to understand everything – and then this passion you call out rears in me and I know you only one way. The rest is a mystery.'

'I am not mysterious, love – it is because I am your first woman, and different from the others you meet.'

'You are right,' he admitted shyly. 'You are my first woman – and even as I know you, you change. Stay and be my first woman and my last woman so that I need never say farewell to you, wherever I am. I thought a lot this summer – all the time I was away from you – and blamed myself for putting you in jeopardy – for perhaps acting dishonourably – so say you are *not* hurt, that I have not harmed you. I was *your* first man, was I not, my dear one?'

'Yes, George,' she said. If only he had been her *only* man.

'Yet you wept last time and seemed so unhappy. I blamed myself – I am sorry, Anna Rosa, if I have made things hard for you.'

'You have not. It was something else – something finished – of no account to me – something else. You have given me nothing but love, George. Don't speak. Don't ask me questions. Please – just believe me. I shall never love anyone else like I love you. I know it. I love your little sister too, but that is different. And I can't see any end to it, George. When you go away it's like you took a bit of me with you. Is it wrong?' She put her arms round him and held him fast.

'You are strong, Anne. It is I who am weak.'

'Nay, you have a conscience. I have no bad worries when I think on you.'

'Is all right then now, Anna Rosa?'

'Aye, as right as it'll ever be,' she replied softly and caressed him gently and then in a sort of loving despair wound herself tightly round him.

'You are *making* me – Annie, temptress that you are. I can't resist you when you hold me,' he groaned, his face muffled against her breast. She was thinking – it's like a child, crying for comfort, but he has to have a whirlwind before he can lie peacefully once more now. And I too – *I* like the whirlwind, but only with George. God forgive me if I am wicked. 'Take me to be yours again, take me, tell me you want only me – tell me no one but *me* can make you feel it.'

'Such joy – such joy,' he moaned and began to kiss her with those strong young kisses and rock her on those inimitable waves of lust and longing beyond desire, beyond words, beyond the world.

Thoughts became disconnected for she had him now and poured out on him all her own youthful passion as though she had been taught how to love, how to abandon herself and receive him in his own abandonment. This time she thrilled in a sensual bliss that she had never before imagined or felt and her lover was roused to a passion he did not understand, or care to understand.

Afterwards he was a little frightened how he had had her but was reassured to see the divine smile on her face and to feel her young hands stroking him.

'Could we be like this for ever?' he said.

'This is for ever,' she replied.

How did such a girl know all these things? Was it planted there by nature needing only to be watered and cultivated?

'The Rose in the Garden of Eden – Rose without a thorn – that is what you are.'

Anne was lying over him propped on her elbows, her eyes never leaving his. She began to hum the tune that Harriet played, the one George said was about love. George began to sing it with her. He had a true voice, a fine voice and they made a good duet. They laughed.

'I know an even better song,' he said. 'They sing it in all the drawing-rooms in London. Listen:

> 'Tis the last rose of summer
> Left blooming alone
> All her lovely companions
> Are faded and gone.

'Go on – sing all the verses,' Anne urged.

'It is too sad,' he said.

'No, please sing it.'

So he sang it all to the last verse:

> When true hearts lie wither'd
> And fond ones are flown,
> Oh! who would inhabit
> This bleak world alone?

His words died away and he turned to her again. 'Now I've made you cry – but *you* are not alone. My rose will be here in the winter when I return, will she not? Promise – whenever I hear those songs I shall think of you. What can I give you, Anne? – you have the little ring. I wish I could give you the opals and emeralds and my uncle's sapphires. All the great jewels.'

'Give me a little locket with your hair,' she replied.

'If you will give me yours – *without* the locket. I shall put it where no one can find it and you must wear the locket under your dress on a ribbon. Promise.'

'I must go George – I don't *want* to go but they will be looking for me. William will want a story and I have to be up early tomorrow to finish the cleaning. Will you wait till the others return?'

'No – I have to go to Oxford. I think they saw enough of me at Norpeth.'

They rose, tidied themselves, took a last look at the little room and walked slowly away.

He managed to steal into the nursery very early next morning to say goodbye. He pressed a little box into her hands and she gave him a tiny tiny tendril of her hair cut from the side near her ear, which he kissed – and kissed the hair and bent to kiss her throat; for a moment they held each other close; he spoke low words to her and then he was off, down into the early dawn courtyard where his carriage awaited him. His tears were still on her cheek as she saw the carriage move away with a large box on its top, presumably containing his books. She knew in her bones, she did not know why, and she knew that George did not know, that never again would they be together as they had been.

'Nothing like you can ever happen to me again – I shall always be thinking of you. Always. Always. My only love … always…' His words, and her thoughts. 'For ever and ever' but 'never more'.

'Don't cry, Anne.' It was William who had got out of his bed and observed the scene, unknown to them both. She held the child and sobbed her heart out.

A few days later the big coach and the small carriages and sundry carts following, arrived home, Lady Georgiana in the first with Mrs Copus and Lizzie and Charlie and the Baby with Dorothy. The rest of the family – with Marie and Curly and Delia in the other two with Blanche, who was always sick in large coaches.

'I rode Bodkin, I rode Bodkin!' shouted Lizzie as the children dashed up to the nursery followed by Delia. She stopped when she saw Anne. Would she remember her? Had she missed her? 'Nanna! Nanna!' she cried joyously. 'I rode Bodkin between Mama and Copus.'

Charlie strode in, sunburnt and boisterous. 'I shot two rabbits.'

'I want to lie down.' This was Blanche.

'Where is William? Hello, William.'

It was hours before they all settled down and Anne was rushed off her feet and had no time to think about anything but sorting underwear, answering questions and washing faces.

'We slept at Uncle Henry's. Do you know our Uncle Henry? He has a peacock.'

Only when the day was over and the children at last in bed did Anne sit down. It had begun to rain. Autumn had suddenly set in.

'Papa is in London,' said Blanche sleepily as Anne tucked her up.

Thank God for that, thought Anne. 'Oh George, George.'

SIX

FAREWELL
1820–1821

Fare thee well! and if for ever,
Still for ever, fare thee well.
                            Byron

It is November and all the roses have gone except one, a Rosa Alba, still struggling, pale and white, hanging its head, its petals braving the late autumn winds. Gone are the tea-roses and the musk-roses, gone the Perpetuals and the Gallicas. The black-red damasks and the moss-roses have bid farewell till next summer and over all the thousand acres of the Earl's land there is a thin cold mist which creeps over and suffocates the fallen leaves from the century-old limes near the Castle and silvers the leaves of the sleeping shrub-roses. It observes the grinning satyrs whose huge mouths loll open at the gate of their name set in one of the Castle walls, and penetrates the great windows of the Castle itself which prepares for winter as though for a siege.

It is not yet as cold as it will be in January but the year seems to have given up; not dead but dying. The inhabitants of the Castle, masters and servants alike, begin to draw to the log fires in the grates, whose flames are bent by the beginnings of winter winds down the chimneystacks. The servants tuck into their rabbit pies and batter puddings washed down with small beer, and crack the filbert nuts the family leave from their dessert; and the family, warmed by beef and fowl and sweetened tarts, their delicate palates pampered by white currants and home-grown pears and port wine, draw together round their candlelit tables with their guests at four o'clock dinner. Charades are proposed but they agree to wait till Christmas when George, the best actor, will be back. Hardow is still in London, dividing his time between the gallery of the Lords – where the Bill of Divorce will soon be presented amidst days of fierce debate – and his club.

Queen Caroline is said to be drinking heavily and the King, long separated from her, shuts himself up and sees nobody. Lady Georgiana is at home still with her children but will move to her brother's country house soon, taking her eldest daughter and others of her children with her before returning to the Castle for Christmas with her lord and master, once the excitements of Bills of Pains and Penalties are over.

George has been to listen to the Lords before going back to Oxford and he is worried and cannot settle to his studies. He has not heard from Anne for some weeks in reply to the letter he wrote her telling her of his distraction and begging for news – if only to say she is well. Today, though, a letter has arrived for him and he will sit reading it whilst the shadows gather in his vast room and the Great Bell tolls out the hours in Tom Quad. There are shouts of revellers in the distance but they fade away and the fog creeps into the quads and up the staircases and into his brain.

'Dearest George – I must see you on your return. I cannot explain now and am rushed preparing Lizzie's wardrobe for her visit away with your Mama but I am ever your loving – Anne.'

This letter does not make George feel better; indeed it makes him feel worse. Oxford is no place for the melancholy; he feels he will be swallowed up by the misty Isis. But he replies post-haste and he takes out the coil of hair she cut for him and kisses it.

William is sitting in the schoolroom, having now been promoted. He has suddenly learned all his letters – or perhaps he knew them before but did not know what they meant. He is talking to Mrs Copus who sits crocheting. The other servants are waving off Lady Georgiana and lifting Charlie and Lizzie into their mama's carriage, for Uncle Duke has asked them to visit.

'There you are, love,' says Mrs Copus, rising and looking at William's slate. 'You see you can write now. Write "Copus loves William".' That'll take him some time, she is thinking, but William is staring at her.

'Grand loves the lady,' he says.

She looks at him closely and decides to say nothing.

'And George loves Nanna!'

'What did you say?'

'George loves Nanna, Nanna loves George,' he intones.

Anne was not sure at first, nor at the end of October, but now it is almost the end of November and she is sure. Fear and dismay alternate in her. If only she could remember dates. But she knows beyond all doubt that a child is to stir within her and is equally certain that it could be the child of Hardow and it could be the child of George, the man she loves. If it is George's she will be overjoyed – but she thinks, I shall never know; and the joy turns to grief and terror. She cannot sleep; she eats because she feels she must. Then she thinks of swallowing poison and rushing to the Mausoleum and lying down there. But – if it is George's child?

It is December now and snow is falling. Georgy and Harriet are at the Castle with their grandfather and grandmother: they are too young for visiting like grown-ups and too old to be taken as children. Miss Harriet is pacing up and down the Long Gallery with Grand, having a conversation with him. Hardow has not yet returned from London, nor George from Oxford. The old man talks on and on to the tall girl, telling her not to marry, to preserve herself, telling her what a lovely woman her mother was, so talented and so musical. And Harriet will give up her music when she marries and she must not. He advises against marriage and Harriet does not take him seriously. They discuss charades and games and art and hunting and shooting and driving and he rambles on about the last century and she thinks, truly he is very amazing, but really she is pleased because he is talking to her as though she were a grown woman, as the light fails and the snow falls and the glowing portraits on the walls fade.

Anne could not bear it. Sometimes she felt that if she were to know for certain that it was Hardow's child she would kill herself rather than bear it. The uncertainty was a black, grim cloud and there was no way of the cloud moving away, ever. And even if she could know the child was George's she would still lose her post; her life would soon change now. She would lose Lizzie – and George of course. Oh, but if it *were* George's child! The torment of being with child, of not knowing whose it would be, of having to tell George, drove her now one way, now the other. Perhaps better never to know and to put an end to it all? But she did not betray herself to any casual observer. Only Delia noticed and said nothing.

On December the 12th she woke with a headache. She had not yet felt sick. Hope rose – perhaps she was not expecting after all? But she had missed two months' blood now, the first time a fortnight after George had returned to Oxford and Hardow to London, and what else could it be? Better perhaps to run away – but whither? The headache went away in the morning. In the afternoon she was to go to her old job of seam-sewing. Distress and despair alternated with the little grain of hope.

'It isn't for another bairn,' said Ellen as they sat sewing. 'They say Harry will be the last.' 'Poor Lady Georgiana's had enough,' said Susan.

Somehow these words brought back the memory of Hardow – his hands and his breath on her and abruptly she got up and went out of the room. They would think she had gone out to relieve herself. She ran down the stairs, gasping for breath. It was like that awful dream she had had. If George were there in the courtyard she would stop – but George was of course in Oxford or calling in London on his way home. She saw Curly's mother in the distance, who did not see her, and she ran across the great court and on to the grass, making for the trees that bowered the East Lake. Away, away from the Temple and all its memories, down the path in the foggy distance, across the sloping field and down, down to the lake shore where George had first seen her, it seemed so long ago. Suddenly she put on a sprint and began to pant. The damp air seemed to be wrenching out her lungs but she determined not to stop and to run right into the water, to wade out until her head was covered, just to end the torment.

But with a little piece of her mind she clung on to the idea of George's baby and she began to cry. Just ahead of her, about ten yards away, was the reedy water's edge and she shut her eyes, intending to go on running until she felt the water round her feet. But some impulse, some final assertion of her identity, made them open again and she saw, curling in the water, as though it had been entangled in the reeds, a little speck of blue. She came to an abrupt stop, the tears still running down her face, and leaning down to the water, bent down and fished out a blue ribbon. Lizzie's hair ornament, lost over a year ago and waiting to be found. She held the ribbon and looked across at the water. Then, her breath still rasping and her knees weak, she slowly turned and walked slowly back to the house, knowing now that she would kill neither herself nor her future baby. And as she trudged back, cold sweat trickling down her back and her heart pounding, the figure of Delia came running towards her and clasped her in her arms. Slowly, Anne leaning her head against the tall girl, they passed indoors.

'I knew it must be something like that,' said Delia, rubbing Anne's face with an old towel. She had made her sit by the fender and take off her boots. Delia asked: 'But who was it, Anne?'

Anne went on crying hot tears, all the anguish of the past five months for the moment dissolving as if confession would remove her predicament. 'I love him. I love him,' she moaned. 'But it might not be his baby, Delia.' Delia waited, saying nothing, and Anne went on: '*He* won't spurn me – *he* wants to marry me . . . but his father – he made me, Delia. I was so miserable – I thought, why not end it? And then I saw Lizzie's hair ribbon and I knew I didn't want to die . . . and – oh!' She buried her face in her hands.

'But *who*, Anne?'

'It's George – he loves me.'

'You mean – Mr George?'

'Yes – and then his father – three times when George was away. He didn't know of course about George, and I'd promised not to tell anyone – I couldn't. And now, how can I tell George? He said he wanted to marry me – I know he can't – don't look at me like that . . . but I don't know, Delia, I don't know whose bairn it is!' Delia sat regarding her and patted her hand now and then and gradually Anne stopped crying. 'But you see, there's nothing I can do, *nothing* – if it's George's bairn, well, I want it – and if it's Hardow's I don't know what to do.'

'Listen.' Delia talked slowly and quietly. Anne found it difficult to concentrate but Delia seemed to be saying that it wasn't the end of the world. She might lose this post but she would find another, even one where a bairn might be accepted. And never mind Mr George – what could *he* do? But Hardow must give her money – that was how they did it. They knew they had to give money in cases like this, enough to see you through. Perhaps enough not to work for a bit till the child was established. Hardow would not want any fuss, he would pay her off. Why tell him about George?

'But Delia, perhaps it *is* George's bairn?'

'Hardow forced you and Hardow will pay. He won't want Lady Georgiana knowing anything.'

'Oh no – of course not!'

'And then he'll say nothing to anyone. Do you think he would let his son *marry* you, Anne? Why, if he did and the bairn were a boy he'd be Eighth Earl!'

'George won't be of age till after the baby's born – and I

wouldn't let him wed me. I love him, Delia, and I know he loves me but even if he could, it wouldn't be right.' Then, thinking over Delia's words again: 'You mean I'd be a *Countess* one day? I never thought of that! But I wouldn't want it. No.' She took Delia's hand. 'You've been right kind to me – how did you know I'd gone out to the lake?'

'I didn't, but I saw your face when they were talking about Lady Georgiana and another bairn. I guessed.' She looked awkwardly at the fire. 'You see Anne, *I* had a bairn once; it was my mistress's brother who got the better of me – oh, not a great lord, but I had to leave. And I hadn't any money.'

'But where is your child?'

'He died, Anne, when he was two years old. I've never told anyone. My mistress took me back after that but *he* tried it again and so I came here.'

'Oh, poor Delia – and I never knew. I'm right sorry.'

'Aye, he was a lovely little lad.' She swallowed and looked out of the window. 'So you see, Anne – with money you can bring a bairn up, give him a start in life. I had to leave my little Jack with a horrible woman in Leeds when I went to look for work. And she didn't feed him properly. I don't talk about it to anyone.'

'But Delia, it was worse for you, I mean' – she was going to say 'he didn't love you, the baby's dad'– but thought better of it.

Delia said, as though guessing her thoughts: 'There was no love between us. Fancy though – you and Mr George!'

'Oh Delia, we could have been happy, I know we could have, if he had not been from a great family, and if he were older. But I must see him first and confess to him. I've got to tell him – I must. I'll try not to say who the other man was – but what if he asks me? It's the not knowing, you see. George will be happy if he thinks I'm going to have *his* bairn – and I've got to take away his happiness if I tell him more. I've prayed, Delia – oh, what will the Rector and Mrs Hart think? – and Mam and Hannah! I'll have to go back.' She began to cry softly again and Delia stole quietly away and made her a cup of tea.

Anne's dread was now centred on George's return. She rehearsed it every way but it never came out right. 'You know,' Delia said awkwardly the next day, 'some lasses get rid of their babies long before they're born. I have to say it. You *could* do that. I know there's a woman in Middlesbrough – at least I heard

202

of it from someone. And look at that Miss Sharpe – don't you think that's what *she* did?'

'I couldn't lose George's child – I couldn't live with what I'd done. I love him so, Delia – if the bairn is his it will be all I've got left of him.'

After that Delia said no more. Privately she thought: 'It could be the child of either of them, but Hardow's already got eleven so it seems more likely! It's probably Hardow's – too much to hope that it's Mr George's.' She even wondered whether Anne had imagined lying with George out of the pain of being forced by Hardow. She never doubted what Hardow had done, had always thought those quiet ones were the worst, had even found him attractive. Now if it had been that *Grand* – that would have been no surprise, even at his age. He was a randy old goat she thought.

Anne's next worry was that the story would get round to the other servants but Delia swore she would say nothing. There'd be plenty of gossip later when Anne had gone but they'd take care to pretend to know nothing as far as the family were concerned. Families got off lightly so long as they paid up.

Anne was very, very grateful to Delia. She wondered sometimes why she had not told Curly. It must be that Curly had grown away from them, becoming a respectable woman: a lady's maid. No one would have dared to seduce Curly! Not with her mum and dad on the estate. And she remembered how Hardow had threatened her with losing her job if he couldn't have his way with her and how she was going to lose it because he had. She was caught.

Delia continued to advise her: 'You must write to that Rector of yours,' she said. 'Tell him you're in trouble and will have to come home. He'll have to do something and he'll tell your mam and dad.'

'But when shall I go? I can't just leave, Delia.'

'Once you've sorted it out with the Viscount he'll be asking you to go, I'm afraid. He'll pay you off!'

'I shall – speak to George first.' She swallowed. 'And then go to Hardow after Christmas. He's not here anyway – when will they all be back?'

'Mrs Copus was saying George is expected soon,' replied Delia. 'If you like, I'll go to him with a message once he's back – as if it were from Mrs C like – I can take Master William along –

and then we'll clear the nursery and you can have your talk with him.'

'Oh Delia, you're so sensible. I was dreading his – just knocking on the door – or meeting him by accident. He hasn't wrote – written – for a bit. I think my last letter must have cast him down. I think I wanted to – prepare his mind like.'

It was snowing hard now and coaches were being delayed. Lady Georgiana and her husband were to return to the Castle for Christmas and in the New Year there were to be further house parties. They had stopped trying to get Miss Caroline a husband till next season, when Georgy would be 'out' too. The Duke was to come and Countess Granville and many more, and supplies of food were being checked and animals being slaughtered in readiness. The French cook did nothing but complain.

The younger children were to be sent home a little earlier but the snow had held them up too. Fortunately they were not in London, only in an adjoining county.

'I did tell George I must see him,' said Anne, 'so he may come straight up to find me.' It was strange confiding their snatched meetings to someone else.

On the morning of the 19th Delia came running up the stairs. Anne was busy washing William. 'He's here – the coach came through in the early morn. They say Mr George travelled up from London as the Great North Road was clearer than the others. Shall I find him once he's up and breakfasted?'

Anne began to tremble so violently that she dropped the hairbrush she had just been going to use on William's tangled locks. 'Yes – yes,' she gasped. Ask him to come up at eleven – say I have to see him – then I've time to prepare myself. Oh, I feel sick – I must get a hold on myself.'

'That's right,' said Delia. 'I'll tell him to knock three times and I'll see Master William is with Mr Coulson. Mrs Copus is down with Mrs Gibson – I don't think she'll come up till Miss Lizzie and Miss Blanche are back.'

'I wish it was Miss Lizzie – I wish she were here! She makes things seem better,' said Anne.

She tried to compose herself; made up the fire, washed her face, put on a clean apron and sat mutely looking out of the window. She heard the Chapel bell strike eleven, its tones muffled by the snow which had now stopped falling but had covered the courtyards and lawns and buildings with a white blanket and weighed down the branches of the trees with frozen icing. The nursery was filled with a white light: everything seemed still and heavy. Then she heard footsteps at the door and the knock: one, two, three. She hardly had the voice to say: 'Come in', and it *might* not be George, so she walked slowly to the outer door and opened it. He was standing there and lost no time in taking her in his arms.

'Anne! Anne!'

She tried to disengage herself but it was so lovely to be in his arms and just for a moment made up for everything. Then she gasped: 'I have to speak to you. Please come – and sit down. I've made a nice fire.'

He looked at her, puzzled, but came in meekly and sat in the armchair by the fire. 'You've got it cosy here – I'm so glad to be back! I thought the coach would never make it. Is no one else here then? What is it, Anne?' He tried to hold her hand and pull her towards him but she sat down opposite him and took a big breath.

'Delia said it would be best this way. You see – I've got something terrible to tell you – and I don't know how.' She paused for a moment and he looked at her with concern.

'You're not *ill*, Anne?'

'No, no, not *ill* – I . . .'

'Anne – can it be? – are you carrying our child? Oh my darling, why didn't you tell me before. Oh, let me kiss you. Don't cry, don't cry . . .'

'No, no,' she tried to speak again. 'I mean, yes I am with child', and then she looked long at him and tried to think how best to break it.

'Then I am *glad*, *glad* – Anne! Did you think I would be angry? Oh my poor darling little Anne!'

She made a great effort, swallowed and looked steadily at him. 'You see, George – it may not be yours!' At last it was out. She saw joy change to incredulity and then to hurt and then to puzzlement.

'Are you speaking the truth – not just trying to spare me anxiety?' he finally said softly.

'It could be another man's. Oh George, I didn't love him. I love *you*. He *made* me – I . . .'

'*Who* made you? Anne, what are you saying? I know you love me – I know you were faithful to me – no one would ever doubt that. Oh, Anne, do you remember, that last time? It wasn't wrong, Anne – aren't you mistaken? Has worry made you imagine things?' Then he saw the anguish in her face and knew that what she had told him was true.

'But I don't understand – someone *made* you – in summer? – when I wasn't here?'

'Oh don't ask me, don't ask me – I mustn't – I can't. Believe me, George, I was forced. The child *may* be yours but I had to tell you this – because it would be terrible for you to think it was yours when it might not be. I had to speak the truth. Oh, forgive me, forgive me – I wanted to kill myself! Lizzie stopped me . . .'

'Lizzie?'

'When I was going to run into the lake Lizzie's hair ribbon was there. I've known now for two months – I didn't know what to do. It's all over – I can't let you love me any more. I'm going away – as soon as – things can be arranged.' She spoke rapidly, disjointedly and he caught at her wrist.

'Anne. You must tell me. You are driving me mad! Your last little letter was so strange – I thought you didn't love me any more – you do, don't you?'

'Oh George, I love you, I love you – but I mustn't – we can't ask anything of each other any more.'

'Anne.' He stood up and then went over to her chair. She sat as though she were a prisoner at the bar awaiting judgement.

'You say it is not your fault – of *course* I believe you – but you must tell me *who*. It must have been a devil, to force *you*. Didn't you tell him you had a lover – a true lover who would avenge you?'

'You made me promise not to tell anyone about us till you were of age – and then – that I had a . . . lover . . . made him worse, you see, because I wasn't a maid any more. Oh Mr George – don't ask me to say any more.'

'Was it that groom, Osborne?'

'Oh no, no!'

'Mr Ross the painter – they say he's not too nice with his models!'

'Oh no, George – no one like that.'

'Then if it's Coulson I'll challenge him – I'll avenge you.' To think of the gentle George with pistols or a sword! What could

206

she say, for George had grown pale with anger and a ferocity showed on his face she had never before seen. 'You must tell me, Anne – for I am going to marry you! Yes, we shall get married! I shall get permission, tell them I love you and it is my child. Even if it is not – it is *yours* my love! Do you think I could allow you to suffer alone when five minutes in church would put all right!'

'No, no, you can't, you can't.'

'But I *can*. I shall go to Papa, not tell him anything, but that you are carrying my child – and it must be legitimized. If I marry you now it will be, and we shall have other children! Anne – this may have happened to force me to see how selfish I have been. Yes, I shall go to Papa – and if Papa will not, I shall go to Grand as head of the family. They can't stop me.'

'No, no, you must not, you *cannot*. I beg you, George, tell no one. I will go away and one day perhaps you will come to me – if you still love me.'

But he went on: 'It is a punishment sent for me. By God – I will kill this man who forced you? How many times – when? – not after I had left you in October?'

'No, before, that is why I don't know – you see,' she took a great breath and averted her face. 'It was only two days before we – we – in the Temple, that last time. I had to have you then, George – just once more – to wipe it all out. But then I found I was with child – at the end of October – and I thought you would think I had tricked you into . . .'

'I wanted *you*, Anne – always I wanted you – you must tell me – WHO? WHO?' He paused and said in a quieter voice: 'You need not have told me – you *have* told me and it is up to me now. You have been honest with me – and you must tell me. It is only right, then I can settle accounts.'

She stood up. All her life seemed to be in the balance, but more than that – all George's life.

'Please trust me – it was not my fault, I swear to you.'

'I believe you, Anne – of course I believe you. I have never doubted your honesty for one moment.' Then a thought struck him and he looked at her face, his gaze travelling over it as though he could discover the truth there. She stared at him and he thought: 'She is so beautiful. Who could do this to her?' He continued to gaze at her and took her hand again. 'Anne – was it, was it – *Grand*? I know he has women – he is old and lives in another age. Was it *Grand*?'

'No, George, no, it was not.'

'Who then?'

Her eyes were burning now and she felt helpless. Then she said, slowly, taking her hand out of his: 'If I tell you – it will – it will – ruin your life George. Don't force me – I cannot ruin your life.' She spoke as though she had a revelation of two futures and both for her were empty, but for George they would make the difference between life and a living death. His spirit – how could it survive her revelation? Wonderingly she looked at her palm as though she held his future in it and prayed for strength. But he took her by the shoulders and the feel of her young body and the swell of her breast against his took him beyond reason. His idealistic desire for truth at all costs drove him on so that he scarce knew what he was doing except that he must know. Whoever it was, he must know – and then he could take care of her.

'Anne, Anne' – his voice rose, almost with a threat in it.

'Oh! do not *make* me – go and have a happy life, my darling,' she whispered, but he went on.

'I have to know. There must be nothing between us that is not true – no lies, no secrets. There cannot be secrets between us – and all children are sacred, all children. Come.' He lowered her into her chair and knelt by her side, holding her hand, his eyes fixed on her face. 'Now you are going to tell me – quietly. I am not angry with you but I must defend my honour. You are a good woman, and you are mine.'

'And I say it will ruin you, George – can you not believe me?'

'Whom are you shielding?'

'I am shielding you,' she replied with a shudder.

'Then,' he went on slowly, 'can it be . . .? On whom could I not avenge myself? Don't speak unless to tell me – I am waiting . . .'

Time seemed to stop.

'I have no right to ruin your life, George. Even if *mine* has been – for it was terrible, awful and nothing could ever change things now.'

'And if so . . .' he said with the impetuosity of youth and also with a presentiment of dread as though a shadow were stalking him which he must turn into flesh and blood, a fatal shadow. 'And if so – *I* will take away the burden from your shoulders Anne, if you tell me!'

'Oh, you can't, you can't. No one can,' she said in the flat accent of complete despair.

'So you will tell me his name, Anne – I must take charge of my own life – I am not a child any longer.' And the shadow crept up and over her face, and what he now saw plainly there were the features of his own father.

His voice would not come out. His world seemed to be turning over into darkness. In an awful whisper he said: 'Tell me if I am wrong. Was it, was it – my – *father*!' He remained staring at her, willing that it should not be true but Anne, her defences finally down, could hold out no longer.

'Yes,' she said simply and bowed her head.

George got up then and smote his breast and the sound that came out of him was like the wail of Abraham when told he must sacrifice Isaac, mingled with the yell of an outraged child. He groped towards his armchair again and fell on his knees, burying his face in it. Anger, grief, amazement, struggled within him but more than that a horror, an incestuous horror. *His* girl, his *love* – and his father. How could it be? But she was not lying, no.

Anne remained facing him across the fire like a seated statue and then she got up and went to him and put her arms around him. He was now completely silent in a blank world. It seemed he could not hear or feel or see. She was frightened and tried to pull his face towards her.

Then suddenly he wrenched away, stood again, trembling from head to foot. 'Nevertheless,' he said in a strange voice, 'I shall marry you. He will have to allow me, he *must* . . . perhaps the child is mine . . . no, even if it is not . . . Oh! I am truly punished for giving way to my lust. Am I no better than he?'

'You must not say such things, George – we loved each other. Your father was . . . lonely . . . perhaps he was drunk . . . he did what men do – so many of them – like, like your grandfather . . . and I could not tell him about us. You know I could not. He wouldn't have believed me . . . and I promised you to say nothing to anyone.'

'Did he hurt you, Anne? Where did he take you? Oh God – don't tell me!' He began now to weep and there was no comfort anywhere. His father, whom he had tried to like, who had never been a bad father to him, rather weak and uninterested perhaps – a picture rose before him of Anne and him, and his gorge rose. 'I shall never be able, never, to stop seeing him and you – oh my God.'

'I didn't want to tell you,' said Anne humbly, but he interrupted her: 'I have brought it all upon myself – you are not to blame.'

He tried to reassert his powers of rationality but great tides of hatred, terror, despair, disgust, jealousy, revenge, engulfed him. His filial piety strove with them, with rage, guilt and sorrow. How could he confront his father? Yet he *would* confront him, by God he would! 'I shall not say to him what I know,' he thought. 'But I shall demand that my honour be satisfied by marrying Anne.' And a picture of a marriage with her, with a child who might not be his, with an estrangement from all his past life, rose and stayed in his mind. Nevertheless he would marry Anne – or would marry no one, never marry, never produce a legitimate heir to all his patrimony. Atone for his sins by marriage – or never marry and punish his father that way. Oh that would be a true revenge!

'Listen. I shall ask for an interview with my – with Hardow on his return. I shall speak to him not of himself but only of me and of you. I shall put the case plainly before him. He will have to choose between his son's happiness and an heir – or his son's misery and a death to his own hopes. Who else knows anything about you and him?'

'My friend Delia knows. She didn't want me to tell you. She said I should receive money from Hard . . . from your father to bring up the baby . . . that he would "pay me off" and I could go away – and perhaps, later, when you are older, you could come to see me. Oh, George, I've lost my post anyroad!' She didn't say, then, 'That was what he threatened me with.'

'Whatever happens, my mother must not suspect. She would suffer terribly. Does anyone else know?'

'I think that Miss Sharpe does – but I don't know if she ever saw me with you – but *she* came with the message, the last time, with . . . your father . . . that I should go to him. He knew I had to do his bidding, George. He knew he could force me to . . .' At last Anne gave way and cried. It was all out. All that mattered now was the baby.

'I shall see my father, demand that I marry under age. Then I shall come to you and . . .' He was going to say 'take you away', but whither?

'Please George – he won't let you – how could he *now*?'

'But no one has yet told him about us?'

'No, but he will know the child could be his.'

'You will wait then till I see him?'

'Please George, don't hurt yourself for my sake. He will refuse you.'

They stood once more silent and the snow began to fall, and George took up his greatcoat that he had flung down in the anteroom before the world had gone dark, and slowly made his way across the white expanse of fallen snow to his rooms, across from one world to another.

Hardow came back two days later.

During that time Anne stayed in the nursery. She felt as though she had just brought the news of a death to a child, a death that would not only orphan the child but strip him of self-respect, reduce him, take away his joy in living, inject the poison of despair in his veins, and most of all fill him with self-loathing.

Yet she was in a curious way lighter of heart after her confession in spite of her anguish. It was anguish for George, not for herself, and one is braver before another's anguish. She was, even so, tortured by the knowledge that she must soon leave Lizzie. Would even George understand how sorrowful that made her? He had left her with many unspoken answers to questions he could not have brought himself to ask her and she had not told him much of her own feelings about losing her post and her little charges. He had enough to bear of his own, poor boy.

George was thinking only that it must all be 'got over', that he must lay his cards on the table. He was not in awe of his father, merely disgusted. More than anything, he dreamt of marrying Anne, as though that would cancel out his father and pull Hardow out of his mind by the roots.

He found himself walking down the corridor at the far end of the Long Gallery to the entrance to the Museum where the slab of stone his great-grandfather had brought back from Greece stood, the stone behind which they had said the Oracle of Delphi spoke. It should not be here, he thought vaguely. It was the Christian God from whom he should ask for answers and comfort. But he could not help placing his hands on the rough cold stone and murmuring: 'Tell me what to do. Tell me what to do. Tell me if it is my child. Tell me.' But the Oracle was silent and he found tears constricting his throat, tears of anger as well as of sorrow.

He could not sleep more than a few minutes at a time at night. He tried to pray but found no words. He tried to confront everything. Then he dozed for a few moments and forgot during that time but was jerked awake again, as though he were going to fight a duel at dawn. Still the hope persisted that he could marry his love before the birth of the child. The thought of not being a child any more himself – he who was Papa's eldest child – the thought of the ignoble acts of that Papa – seemed to cancel out all the past happiness of his life. He had just managed to become on good terms with his own body, to begin to sort out love and lust, and to find both with one person, with dear Anne – and now he was forced into a guilt and shame he felt he truly did not deserve, because of the conduct of his father. How could he bear to see the shame on his father's face if he knew that George knew? The driving force of bodily lust was no excuse for a so-called Christian gentleman. And he had thought his father both a Christian and a gentleman. All he could think of to spare his father would be to insinuate to him that he thought Grand might be responsible, as well as himself, for Anne's predicament. That would save his father's face. But why should he worry about saving his now despicable father's face? If Papa persisted in disallowing a marriage, he would make it plain that he knew the real seducer – but only if Papa himself insinuated that anyone but George was the father. It was all so undignified, such a mess. Then he thought, as dawn broke, that even if he had never fallen in love with Anne, his father's crime would still have taken place and Anne would have been without love and with only the memory of a hateful seducer. This gave him a small paradoxical pool of comfort in the desert of his own distress.

He could not wait to get it all over and yet dreaded the confrontation more than he had ever dreaded anything in his life. Stripped of robes and the Garter Star, without land and money, fine food and jewels, books and travels, his father like all noblemen was just a man. If Anne had been born a Lady Anne, brought up to be presented at Court and go to balls and find a husband, a Duke or an Earl, would she have been any different? And the little baby – it would come into the world naked, whoever had sired it. And unless he could marry Anne, or at least take care of her, that baby would be a baby in a poor village and never know the benefits of so-called civilized life. But if that life were not civilized, and if it was in any case the baby of a good woman, well, would everything be all right? He thought: 'Perhaps he'll be *my* little son', and felt both humble and proud. Then he remembered again – perhaps he would be the child of a hateful act, his mother a victim of male power; and was once more in despair.

Once he knew his father was back and that his mother and her retinue would return a day later, George found it hard to wait. He had deliberately not been there to greet his father in the Great Hall on his return and had stayed in his own apartments until the afternoon, by which time he felt Hardow would be rested from his journey. Hardow hated journeys and always took a long time to recover from them. By four o'clock George could wait no longer and went to search him out in his private study. As he went into the anteroom he saw John the footman was there with a box of silver buckles ready to take down to the odd-job boys for cleaning.

'Is my father alone?' he asked, nervous now that it had come to the point.

'No, Mr George – Mrs Copus is in with him. Would you like to wait in the music room and I shall call you when she has gone?'

What could Mrs Copus be wanting? It was not the hour for receiving the housekeeper or the steward. George sighed with annoyance; he had screwed his courage up to sticking-point and now must wind it down a little.

'Fair enough, John. Come for me when his lordship is free.'

He went into the music room and found he could not sit, must walk up and down, riffle through the pages on Harriet's music stand and look out of the window. Here his sister had played 'Plaisir d'Amour'. Tears came into his eyes. It was Chagrin d'Amour now, indeed. But he must be cold, distant, polite, present his case to Papa as a man. After all he was now twenty and in only a year could marry whom he pleased. But he could not legitimize Anne's baby – what a ridiculous circumstance. He felt alternately angry and miserable. How could he bear even to look at Hardow? Fortunately Hardow would know nothing about his feelings, for he was going to have to tread carefully, not mention any doubts over the future baby's parentage unless he were forced to pretend it might involve Grand. Poor old man – should one make use of him in this way? It was immoral. But what was morality, when there was future happiness at stake? The snow light filled the afternoon room as he paced up and down. He was sure his Papa would listen to reason, if only to purge himself of is own guilt.

Hardow had just said goodbye to Mrs Copus, who had come to cast accounts when he had wanted a doze. And she had also 'felt it her duty to report' that, 'not to put too fine a point on it, sir, I am told that one of my maids, Tesseyman, is carrying on with Mr George. We are a respectable house, my lord, and I thought fit to inform you before I spoke to the girl.' It would be most unfortunate – otherwise she would have held her tongue – but dear Master George (though she supposed he was a grown man now, she always thought of him as her little boy that she had looked after till he went off to school, her *first* little boy) – dear Master George must be warned. These girls were not always as prim and proper as they looked and she had been very worried lest my lady should hear aught of it – Mr George should perhaps be spoken to, and the girl dismissed. Not that she knew for certain that anything had been going on but, as she had said, she felt it her duty . . .'

Hardow had listened with apparent languor but inside he was turned to ice. If it were true? If his own son had been the 'lover' Anne Tesseyman had spoken of! He would have to find out. How could he? It was most unseemly. More it was a disaster. George must not know of his own seduction of Anne. Surely the girl would not tell him? All was not lost. But if his wife were to hear of his own affair! His blood ran cold.

'You may go, Mrs Copus. I am indeed grateful for your taking such a kindly interest in our Mr George. Do nothing. Now perhaps on Friday you could bring me the completed receipts?' Interfering busybody.

Mrs Copus had gone, feeling full of virtue. The Viscount would sort it out. George was young and hotheaded. 'Nanna loves George,' indeed! But she was uncertain about how to deal with Tesseyman; she had thought her such a good girl.

Hardow had no intention of speaking to George, certainly not. Better let sleeping dogs lie. George would have plenty of other girls before he settled down – though it was deuced strange, he never would have thought his gentle, scholarly son capable of an emotional attachment with a servant. Perhaps there was no truth in it and it was just Copus getting all hot and bothered over gossip. Pity the only person to whom he could mention it and perhaps get some advice was his own wife. She wouldn't believe anything derogatory of her beloved eldest son but he scarcely wished to introduce the name of Anne to her.

He was just putting his papers away and thinking he would go to look at those new folios the Duke had sent to him in his absence when the footman knocked and announced: 'Mr George, my lord.' Hardow started up as though he had been rifling his own desk, but covered his confusion by bending down again over his papers.

'Well, my boy – back are you? Thought you'd have come up earlier. Deuced weather, ain't it?'

George advanced, stopped, cleared his throat and summoning all his courage managed to get out: 'I have to speak to you, sir. It is a matter of some importance.'

'Well then, sit down. Have a cigar. And Johnny sent me the new *Edinburgh Review* – specially bound with the arms in gold. Want to see it?'

'Not now Papa.' George decided not to sit and shook his head at the proffered cigar. 'I'll be plain sir. I love a woman and I wish to marry her. I am not of age as you know and I come to beg your permission in – exceptional circumstances. I am not asking for money, or for a settlement, simply for your permission.'

Hardow stared at him. 'May I ask the name of this woman? Who is she? A sister of one of your Oxford friends?'

'No sir. Her name is Anne Tesseyman. She is in my sister Lizzie and my brother William's nursery. She is a good woman and I love her and she loves me.' He stopped and did not look at his father but Hardow was looking at him.

'Are you telling me – asking me for permission to *marry* a servant?'

'Yes sir, I am. I cannot marry without your permission.' He still did not look at his father.

'George – recollect yourself. What may be your – relations – with this girl I do not enquire, but you are out of your mind, my son. You know, you *must* know, that if you marry, and I hope you will, it will be to a girl of your, our, own kind. You – the heir to one of the premier Earldoms of England! I never thought to hear such nonsense. Your study of classical myths has unmanned you. Let us have no more of this nonsense.' He spoke calmly but he was rubbing the cuticle of his thumbnail with his finger and a little muscle twitched under his eye.

'There is a reason, sir,' replied George quietly.

'There can be no reason – reason does not enter this matter!'

'The reason is,' and George paused and looked full in his father's face, 'she is carrying my child, sir.'

Hardow gasped and fell back in his chair.

'Your child sir – what a tale!' he managed.

'I believe,' stated George, a tremble in his voice, 'I believe she may have been wronged.' He must play another card. 'I believe some – person – wronged her. There are those in this house whose manners and morals are not of the Enlightenment.' He hoped this reference would not escape his father who had himself found Grand's conduct often reprehensible.

'Are you telling *me*, your *father*, George, that you are about to rescue a maiden in distress, that you would marry some girl from nowhere to give a name to her child? Come, my boy, that will not do. Could this – this bastard be yours? I can scarce believe it! *Your* morals *are* of the Enlightenment as you put it, I am sure.'

'I have loved her for many months, father. I am guilty of taking her honour away from her. She was a maid when I first loved her – and she is the only woman in the world for me.'

Hardow stared at him. What Mrs Copus had suspected was true then. An affair of passion between his own son and that frightened girl! Gracious gods, how was he to get out of this. But there would be no question of marriage, absolutely not. A settlement of money . . .

George was waiting for an answer.

'I refuse you, sir. Set yourself up with her if you wish in some rural spot till you tire of her. Or pay her off. Are you so unworldly that you do not know that is how these things are done?' *Did* George know who had wronged her? George's next words seemed to indicate that he might.

'Sir, I am your son. I come to you not as a man wronged but as a man who cannot see a woman wronged. By marrying Anne, all can be put right.'

'I tell you, there can be no question of marriage. When you are of age that will be your own affair but if you persist then you will find you are cut off from your settlement, I'm afraid. You do not know the child is yours, do you?' he added slyly.

'If I marry her, the child is mine. But only if I marry her before the baby comes into the world – and that I cannot do sir unless you allow me. Will you or will you not give me your blessing?'

'George – that is enough, quite enough.'

'The child would be my heir, father!'

'I am aware of that and nothing in the world will allow me to let that happen.'

'And do you not think of the judgement of Heaven?' cried George, now out of control.

Hardow got up and moved to the window. What if his son struck him?

George knew his father was afraid but that even his fear would not by one whit change his mind. In despair he cried out: 'Then father, if you do not allow me to make an honest woman of her – as though she were not already the most honest woman on earth – I swear to you, I swear that I shall never marry – no, never. Either Anne, or no one. If Anne consents to marry me when I am twenty-one, I shall marry her – and if I do not, *never, no one.* You will have to find your heir elsewhere.' He had not meant to say it but it was all out before he could help himself.

'For God's sake, do not say these things, and especially not to your poor mother . . .'

'No sir, not to her,' said George. 'Anne said I would not be allowed to marry – and even, father, she said she *would* not, that it was wrong. So she was right. And we are fated to part. Father, how can you be so cruel?'

Hardow turned. 'Do not *beg* of me, George. It is not the conduct of a gentleman.'

'No,' cried George. 'It is *not* the conduct of a gentleman. Do you remember, sir, when last year I spoke to you of Grand's conduct in the matter of another servant – an older woman – and one not like Anne Tesseyman – you told me to mind my own affairs? Well, now I am minding my affairs, by God I am and I swear to you once more – it is my last word to you as a dutiful son – I shall not marry. Think what you have done when you confront your Maker. You have robbed me and *her* of all happiness – I shall not forgive you, Father, and I shall never forgive myself.'

'Go – George, go. And speak to me again only when you have recovered yourself.'

After a pause, as George turned to go, he said: 'Don't tell your mama, my son', and George knew then that Hardow knew he knew but that there was nothing to be done. He did not know how he got to the door, how he found his room again. He flung himself on his couch, weeping, and a great hatred of his father made him clench his fists, imagine he was in mortal combat with him, that he killed him even. 'I shall keep my word, keep my word. Never marry. Never. No,' he cried. 'And between me and him now, the rest is silence.'

Hardow sat long in the darkness of his study before passing into his dressing-room. George. The best-favoured, most intelligent and gifted of all his children through whom the line must be carried on. For if George died without a son, Fred would be next earl and Fred was a nincompoop, an oddity – rash, well enough in face and figure, but a cipher, a nothing. And after him, William, who would certainly never marry. Hardow envisaged the result of his own folly and evil for a brief moment, then closed his mind to it. He would pay the girl off, enjoin silence, joke with Lady Georgiana perhaps about George's delusions and all would go on as before. The devil take women! Sent into the world with their charms to trap men. And George – well and truly trapped too – George who was a better man than he was, that he knew. If anything came out they would all tacitly blame old Grand. How much did Selina Sharpe know? He would have to pay *her* off too to avoid any further trouble. And who had told Copus? Taking your son's woman – that was what he had done. And George – with his father's whore!

And whose child was it? Could it be his? By God it could. He could hardly ask the girl – she didn't know either. It must have been that last time – but George had had her since, had he? It was worse than Queen Caroline – but Anne Tesseyman was no Caroline. He had besmirched and befouled his own son's sweetheart. How could he have known? She ought to have told him – but of course she *could* not. This was the last entanglement he would get himself into; he swore George would come round as he grew older. He was only a stripling. But he himself would have to see the girl. Wait until after Christmas? See her first, then pay her off in the New Year. With that he rang for his valet and dined alone trying to drown his anger and annoyance in port. But still the thoughts went round his head. Why had the wretched girl not told him it was George? It would have stopped him like a cold hand on his lust. He supposed she would have thought he would be angry – and well he might. And of course the boy had probably told her to say nothing to anyone. It was when he had threatened her with loss of her work at the Castle that she had seemed most frightened. What's past was past – it was too late now! What if it *were* his child? A little step-brother for George. He had it in his heart to be sorry for that young man: having a fancy for a girl was good and well – but falling in love with her, that was not done. By God though he envied him that. What he would not give to be young again! The thoughts struggled round his head till the port finished them off and he slept.

The next morning George rose at dawn and went out into the snow-covered gardens to try and avoid meeting anyone before he had spoken to Anne. She would be waiting and wondering what had passed between his father and him. Well, all that was over now, there was nothing more to say to Hardow and he hoped Hardow would not address him. It was a pity the others were returning home tomorrow: he could not inflict his misery upon his mother and sisters. How could he break it to Anne when he could not even face it himself? He could offer her all the money he had to give, to make things easier for her; he could promise to wed her on his twenty-first birthday. But how to get through the next year? He walked wearily on, not noticing that a weak sun had come out and that the snow might thaw a little. Wretched sun, to shine on over all this weary world! He looked up, passing statues who looked like gigantic snowmen striding across the park. Where was he going? He found that his feet had led him to the Temple path. The Temple would be surely locked today. Yet there would be a breathtaking view from the Belvedere. How could he think of views when he had to break the ghastly news to Anne? Then he saw her, waiting motionlessly by the Temple trees, wrapped in her black cape. He advanced slowly without greeting her and she could see from his dejection what had happened.

'I knew you would come if I thought on you long enow,' she said. 'Don't tell me – I can guess what has happened. I never expected it different.'

'He is going to pay you off' – George's voice came out husky. She took his hand and held it to her lips. 'Did you show him you knew – about what he did to me?'

'I think so, though nothing was said . . . You are cold – come – let us see if the Temple is open on this side.'

She put her arm through his and they walked up the familiar steps and tried the door. It creaked open.

'We are lucky.'

'I can't stay, love. *Should* I take your father's money, George?'

'I want you to take all mine,' said George dully.

'You know I couldn't do that. No, George, I'll take nowt from you but your love. You don't owe me a penny. How could I!' Suddenly great sobs began to heave out of him and he bawled like a child. It was dreadful – it seemed they would tear him in two, rasping his throat. 'Nay George, it's not your fault. We must think on the bairn. I'll go whenever *he* tells me to – I'll write to our Rector and ask him if Hannah can find me work with her for a bit.' She consoled him in her arms.

'You're going away and I shall never see you again – I know it. I told my father I'd marry you when I was of age if he wouldn't let me marry you now, but I'm frightened – I shall die – I feel so terrible – like a great black fog all round me.'

'George – you'll carry on because you *must*, and if you like, I swear – if you still want me when you can marry me – I'll wed you. There, don't take on so.' She soothed him, seemed suddenly motherly. But, she was thinking, he mustn't throw his life away, there were grand things for him to do, without her. She would manage. Little by little she calmed him down. Even so, she was a little frightened in spite of her words for he looked so distracted. The scene with his father had bit deep, to the bone of his being.

'You must stay over Christmas, Annie – don't go till New Year, till *I* go – I won't let you – I shall make a disturbance if father tries to make you go before you want.'

'And you won't say anything to your mother, George? Promise me, love.'

'I promise.' He put his hand on hers which was lying on her lap. 'What is it like, Anne, to feel a baby inside you? What power women have!'

'I can't feel anything yet. Nay – it's *men* who have the power!'

'Annie – let's pretend it's our baby even if it isn't. I can't bear to think of you suffering for *him*.'

'If it's a love-child, then it's yours. You are cold – come, we must go.'

He marvelled at her calm. She seemed to have changed overnight from the girl he knew, seemed assured, resigned. How strange people were. But it would be different when they said goodbye, he knew.

Hardow sent for her the next day, before his wife and family returned. He sat at his desk and called her in brusquely. I am ready if he insults me, she was thinking, still on the wave of strange confidence which her confession to George had brought her. How much was he going to admit?

'I am to give you some money, Tesseyman,' he said. 'I hope no one else has given you any.'

'It was offered and was refused, sir.'

'There are fifty pounds here – enough for you to live on for a pretty long time if I know you people. This is on the understanding you say no more about anything that may have taken place this summer and autumn during my residence at the Castle.' He turned away and whispered: 'Particularly to my wife, if you don't want to be responsible for her death, for I think it would kill her!'

'I never, never shall.'

'And as for my eldest son...' he paused and turned round and stared at her. She felt the bright blush flame over her face and neck. 'I cannot make you promise not to marry him but it would not be, shall we say, in *his* best interests. In any case he cannot marry for another year without my permission.'

'I know that, sir. May I speak, sir, since I shall not speak with you again. I think I have the right. You have the best son in the world, my lord – '

'And *you* have ruined his life,' interjected Hardow angrily.

'No sir, *you* have.'

'Take the money and go. Leave in the first week of the New Year. We shall not speak of this again. Don't speak to me like that. Don't look at me so...'

'I wish it had been your father, sir – not you,' she said. 'I am taking your money and thank you for it. I would not take money from Mr George because I love him. But I cannot live without work. I never wanted to leave here but I can't carry on with a child of the Fountaynes at my skirts. I hope and pray the bairn is Mr George's, sir – if he does wed me, I shall send your money back to you. But, sir, when I take your sovereigns I am not agreeing this child is yourn. I will not have that. I'd rather be hanged. I shall spend it only on keeping alive and on the child.'

She spoke with rare dignity and he was impressed and began to understand why his son loved her. But her knees were knocking together and after she had left with the sovereigns in her kerchief she did not know how she had dared.

Lady Georgiana noticed how strangely quiet her eldest son was. All the life seemed to have been drained out of him. Copus had been odd too, rambling on about the Tesseyman girl, Lizzie's maid, and how she was leaving – had to go and look after her own mother. Was the girl in some sort of trouble? She had little time to probe any more deeply into the matter of George or into the moods of Mrs Copus for the day after Christmas the New Year house guests would begin to arrive and she was determined to present Caro in a good light to the Marquis of H, who had a pleasant son. Georgy was in good form, had thoroughly enjoyed her visits, and so had Harriet. Fred was out most of the time planning his next shoot and dear little William had much improved. Mr Ross the painter was to paint them all – he had already worked on the background. She sighed. Soon the younger boys would be away too. Edward and Charlie would both be off again to school – next year even Edward would be going to Eton, though she doubted whether he would carry off as many prizes as dear George. Blanche seemed in better health and Lizzie was growing fast, even quite tall, perhaps a little too thin for comfort. Baby Harry had celebrated his second birthday with his first proper sentence: all in all, the family were in good spirits. What *was* the matter with George? Perhaps a long visit abroad in spring would cheer him up? Perhaps he thought he was in love – with the young Spencer girl he had played charades with so charmingly, at her brother's. George hadn't had a nice chat with her for months. She must try to find time to have a heart to heart, though it was difficult with such a large party arriving. Thank God Gibson and Copus were back in charge. It was really too tedious, all this moving around and there would be even more when Georgy came out this spring – and then Harriet. It was satisfactory to have such excellent servants: *Mrs*

Gibson and *Mrs* Copus were married to the castle, she supposed.

She noticed in Chapel on Christmas Day that George and Lizzie sat together and that Lizzie looked as though she had been crying. After all, she was only five: her remarkable speech always made one think she was older. She mentioned it to George after dinner.

'Is something amiss with Liz? She looked very "down" this morning, I thought.'

George took his time replying. 'It is her maid, Mama – Lizzie is *so* fond of her and I'm afraid she's leaving.'

'Can we not persuade her to stay?'

A pause. 'I'm afraid not, Mama. Mrs Copus has told Lizzie that Anne – the girl – is needed at home.'

'Oh what a pity. I remember her – such a pretty gel. Lizzie does get so fond of people. In summer she was missing her – do you recall?'

'Yes, Mama. I expect *she* will miss *Lizzie*, too.'

Next day at dinner, Lady Georgiana's brother the Duke, who had just arrived, was holding the guests in rapt attention. He was a witty raconteur and bon viveur but at bottom a serious-minded man who, they said, had never recovered from the death of the King's daughter Princess Charlotte, though he kept a string of mistresses. Harriet, who had been allowed at grown-up dinner for the first time, had been recounting her conversation with Grand in the Gallery.

'If we all did as he advised,' she said gaily, 'we should remain celibate – and then there'd be an end to the world!'

'I'm sure Grand wasn't speaking seriously!' said Lady Georgiana.

'Ah,' said the Duke, stroking his chin. 'What did the great Bacon say?' ('The great Bacon,' tittered the ladies.)

'The noblest works and foundations have proceeded from childless men, which have sought to express the images of their minds where those of their bodies have failed . . .'

'But that isn't the same as being unmarried, is it?' trilled the Marchioness of Lansdowne. 'Many men are married and childless and many unmarried men have children!'

'La, la,' reproved a young spark, sent up north to gaze at Georgy.

George suddenly left the table, muttering an excuse.

'Is he not well?' asked Caro. 'I thought he was looking a little seedy this afternoon.'

The conversation turned to the card games they would play after dinner.

'Perhaps George is in love?' suggested the irrepressible Harriet to her mother over a game of chess which they both played rather well.

'Oh – I expect George will always take life too seriously,' answered his mother. 'Look at how fond he is of the little ones.'

'And they of him, Mama!'

George excused himself from some of the festivities during the next few days: he had much studying to do, he said.

'It is not fun without you,' pouted Harriet.

'George is such an *honourable* man,' sighed his other sister Georgy. 'I wonder whom *he* will marry. A good thing men don't have to "come out" at seventeen! He was such a dear old serious face then.'

'Still is,' said Caro.

Lizzie was inconsolable. Her Nanna was going. Why couldn't she stay – or take Lizzie with her? Anne kissed the child and said she would think of her often and Mrs Copus would find a nice new girl to do Lizzie's hair. But she was as sad as the little girl. Never had she realized quite how much she loved the children, but particularly Lizzie whose hair ribbon had perhaps saved her life. In a week, provided she had heard from the Rector, she would be back in Stockton and would then go on to Alne to Hannah's place. They might need another servant and might take her on till July. She calculated the baby should be born somewhere around the middle or end of July, helped by Delia who made discreet enquiries about the date of the beginning of Mr George's Oxford term last autumn, and worked back from there.

Anne kept up the fiction that she was needed at home to all the servants but Delia. Even to Curly.

'Promise me you'll talk to Miss Lizzie about me – don't let her forget me, Curly!'

'It's a shame, that's what it is,' said Dorothy. 'Why can't your Mam have your sister home instead of you?'

'Oh, it's Hannah's turn to be away,' replied Anne evasively.

'Perhaps you'll come back?' Ellen suggested.

Anne knew she would never see them again, unless perhaps one of them came on a visit. She could swear them to secrecy if they did come over to Stockton.

'Curly – come and see me next summer!' she said.

'Oh, I'd love to – if they can spare me. Why it seems like yesterday when you came.'

'Two years – more,' said Delia. 'Seems a long time to me.'

It was strange. Anne was sad but she was no longer tormented, except on George's account. The words she had found to say to Hardow amazed her! That she had dared to say them amazed her even more.

'I s'll look forward, Delia. What's the use of looking back?'

'Aye – when you hold the bairn in your arms and if he has the look of Master George – that'll be a happy day for you, love.'

'I do pray so that it will be George's, Delia. But it's the one thing left to bring me down – that he should look like Viscount Hardow. But I say to myself – even if the bairn is Hardow's, he's still my George's little brother – or sister!'

The New Year's Day and Epiphany service was over. George had not attended the Chapel and neither had Anne. The day for her departure grew near and still she had not glimpsed her lover since the day in the snow.

'I'm afraid he might be ill, Deely – how would I know?'

'He'll be downhearted – that's all,' replied Delia. 'He'll have a way of finding out when you go, don't worry.'

'Oh – I must say goodbye – but it will only cast me down again. I've got to bear up for the baby!'

Anne had had a letter from Mrs Hart, a kind letter. The family in the village were expecting her on January the 7th. Anne had said she was leaving for a special reason and would tell Mam later. They would have guessed – pregnancy was the only reason girls forsook work in castles! She felt she couldn't have explained in a letter. Hannah again was mentioned – and her work with the Rector of Alne. Anne felt she was lucky to go straight from one post to another. But she must have a few days with Mam first and worked out how much money she might give her without Dad's knowledge. The beer-house had had quite enough of his money when he was living at home.

Lizzie continued to be the worst hit.

'Hush, Miss Lizzie – you were away from Nanna a long time in the summer, and at Chatsworth. You didn't miss Nanna then.'

'I did, I did – and I knew I was coming back and she'd be *here*. And now, she won't be here. Nanna, Nanna, don't go!' Lizzie was so fierce in her grief that she wore Anne down. She took the child on her knee.

'Look Miss Lizzie – listen to Nanna. One day when you are a big girl, you will ask your brother, your kind brother George, to take you on a visit to Nanna. It is a secret between you and me. Don't forget – when you are a big girl – if you haven't forgotten me, Mr George will tell you how to find me. But you mustn't tell *anybody* – except Delia.' It was a strategy of desperation. Anne said to Delia: 'I didn't promise, but I hope one day he'll bring her – if ever they could slip away. Warn her to say nothing to anyone else. It'll keep her going!'

Lizzie came up again then and asked what Anne would like for a present.

'Could I have your blue hair-ribbon that you lost last year and that I found for you?'

Lizzie went to her chest of drawers and found it. 'I've drawn a picture for you,' she said. 'It's my brother George in a big coat – would you like it?'

Anne drew the child to her, her heart full to overflowing, kissed her and took the drawing, a strange pencil sketch of a man standing by a tree. 'Bless you, my little Lizzie,' she said and took the child on her lap. Thank God this could not go on for long – she began to long for the day of her departure.

It came and it was a sparkling frosty afternoon. Her small possessions packed and farewells said in the Servants' Hall, a little walk in the morning with Curly, an awkward silence between them, no last look at the Temple, the lake frozen over – it all passed quickly enough.

'He'll come – he's been in bed,' said Delia briefly after early servants' dinner. 'John told me to tell you – he'll be in the stable courtyard.'

'Oh – he's ill! And I didn't know. Oh, Delia, he mustn't go out!'

'He'll be there,' repeated Delia.

It was two o'clock; the children had said goodbye. No sign of Mrs Copus till Delia said: 'Mrs C asked me to say she's been pleased with your work and she's sorry you're off – but it's for the best.'

'How much does she know, Delia?'

'Mrs C usually knows everything, Anne. Look – here's Master William. We thought you'd forgotten! Anne's off today. Say goodbye, Master William.'

William stood quietly looking at her. He had grown in the past year and his arms shot out of his sleeves. Soon he would be a youth, not a child. Suddenly in his strange flat voice he said 'William loves Nanna', and continued to stare at her. Then Lizzie began to cry piteously.

'Best get it over,' muttered Delia. 'Don't forget us – we won't come down – the old coach'll take you to the diligence from Malton.'

'Oh Delia – thank you Delia – for everything. Please take this – no *do* – in remembrance.' She pressed five shillings of her earnings into Delia's hands. 'And say goodbye again to Curly – and if either of you are near Stockton – or Alne – even if it's years and years – come and see me.' She was determined not to break down but stooped and kissed Lizzie again.

'Goodbye,' said Blanche politely and returned to *Mangall's Questions*.

'Bless you, Miss Lizzie – and be a good lad, Master William. Now I'm off.' Without a backward glance, head held high, the lump in her throat almost past bearing, she was out of the room and down the stairs and trudging across the vast courtyard and round by the West Wing to the Stable Courtyard. At the turning she waved and then took up again her bundle and her basket and her box.

But what was this? Surely the carriage was not going without her? No, a post-chaise suddenly swerved round from the stables in the direction of the North Road and Anne saw, lying back on the seat, a box at her feet, the figure of Selina Sharpe. That lady did not look in her direction but stared fixedly in front of her. As the chaise slowed down at the outer gate a man jumped off his horse and tried to stop it from going on. The post-chaise driver took no notice and Selina was swept away.

But Anne had no time for mysteries. The coach was waiting, she thought. She looked round in case George were waiting but there was no one. Only the coachman, and she was the only passenger.

'Best get in, luv,' he said. 'I have my orders.'

There was nothing else for it so Anne got in and her possessions were put on the seat. He must still be poorly, she thought. I should have gone to see. I was too frightened of seeing Hardow again. Oh George, where are you?

With a 'gee up', the coach started off. She would never see him again. She leaned out of the window and shouted: 'Please – please stop – I've forgotten something – I must go back'. . .'

'My orders are to stop at the lime avenue,' he shouted back.

'At the lime avenue?' This was outside the inner gate along the outer boundary road beyond the obelisk.

She saw the high mock-fortified walls rattle past with a sight of the dome above them and then the coach went a little way up the tree-lined avenue and came to a sudden stop. 'You can wait here – but not long, mind. I'm to be at the crossroads at four, come rain, come shine.'

She looked out of the window and a figure detached itself from the wall and stumbled towards the coach. She opened the door and George flung himself into her arms. He clung to her as though she were his last hope of salvation.

'George – your face is all hot. What ails you, my darling?'

'I was in bed – I couldn't let you know – I had a bit of a fever – Edward had it too, don't worry. I had John bribe the coachman. I couldn't let you go without another word. I'll write to you where you said – the Rector of Stockton – and then to your sister's employer in Alne. Oh Anne, Anne, take me with you – no I'm not mad . . . Why can't I take you away? As soon as I am well again, let me come to see you . . . I'll write every week, and get my valet to bring my letters to you.'

'George,' said Anne quietly, 'I can't bear to leave you when you've got a fever. It makes it *all* worse – leaving you and Lizzie – and the baby – and your father and all . . . but I think it wouldn't be right for me to see you until the bairn's born.'

'But why, Anne?'

'I just think I shall know whose it is then – when it's born – and then you can come and I can give your father his money back and . . .'

'And we can marry – but you know I'll marry you when I'm twenty-one whoever is the father of your child.'

'Yes, I know, love, but I think it's better this way. I'm not far away, love, and I'll write if I get the chance. In a week I'll be with

Hannah — and will stay till — till, the baby . . .' The numbness she had been feeling for the past week or two suddenly changed into a blinding wordless misery. Now *she* clung to him. 'Tell me you love me, say it again,' she whispered. For answer he pressed his hot forehead against her hand.

'Oh yes, oh yes — oh — for ever Anna Rosa — and I shall come to you when our child is in the world. And I shan't leave you, not ever — no. You know, I told father — I'll never marry if I can't have Anne . . .' His eyes were glittering.

'George, you must go back. You mustn't fall ill — I shan't be able to bear that and me not knowing . . . don't take on, George — keep calm — as I will, I swear. You are more to me than my own life — and I'll keep faith. You write to me — and you will be told when the baby comes — Mrs Hart will help me I'm sure — and, George, look after Lizzie, she's been like my own child.'

She thought he was rambling for he was muttering and indeed looked delirious.

'Go straight back and get your valet to make you a hot caudle — I've told Delia to keep an eye on you,' she said with a mighty effort at a smile. 'I feel it's right, George love,' she went on as he continued to groan. She sat with her arms around him. 'I just feel that it will all be all right when I've got the bairn — I shall know then, I know I shall. And you just go and get rid of that fever and tell me when you're better and I'll go home.' She was desperately trying to comfort him. But he must not seek her out before the summer, must get on with his life. 'Promise me you'll send for me to come as soon as you're delivered and I promise to come — and I'll write to you every day if I can.' 'You'll make me sad if you don't do your studies, love — I don't want anything to change because of me.' She was distressed, but more upset that he seemed so wild and uncontrolled. 'I shall know then,' she kept on saying, 'and then I'll do whatever you want. It might be under false pretences if you saw me before — I don't want you to quarrel with your dad — promise me, George.' Anne felt obscurely that she must suffer for her love. George raised his head 'Nun scio quid sit amor,' he whispered. 'But don't leave me, don't go!' 'Hush, I have to go.' 'You are going to your own,' he said slowly and wondered why he had said it. 'George — don't keep your hurt green you know — with your dad — he didn't know — try and forget — it's better that way.'

'You ready, luv?' The coachman poked his head in. They

slowly untwined themselves. The moment had come and Anne could have wished George was in better health and spirits.

'Go now, sweetheart. I'll be all right. Don't fret.'

He nodded, brushed tears away from his eyes with his sleeve.

'Promise – go to bed, keep warm – I'll be right worried if you don't.'

'I promise – and I'll love you for ever,' he said in a broken voice before slowly and reluctantly backing out of the carriage.

'Farewell,' she said.

'Oh, don't say that! Remember, remember, Annie – the happiest days of my life. Forgive me – I'm too upset to think straight.' For his sake Anne kept the tears back and kissed him again and then with a crack of the whip the coach and two horses moved away and George watched it dwindle on the road and then fade away quite, and Anne, looking out of the window in the cold afternoon, saw the figure of George dwindle too until the coach turned on the road to York. Then blind misery overtook her. I can't bear it . . . I can't bear it. The agony of parting swelled and swelled in her. And there was no relief. There never would be, unless one day they could be together again. But, the baby? Please God, please God, let it be George's. Oh, let it be George's.

The thought of the baby just enabled her to keep going and put an end to her sobbing so that when she finally arrived in poor familiar old Stockton she held her head high and did not break down.

George was put to bed and became delirious. When he recovered a little he kept asking for light. 'Where is the light?' he said to his valet and to the doctor. 'They have taken the light away. It's all dark. Why is it all dark?' Hardow never entered his chamber.

After a week his fever left him and he staggered out of bed, managed to keep going for ten days, was taken ill again when acting charades with Harriet and Caro, put to bed and bled. They said it was 'brain fever,' brought on by too much study. For two months he kept to his room but by April was well enough to go on a short holiday with Mama. Back in Oxford in May and June he rallied but was still not himself when he went to London in mid July for the coronation of George IV. He had managed to write to Anne as soon as he could frame a coherent sentence and his valet had delivered his letters.

'George was always too sensitive – this absurd chimera he entertained when he was delirious, that he had seduced a 'maiden' – always raving about love. He's far too refined for such matters. I think his imagination has worked on him from too much reading, don't you agree, Hardow?' said Lady Georgiana to her husband. But Hardow was buried in his new book and seemed not to hear her.

The Castle
March 21st 1821

My beloved Anne –
I was ill, and could not write. I hope you got the message I sent by John two weeks ago. They say I had fever on the brain but I know better. In truth I think I am pursued by some fatal shadow – not yours my darling. I think it is receding now and in a few weeks I shall be stronger. Write to me here or in Oxford after the end of April.
   Ever your own GH.

Aprill 1821 Alne Rectory

My dearest George,
I have little time to write but I send you all my love dearest. I am so worried about you. Do not worry about *me* – I shall be all wright. Do not tire yourself and try to get stronger. I am well and the work is not too heavy. It is a pretty place. I think on you every night before I sleep,
   Your own loving Anne.

Christ Church, Oxford
May 31st 1821

My darling,
I am truly much improved but am plagued from time to time with a dizziness and a slight fever if I do over much. I am going for a short while to Uncle Duke's at the end of term. Then I have to attend the Coronation with the Family but I shall return speedily to the Castle in July and await your letter

which I hope will be from Stockton. You must not work to the end of your time. I am impatient for news of you and think of you every hour. The world is cruel. You are an angel.

> God bless you,
>> Your,
>>> George.

Dearest George – I do not like to write when I am low as I was last week when I did not hear from you and was thinking you were dead. But now I have your letter that Mr Thorne brought and my sperrits have perked up. I was tormented by your fever more than I was about the baby and leaving you all. Sometimes though I cry over leaving little Lizzie. Please George send her my love and tell her it is a secret and she is not to forget me. Do not wurry about me my darling I am alright. Just wait it is all we can do. I have a good post and am very lucky and in the evening Hannah sits with me by the stream at the bottom of the garden and we dip our feet in the watter and I tell her about you. I hope you do not mind, I think of you all-ways. Write to tell me you are quite well now. I love you. Your Anne.

I shall go home in two weeks and will write to you from there and send it to the Castle.

SEVEN

THE CORONATION
July 1821

God save our gracious king!
Long live our noble king!
God save the king!
                    Henry Carey

All night the preparations for the most splendid coronation in English history had been under way, the culmination of months of planning. The King had produced the ideas, down to the tiniest detail of his peers' costume.

Most peers, heroes, and statesmen never got to bed at all the night before and if they did it was to rise again before dawn and make their way in their creaking coaches to Westminster Hall. The bells of St Margaret's pealed out every half an hour after midnight and all noblemen and their wives and families had to be ready in Westminster Hall by seven o'clock. They had mostly arrived hours before to the distant sound of guns firing, the nearer tramp of soldiers and the squeaky clatter of thousands of carriages on the cobblestones. The crowds were already immense and there were barriers across Parliament Street. Cockspur Street and Pall Mall were seething with the mob, out to see if the discredited Queen Caroline would arrive. In Westminster Hall distracted officials were darting hither and thither and they would have been even more distracted if they had known that Queen Caroline was to leave her house at a quarter past five in the morning with a following mob. In the Abbey all was for the moment quiet but soon the choir would be in to rehearse their Hallelujah Chorus (demanded by the King) and their anthems and responses.

Outside Westminster Hall a platform had been set up, linking the Hall with the north door of Westminster Abbey, and across which the King and the peerage and knights and other notables were to parade at the least inconvenience to themselves and with maximum visibility. Their velvet and satin would appear for a moment on a stage as though they were actors, which indeed they were. Everything by five o'clock was sparkling in the morning sun, and indoors coffee was being served to the peers who had arrived. It had not made their lordships any cooler. Outside was more pleasant. Three great 'pavilions' had been erected near enough for those who could pay to see the elevated noblemen and their King as they passed into and out of the Abbey. Seven thousand people had been allowed for, but they were as yet half empty since the soberer and richer citizens of London had feared there would be trouble if the Queen arrived and tried to join her husband at the Abbey service. Also the seats were not cheap.

At first peers could be seen arriving in twos and threes at

Westminster Hall from their town residences. Then they began to arrive in greater numbers, accompanied by their servants in livery, basking in a moment of glory before their masters passed inside. Most of the latter were already wearing their dark red velvet imitation Tudor surcoats over their crimson robes and ermine capes, with the exact number of spots according to rank. Their legs emerged under all this in white hose slashed with gold. Those privy councillors who were not peers were in white and blue satin and fancy hose. Their ladies, who would follow them, would of course be in court dress, their hair dressed high and topped by waving ostrich plumes.

Hardow and his father had arrived early. George was with them, looking pale and tired, a slight figure in a dark velvet suit befitting the eldest grandson of an Earl. Occasionally he would reply politely to his grandfather, who at seventy-three was not the oldest of the ancient noblemen and not the most bowed or feeble. Many of the old peers looked weak as well as venerable. At four o'clock the doors of the Hall had been opened by the doorkeepers who were on this day famed pugilists ready to bounce out those who should not be there. They seemed to have dosed themselves liberally with spirits throughout the night in anticipation of the day's doings. As the rising sun flooded the long windows the galleries were beginning to fill. Hardow strolled in with Grand on his arm and was soon joined by his noble friends with whom he chatted casually, keeping an eye out for the arrival of his lady wife and two eldest daughters. Harriet, to her great chagrin, was not yet old enough to attend. She had tried to bribe her sister Georgy to let her go instead of her but Georgy was scandalized and would not hear of it.

'I am taller than you and look older than you,' said Harriet. Georgy and Caro had promised to give her a full description on their return to Grosvenor Place and Mama had offered to let her try on the peeresses' robes that evening in private.

'*I* shall be a Mistress of Robes one day,' said Harriet to Caro. 'Would you like a wager on it?'

'I don't doubt that, my dear,' Caro had replied with unusual tactness. 'But today is Mama's day and we are just allowed on sufferance.'

The Whigs were providing the King's pages too and Grand was now grumbling that Ned should have been chosen since he was now twelve years old and a fine handsome boy. But Lady

Conyngham, the King's present favourite, had been entrusted with the choice and she had no special love for Lady Hardow and her children. Little Child Villiers and gangling Russell had been her choice.

Outside, the crowd had become denser and from within the Hall a great hubbub could be heard even over the noise of hearty greetings, and arguments over the seating arrangements.

'What is it?' murmured a cousin to Hardow.

'The Queen, I expect,' that nobleman replied.

''Tis only a rumour,' said another.

George, standing by his grandfather, could not help hoping the rumour was true. If Queen Caroline were below it might make the King a little more humble. He did not wish the King's great day to be spoiled, but surely something from his past must just gently remind him of all that had led to this day? After all, she was the mother of his dear dead daughter.

'Yes,' said Granville, coming up. 'It is the coarse Caroline.'

'Not with Brougham, I hope?' said Grand.

'That is not likely, Fountaynes,' replied Granville. 'Brougham knows when to cast his net and when to take it up. She's down in Dean's Yard with one or two of her party.'

'Brougham knows nothing of it, I'm sure,' said Hardow, blowing an imaginary speck of dust from his wristband. Arrayed in his red velvet he looked a noble figure, with his long nose and deep-set eyes, his hair just beginning to show iron grey at the cheek and forehead.

George was thinking it was all a mummery and wondered if his father thought so too. But anything to preserve the *convenances*. The Queen had not won her case but neither had the King; it was an example of hypocrisy they called compromise. There was no possibility the Queen would be allowed in, and they all knew it.

Grand turned to George. The fellow studied too much, looked tired. 'Sixty years,' he said as he had said many times already this morning, to anyone who would listen. 'I was a lad of thirteen last time – hrrmph – thought I should see through a few coronations, but this is the only one and I shan't see another.'

Just then Granville's cousin arrived, greatly excited. Knots of noblemen were at all the doors now pushing out for news. The family stayed in their seats in the Chamberlain's box between the doors and the throne.

'Refused at all doors of the Abbey they say.' He laughed. 'Poor thing. She was applauded by the pavilions, in a mild sort of way, I gather – handkerchiefs waving and all – but no end of huzzaing from the mob.'

'Could be trouble there,' interjected Grand.

'The handkerchief waving was to no avail, I gather?' said Hardow.

'No – she'll have gone back by Whitehall,' replied Granville. 'The mob will please her there. But there's nothing to it – she's failed – hadn't got a ticket.' He laughed and there were smiles on all the gentlemen's faces but they looked a little uneasy, George thought.

'Wouldn't agree she *needed* a ticket,' said Lord Gower coming up. 'Said she was the Queen.' Which she is – in name, thought George.

'Am I to gather,' said Grand, 'that the lady has been tramping up and down outside in all this mêlée, getting herself refused?'

'Indeed,' said Granville. 'But you will soon see she will not have damaged the coronation.'

'No – she's made history,' said George suddenly.

His father looked at him but said nothing. 'Where is *He*?' asked Grand. It was now after seven.

'I am more worried as to the whereabouts of my dear wife,' said Hardow.

Prince Leopold could be seen in the royal doorway looking grave.

'York is very affected too, poor fellow,' said Granville.

'We are all affected,' replied Gower.

'When will He arrive?' asked Grand again.

'In His own good time, Papa,' replied Hardow.

'Damn lucky if anyone can get through now,' said another Fountaynes cousin. The family and their in-laws had now drawn together as families do on great occasions. Indeed the whole Hall was full of families, mostly known to each other for several generations.

Lady Georgiana and the girls finally got through at some cost to Caro's hair which Curly had spent two hours dressing that morning. The tension was mounting.

And at a time only a little later than promised, when they were all longing for another cup of coffee, He, The King, arrived.

From near the platform prepared for His Majesty at the Abbey end of the Hall, Norry, King of Arms, and Lord Willoughby were still giving directions, the latter waving his Great Chamberlain's wand to and fro. George thought he looked like the magician in a pantomime. All the officials were beside themselves with their caps half falling off their heads as they tried to circulate the orders for the placement in the procession to the Abbey.

As usual in these affairs there had been many false alarms and all eyes were on the empty throne. But the space round the throne suddenly seemed to be the empty heart of a whirlpool. A few nobles near it rose with their heads turned towards the door. Several others near the throne stepped back. There was a pause. Was it another alarm? Talk had begun again but more muted this time and the Earl Marshal was again seen pointing his arms in all directions. A few courtiers hurried up from nowhere, a few more turned on the balls of their feet; one or two better apprised disappeared through the door. Then suddenly a hush fell – the royal dukes and three or four favoured friends appeared from behind the great throne walking backwards. Dead silence now. Then they all parted to reveal a dazzling white-satin diamond-gleaming feather-waving object, the person of His Majesty, attended by his household and the great officers of state. He lowered his immense bulk on to the throne with the grace of long practice, despite his weight, and the whole room rose to greet him with the susurration of silk sliding against silk and the faintest sound of plumes. There were universal cheers and the trumpets sounded from the back of the Hall. A great sunbeam seemed to open out over all the chamber and the feathered heads of the ladies waved atop the sea of faces. Rank upon rank, orderly now in appearance, with their heat and thirst forgotten, they watched the King as he rose once more to greet them, to bow towards the nearest line of ladies and towards the foreign ambassadors in a posse together. He was smiling like a bird of paradise, arrayed in cloth of gold, red velvet over the white, all scarlet and white like blood and snow, and encrusted with diamond upon diamond.

'By Gad!' murmured Grand. But they were all equally affected. It seemed that they had lost their individuality, were become a mass of adulation and that the uppermost feeling in all hearts, personal lives for a moment forgotten, was of adoration for the strange glorious figure seated before them.

The ceremonies took place – presentations, arrangements for the great procession which was to wind over to the Abbey where their feelings would be sanctified. George was thinking with that critical part of his mind which would not let go that here were gathered the two thousand members of society who counted in the realm. If an act of God had made a thunderbolt to fall upon that edifice, the whole social system of the realm would have collapsed. He hid himself behind his family and there was sadness in his heart. The music began again and finally the long line of nobility slowly began to move in strictest order of rank, but Whig with Whig, Tory with Tory. The Queen was forgotten. This was the day of the King and his supporters of all parties, those who existed in sure and certain hope of having found favour, and determined to keep it. On their backs was poured the wealth of the shires, backs now resplendent in that medieval costume whose very pattern the King with his exquisite taste had ordered. Trumpets sounded again and the King's herb woman and her maidens, lissom young women in white, entered the doors strewing their blossoms like nymphs, slowly, with the gestures found on Grecian urns. They came and went against the dark Gothic arches and then the peeresses passed through their special door, all arrayed too in their crimson velvet, and moving capillary-like out towards the open-air platform on their way to the Abbey.

Nothing could now stop every person remaining in the Hall from following his neighbour as the whole great assembly made its way slowly out to the sanctification and enthronement. In front of the King the three bishops carried the paten and the chalice and the Holy Bible and in front of them were the great officers of state carrying the orb and sceptre and the great sword of state. The long, brilliant procession glided out like a snake over the blue carpet of the covered walk. When those in the outside viewing galleries (named the Royal George and the Ladies' Fancy) saw the King approach under a canopy of cloth of gold borne by the barons of the Cinque Ports, they were for a moment silent, overcome by the beauty of the whole. It was not the King alone they felt they venerated, but the crown of England in a cameo of history motionless for a moment. But the Monarch in his black Spanish hat with its spreading plume of white ostrich feathers surmounted by a heron's plume and revealing a long curled wig both behind and curling over his forehead, brought them back to the earthly representative of God's people and they cheered then, and cheered the nine yards train of crimson velvet embroidered with golden stars. George the Fourth, by the grace of God the Christian King of England, George of all the graces, ruling not by divine right but by the acceptation of his lords. Even George Hardow felt it in the dusty glare of that hot July morning as he entered the Abbey behind his father and grandfather and heard the loud cheers from outside from the thousands of ordinary people who had no good view but had glimpsed the procession pass like a coloured jewel hanging against the blue of the summer sky. The hurrahs and huzzahs were like the distant sound of rolling breakers. Then the light of the sun was clamped out as all the heavy doors shut and George half wished he were outside again with common people, away from the ceremonies of which he, by reason of his birth, was a part.

The confusion in his head from early rising and the din and the crowds and the sun and the emotional sight of the King gave way to an inner darkness for his illness still lingered on. It alternated between making him lethargic and heightening his emotions. Not one night had passed since the winter without his waking untimely and yearning for Anne, Anne who would not call for him until her baby was born. He had kept his feelings to himself in the daytime by distancing himself from himself but they were liable to break out in bodily weakness and fatigue when tears would suddenly prick his eyes. When he entered the Abbey he was thinking of her. He had thought it would be an oasis of calm where he could forget the world and the events of the day, but he felt the very roof press down on him. Here in the very bastion of the church and national glory, there was no escape from himself, and he felt himself small and of no account, only a receptacle for feelings for his beloved. Had that very monarch now entering his own abbey felt such things, in a life devoted to the fair sex in one way or other?

At first he was aware only of glimmers and scents, both of which were making him feel dizzy as he came into the darkness from the dazzle of the sun. They had found their pews and George clutched the carved curve of the wooden stall before him, his knuckles taut and fingers trembling. By degrees he began to feel better and looked round the dark cave of the Abbey which was yet lit at present in great corona-like clusters of candelabra which smoked and flared. So it must have looked and smelt in the days of the Catholic monarchs, strange candlelight in contrast to God's own light outside. Drifts of scents – of burning wax, pomade, violets, camphor and the sweat of ermine – seemed almost tangible. The great company still arriving in all the muted dazzle of their gold and diamonds, their sapphires, rubies and emeralds served only to make George feel more isolated. One day it was intended that he too should wear the garter star which Grand now wore. He could not believe it. 'Yet I am one of them,' he thought and then wondered if he had said it out aloud. Grandson of a peer of the realm, one of the two thousand, the privileged, who were now rising on the appearance of the Archbishop as on a tidal wave. When the King appeared again he thought they would all lean towards him like lemmings. And he did appear, grotesque yet somehow marvellous in his beautiful robes and bearing the marks of all the sixty years of his misspent life, he who had been Prinny and a friend of Grandmama's, and his sister Georgy's own godfather. He saw Georgy over the aisle with the ladies, looking in great beauty. Even Mama looked happy today. If anything went wrong she was not responsible. She could sit and enjoy herself, not tortured that the arrangements were somehow her own responsibility.

As the Archbishop entered from the choir, the nave and all the transepts stood still in attitudes of trance before recollecting themselves and beginning the ceremonial which was to last over four hours, homages, crowning, anthems, and all. For a moment George wondered if he could perhaps float away. When he was a little boy he had been sure he could rise from the ground as a matter of will. Mama had been quite worried about him. Now he wished he could levitate out through the door, which would open at his magic touch; float far away over London, over the lanes and roads of the realm, past the valleys and parks and fields heavy with harvest, over the cottages and the great houses, over the hills and far away north, ever more north, towards the magnet of his love. His love, his Anne, who would never be allowed at a coronation unless she were behind the scenes washing the feet of the worshippers. She would have been more beautiful than any of those flower girls, he thought, and suddenly saw her amongst the roses and held on to his pew as the anthem began to peal and the great orchestra and choir began with a sound like trumpets.

As he could not float away he first of all tried to follow the ceremony closely. That would at least please his mother if he were later able to converse upon it intelligently. But in spite of the magnificent view afforded to him from the peers' special seats he still found it hard to concentrate and to enter into the spirit of the occasion except to regard it as a spectacle like a theatrical performance. The King, having been presented to and recognized by the people, or rather the gathered nobility, prayers introduced the religious part of the affair. George found himself praying not for the King who seemed now to rise like some wreck from the deeps encrusted with barnacle diamonds and robes of seaweed, not for this pendulous old man, but for himself who had been called by his name.

He swallowed and tried to take a hold of himself. As the first responses were made he found he was praying for Anne. The sound around him of the murmuring multitude was like the sound of a swarm of wild bees. The congregation was once more seated and he opened his eyes and saw his mother, in front with the peeresses, look up for a moment, and glimpsed his aunt sitting with her husband as befitted an ex-ambassador. He averted his eyes from Grand and Hardow and looked again at his sisters whom he could now just see at the back with daughters and viscounts' wives. Poor Caro – still without a husband. But perhaps that was a mercy. He shut his eyes again and straight away he was with Anne again. As soon as the child was born he was to go to her. He had told his parents he had work to do and could not stay for the balls of the coming weeks; pleading tiredness. 'O Lord', he prayed, 'may our long night of pain soon be over. May you give me the strength to go to her and stay with her if she will have me.' Better a life with his father's bastard and a marriage next year when he came of age than the torment and misery he had suffered. He had thought he would go out of his mind. He thought of the Queen who had lately tried to enter these sacred precincts. Vulgar as she was, the people had pitied her. How much more should an abandoned virtuous woman be pitied! No more should Anne's scruples and his own weakness and illness come between his love and himself; no more must she expiate an imagined guilt. Her mystic feeling that once the child were born and she beheld it she would know its father was one he understood. But 'O God,' he prayed, 'let her feel it is mine whether that be the truth or no.' For if not there was nothing for him in the world. No power, no glory, no riches, no ceremony could make up for that . . . He opened his eyes again and saw the Monarch looking steadily ahead and his favourite Lady Conyngham placed some paces away looking fixedly at him with her white globe face. Poor man, he is lonely too, he thought. But *quelle farce*, he went on to think as the Archbishop intoned. The Christian Monarch had left outside the Abbey doors all the dross of his former attachments, a King without a Queen. 'And I am a man without a woman,' he said to himself and suddenly had the involuntary vision of the back of Anne's upper arm, faintly speckled like a brown eggshell, and saw the blue of her eyes with their gold-encircled pupil.

He sought once again for the words as he tried to pray for her in the moment of her travail and for that unborn child whom rank and ceremony prevented his recognizing as his own. The same rank and ceremony as perpetuated this noble farce. 'Dear God let me see her soon. I promise you that my soul will never be parted from hers, for I pledge myself to her. Forgive me Father; forgive me.'

He saw Hardow sitting glancing vaguely up at the timbers. Not a word other than the formal or trivial had passed between them since that fateful winter day. Yet he would have wished to forgive him, except that Hardow saw no necessity for foregiveness.

As the choir began to intone another response before the sermon, George seemed to hear other music in his head in counterpoint to it; those lyrics which the King's favourite musician had composed, those songs which he had so passionately murmured to Anne. He heard them now all jumbled up – 'believe me if all those endearing young charms which I gaze on so fondly to-day . . . dear ruin . . . friends of my youth . . . some banquet hall deserted . . . the last rose of summer . . . the sorrow of love which lasts for ever . . . tell me our love is remember'd . . .' This monarch had loved those songs too. Perhaps it was not his fault that his loves had not lasted. But mine will last, however many summers will pass – all my life, he thought, all my life I shall remember and raised his head again and saw the Archbishop entering the pulpit to speak.

And O Heavens he was speaking of encouraging morality and religion – of the depravity of morals (George stole another glance at Hardow who had his eyes shut), of the dignity of virtue

(Lady Georgiana was smiling, her eyes bright) and George IV was admonished to rule in the fear of God.

When would it be over? The oath was now to be administered. After almost four hours in the Abbey, George saw his namesake anointed with holy oil, his spurs presented to him and returned and offered up to God, the sword of state placed by the King's own hand on the altar.

The great state robes were now put on; the orb, the ring and the sceptre and the rod were given him too—and then the final climax of climaxes: the crown of England, made holy with the prayers of all Englishmen past and present, descended on the royal head. With a great shout that sent shivers down the back, the peers all put on their coronets and the ladies theirs too and George put on his own cap and muttered 'God Save the King' with them all. And again and again they cried 'God Save the King'. God Save the King.

Several ladies were weeping with emotion and there were still blessings to come, and then the *Te Deum* suddenly subdued them all. And George in the midst of it all still saw Anne and she had a crown on her head and he was worshipping her as these people were worshipping this new King. Yet even so he too felt the glory of the occasion; that they were somehow transported beyond themselves – and all hearts were one, all bent upon a single object, the power of history continuing the story of the race. The King kissed the lords spiritual and received the homage of his peers from the throne. Gold medallions were scattered in largesse, the choir sang again and the ceremony ended with a final solemn prayer.

As they slowly and finally processed back to Westminster Hall, the peers to attend the great banquet and their sons and daughters and wives to watch it from above if they had the strength, Lady Georgiana turned to Caro. 'George seems much affected,' she said. And she did not mean the King.

Stockton July 15 1821

Dearest George,
God bless you sweetheart. You will be better now. I am fine and it will not be long now I hope. Mrs Hart has been right kind to me but I shall have the bairn at home with Mam. I have hardly used the money but have paid Mam my wages from

Alne. She thinks the bairn is a boy for I am so big! I am feeling it is a bit of you my love. I shall ask Mr Hart to write to you if I cannot when I am abed. I pray for us both and for the little one. Send kisses to little Lizzie from me if she is not at your other place.

> Your own
> Anne T.

Hardow Castle
July 31st 1821

To Mr Hart, the Rector of Stockton,
Dear Mr Hart, Reverend Sir,
I have been waiting impatiently for news of your parishioner Anne Tesseyman from whom I received a letter on the 24th written on July 15th. I nearly rode over but felt it best to wait for news and not upset her before her lying-in. I beg news of her from you and if you should see her, would you convey to her my deepest feelings of respect and love? I hope you will forgive my writing to you dear Sir but I must speak plainly so that you as a gentleman of the cloth may witness that if it were within my power you would have married us in January. I shall wait for news of her from you or from Anne herself if she is recovered. Surely there is another little soul in the world now? Tell her I am now recovered from my illness.

Please convey to her, if you are able, my deepest and undying devotion – and forgive my writing to you.

> I am Reverend Sir
> most sincerely yours
> Geo. W. F. Hardow.

Stockton,
17th August, 1821

To The Honourable George Hardow,
at Fountaynes Castle
Honourable Sir,
Your letter of the 31st of this July was received by me on the 2nd August the very day Anne Tesseyman gave birth to a daughter whom I baptized Elizabeth at her request. I read her your letter the day after. The birth was not difficult, though late, but after a few days she took a fever and yesterday, August 8th, to our great distress, she died of an infection. Her

home is poor, as you know, and we think the well water was none too clean. My wife and I had offered her to lie-in at our home but she wished not to be a burden and chose to remain in her mother's cottage. Just before she died, being quite lucid and after receiving the Holy Sacrament, knowing you were waiting for news of her, she begged me to write to you. I was to say 'Tell George I love him. Tell him I have a little girl. We could all have been happy. If I am judged worthy of heaven I know I shall meet George there.' Shortly after this she expired in her mother's arms. I stayed to pray with her mother and sister.

I am aware that this letter will come as a great shock. I can say only that Anne did not suffer over much and the fever was most unexpected. The little girl has been taken by Anne's sister Hannah to be brought up by her in the family where she works. The Rector of Alne is a friend of mine.

I must tell you that the funeral is tomorrow – I delayed writing to you, for Anne wanted to answer your letter herself. By the time you receive this she will be buried. I thought it best to spare you the funeral dear Sir and I hope you will forgive me that.

I am aware of course of the tragic circumstances surrounding Anne's recent life and I hope this chapter will now be closed. Hannah Tesseyman was given Anne's money for the upkeep of the child and will, I am sure, be a loving and capable foster mother. The child seems healthy and strong and my wife has found a wet nurse in the village until she is established.

May I also send you my deepest condolences. Anne was for many years, though a servant, more like an older daughter to us at the Rectory and the loss to us in inestimable. May you and ourselves be enabled to bear it through the love of our Saviour and, in the words of our holy Prayer Book, let it please Our Lord to defend and provide for the fatherless children and all that are desolate and oppressed.

I regret that I am the bearer and writer of these sad news. Let us pray that our sins may be forgiven us.

> I am, Honourable Sir
> Yours faithfully
> James Hart

On the 8th day of August 1821 Queen Caroline had died of appendicitis.

On the 18th day of August of that year, Anne Tesseyman, single woman, was buried in Stockton churchyard.

There was no paper garland carried on her coffin, as for the burial of a maiden.

On the 21st day of August 1821 George Hardow was accompanied to Italy by his old tutor and stayed in Rome for a year.

In January 1823, Hardow and Lady Georgiana had their twelfth and last child, a daughter.

Miss Caro was asked for by a younger son, and on accepting him, the fate which has been implicit from the beginning of her woman's life was sealed. She went virgin to the altar with the man who had chosen her, a man she did not love and by whom she had eleven children. Her brother George often wondered whether she had had as little choice as Anne Tesseyman in the matter of her destiny.

EPILOGUE

Two Women
1848

The inseparable propriety of time, which is
ever more and more to disclose truth.
Bacon: *Advancement of Learning*

The little farmhouse stood back from the lane, wide fields behind and on every side. A little way down the same lane stood the church. In the farm porch a young woman was standing, a child in her arms and another at her skirts, watching a carriage wobble slowly towards the farm from the church end. There was nothing and no one else in sight.

Well, they would find her here as the Rector had told them. But what could they want? Whom would they send? She had nothing to be ashamed of, had done nothing wrong.

Not for the first time she put her hand up to her hair to tidy it and shifted the baby in its shawl. It was a winter afternoon and the men were all out in the fields. She looked behind her nervously at the little room with its range, all spotless, the settle by the window, the two oak chairs and the scrubbed table on which she had put her best tablecloth, the one crocheted by Aunt Hannah and left to her when she died three years before. If only she had a parlour.

Suddenly she decided to go back in to lay the baby, little Anne, in her cradle. 'Harry, go play in the yard,' she said, and smoothed her apron once again. She sat on the edge of one of the chairs and saw the carriage stop outside. Two ladies got down and then the carriage went on.

She waited for the knock, her heart thudding. What would they think of her little place which might be a palace to her but was only the small farm of a poor man and his wife? Never mind! She had thought of a moment like this ever since Hannah had told her the secret years ago, the terrible, thrilling secret which she was proud of, yet which frightened her. Oh if only her own mother had been there to tell her what to do! But Hannah had been the only mother she had ever known.

The knock came and she went slowly to the door and opened it. The ladies wore veils and there was fur on their mantles. She could see that one was middle-aged and the other a little older than herself.

'Will you please to come in, your, your – ladyships.' They followed her in quietly and she motioned them to sit. The older lady sat on the settle by the window, staring at her through her veil.

'Will you take tea, ma'am?'

'Please don't worry yourself, Mrs Clayton,' said the younger, taller lady. She seemed very ill at ease. She had probably never been in a cottage before.

'You are Elizabeth Clayton, the Rector tells me?'

'Yes – my lady.'

The tall lady seemed to decide to plunge. 'I am Lady Elizabeth and this is my personal maid, Mrs Currey. Please don't be nervous. You have done nothing wrong. You may have *some* idea why we have come?'

Elizabeth Clayton, who had been standing in the shadow as they settled themselves, came forward as the tall lady lifted up her veil and looked at her. The lady went on staring at her. Then suddenly: 'Oh God', she said, and clutched at her throat.

'What is it, ma'am? Are you ill?'

'No, no.' She went on gazing at her and tears slowly filled her eyes. She half rose up.

'Please sit down, ma'am. Please. What can I do?'

Slowly Lady Elizabeth sat, keeping her eyes on Elizabeth Clayton.

Then she spoke, slowly, carefully as though she had rehearsed something but something else had almost put it out of her mind.

'You must forgive me. I will tell you from whom I come and then you may understand. My brother became Seventh Earl of Fountaynes last month on the death of our father.'

'Yes, my lady. Your *father* was spoken of by my aunt.'

'But can you guess why I have come, why my brother has sent me to you?'

'No, ma'am, not really. You do not need to worry about me. All that was over long ago.'

'But it is not over. Nothing is ever over. My brother George sent me to you and now I see you I know what I came for.'

The other lady now stood up and came up to Elizabeth Clayton.

'*You* see, Mrs Currey? Oh God.' Lady Elizabeth was pale and trembling.

'But what *is* it, ma'am?' asked Elizabeth Clayton once more.

'It is – that – Mrs Currey – you see what I mean?'

Mrs Currey, who had a round smiling face and curly hair, put a hand on Elizabeth's cotton sleeve. 'Forgive us. Let us have the tea. And we must see your children ... What her ladyship is trying to say – and we could not know this before we came – is that you are the image of –'

'No, don't say it, Currey – let me say it,' interrupted Lady Elizabeth. Elizabeth Clayton went up to her: 'Please ma'am, – your ladyship – is it something very terrible?'

'My dear Mrs Clayton, you are the image of my mother when she was young!' said Lady Elizabeth. She went on: 'Oh, no – not terrible – a wonderful thing!'

Elizabeth Clayton, tall and fair and buxom, stood in her own parlour, just about to fetch the teapot, the words sinking into her brain and making a kind of sense she could not put words to.

'Oh, my lady,' she said, finally. 'Then we are not half-sisters?'

Mrs Currey, in her downright way, said: 'What her ladyship means . . .'

'No, let *me*,' said Lady Elizabeth quietly. 'I am sorry, Mrs Clayton. May I call you Elizabeth?'

'They call me Lizzie at home,' said the farmer's wife.

'That was *my* name. When your mother was my Nanna. Oh I do remember her so well! Though I was only a little girl when she left me.'

'I believe she called me after you, my lady!'

'How strange it all is. You ought to hate us – and yet I don't believe you do. If only your mother were alive. She could not have known that – ' she gathered her forces ' – that your father was not my father the Earl, but my *brother* – my dear George!'

Now it was out.

'*He* is an Earl too now, ma'am! My aunt told me that my father might have been the man who gave my mother the money, the one who became Earl of Fountaynes, but that my mother loved his son,' replied Elizabeth.

'Lizzie, now that we see you – and you must forgive us if we have stirred up old unhappiness – there is no doubt. My brother George – your *father*, Lizzie! – is very like his dear mother – not so fair of course – but *you* are even more like her. So you cannot be my *father*'s daughter. You must be George's daughter.'

It was beginning to make rational sense to Lizzie. All Aunt Hannah had told her when she was a little girl – not about her mother being seduced of course, not then, but that she had been loved by a wonderful young man, the Earl's son – was that she had been born in shame and that the money they had used to live on had been from his father Viscount Hardow who became an Earl . . . And that she must never, never mention the young man or the Earl to anyone. It had not been the young man's fault.

None of it had been his fault. The old Rector in Stockton had told her to be a good girl and thankful to her mother's sister Hannah for bringing her up.

'You must be my aunt then, my lady,' she said carefully.

Then a little boy suddenly toddled in from the back. 'This is my little Harry,' said Lizzie. 'And Anne is in the cradle.'

'Did you call her after your mother, then?' said Mrs Currey, making conversation.

'My mother Anne left me nothing but her name,' said Lizzie slowly. 'Aunt Hannah brought me up. She often said mother had called me Elizabeth after the little girl she looked after at the Castle. She was heartbroken to leave her.'

'And *I* was heartbroken when she went!' said Lady Elizabeth. She turned to Mrs Currey again. 'Oh, Maria, how like Lady Georgiana she is. I cannot believe it. If only things had been different. And they can never meet, can they?'

Lizzie Clayton had filled the kettle and put it on the hob.

'But – why did you come? You didn't know I was going to look like your ladyship's mother – you had no idea?'

'We never thought of it. We came on an errand – to ask forgiveness – from my brother George. You know that he – your father – is a great man – a scholar, a writer – and that he was for many years in Parliament? No, how could you know these things. How can we talk to you of him? Yet – it does not seem strange, does it? We are all children in the sight of God.'

Lizzie remained silent, thinking it over.

'But why did he send you? You know madam that I should never use any – any *knowledge* I have, against him. Our family have always remained loyal to your family. It was my mother's last wish – to forgive the past and make the best of the future. She was remorseful – oh, she was, Auntie Hannah told me – but she had nothing against you. She said "they were the happiest days of my life, Hannah" – that's what Aunt Hannah told me.'

'Your mother was a good woman,' said Mrs Maria Currey, alias Curly, speaking at last of her dear friend Anne Tesseyman.

'You knew her then?'

'Yes,' said Curly. 'She was my friend.'

They drank the tea; all had dry throats. The feelings stirred up in them all were almost palpable: the old friend Curly, little Lady Lizzie, now grown up, and Anne's daughter, herself now a mother.

'His lordship – my brother George – could not rest till he had found out if you were alive,' continued Lady Elizabeth. 'All these years *I* never knew anything about it till last year, when father was ill, George told me why he had never married – and never would marry. You see – he could never love anyone else. He blamed himself as well as his father but, being so young, there was nothing he could do. He tried to forgive and to forget but he could not forget – and never could forgive himself. When he heard from your mother's Rector at Stockton that she had died shortly after your birth, he nearly went mad with grief. He travelled and wrote and became famous and all the time he thought of your mother, Anne Tesseyman. The remorse has gnawed at him all these years. He has never been happy. And when father died he knew he must find out about you. He knows he has no claim on you but he is a good man, Lizzie. He never dared believe you were his. Now I think he will believe it. You are married, with children; I have never been blessed with them. You belong to your husband as I do to mine . . . George would never interfere, I know – but to know that he has grand-children when the world knows him for a pious bachelor! . . . The world must never know . . . it would do him no good . . . But *he* must know . . . This is not the only world, Lizzie . . . I am married to a man of the church myself . . .' She spoke dis-jointedly, distractedly.

Suddenly Lizzie put down her teacup and went impulsively up to Lady Elizabeth and kissed her. There were no barriers of rank or wealth that could stop her. This was another Lizzie, the one she was named after, the one whose ribbon had stopped her mother throwing herself in the lake. Hannah had told her that.

'Oh, ma'am – you were my mother's favourite little girl and I feel you are like a sister to me, even though it turns out you are my aunt. We are like sisters in our hearts.'

Lady Elizabeth was crying. 'They are tears of happiness,' she said, wiping them away with her fingers. 'That my dear Nanna's little girl has grown up and is also the child of my dearest and most favourite brother. It is too much. The best and kindest of men. And his little grandchildren! Oh the world is so cruel – I was so unhappy when she went away – I've never for-gotten her.'

'No – *men* are cruel,' said Lizzie slowly. 'They break our hearts one way or another. I can't be his daughter now – why,

255

your world is like a fairytale to me! I don't want to be any different,' she said proudly. 'But tell him what Hannah told me – that mam loved him like she loved the sunshine. That she died happy – that's what she said.'

The three women were all silent. The strangeness of life seemed to fill the room and themselves. It was like a moment stopped in time, till the baby, little Anne, woke and cried and broke the spell.

Lady Elizabeth was struggling to put into words what could not perhaps be put into words: that a great wrong had been done by her father whom she had always been taught to respect and obey. No one had mentioned Hardow – and Lady Georgiana, who had also been wronged. That her brother had been wronged. That Anne had died, somehow giving a meaning to them all sitting there – to her daughter, to her friend and to her little charge of so long ago.

'They say time rights all,' said Curly finally. '*We* have survived and *I* shall keep in touch with you, Lizzie Clayton. *I* can see your children, can't I, Lizzie, for I should have seen you long ago if Anne had told me about it.'

The ladies finally left as dusk was falling. Elizabeth Clayton sat then at her window in darkness until her children crept in. Now, she thought, she had a real father. 'You've a grandad, love!' she said to baby Anne. But the baby looked back at her as if to say 'A mother is enough for me.'

A young man with a large head and a strange gait often used to walk by the Temple of the Four Winds, and when, after his brother's death, he became Eighth Earl of Fountaynes, he would go there to remember – still as bright as yesterday in his curious mind – a young woman who had been kind to him and who had gone away and never come back. Like his brother Fred she had died young, but he did not know that and used to look for her there until he was an old man. When he died his brother Charlie's son succeeded him as Ninth Earl of Fountaynes.